REGINA'S FIRST VIEW
OF THE CHÂTEAU DE VERLAINE
LEFT HER TREMBLING
WITH AWE
AND EXCITEMENT.

HER FIRST NIGHT
IN THE ARMS OF ITS MASTER
OPENED THE DOOR
TO RAPTURES
SHE HAD NEVER IMAGINED. . . .

As his kisses grew in intensity, she forgot the outside world. She could see dimly the lights on the street outside the windows, but Julian was so close, so strong, his arms moving about her, his hands caressing her slim body. The rose nightdress was removed; he tossed off his robe. She felt heat in her body, and a softness that welcomed him. He must have known, because he went on and on, kissing her, holding her, until her arms came up and closed about him.

"My love," he whispered softly. "My beautiful love."

Dell books by Janette Radcliffe

STORMY SURRENDER
HIDDEN FIRES
LOVERS AND LIARS
AMERICAN BARONESS

AMERICAN BARONESS

Janette Radcliffe

A DELL BOOK

Published by
Dell Publishing Co., Inc.
1 Dag Hammarskjold Plaza
New York, New York 10017

Dell ® TM 681510, Dell Publishing Co., Inc.

ISBN: 0-440-10267-7

Printed in the United States of America

First printing—August 1980

CHAPTER ONE

Regina Pierce came slowly into the drawing room, her silk skirts rustling as she moved gracefully toward the window that opened onto Fifth Avenue. With a practiced eye she adjusted the flowers on the table and rearranged the jade figurines beside the blue china vase. Everything had to be perfect or her stepmother would be furious with the maids—and with her.

Regina had dressed early in the pale blue silk, arranged her hair in a coronet, and had her maid set a wreath of small yellow roses in her hair. She had very long curly chestnut-brown hair, an ordinary color, she thought. With blonde hair in fashion, it seemed very drab. And her eyes were dark brown, not a vivid blue. Sometimes her stepmother mourned that Regina did not have the coloring or the presence of many of the famous beauties of the day.

"But she'll have plenty of money," her father would reply laughing at Emilia's pained expression. Then he would give Regina a wink, but she could scarcely summon up a smile.

The money. The hateful money. If they had not had so much money, she could have stayed in the Rocky Mountains, where she had been born in a log cabin daubed with mud to keep out the cold, howling winds of winter. She would not have been forced to endure the miseries and formality of the girls' school where dress was more important than brains.

Frederick Pierce had been gold mining for years when Regina was born, the youngest of his three children. She had been happy paddling barefoot in creeks in the summer, gathering berries, gossiping with Indian women, clinging to the bearded old miner Tumbleweed who was her "best friend," as she had announced proudly to her older brothers, George and Bernard. But all that was part of the past now. Everything had changed.

Emilia Pierce swept into the drawing room. In her forties, graying, formidable, she seemed to sweep into situations like a brisk north wind. She was actually a distant cousin of Frederick Pierce, a calculating and ambitious woman. When he had moved back East after the death of his wife, bought a bank, and asked his cousin Emilia to help "raise Regina," she had seen her chance. Within six months Emilia and Frederick were married, and she, the despised spinster and poor cousin, had started making her fierce secret dreams come true.

Frederick didn't care what Emilia did so long as she left him and his study alone. When she nagged at him too often, he escaped to his bank and roared at his employees. His sons escaped early to the marriages Emilia had arranged. Only Regina had quietly defied her matchmaking. She had insisted on finishing her education, and had gone to college, graduating just a year ago. In history, art, French, and Spanish, she had excelled.

Now Emilia had her back, and with her the opportunity of a lifetime. Regina was wealthy in her own right, and her father would make a generous marriage settlement; he adored the girl. Emilia had been observing the ways of the wealthy, and in the past few years had seen some of the most brilliant marriages ever made—international marriages. An American girl marrying an Italian count, another marrying a British duke. Emilia fiercely craved a title—a title! Her dear Regina should be a duchess, a princess, at least a marquise.

These ambitions, confided in Regina, had wakened only horror in the young girl's breast. She had evaded a duke of forty, a French count of fifty. She had escaped by explaining to her father that she wanted to marry someone as nice as he was. Proudly he had rejected the fatuous duke and the rake of a count.

"You've got to find someone decent and nice, Emilia," he told his frustrated wife. "Regina ain't the kind to enjoy their carryings-on. Can't you find someone nice for her?"

Emilia deserved credit for trying. She had tried a Spanish grandee, a German graf, several English viscounts. Regina had turned them all down or managed to offend them in her quiet, innocent manner. Emilia was never sure if the girl did it deliberately or by instinct. But she turned them away.

Emilia eyed Regina suspiciously this evening. She found no fault with the pale blue silk or the yellow roses. The girl

looked rather sweet, her oval face clear of makeup, showing her own lovely pink-and-white complexion. Her carriage was good, erect, and proud. Emilia could imagine her
on the arm of a count, a duke—*someone* important. The
slim arched eyebrows set off her large dark eyes, luminous
now in the candlelight as she greeted her stepmother.

"Is there anybody special coming tonight, Mother?"
asked Regina.

Emilia gazed at her suspiciously. "Well, your cousins
from Massachusetts. I had to invite them, since they are in
town. And that nice young man from your father's bank."

Regina concealed a smile. She already knew that a
French baron was coming as well. She had met the handsome Baron de Verlaine several times last year when he
had come to New York. He had appeared at several func-
tions, then suddenly disappeared around August. She had
thought he was going to the seashore or the mountains,
but one of the men who had become friendly with him had
said, "Oh, Julian has gone home to his precious vines!"

Julian Herriot, the Baron de Verlaine, was the owner of
a large vineyard in the Loire Valley of France. He was also
part of a long and cherished lineage, dating back to the
Middle Ages—or so Emilia had told her. She had sent
Frederick's competent secretary to the library, and he had
looked up peerage books and discovered it. Imagine,
thought Regina, a line going back to 1200. What a responsibility! Her father's people had come over from England
during some depressed times, Frederick had said loudly
and cheerfully to Emilia's horror. Her mother had been of
French descent and could trace back several generations.

Emilia carefully arranged the Valenciennes lace at her
throat so that the pearl brooch that fastened it was set
more exactly in the center. The dangling pearl earrings
softened her excellent though severe features.

"There is also that French baron you liked last year,"
said Emilia, watching her stepdaughter in the mirror. Regina carefully kept her expression neutral.

"The Baron de Verlaine," said Regina.

"Yes. Do speak French to him tonight, Regina. It might
make him feel more comfortable. Not that his English
isn't good," Emilia added hastily.

"Yes, Mother."

"And be sure not to talk about your early upbringing!" Emilia reproached. "Do be sensible about it, Regina. Some people know your father made his money out West, but you don't have to talk about growing up in a log cabin, or paddling in water, barefoot! Or riding a donkey, without a sidesaddle."

"Without any saddle at all," said Regina cheerfully.

"Please, Regina!"

When her stepmother groaned in that way, Regina gave in. "Yes, Mother, I'll be careful. I expect my stories bore people anyway. New Yorkers just like to talk about money and jewels and stocks," she said bitterly.

"And opera, music, don't forget that! And art, you can talk nicely about art. Only not about nude paintings, or Greek sculpture. I'm sure I don't know why girls had to get undressed to be done in marble," Emilia fretted. "I don't know what their mothers were thinking about."

Regina was silent. She had some idea about that, having read more about the ancient Greeks than her stepmother had.

"Well—let's go to the hallway. I do wish it would stop snowing. Your father said it was a foot deep when he came home from the bank. These winters are getting worse and worse. Perhaps we should go to the Mediterranean until spring."

That was her latest idea; Europe in the winters. Regina sighed. She loved New York, and she enjoyed going up to Connecticut to visit her brother Bernard even more. She liked her sister-in-law, Sally, and their little girl. Not much chance of going this year, with her stepmother set on presenting Regina to society all year.

The snow was still coming down, in big fat flakes that showed little sign of melting. When Regina peered out the large front windows, drawing back the golden draperies, she saw that the gate posts were piled high with the snow and the garden was covered so that only the taller shrubs could be seen. In the street, carriages were slipping and sliding. The poor horses, Regina thought, hearing the shrill neigh of terror as a horse lost its footing on the ice. It was a terrible night to be out. Nevertheless, the carriages were beginning to draw up in front of their grand Fifth Avenue mansion.

As the first guests arrived, Emilia led them into the

drawing room, but Regina lagged behind to confer with the butler. A dozen persons were expected. They might have to postpone dinner if they could not all come in time.

Her father came down the stairs, his finger under his tight high collar, his grimace telling what he thought of his outfit. Regina went up to him, smiling. "You look very handsome tonight, Papa," she said, as she adjusted his collar and flowing tie and smoothed his jacket in front. He grinned down at her, his broad shoulders moving uneasily.

"Don't know how I'll stand it for a whole evening," he grumbled. "Emilia talks about having two dinners a week! My God!"

"She's enjoying herself immensely," said Regina tactfully. "And you don't have to go to the opera on Friday. She agreed to let your secretary fill in, and my maid will go with me."

Frederick Pierce did not disguise his relief. "One of the bad things about getting money is all that nonsense goes along," he said gruffly. "Never thought when I was out hip-deep in cold mountain streams that the gold I found would land me here. Dressed up fit to kill, uncomfortable as a bear in a wolf's coat, having to say nice things to people I don't care much about. In the old days—"

"Mother is waiting, Papa!" Regina hated to cut him off, but once started on the old days, her father hated to stop.

"Don't you miss the old days, baby?" he asked in a low voice, patting her shoulder.

Regina bit her lips. She missed them terribly, the laughter-filled sunlit days, even the bad days when the food ran short, and the mountain passes were closed, and they couldn't get out except to feed the animals.

"Frederick, your guests are here," said Emilia, appearing majestically in the hallway, her eyes frosty with anxiety.

"Coming, dear!" Frederick marched forward, his shoulders held back.

Regina was about to follow when the butler motioned to her worriedly.

"Yes, Horace?"

"Excuse me, Miss Gina," he whispered. "A guest came in—he's covered with snow. I put him in the little room, but there's no fire, and he's fair shivering with cold and his boots are a sight—"

"I'll see to him," she said quickly, thinking it might be

one of her cousins. One of them, Tom, was very young; he might have been playing one of his pranks, making a snowman or something—

She went to the small room off the entryway and stepped inside. In the dim light she could see a man standing there, a tall slim man with a mustache, tugging at his snow-covered boots.

The rustling of her skirts as she entered caught the man's attention, and he stood up so quickly that he almost fell over, one boot in hand.

"Mademoiselle Pierce!" he gasped. "I beg pardon—"

It was the Baron de Verlaine. Regina gazed at him, as surprised as he was. "Good heavens," she managed to say. "Have you been in an accident, Monsieur?"

"*Non, non,* Mademoiselle," he said, flushing. "I walked—"

"Walked! In this snow!"

"I did not want to make the horses go out in this," he explained simply. "There were so many slipping on the ice. I decided to walk, it is but ten blocks—"

"But the wind and the snow! Oh, you must be frozen," she said impulsively. He was shivering a little, and Regina noticed that his coat did not look very warm. "You are not accustomed to this weather, I fear."

He grimaced. "No, but it is very exhilarating! We do not have such wind and thick snow in the Loire."

"You must get warm." She thought quickly. "I know. Come to Papa's study. Bring your boots. I'll make sure no one sees—" She peered out the door, around the corner. Only the butler was in sight, looking anxiously toward her.

"Stand in front of the drawing-room door!" she whispered to him.

He nodded and obeyed at once. Regina beckoned to the shivering man behind her. "Come along, quick!" she said and took his hand. "Oh, you are cold!"

Imperiously, she pulled him with her, and they dashed along the corridor to the back hall. A footman saw them, and Regina put her finger to her lips to signal silence. He nodded and grinned.

"Bring a hot drink to the gentleman in the study!" she whispered. The footman sped away.

Regina opened the door of the study, and all but pushed the baron inside. "There, the fire is lit. I knew it would be," she said with satisfaction. "Papa likes to sneak away from parties and take refuge in here." Then suddenly she realized who she was speaking to, and went crimson.

The baron was smiling. "You are most kind to me," he said, walking toward the fire. He placed his boots before the hearth and held out his hands to the flames.

Regina hovered between the baron and the door. She should not remain, it was not proper. But she was worried about him. He was not accustomed to this terribly cold weather. "You really should not walk far in the snow," she scolded softly. "You could freeze your hands and feet! I know, one time—" She stopped quickly. She was not supposed to talk about the years in the Rockies. "I mean people get very cold, and it is dangerous."

The footman brought in a hot mug on a silver tray and handed it to the baron. He took it, sipped tentatively, then nodded. "Excellent," he said approvingly.

"Would you take his boots, please, and get them dry and clean?" Regina asked. "He can wait here for a little while."

"Yes, Miss Gina," the footman said and took the boots away.

She sat down on the edge of the overstuffed chair as the baron sipped his drink slowly, looking about the study with interest.

"So many books. I did not know your father was a scholar, Mademoiselle Pierce," he said.

"Oh, he isn't. He would be the first to say so. But he loves and respects books. We couldn't—I mean, in the early years, we had very few books. I used to read to him and my brothers in the evenings, after work," she said carefully.

She worried that he might ask questions about where this was, but instead he strolled over to the bookshelves in his stocking feet and said, "What was your favorite reading, Mademoiselle?"

He had a nice deep voice with a strong French accent. She thought he looked nice also, rather tall and slim, with the nervous energy of a thoroughbred horse. He had light-brown hair and pale green eyes, and his mouth seemed almost stern except when he smiled. Regina thought he looked like a serious man. Tonight he seemed more relaxed than she remembered him, though.

"We liked the essays of Ralph Waldo Emerson," she told

him. It was also one of the few books they had had in their mountain cabin. "And the book by Henry David Thoreau, called *Walden*. We all liked that one, even my brothers. And the plays of Shakespeare. We took turns reading the roles out loud. We also had a book of poetry, and we liked James Lowell and Mr. Tennyson from England."

"Ah, yes," he said, and amazingly, he began to recite:

> "Come into the garden, Maud,
> For the black bat, night, has flown,
> Come into the garden, Maud,
> I am here at the gate alone;
> And the woodbine spices are wafted abroad,
> And the musk of the rose is blown."

She stared at him in surprise, touched by the sound of the English words spoken so beautifully by the Frenchman.

He smiled a little, glancing at the row of books, and said, "Do you know the last verse of that poem?"

"I—well—I have read it," she said in a low tone. She could not admit she had memorized it. She blushed and put her hand to her cheek.

Turning away from her shyly, he said the words:

> "She is coming, my own, my sweet;
> Were it ever so airy a tread,
> My heart would hear her and beat,
> Were it earth in an earthy bed;
> My dust would hear her and beat,
> Had I lain for a century dead,
> Would start and tremble under her feet,
> And blossom in purple and red."

There was silence in the study when he had finished; Regina did not know what to say. She was shivering a little, not with cold. She had never been so moved, not by that poem or any other. It seemed to mean—to mean more than he said.

"I have never said that poem to anyone," he said aloud, as though reading her thoughts. He turned around and gazed at her across the room. "I wanted you to know that—I have never said it to anyone, not before today."

"I—I believe you," she said in a hushed voice. What else

was there to say? "I—I should get back—to the drawing room. My stepmother—I mean, my mother—"

"Yes, of course," he said. "We will talk again, another time, yes?"

Impulsively, before she could stop the words, she said, "Do you enjoy opera?"

His green eyes widened, glowing almost golden in the firelight. "Yes, I enjoy it very much. Should you like to attend?"

"I have tickets. I mean, Papa hates it, and I was going on Friday. Would you like—I mean—to escort me and my maid—" She blundered to a halt, then added, "It's the *Magic Flute* by Mozart."

"Ah, I should like it immensely. May I come, truly? And for dinner first, that is permitted? May I speak to your mother about this?"

"Yes, if you wish," she said shyly.

Before she could say more, the footman came in with the baron's boots. His impassive face said nothing of his curiosity. Regina moved hastily to the door. "I'll go back to the drawing room now. You can come in as though—I mean—you have just arrived. If you want to—"

He bowed deeply. "Thank you for your kindness."

Once in the drawing room, Regina waited nervously for the butler to announce the baron. Emilia Pierce's face relaxed when she heard his name, and she whispered, "Oh, he is here," as though speaking to herself.

The Baron de Verlaine entered, very correct in his black suit and striped trousers, his high boots polished to a gleam.

He went directly to Mrs. Pierce and bowed over her hand. She fluttered like a mere girl. "I beg your pardon for my late arrival. It is terrible of me. The snow was quite deep."

"Oh, not at all! A dreadful night, I must apologize for our awful weather. Allow me to introduce my other guests. . . ."

She took him around the room. Regina watched them curiously from beneath the shadows of her long lashes. He is graceful as a slim dark panther, she thought. She noted the flexing of his long fingers, the rare smile, the gravity of his appearance. He had smiled more often in the study. Perhaps, like her father, he was not comfortable at parties.

Everyone was very much impressed by him. He was noble, formal, a French baron of a long line. And he was unmarried. Curious looks went from him to the three eligible girls in the room. It was a relief when Horace announced that dinner was served, and the baron took Mrs. Pierce in on his arm.

Placed between an elderly banker and a second cousin, Regina found her gaze wandering to the head of the table where her mother and the baron were seated. Between the interminable courses that were now fashionable—the appetizer of shrimp and oyster, the fish course, the side of beef, and three rounds of sweets and puddings and cakes—it was all she could do to make pleasant conversation with the other guests.

Sometime during that long dinner, the Baron de Verlaine must have asked to take Regina to the opera. Before he left that evening, toward midnight, he shook Regina's hand lightly. "Your mother has consented that I escort you to the opera on Friday evening, and to take you for dinner first. May I come for you at five o'clock?"

"Thank you," she said formally, "I should enjoy that."

"Until then." He bowed deeply over her hand but did not kiss it, and she found herself wondering how it would feel to have his lips on her fingers. His lips were neither thin nor full under the light-brown mustache.

On Friday evening, Regina dressed very carefully. She had been scanning a French textbook feverishly for three days. Tonight she would dare to speak French to him. He would not laugh at her accent, she felt sure; he was too nice.

Her stepmother came to approve her gown and to warn her of her manners. "Yes, very nice. That ivory brocade is good on you, a warm tone, and the embroidery is exquisite. You will wear your brocade opera cloak with the ermine fur. That should look impressive. You have your opera glasses?"

Regina showed her the mother-of-pearl glasses. "Yes, yes, very nice. And Giulia goes with you?" Mrs. Pierce half frowned at the eager Italian maid. "You will not become so absorbed in the music, Giulia, that you forget your first duty is to chaperone your mistress," she said sharply.

Giulia made a deep curtsey, and Mrs. Pierce relaxed. She enjoyed all the formalities her position entitled her to, especially since before her marriage she had been a chaperone for wealthier cousins and relatives, the poor relation who sat in the corner of the box and kept an eye on cloaks and candy boxes.

The Baron de Verlaine arrived early, with a smart black carriage and two matched black horses. The snow had nearly melted, and only patches remained, making travel safe.

"I am amazed that the snow goes away so soon. It looked as though it would stay forever," he commented as he helped the women into the carriage.

The weather was a safe topic. "Yes, sometimes it goes away at once, and other times it remains for two weeks or more. The ice is the worst," Regina agreed.

He took her to a fine French restaurant near the opera, and at her shy request he ordered for her, explaining the dishes. As they were discussing the menu, she asked, "May I try to speak French to you this evening? I studied it in college, but I fear I do not use it enough."

His quick smile was approving and heart-warming. He answered in French. "I shall enjoy it immensely. I did not know you had studied my language."

She answered slowly, but correctly, watching his expression to see if he approved of her accent. "I studied French for three years, Monsieur le Baron. I also studied Spanish. Art was my favorite subject, and also history."

"Very good," he said. "And do you read French literature?"

"Yes, Monsieur le Baron. I often read stories and essays in French."

"I shall be pleased to give you several books to read, if your mother approves."

The French waiter beamed to find them speaking French, and in his enthusiasm he rattled off something that Regina could not understand at all. The baron reproved him gently, and asked him to speak slowly. "The mademoiselle is pleasing me this evening by speaking my language. I do not wish her to become discouraged."

"Ah, *oui, oui, Monsieur, je comprends.*" He smiled down at them knowingly, observing the maid seated dis-

creetly at the next table, then returning his gaze once again
to the elegantly dressed Frenchman and his radiant companion arrayed in diamonds. He waited on them alone the
entire evening, dashing from kitchen to table to bring them
excellent sole almondine, chicken in a white wine sauce,
small potatoes, and flaming crêpes in strawberry syrup for
dessert. With it he served them a white wine that had a
little sparkle to it; the baron called it *petillant.*

"That means it still sparkles a little, it still ferments even
in the bottle," explained the baron, within the waiter's
hearing.

"Ah, the monsieur understands his wines! This is a fine
dry white wine from the Loire Valley—"

"Yes," said the baron. "From one of my neighbors."

"Monsieur is a *vigneron?*" asked the waiter a little
doubtfully. Monsieur was evidently a nobleman.

The baron nodded. "The vines were destroyed in recent
years. Again, we build them up, using American root
stocks. It may be years before my name is known again in
the wine trade."

"May I be permitted to know the name of monsieur?"
asked the waiter.

"It is Verlaine. The château de Verlaine was once
known—"

"But I know it! My father knew it! The wines were most
excellent—white, dry, with a little of the green color—"

The baron half rose and bowed in acknowledgment. "We
are now working to make a fine rosé. The old wines are
gone," he said. "I hope one day soon you will hear the
Verlaine name again."

"One hopes so," the waiter agreed, as happily as though
he himself would work toward that goal. With great care
he poured more wine into their glasses, urged them to eat a
little more of the crêpes, poured out hot black coffee, and
then stood back, hands folded, to wait for their approval.

"I did not know you had had trouble—in your vineyards," said Regina, in French. "I am so sorry."

"Yes, it is a long, sad story," he said, and there was a
mournful look in his eyes. "One day I should like to tell
you."

After a second cup of coffee Regina and the baron left
for the opera, arriving in time to settle themselves and look
at their programs, and also to study the other opera lovers.

They talked a little, but all the while Regina was wondering about the look on his face as he spoke of his vineyards. She thought she would never forget that look of sadness.

"Julian has gone home to look after his precious vines." The words echoed in her mind. Julian. And his precious vines.

She would indeed like to hear the story of his vines one day. She sensed there was a story behind them that affected him very deeply. And somehow she wanted to know about anything that meant so much to him.

CHAPTER TWO

Regina rose very early on Tuesday morning two weeks later. She had to talk to her father, it was imperative. She asked Giulia to bring her a warm dress, and the maid set out the cinnamon wool embroidered in black.

"This will look lovely with your hair, Miss Gina," said the maid happily. "And how warm for this so-cold day."

"Thank you, Giulia, that will be fine." Regina planned to wear it that afternoon. She was to attend a concert with the Baron de Verlaine.

She frowned to herself, lost in thought, as the maid brushed her curly hair, which fell in waves below her waist. At last it was smoothly coiled into a neat chignon at the back of her slim neck. But Regina scarcely noticed.

"We have seen a great deal of each other these two weeks, but I never dreamed—" The silent words broke off in her mind.

An item in yesterday's newspaper had disturbed her a great deal. She could recite it, she had read it so often since the previous morning.

> The Baron de V. is showing much interest in one of our long-stemmed American Beauty roses. Is another international marriage about to be made? We understand he is heiress-hunting and she has a rich and indulgent papa. We will watch with much interest— especially at the opera, where they have been seen alone but for her maid.

It was enough to make her blood boil. She hoped the baron had not seen it. She had thought and thought, but she knew no other "Baron de V." in New York at this time. Nothing had been said of marriage, and she had gone only twice to the opera with him. She had enjoyed it, she had to admit that. He listened to the music in silence, only exchanging a smile of satisfaction with her at the end of a particularly fine aria. Regina was impressed with his obvious knowledge and appreciation of the music.

As a matter of fact, it had been a pleasure to go with him. He did not fall asleep and snore, as her papa did. He did not rustle about and stare more at the audience than at the stage, as her stepmother did. He did not care much about strolling during the intermissions, but rather seemed quite content to remain in the box, ordering hot chocolate for the two of them and talking about the music.

She also liked the way he treated Giulia. When he realized she knew about music, he had drawn her discreetly into the conversation. He had also supplied her with her own tray of hot chocolate, and made sure she could see the stage from the back of the box.

He was kind; he seemed intelligent and thoughtful. But Regina was not going to have her name coupled with his in the gossip columns! Her father had some influence with the press, and she would ask him this morning to do something about it. And she would not see the baron alone again!

She scowled into the mirror. "Something is wrong, Miss Gina?" Giulia asked timidly, her dark eyes peering past Regina into the mirror. "You look splendid, I think."

"Yes, yes, my hair is fine. I must see Papa," she said.

"Yes, Miss Gina."

Regina swept down the stairs. The cinnamon wool dress was warm and comfortable, perfect for today's cold weather. During the night there had been another snowfall, and now the wind blew the snow in gusts against the house.

She found her father finishing his hearty breakfast in the small breakfast room in the east wing of the mansion. It was his favorite room; he hated the huge formal dining room that seated twenty-four comfortably. He cast down the newspaper as Regina came in.

"Ah, good morning, my dear. How splendid you look today! And up early also. I would think you would want to sleep late today."

She had come in at midnight from a tiresome dinner.

"I wanted to speak to you, Papa," she said firmly. "May I see you in your study after breakfast?"

He gave a quick, almost guilty, look at the newspaper. "Well—ah—I have to make an early start to the office—"

"I must speak to you today, Papa!" She rarely spoke to

him like that, but she refused to give in to her father's excuses when she had an important matter to discuss.

"Well, with the weather like this, I suppose it won't hurt to stay home a bit this morning," he said reluctantly. "What do you want to talk about, Gina?"

The footman was serving her breakfast, his face impassive. She glanced at him and shook her head at her father. "Coffee, thank you," she murmured.

He poured the coffee into the white and gold-banded china cup, set the cream and sugar close to her hand. The silver service gleamed in the light of the gas chandelier above their heads. She remembered the battered coffee pot in the log cabin in the mountains. How the wind had howled about their heads! Yet they had been cozy and warm, and laughter had filled the house. It had been a pleasure to stay indoors, to eat the plain fare of beans and thick bacon, to tell stories, to listen to the adventures of Tumbleweed and the other miners.

Deep in thought, Regina toyed absently with her breakfast of an egg, bacon, and a muffin while her father had another cup of coffee. He was ready when she glanced up.

"My study?" he murmured, and stood aside for her to precede him down the hallway. As she entered the study, she had a sudden memory of that January night only a few weeks ago when she had rushed the baron into the room and told him to give his boots to the footman.

What must he have thought of her informality? She shook her head. Perhaps she had amused him with her impulsiveness—or shocked him, though his face had never revealed that.

Regina sat down opposite her father's large mahogany desk, which was bare but for a pen set. He liked a neat desk. In fact, he did not make much use of the desk at all. He kept everything in his head, where it would not tempt people to steal a peek, as he said.

"Well, now, Regina, what's on your mind this morning?" he asked indulgently. "A bit more allowance, eh?"

"No, Papa, I have more than enough," she said. "No, it is about that note in the paper. About the Baron de V."

"And the long-stemmed American beauty," her father murmured glancing over her slim figure as she leaned back in the chair.

"So it did mean me?" she asked, her fingers laced together. Her dark-brown eyes met his. They had never needed to fence with words; they were too much alike.

"Papa—is the baron a . . . a fortunehunter?" she asked finally, twisting her fingers.

Her father frowned. "Well, I wouldn't say that. No, of course not. When I had him investigated last year—"

"You had him investigated!" She sat up straight. "Papa, you didn't!"

"Nonsense, of course I did," he said, scowling to cover his embarrassment. "When anyone shows an interest in you, I check up on him. Of course. I sent a man to France—"

She stared at her father helplessly. He was incredible! Last year she had scarcely noticed the baron. "And what did your invaluable man find? That he was short of money, hunting for an heiress—"

Her father nodded. "That's about it." He did not seem to notice her shock. "It seems that he inherited a title and hundreds of acres along with the château, which was built in about 1200. That takes a lot of money to keep up. My man spun some tale about the European vines having been ruined twenty years ago, by some louse—don't know what it was—anyway, they couldn't produce wines. The baron's short of money. Thought last year's harvest would be good, but it rained and that ruined it. He owes money. The way I see it—"

Regina had gone as white as a camellia. "Papa, you are not considering *selling* me for a title?" she whispered. "Not the way Mother wants?"

Frederick Pierce coughed uneasily. "Now, Regina. Don't look at it like that. You have a bit of money, and you'll have more when I give you a dowry. It's only natural that men will come looking at you for the money you have. Money marries money, or a title, that's the way of it."

"Father, I don't want to be married—not for money. I don't want it! I don't want *any* arranged marriage. How could you do this? You know how I feel. That I wanted a marriage—like you and Mother—"

"Emilia?"

"No—Mother, my mother."

They were both silent. A shadow passed over Frederick's broad, hearty face. He put his hand to his eyes. He did not often think back to the early days anymore; they hurt too much. He had married lovely gentle Virginia in his youth, and she had given him two fine sons and a daughter. She had gone out West with him, lived in rough cabins, had never complained about the dangers or the hardships. When Regina was eleven, Virginia had fallen sick with fever, and in a matter of days she was gone. His pretty sweet Ginny. Gone. For months he had been dazed with shock.

Regina had taken over. Gina, so like her mother. She looked delicate, but she was smart and strong. She was able to cook on a wood stove, to carry buckets of water from a cold mountain stream, to sew coarse shirts with pieces of thread and a broken needle. And still she could laugh at the mischief of her brothers, or the tales of the rough miners, her eyes bright in the firelight as she encouraged them to talk.

"The old days are gone," he said finally, wearily, with an evident effort. "This is now, today. I want a bright future for you. All the money you want, clothes, jewels—"

Love, thought Regina rebelliously. That was what she wanted. Love, and affection, and caring, and laughter, like the marriage her parents had once had. She had to make one final effort.

"Papa, I told you, I wanted to marry someone fine and decent, a man I could respect—"

"Well, he is one, Gina," said her father reasonably. "I looked him up, I've talked to him. Get him to talk about his vines; he is damned interesting about that. And he has a big family, he looks after them all. He is sober, industrious, and that title of his is a real one, not bought. He had to borrow for some debts, but I figure in a few more years, with a couple good harvests, he could pay it all back. If he came to me at the bank, I'd loan him the money like a shot. Of course—" He gave her a guilty look. "That isn't what we had in mind."

"Couldn't you do it like that, Papa?" she pleaded. "Give him the money he wants as a loan? He probably wants to marry a French girl, not a strange American—"

"It's up to you, Gina, whether he gets the money from me or not," said Frederick bluntly. "I might as well tell you. He has borrowed to the hilt. He came to me, told me frankly what his situation was. I told him if he married you, he could count on me to the tune of two million dollars. That will let him pay his debts in France, buy more rootstocks in America, make some renovations on the château—"

Regina was shaking. "You mean—he came to you—"

"And asked permission to court you. I like him, Gina. He put his cards right on the table. He has to marry money. He looked around Europe, didn't like the gals he met there. But he likes you, he respects you, he said you have a fine mind. He thinks you will fit into his life. You speak French fine, he told me that. And he will be a good investment for me," Frederick said with satisfaction. "He'll recover his fortunes eventually, I'll bet on it. Good stuff in him."

"Father, I will not be sold!" she choked. How humiliating, to have been discussed like this! How horrible! Like the security on a loan! "Papa, did he act like that? Like I was a loan?"

"No, no, Gina," he said hastily, reaching out to pat her slim fingers. "Don't be silly. Men don't talk like that. And I'm damned fond of you, my gal! But Emilia pointed out to me, you've been turning up your nose at most of the young men you meet. She thought you were discouraging them somehow. I know a couple men started to court you, then stopped coming." He gave her a shrewd look. "Wouldn't be up to your tricks, would you?"

She could not look him in the eye. He gave a short laugh.

"Thought so. Now, Gina, if it ain't this young man, it'll be another one, maybe worse. He doesn't have bad habits, doesn't drink much, he's clean and decent. You could do far worse! And your mother is set on having a title for you. Baroness! That ain't bad!" he said proudly and stuck a cigar in his mouth to light it. "My daughter, a baroness! And me a gold miner, up to my hips in icy water. Never would have thought it."

His words rang in her ears that afternoon as she waited for the baron to come in his carriage. *"You could do far worse!"*

How horrible. To be sold at auction. Discussing her cold-bloodedly behind her back. Two million dollars in exchange for her. Well, at least she was worth a good price. She bit her lips until they stung.

She wanted to act so cold and hateful to him that he

would be discouraged and drop her. But the words kept
ringing in her ears: *"You could do far worse!"*

The baron arrived promptly, and Regina and Giulia
went out to meet the carriage so the horses would not be
kept standing in the ice and snow. When he jumped down
to greet her, there was a smile on his lips and the stinging
wind had brought color to his cheeks.

The baron glanced over her, apparently pleased with the
mink cloak she wore over her cinnamon wool. She wondered bitterly if she could match the chic of the French
women he knew. Probably not. Money could not make up
for style, elegance. But the baron had to have money. Two
million dollars.

"May I say you are looking most elegant today, Miss
Pierce?"

"Thank you," she said briefly, as he placed a warm rug
over her knees. Giulia gave him a shy smile when he did
the same for her.

"I am looking forward to this concert. Beethoven and
Brahms, and some Chopin. Afterward, your mother has
given me permission to take you to dinner again."

Emilia hadn't mentioned a word of it to her. "That is
most kind of you."

He gave her a keen look, noticing that her replies were
brief and chilly. He turned his gaze to the city streets then,
and Regina put her gloved hands in her mink muff and
huddled back into the folds of her cloak. She shivered.
How could he be so friendly and nice when he was thinking
of her dowry?

You could do worse—you *would* do worse—

Although Regina had never wanted to believe it, her
mother was set on a titled marriage for her. She thought
with distaste of the dukes, the viscounts, the German graf
she had met in the past year. Much worse, she thought.
She roused herself. She must be polite. It would do no
harm to get to know him better. Perhaps she could find out
something about him that would turn her father against
him.

"My father was telling me about your vineyards. He said
there was some trouble with them a few years ago? I
should like to hear about that."

The baron turned from his somber contemplation of the
icy streets to look at her in surprise and growing under-

standing. He must realize that her father had spoken of more than vineyards.

"I should like to tell you about them," he said. "But it is a business matter, and I am afraid you would find it boring."

"Nevertheless, I should like to hear," she said, with a set smile. "Father mentioned that about twenty years ago there was a blight, or louse—"

"Yes. Both. Some vineyards were blighted by a black rot. We recovered from that at Verlaine, but then another disaster struck. The louse, called phylloxera, began to destroy many of the vineyards of France and Germany. We hoped to keep it away. I was still a child, but I well remember the many efforts of the *vignerons* in the Loire, the chemical solutions, the many attempts to wash it off, to kill it. Nothing worked. The louse swept through and all the vines had to be burned. There was nothing left."

She found she was interested in spite of herself. "So what did you do then? You have vineyards now, I understand."

"It was a long, slow rebuilding process. Word came that some of the American rootstocks that were thin and wiry were able to resist this louse. People began to import them and graft them on the European roots. We tried this in our best field, a southern-exposure field, and it began to work. We were encouraged, but the stocks were expensive. My father worked night and day. He finally took ill, and died, I believe, of exhaustion."

"Oh—I am sorry," she said softly.

He waved his gloved hand, as though to refuse sympathy. His jaw was hard. "Forgive me, I did not mean to become personal."

She hesitated, then asked, "What happened next? You took over the vineyards and kept on with the work?"

"Yes. We continued to experiment. But I also raise thoroughbred racing animals. With clever buying and selling— not my cleverness—that of my manager," he added quickly, "with his good work, we were able to manage, until three years ago. Our harvest failed, just as we thought—no matter. It is as God wills. One good year can carry several bad ones. But we have only had one good year, 1893, and unfortunately we did not have enough vines out then. We have good wine from that year, but not enough to export. Last year, the rains came at the wrong time, just as the grapes were about to be harvested. So they were ruined."

As the baron finished his explanation, they arrived at the concert hall. Silently, he escorted Regina and Giulia inside to their box. Then he spoke of concert music and asked Regina's preferences, seeming pleased when she named Beethoven, Mozart, and Chopin.

"Yes, I like them also. In Paris we have some fine concert houses. I think you would like the opera there. It is splendid. And the Opera House is magnificent."

As soon as the music began, he ceased talking and gave his full attention to the music. Regina usually could lose herself in the performance, but today her thoughts were so confused she could scarcely concentrate. She was very conscious of the man on the velvet seat next to hers. She noted the strong brown hands on his knees, the perfect posture, the attentive bent of his head, the long legs in neat gray trousers, and the close-fitting black suit coat. When he leaned toward her to whisper at the end of the first piece, she was aware of the warmth of his body, the faint scent of a masculine cologne.

"You are quite comfortable? Is the chair not all right? Perhaps you would like a refreshment."

She was aware that she had been shifting restlessly with her thoughts. "It is fine, thank you. No, no refreshment, thank you. What about you, Giulia?"

"Oh, no, Miss Gina. Thank you very much." The maid was caught up in the beauty of the music. Giulia exchanged a quick understanding smile with the baron. "It is no hardship for her to attend you, Miss Regina." His murmur of her name made her aware of their closeness.

"No, she enjoys music," said Regina hurriedly.

"That—and she is fond of her mistress."

She smiled slightly, looking away, pretending to be interested in the crowd below them. People were looking up at their box; two women, stout and velvet-clad, were studying her frankly with their lorgnettes.

The concert was wonderful, but Regina missed half of it, unable to concentrate. She was impatient with herself and almost wished she could go directly home, but the baron had arranged to take them to dinner. Again he chose a French restaurant and he spoke to her in French as though it delighted him, and she shyly used her French to answer.

After the meal had been chosen, and the wine brought, approved, and poured, he leaned back as if to study her. "I am afraid I have bored you tonight with my talk of the vines."

"Not at all. I would not have asked if I had not been interested," she answered calmly. "I am more like my father than people think. He is a businessman, and very much absorbed in all matters of commerce and industry."

He did not flinch at that admission as some men had done. He only nodded, sipping his white wine. "And you enjoyed your college years and studies, I can see that."

"Is it not usual for French girls to attend college?"

He smiled, a genuine heart-warming grin that strangely attracted her. "My sister would have been horrified at the idea! Some French women do attend university, but they are—what do you call it?—bluestocking?"

"I think I know what you mean. What did your sister do?"

"She went to a finishing school, run by some fine Catholic sisters, and then she married. She is the mother of a lovely little girl, my niece Jeannette." His face softened as he spoke of the girl.

"Ah, she is the one for whom you bought the doll last year."

"You remembered? It was most kind of you to assist me in choosing the doll." That was the one time they had gone out alone, and Regina remembered how surprised she had been when he asked her help in choosing the doll. They had found one with blonde flaxen hair and wide blue eyes, in a pretty blue dress. "She is most fond of the doll. She calls her Regina. I hope you do not mind." He gave her a questioning look.

"Oh! I am surprised—but it is flattering, of course. Only I do not have blonde hair and blue eyes!"

"No, you have hair with red lights in it in the sunshine, so soft one wishes to touch it. And eyes like the dark pools in a quiet woods."

She swallowed. She had not wanted flattery, but his voice sounded sincere.

He went on to speak of Jeannette and some amusing things she had done. The dinner sped past. They spoke of music, the baron telling her about the opera in Paris and then about some artists he had met who were doing something quite new in painting. "They attempt to capture a scene as it appears in a particular light, before it disappears. It is most fascinating to watch them work."

He encouraged her to talk, but somehow she was wary of him now. When he took her home, it was quite dark, and the gas lights shone on the banked-up snows.

"I understand I am to have the honor of escorting you to the ball at the Astor residence this Friday."

She turned in surprise. "I didn't know—"

"Your mother gave me permission," he said firmly. She closed her mouth on a quick retort.

"Thank you for a most pleasant day," she managed to say.

"So until Friday!" he said, handing her out of the carriage to the butler, who was waiting to help her inside. Then he handed out Giulia. "Good night, Mademoiselle Regina!"

"Good night."

"My name is Julian, you know," he added unexpectedly, giving her that warm smile that made her heart feel strange.

"I—I do not usually address young men—" she began.

"I hope, in private, you will not hesitate to call me by my Christian name. It makes me feel more to home."

"Perhaps," she said with a smile. The way he said "to home" made her feel funny again.

Julian came for her on Friday evening, promptly as usual. Regina was dressed in a magnificent rose brocade gown with a wide lace bertha and diamonds at her throat and in her ears. He gazed at her unwaveringly as she descended the wide stairway. Giulia followed with her mistress's mink cloak draped over her arm.

"You are magnificent," he said in French. Emilia came into the hallway. She did not pretend to understand French, but she could easily understand that. She gave the baron a beaming smile.

"Doesn't Regina look like a princess?" she asked coyly.

"Yes, she does," he agreed.

Frederick Pierce followed his wife, grumbling. "I don't see why I have to go tonight. The baron can escort you both. Damn it, I hate to get all gussied up—"

"Mr. Pierce!" said his wife, embarrassed. "It is the Astors, after all!"

Julian gave Regina a tiny wink. He did not try to enter the argument, but held out his arm to escort Regina to his carriage. The others would follow in the Pierces' carriage.

Once they were on their way, Julian Herriot said, "Your father does not care much about society, I believe."

"He would rather face a dozen board fights against a hundred corporations! You watch, he'll find a way to closet himself in a study with Mr. Astor or to go home early."

The baron chuckled softly. "I am not so fond of balls myself, unless I have someone as lovely as yourself on my arm," he said. "In the country, at Verlaine, we have to make our own amusements. There are hunts and dinners to follow. But for the most part, we are rather dull."

Was he warning her? Or hoping to scare her off? Did he think she was chasing *him*? She did not know what to answer.

He leaned forward in his seat. "I cannot see your face in the darkness," he complained. "Do you enjoy these balls as your mother does? Would you miss the excitement of society?"

"I don't know," she said evasively. "This is my first year in society. I do enjoy the musical outings."

He was silent for a second and then said, "That reminds me. I have tickets to a Beethoven concert on Sunday afternoon. May I hope you will attend with me?"

She had just about made up her mind to discourage him, to start refusing his invitations. Weakly, she said, "I am not sure of my schedule—"

"I spoke to your mother. She said you were free."

Regina stifled a sigh. It seemed he was determined. "In that case, I shall be . . . delighted to accompany you."

"Good." There was a smile on his face as he lifted her down from the carriage at the lighted mansion of the Astors.

Together, they went into the elegant hallway to be greeted by their host and hostess. "Ah, Miss Pierce! And Baron de Verlaine!" gushed Mrs. Astor, taking their hands in a quick nervous clasp. "How splendid to see you—and together again!" she added significantly.

"Splendid indeed," Julian murmured as he tucked Regina's hand in the crook of his arm and moved with her toward the ballroom. There was something in his manner tonight that seemed almost possessive. If he was determined to have her, what could she do?

You could do worse . . . you could do worse . . . She felt the warmth of his body against her hand, and when he swept her into a waltz, she felt dizzy with the pleasure of it. He moved so well, so lightly on his feet. When he smiled down at her, in that amused way as if they were sharing a secret, she felt warm all over.

Throughout the evening Regina was conscious of people staring at them. She saw Emilia, her head bent conspiratorially in a circle of her own cronies, beaming complacently. A baroness, my daughter the baroness! It could come true—

Julian did not release her when the waltz was over. "Again?" he murmured. "You dance like a dream come true!"

"You are very kind."

"I am thankful." He smiled, and his green eyes were glowing like gold in the light of the chandeliers.

CHAPTER THREE

After the Astors' ball, the pressure on Regina seemed to mount steadily. The baron came almost daily. He brought her flowers, yellow or red long-stemmed roses, always with a charming note.

"I beg to present these blossoms to you, though you will outshine their beauty." "May I hope that you will accept these roses and keep them close to you."

With a small round bouquet encircled in lace, he noted, "For your exquisite gown—will you wear my flowers tonight?" And of course she did, at her mother's urging.

Emilia was radiant. One morning in February she called Regina into her small sitting room. "Regina, you are deciding on the baron, are you not? He is so very attentive, and most charming. He speaks of you with such flattering devotion!"

Of me—or of the money? Regina thought bitterly.

"He seems—most pleasant," she said coolly.

Her mother gave an impatient sigh, but retained her smile. "He is a fine gentleman. Your father approves of him," she said significantly. "And he is a French baron, a real baron! With a château, Regina, think of it! You will live like a queen!"

"I would rather live in America."

"There are no titles in America," her mother said. "Just imagine, Regina. You would be the Baroness de Verlaine. Accepted in society. Received by the Queen of England and other nobility."

"I don't imagine we would go to England to be received by the queen," said Regina perversely. "Isn't she always in mourning?"

"No matter! There are other queens," Mrs. Pierce said recklessly. "And you would rule over your subjects in France—"

Exasperated, Regina went to her father in his study. He was sitting at his desk, a frown of concentration wrinkling his broad brow.

"Ah, Gina. Want something, honey? More money for clothes? I like that dress." He gazed with approval at the simple peach wool dress that clung to her tall slim body, gently molding her rounded breasts and hips.

"No, Papa. I wanted to talk about the Baron de Verlaine." She sat down in a big chair opposite his desk.

"Ah, yes. I have accepted his offer for you, Gina," he said absently, his eyes returning to the papers he had been reading. "Seems a fine man. I have his financial reports before me."

"You—have—accepted—"

"Yes, yes, he means to speak to you this afternoon. I believe he comes at four. Did your mother say anything?"

Regina shook her head, feeling numb and lifeless. Sold, she thought. Sold like a—like a race horse! For two million dollars.

"Now, Regina, don't fret. He's a nice chap. Like him myself. What's bothering you?" His kindly face furrowed; he hated personal upsets. Since the death of his first wife, Frederick had avoided emotional confrontations whenever possible. Though he loved his children, he kept their relationships on a brisk, practical level. It was best that way. No fussing and fuming.

"Going away to France, so far away," she said, almost in a whisper. "Being—away from—all my friends—my family—"

"Why, you'll come home often and visit. Might come over myself and see you," he said heartily, though she knew he hated ocean voyages. He didn't even like to travel on the canals and railroads, and did so only when urged by business.

"I might—find someone—an American, maybe," she said hopelessly, futilely. "If we could only wait—"

"Now Regina!" he objected sternly. "Emilia says you're getting quite fond of Julian. You go out every day, and you both like music and dancing and all that. Don't you be pouting and sulking about this! Your mother has worked hard to find a nice young man for you."

"But I don't want to marry. Not yet."

He glared, then frowned. "You are twenty-two," he accused. "When did you think you *would* be ready?"

For once her father was not on her side, Regina realized.

There was no hope in arguing; it would only make him more determined. He was satisfied with the Baron de Verlaine, and her mother was delighted over the match. If she did not accept him, there would be another suitor presented, and another—and another—until eventually she would have to give in.

When the baron was announced that afternoon, she rose to meet him. She felt pale and listless, cold as the dreary February day outside. She thought he looked drawn also, though his face was reddened by the wind. After he had removed his heavy coat and the footman had taken it away, he bowed over her hand, and this time he kissed it.

She was surprised by the gesture; he had never done it before. She was also amazed at the small thrill that went through her at the touch of his lips on her fingers. He held her hand and gazed deeply into her eyes, thoughtfully, without smiling.

"Good afternoon, Miss Regina."

"Good afternoon, Monsieur."

"I thought you had agreed to call me Julian to make me feel more to home," he said, a glimmer of a smile coming first to his golden-green eyes, then to his lips.

She managed to smile in return but drew her hand gently from his. "Please be seated, Mon—I mean, Julian. My mother will come at once."

"I asked to see you alone," he said, grave again.

She took a deep breath. It was true then; he had come to propose. And he already had her parents' permission.

The footman had closed the door behind him, leaving Julian and Regina alone in the formal drawing room. She sat down shakily on a gilt-edged chair and looked helplessly up at him. She hoped he would not go down on his knees. She would hate that.

He did not. He hitched up his smart gray-striped trousers and sat down on a chair facing her.

"Miss Regina, I have the permission of your father to present myself to you," he began. His accent seemed very strong today, and his long fingers clenched and unclenched. Why, she thought, he was almost as nervous as she was. "Your beauty and charm have attracted me to you. It is so very pleasant that you share my interest in music. We have been able to converse easily. May I say that I admire your intelligence and knowledge as well as your beauty?"

She swallowed hard. She had never received a proposal before, always having been able to avoid that crucial moment. Now she looked away from Julian, her hands folded in her lap. She was startled when he reached over and put his hand on hers.

Regina wondered if he would speak of the money. How would he say it? I have long admired your father's ability to make money, and I long to have two million dollars of it. No, of course not. She felt a little feverish as she waited for him to continue.

"I have been longing to tell you of my deep regard for you," he went on slowly, anxiously studying her averted face. She gazed at the blazing fire in the large fireplace, at the marble mantel with the huge blue porcelain vases set there. "I wish to assure you that if you will consent to marry me, I shall always care for you and protect you. You will be welcomed into my family, and receive love and devotion from my mother and sister and brother. I have written to them and spoken to them of you. They are eager to meet you and to welcome you to Verlaine."

Regina wet her lips. She must say something. "It is most kind—of you—to say so. I have wondered—that is, I have not wanted to leave—my country. I have never been to France—"

"You would like it," he assured her. His warm hand remained clasped on her cold ones. "The life is a quiet one, there on our land in the country. But we shall have music, Regina. My sister plays the piano, and her husband the flute. And when you tire of our quiet life, I shall take you to Paris for a more exciting time—"

"It is not that," she hurried to assure him. "I do not have to have a gay time, or to be surrounded by people but I—" Squeezing her eyes shut, she struggled to collect her thoughts. She did not want to marry at all! She was terrified of taking such a big step. She was still young.

"I understand," he said quietly, releasing her hands. "You have many tastes like mine, I believe. You like to read, to think, to talk with a few good friends, to attend concerts. That is what encouraged me to ask for your hand in marriage. You already speak French well—"

"Not very well," she whispered, in one last feeble protest. She did like him, he could be so nice. And they did have a lot in common. Perhaps he would be better than a fortune-hunting American, certainly better than any of the other titled men she'd met.

"Quite well," he said firmly. "And you would grace my home. You have reserve, dignity, as well as loveliness. My mother would willingly teach you to take over as baroness; she has grown tired and is sometimes ill. Do not worry that she would not welcome you. And—forgive me for speaking so bluntly. But I believe you appreciate honesty as your father does. I long for children, for sons to follow me in the care of the estate, for daughters to love and enjoy. And you also seem to care for children."

Regina blushed hotly, yet she was somehow reassured. He did not speak of money, but of love and caring. He wanted a real home, a family, children.

Julian sat back, his hands on his strong thighs. "I have probably bungled this proposal," he said with a grin that warmed her. "To speak of children as one proposes! I know it is not done. But I want honesty and truth between us always. You value it, and I think it is essential in a good marriage. To have similar wishes, tastes, and wants, to speak frankly of any problems, to be honest with each other."

"Oh, I think so too!" she blurted out, still crimson. She put her hands to her cheeks. He had a nice sense of humor, he was more human than he had seemed at first. She could do worse, much worse—

"And you will consider this seriously?" he asked. "You will . . . perhaps you will agree today, to marry me? I may seem to be in haste. But I have been considering this matter since I met you last year. You are not like some of those others, the frivolous empty-headed darlings—" he caught himself up, wiped the contempt from his tone. "No, you are not like those who enjoy only appearing at balls and in the pages of society columns. I noticed you at once, and it was not long before I decided that I must come to know you better. I should be honored and grateful if you would consent to marry me."

There was silence in the room. Regina clasped her hands tightly. She must say something, she must. But what should she say? She glanced at him under her lashes, to find him wiping his forehead, his face pale and anxious. It had been

an effort for him, and somehow that endeared him to her.
He was real, human, warm. He had a family he was fond
of. Perhaps one day, he would be fond of her also. "I—
Julian—I will—I will marry you." She felt numb. When he
took her hand, raised it to his lips, and thanked her, she
felt nothing.

"I am grateful to you. You have made me very happy,"
he said quietly. "I will try to make you as happy as I possibly can, and you shall not feel homesick in my France.
You will be at home there, and my family shall be your
family."

Dazed, she could not say much then, even when her father and mother congratulated them. She was exclaimed
over, kissed, and hugged, but still she could hardly believe
what had happened. She was going to be married. Perhaps
in time she would become accustomed to the idea. Perhaps
in time. . . . But at dinner that evening, she realized she
had little time. Julian, his voice sounding more like the
Baron de Verlaine, was calmly insisting on a March wedding.

"But it is too soon to prepare!" her mother protested,
torn between a great excitement and a reluctance to rush
the lavish preparations she envisioned. "It must take
months. The bridesmaids, the caterers, the church, the dec-
orations—and—"

"I must go home to France by late March," Julian said
firmly. "I am a *vigneron*. I must work the fields and see
that the vines are prepared." He turned to Regina's father
appealingly. "You understand, Monsieur Pierce, the work
must be done at the right time. I wish to marry Regina
soon, so we may have a honeymoon in Paris, then arrive at
the château in time for the preparations of the vines."

"Of course, of course," said her father heartily; business
reasons he could comprehend. "That is necessary. Emilia,
do not make such a fuss! She can be married quietly—"

Emilia was shocked and horrified. A quiet wedding? Her
daughter was marrying a baron! "I shall manage," she said
with dignity. "But it shall not be a small wedding! Never!"

And it was not. The gazettes reported the engagement
parties, the balls, the dances, and the teas Emilia gave in
celebration. They commented gleefully on the baron's long
lineage, and on his magnificent château. In fact Regina

learned more about her future husband from the gazettes than she did from him.

Also, there was endless commentary on the preparations for the wedding. Regina clipped the items, and her father's secretary helped her arrange them all in a large album for the future. Still, it seemed unreal, as though it were happening to someone else. Even the fittings for her trousseau and for the ivory brocade wedding dress with French lace at the throat and wrists seemed oddly like a charade.

To Emilia's satisfaction, Frederick Pierce spared no expense for his only daughter's wedding. Without a murmur, he paid for eight bridesmaids' gowns, the reception for two-hundred guests at a huge hotel, hired carriages, imported champagne, and miles of red carpet for the church and reception rooms.

While these preparations were being made, Julian Herriot sent for some relatives and friends, who arrived during the last week of March, only two days before the wedding. Regina met them nervously and was dismayed that they chattered in rapid French, ignoring the fact that she could barely follow it.

Claude Herriot was a charming man of thirty-six, handsome and still single, who kept saying that his cousin had stolen the most beautiful girl in America and repeatedly tried to kiss her hand. Julian watched in silence, frowning as though he didn't quite like it.

Madame Simone de Lamartine was smart, chic, with black hair, magnolia-petal skin, and the most glorious clothes New York had ever witnessed. At first Regina thought she was a relative, but Claude informed her that she lived on an estate nearby, "across the hill," as he put it. "Her father died penniless," he said distinctly. "Poor Simone had to marry an elderly man. Fortunately, he died years ago."

Regina caught her breath, and Claude grinned at her engagingly.

"Ah, I must not shock you so soon!" he teased. "You are not accustomed to us French! We speak so frankly. It is our way."

Regina tried to smile, then moved away to greet the other French guests. Apparently Julian's immediate family—his mother, sister, and brother—had not come. Emilia, of course, considered their absence a slight and fretted about it, whispering her concern to Regina.

Julian soon realized this and told them gently, "My mother has been ill. She is too frail for the ocean voyage, but she sent many messages and is anxious to receive Regina. My sister and brother-in-law must remain to care for the château and the vineyards. And my brother—" A shadow crossed his face. "I never told you about my poor Eric. When he was but a small boy he had a critical illness which left him crippled. He has very little use of his legs and must remain in a wheelchair. He is most shy about it, so we shall not see much of him, even at the château. He lives more and more with his books."

"I'm so sorry," Regina said, seeing the pain on Julian's face. "Shall we choose some books to take to him? Perhaps I could pick some out at a store that carries both English and French—"

"That would be most kind," said Julian, pressing her arm warmly to his side.

It was practically the only intimate conversation she had with him before the wedding. The day approached so fast, she had no time to think. But perhaps it was for the best; she might have panicked and collapsed, or wanted to run away. Marriage—to a Frenchman—and life in a strange country; it did not bear thinking about.

On the day before her wedding, Regina suddenly realized that she was not the only one with problems. Giulia went about with red eyes and a subdued look, hardly speaking and never smiling at all. Regina finally said to her, "What is it, my dear? Don't you want to come to France with me?"

Regina knew that Giulia was very devoted to her family and would miss them terribly. She was accustomed to spending one day a week at home, and always looked forward to it.

"Oh, no, Miss Gina! I want to come with you! But you are to have a new maid, a French maid! I am being sent to your brother's family in Connecticut!" She burst out in sobs, which she tried to smother in her handkerchief.

Regina caught her breath in shock. "You are? You must have misunderstood! I especially wished for you to come with me!"

The girl shook her head vigorously, wiping her face and sniffing. "It is not to be, Miss Gina," she struggled to say quietly. "Mrs. Pierce told me that—he—the baron—he hired a French maid. She came over on the ship with them. That Madame de Lamartine hired her, and she'll be—be dressing you—for the wedding tomorrow!"

Regina went right to her mother, only to have Giulia's news confirmed. "Yes, of course, dear. You can't take an Italian maid to France! She won't speak French, and she just isn't right for a *baroness*! It was terribly kind of Madame de Lamartine to bring Ninette. Didn't I tell you?"

"No, you didn't! Am I not to be told anything about my own future? Who dared to hire a maid for me, as though I were a child? Giulia has been with me for four years. She knows my tastes—"

Mrs. Pierce turned uneasily from her contemplation of the wedding gifts of silver, china, lace, a gold coffee service. "My dear child, why should you be bothered with this? Your husband decided you should have a French maid and asked his friend to hire one and train her. I think it was very thoughtful of him."

"Without telling me?"

When Julian came that afternoon, she was cool to him. He noticed it immediately, eyeing her uneasily. The damage had been done so it was too late to speak her mind, but she wouldn't soon forget what had happened. She was glad when he went off to a bachelor's dinner that her elder brother George had arranged, and she went to bed early, but not to sleep.

In the morning, the French maid Ninette came to Regina. She was not an arrogant, disdainful woman, as Regina had feared, but a small, thin, nervous girl of about eighteen. She had been well trained, however, and was silent unless spoken to, neat and deft in her work, a marvelous hairdresser. Regina had asked Giulia to remain, and to her surprise and relief the two girls got along fairly well.

Ninette put up Regina's thick chestnut hair and adjusted the coronet of diamonds and the lace veil, which fell down past her shoulders to the hem of the ivory brocade gown, and made Regina feel as if she were drowning in a white mist. The girls exclaimed over her, and Mrs. Pierce nodded her approval.

After Regina was dressed, time seemed to fly. Soon she was alone with her father in the black carriage, riding to the church, but there was no time for words. Frederick Pierce was afraid to touch the beautiful stranger beside him and, besides, hugging would have mussed her hair or crushed her gown. He muttered something about hoping she would be happy.

Regina wondered if she would be; drearily, she supposed it was a bit late to consider that.

The red carpet was laid at the church. Eight brides-maids, cleverly chosen by Emilia for their positions in society and their appearance, led the way up the aisle, each wearing a different shade of pink, from deep rose to palest shell pink.

Julian and Claude waited at the minister's side as Regina moved slowly up the aisle to the traditional wedding music. She felt outside herself, as if she were looking in on a stranger's wedding, and when Julian finally took her hand to put on the ring, he started at the coldness of her fingers. When he released her hand, she put it back inside the white muff covered with orchids, wondering if she would ever be warm again.

Outside, the March sky was cloudy and it looked like it might rain any time. The wind blew in chill gusts across Manhattan, picking up Regina's skirts and blowing her veil in Julian's face as well-wishers showered the newlyweds with rice.

The reception was a flurry of noise: popping champagne corks, laughter from the men, and shrill giggles from the ladies as wine and whiskey were rapidly consumed. Julian and Regina cut the towering white cake, but she ate little, feeling slightly nauseous.

"You look a bit white, Gina," her brother George said in her ear. "Not feeling quite the thing?"

"I'm all right, George."

"We might come over and visit you, you know!" he said, trying to boost her spirits. He had felt all along that Regina was being pushed into marriage. "All we have to do is talk Sally and Betsy into facing the ocean voyage. Then we might come see you."

"You must come, to be sure," said Julian, overhearing George as he approached from the far side of the room. "You will be most welcome."

"Regina might get homesick so we'll have to come to cheer her up. She ain't used to living abroad."

"I shall try to make her feel at home," Julian responded in his quiet way, but Regina felt he was displeased. Before she could intercede, Simone de Lamartine appeared at Julian's side and took his arm, clinging to it and smiling into his bright green eyes. She was fashionably gowned in beige lace, with a big picture hat of lace and feathers that made everyone else look dowdy in comparison. Her gloves and shoes were dark brown, and her glossy black hair was dressed high, with small curls hanging beside her delicate ears.

She said swiftly in French—Regina just caught the words—"My dearest Julian, to think of you marrying like this! To a common American, when you could have—"

He stopped her, his tone angry. "Guard your tongue, Simone. You shall not make trouble here!"

Regina pretended not to understand, turning with a smile to an elderly guest, a friend of her father's. But she was burning inside. What had that woman been about to say? When you could have married nobility? What a nerve she had! An enemy, thought Regina, catching the woman's cold calculated glance above the sweet red-lipped smile.

Simone managed to hold on to Julian's arm long enough for an alert photographer to snap their picture together, but Julian was obviously displeased. He said something to her in a furious whisper, and Simone shrugged, smiling as she slipped away. She looks like a cat that swallowed a bird, Regina thought uneasily. She had *wanted* that picture taken. Why?

The afternoon wore on. Emilia did not want it to end; she was in her glory. The Astors had come! Mrs. Astor had been gracious and had spoken of inviting the Pierces to dinner the following week. Mr. Astor enjoyed talking business with Mr. Pierce. Emilia's cup overflowed. She was made. Every major newspaper had sent a society reporter and a photographer. Crowds hung about the doorways to see who came in and out. She could ask no more today. But already she anticipated mentioning her daughter casually in conversation, saying, "My daughter, the Baroness de Verlaine, writes that—"

Regina returned to her parents' home on Fifth Avenue for the last time, to change into her going-away dress. Giulia was not there so Ninette helped her, saying that Giulia had gone to the hotel to assist her new mistress, Madame Sally Pierce. Regina bit her lips. They had not even let her know! She hadn't a chance to thank Giulia for the years of care, or to say good-bye.

She sat down and wrote a quick note to Giulia, entrusting it to the butler, Horace. He assured her that he would see that Giulia received the note and the enclosed money that was a gift from Regina. "Tell her I'm sorry not to have seen her again. I didn't know—" Regina's voice faltered.

It was a little thing, but to the tired, frightened girl it loomed large. Her husband had chosen a new maid, dismissed the other, and had not even told her. To Regina it was an ominous warning of the events ahead.

Finally Regina was dressed in a gown of cream brocade, full skirted and sweeping. Over it she wore her full-length mink cloak. Her hat was wide-brimmed beige straw ringed with red roses. As soon as she was ready, the carriage arrived to take them to the ship, which was already in the harbor. It would leave early in the morning.

Frederick Pierce stared at his daughter's pale face and finally caught her in a bear hug and kissed her. "You'll be fine. You'll be just fine," he whispered hoarsely.

Julian took her arm and drew her gently away. "I will take care of her, sir," he assured Mr. Pierce. "And she will write often, I am sure of it."

They departed, Ninette sitting in the seat opposite her mistress, her face taut with anxiety and excitement. At the ocean liner, an officer showed them to their suite of rooms. Regina had just turned to speak casually to Julian, something about supper plans, when their door burst open.

Claude came in, followed by Simone de Lamartine. Regina stared in surprise. It was so rude of them, surely Julian would scold them.

"So here you are! How smart you were to get a suite," cried Claude. "I have a pokey hole of a cabin, and Simone is miserable! We *must* share your sitting room. Regina will not mind, will you, dear?" He tossed her a careless kiss from his lips.

Regina froze.

"I imagine we will wish to be private here," Julian said amiably. "However, there is a large first-class lounge, Claude, and you may order as many drinks as you wish!"

As Regina stood rigidly at the door of the bedroom, Simone sat down without being invited. "Such a beautiful suite," she purred in French. "Julian, you have done well for yourself!" Every word she spoke seemed to contain a hidden meaning and a little dart for Regina.

"About dinner this evening," Claude said. "I looked over the dining room and chose three tables close together. I ordered the wine for tonight."

He strolled about the room as though he belonged there.

Regina couldn't stand it any longer. "Please excuse me," she said, avoiding Julian's gaze as she retreated to the bedroom and shut the door. She could hear the voices as they laughed and joked in French, and talked about the evening ahead. Soon she stopped listening. Her head ached. She didn't want to concentrate on translating all their chatter.

Some time later there was a tap on her door and Julian came in, giving her a keen look. "It is time to go down to dinner, Regina. Are you ready?"

"Yes. I suppose so."

"You have not even removed your hat," he said quietly. "Shall I help you?"

Silently she turned to the mirror and removed her hat, stuck the hat pins viciously into the roses that trimmed it, and brushed back her hair with her hands. Julian was gazing at her thoughtfully in the mirror, and his face had a cool, distant look to it.

"I hope you will like my friends and relatives," he said, and it seemed to her like a warning. "They think you are stunning, but either shy or reserved. I want you to come to like them all."

"Yes, Julian." He offered her his arm.

They went down to dinner. She was seated at Julian's right, at a table just the right distance from the orchestra. Simone de Lamartine in a stunning low-cut crimson dress, was on his left. She was so elegant, so smart, and her conversation in rapid French seemed to amuse everyone.

The older relatives were at another table, and Regina found herself wishing she could be with them instead. They seemed kind and much more friendly. But no, she must sit with Julian and smile and be polite, and even try to eat after that huge wedding reception. She did refuse all the wines pressed on her.

"You do not care for wine, *chérie*?" drawled Simone in

English, her eyes narrowed on Regina. "You will seem
strange to those of us in the country of fine wines! Perhaps
we can change you."

"No doubt," said Regina, with cool emphasis.

Julian looked at her thoughtfully.

And that was her wedding evening.

CHAPTER FOUR

Regina retired to the bedroom. Ninette was waiting for her, so pale and shaky that Regina finally realized the maid was as nervous as the bride.

"Madame la Baronne approves this nightdress?" she asked timidly, indicating the fluff of white lace laid out on the bed nearest the porthole. "Madame la Baronne wishes me to aid her with her hair? Madame la Baronne—"

"Please call me Miss Regina," interrupted Regina impatiently, beginning to pull the many pins from her heavy chestnut hair. "There, that's better. Yes, please brush it for me."

Ninette helped her undress and put on the nightdress and negligee. Regina sat down before the mirror, and the maid began to brush out her hair in long sure strokes that were somehow soothing.

"If I do anything you dislike, please tell me," the girl said softly. Regina met her nervous look in the mirror.

She could not help smiling. "You do very well, Ninette. Who trained you?" she added, with seeming casualness. "Madame de Lamartine?"

"Oh, *non, non, non, non, non!*" sputtered the girl. "*Non,* not that one! It was Madame la Baronne, the Dowager Baronness, your mother-in-law," she explained. "She brings me from the village when I am fourteen. She says, so kindly, 'You are smart girl, you are clever with the needle. I teach you, good, so you do well in the service of the château de Verlaine.' I work hard, I try, I learn. She is pleased with me, I think. She is so kind, the Dowager Baroness. When Monsieur le Baron send for a maid, Madame, she say to me, 'You will go, Ninette. Across the ocean you will go, and assist the new Madame la Baronne.' " She beamed happily at Regina.

Regina was so happy to learn that the girl had been chosen by her mother-in-law and not Simone de Lamartine that she beamed back at her, cementing a timid friendship between them.

"I am so glad you came, Ninette. You are—very good—a very good maid. I will be glad of your assistance."

"Madame la Baronne is most kind," said Ninette, heaving a sigh of relief.

Julian entered the room without knocking and began to remove his black jacket. Regina stiffened. He said casually, "Ninette, I heard you speaking English. I know you wish to speak it at times. However, I wish you to speak French to Madame. She is trying to become more familiar with French."

Ninette bobbed a curtsey to him. *"Oui, Monsieur le Baron,"* she said obediently. "Always as you wish."

She disappeared at his nod, and Regina continued to brush her long thick hair. She saw Julian glancing at her, studying her in the mirror.

"Your hair is even more glorious than I had imagined."

"Merci, Monsieur."

"Julian," he said with a smile. "Now we are married, you surely will not call me Monsieur!"

She continued to brush her hair nervously, stroking more than the required one hundred times. He came up behind her, took the brush from her hand, and set it down. "Regina," he said softly, "you are very lovely. You are not too tired, are you?"

She shook her head. She felt numb, and weary, but he seemed to want her to reject her tiredness. He drew her up into his arms.

With a shock, she felt his lean hard body pressed against her soft one, his warmth penetrating the silk of the nightdress and negligee. His mouth came down on hers, slowly seeking her response. She had never been kissed on the lips before. Even her father and brothers merely brushed her cheek with their lips. She felt the jolt of it race through her body.

His lips moved to the softness of her cheeks and then to the lobe of her ear. His tongue darted lightly into her ear and she thought it was the most sensuous thing she had ever felt. She shivered. He drew her over to the bed and lay down with her. Then he moved impatiently. "I haven't undressed," he muttered, and got up again, leaving her lying in the middle of the bed near the porthole. She didn't know whether to get up again or lie there. Embarrassed, she moved into the bed, pulling the blankets over her. She felt cold.

He undressed, turned down the lights, and came to the bed. He laughed softly as he pulled her out of the blankets. "We don't need this," he murmured, and helped her remove the lacy negligee that covered her nightdress, unfastening the ribbons that tied it at her waist and throat. He tossed it aside and slid into bed with her.

Involuntarily, she stiffened in fear. He felt it, and his hands were gentle on her back and shoulders, stroking her.

"Regina? Did your mother talk to you—about this?" he asked.

She gulped and managed to mutter, "Yes."

"Good. But it will still be a shock for you, as it is for any gently brought up girl," he said soothingly. "I will be very slow and careful, and not hurt you very much, I believe. I am afraid it is a necessary part of marriage, the hurting at first. Later, you will come to enjoy the love and the caresses."

His lips moved on her chin, down over her throat, and his hands slid over her silky nightdress, gently sliding it from her shoulders and breasts. With a shock, she felt his hands on her rounded breasts. He cupped them, teased the nipples until they were taut, then softly kissed them.

"You are so beautiful," he murmured in French; his words that night were all in French. Sometimes his emotion overcame him and the passion blurred his words so that she could not understand them. Somehow, oddly, she resented it bitterly that he did not speak in English that first night, when she felt so strange.

His arms tightened about her, and he moved his body over hers. She was frightened as he pressed himself down on her, and she squeezed her eyes shut to block out the pain as he pushed himself into her tender body. She fought against crying out, but then came a final thrust, forcing a moan to escape her lips.

"Oh—don't—don't—it hurts—please—"

But it was done. He lay on her, panting, as the tears coursed down her hot cheeks. She was shaking, but so was he. Finally he moved and drew back from her.

"I am so sorry, my darling. You are so very small. But it is done now," he said soothingly. "There will be no more pain, I think. Come now, Regina, do not weep, it distresses me."

He soothed her, and to her deep embarrassment, he even got up and brought some ointment to put between her thighs. Then he kissed her forehead and crossed to the other bed to go to sleep.

She pressed her hand to her mouth, to keep back sobs. What a horrible thing marriage was! She hated it. And she felt so strange, so terrible, as if she had been somehow violated. Her body had been a private matter—before today. Only her maid saw her, and she only briefly. But now a man had gazed at her, held her with his hard hands, pressed himself on her, forced her to receive him. She felt ashamed, as though she were now unclean. She wished she could get up and bathe.

She lay rigidly in the narrow bed as Julian slept peacefully, his breathing even. So this was what marriage meant; the man satisfied his desires and went to sleep. Her mother had told her, briskly and practically, that she must satisfy her husband, and that in return he would be peaceful and gentle with her.

"But what about me?" Regina asked herself passionately. "Is a woman nothing? Is she only made to—lie there—and give in to whatever her husband wishes to do? It is degrading! It makes me feel like I'm just something to be used for his pleasure!"

She felt such rage that she could not lie still. She tossed from one side to the other but she only succeeded in hurting herself, increasing the pain between her soft thighs and the soreness of her breasts. He had bitten her nipples with enjoyment, and she had felt both horror and an odd pleasure. What did it all mean?

If only he had loved her. If only there had been kisses and embraces between them before their marriage, but society did not permit such freedom. She put her hand wonderingly to her breasts and closed her eyes. It was a long time before she slept.

When she wakened, she knew by the sunshine streaming in the porthole that it was late morning. Julian was dressed and standing beside the bed. He smiled as he looked down at her.

"You are beautiful, even in the morning," he said, "with your hair mussed and tossed on the pillow." He sat down on the side of the bed and bent to kiss her. She endured it, and when his kisses became more passionate, his tongue darting between her lips, she was shocked to discover that she enjoyed it.

Then she heard a voice from their sitting room. "Julian, Julian! Aren't we going to do some shooting this morning?"

It was Claude! Regina jerked herself from Julian's hold, her cheeks scarlet. Julian stood up, frowning.

"This is too much," he said. "He should not disturb us in our own room." He hesitated. "Do you wish to come to breakfast, or shall I send Ninette to you with something?"

"Send Ninette," she murmured, and turned over to face the window. She could have killed Claude!

Julian went out, and she heard the rumble of voices. She caught Claude saying, "But my dear Julian, it is past eleven o'clock!"

"This is our private suite, Claude, and I do not wish—" The voices lowered, but Regina sighed in relief. She hoped he would put his foot down, and keep something of their lives private.

Ninette came in soon with a tray of hot chocolate, some sweet rolls and butter. Regina eyed the tray in dismay. "It is the French way," murmured Ninette soothingly. "If you wish something more—"

"I suppose I had best become accustomed." Regina sighed.

She found the breakfast too sweet but she ate everything Ninette had brought, and then requested a bath. Although it was a curious sensation to bathe while the ship lurched about, Regina tried to relax in the warm, soothing water. Her thighs stung, and her legs ached. There were faint bruises on her body also. So far she didn't think she cared much for marriage. Like so many other things, it seemed to be made for the pleasure and convenience of men.

Ninette laid out a smart outfit of navy blue with white piping, and a little hat that would hold down flying locks of hair against the wind. Regina dressed; Ninette arranged her hair cleverly and set the hat on her head. Then Regina went out onto the windy deck.

She found no one she knew. She walked for a while, briskly, and at one point she heard strange whooshing sounds and someone spoke of "skeet shooting," but she couldn't see where the noises were coming from. She wondered if that was where Julian was, and felt very much alone.

Presently a little boy in uniform circled the deck, ringing a bell to announce luncheon. Regina waited, not knowing where to go. Everyone around her seemed to be leaving the first-class deck. She decided to follow them, and found herself in the dining room.

She hesitated in the doorway, looking at the table where she had dined last night. Julian sat at the head with Simone de Lamartine at his right. A stabbing pain tore Regina's chest.

She almost fled, but instead courage came to her, and anger. She lifted her chin and strolled slowly toward the table. Julian saw her and came to his feet, his face flushed.

"My dear, I did not know you had arisen," he said, taking her hand. He looked uneasily down at Simone, who smiled and sat still.

"No matter, there is a place at the next table," Regina said coldly, pulling her hand from Julian's and walking away. He followed, to see her to her seat and introduce her to the others there.

"I am sorry about this," he muttered in her ear. She shrugged and turned to her companion with a smile.

The relative was elderly and spoke only French, so the effort of speaking to him and to the others at the table occupied her. She pushed the food on her plate around with a fork; her appetite had gone.

Julian finished his meal quickly and soon came to her side, drawing up an extra chair and joining in their conversation.

"Would you care to walk on deck?" Julian asked, when she had finished her coffee.

"Yes, I believe so," she said. He sent someone down to their cabin to fetch her cloak and hood, as the wind had grown cold. Julian set the cloak about Regina's shoulders with great care.

Regina felt so angry and confused, she did not know herself. She was curious about Simone, but was too proud to even mention her name. Instead she took the arm Julian held out to her and strolled the deck with him. She answered his remarks mechanically.

"Yes, the sea is beautiful. It does look rather stormy to

the west. . . . Yes, the food is delicious. . . . No, I am
quite warm, thank you."

Moments later, Claude came along, and Regina was actually glad to see him. She felt awkward with Julian, and
he seemed more reserved than ever. Claude's gay remarks
made them laugh, and she relaxed a little.

Another couple was strolling toward them, smiling at
Julian. He stopped short when he saw them and cried,
"Kenneth and Victoria!" with unmistakable pleasure.

The two newcomers smiled warmly, and paused to shake
hands.

"Regina, I wish to introduce to you these dear friends,
Americans who live in Paris. Mrs. Longstreth and Mr.
Longstreth," Julian said formally. "Vicky and Ken—my
wife, Regina."

They shook hands, and Regina looked them over shyly.
Victoria was about thirty, and Kenneth perhaps thirty-five.
She was dark haired, with a clear complexion and brown
eyes. He was blond with blue eyes and a red face, rather
plump and hearty. Claude had grown silent, and soon left
them, moving away to lean on the railing.

"We heard you had married, Julian—about time, old
boy!" Ken teased. "And what a beauty!"

"We saw your pictures in the newspapers but we never
dreamed we would be on the same ship," Vicky added,
sending a sweet smile and a gently critical look over Regina. "You *are* a real beauty—Julian, you are so lucky!"

"I know I am," he said, and put his arm about Regina,
drawing her closer to him. "And as pretty as she is, she has
a brain also! And she loves music! Won't Maman and
Thérèse be pleased with my bride?" He sounded proud and
happy.

"Are you staying in Paris for a while? Why don't we
show you around?" Ken suggested.

Julian accepted before Regina could speak. "That would
be a pleasure. Darling"—he turned to Regina—"these people know Paris like the backs of their hands. They know
artists and musicians, the—shall we say—seamy side of
Paris as well as the social. Ken is an undersecretary at the
American Embassy, and I verily believe he knows everybody in the city."

Longstreth grinned and took the compliment in stride.

"What a great time we can have," he said. "We shall not impose on you—don't think it—this is your honeymoon, after all. But it would be a pleasure for us to take you out some evening when you have the time."

Regina could have kissed him for his tact. He was the first person who seemed to take for granted that a honeymoon couple should be left alone!

They found deck chairs together, Ken organizing it all efficiently. Regina lay back in the sunshine and opened her cloak. She felt cozy and warm, with Julian lying silently, eyes closed, on one side, and Vicky chattering amiably on the other. Ken was sitting up, telling them enthusiastically about a new wave of painters in France called the Impressionists, among them men named Cézanne, Manet, and Monet, whom Ken predicted would be famous. Evidently he respected them, but the art critics did not.

Vicky told them about the new operas by Delibes, Bizet, and Saint-Saëns. There seemed a wealth of culture in Paris, and the Longstreths were familiar with it all.

Tea was served in the afternoon while they relaxed in their chairs. Afterward, Julian decided to stroll the deck, and Regina walked with him for a time, but the wind was blustery and she soon retreated to her deck chair for another talk with Vicky. It was so good to be able to talk with someone, to feel at ease in conversation.

Some of Julian's elderly relatives had ventured out of their cabins and were sitting nearby, talking in French. Regina paid them little attention, as they were not speaking to her and she was engrossed in Vicky's story about an American divorcee who had made a scandal in Paris.

"Look at her," muttered one of Julian's great aunts in French. "That shameless one, see how she clings to him!"

Regina idly turned her gaze and was startled to see Julian coming round the bow of the ship with Simone on his arm. Clutching her fashionable scarlet hat to her head, Simone laughed up at Julian coquettishly.

"Shameless! He's married now, the past is dead. She shouldn't have come. After all, he would never have married her, so why does she not let him go?"

Regina could not believe what she had heard. Vicky, on her other side, leaning back with eyes closed, did not seem to have heard. Perhaps, thought Regina desperately, she misunderstood. But as Simone and Julian came closer, she heard one of the older women say harshly, "That Simone de Lamartine, she's a troublemaker. Julian is well rid of her. Why did he allow her to come to America for his wedding? His bride is young and innocent, but even she will guess—"

"Hush, hush," her companion warned. "She may hear you!"

"She does not understand much French yet, thank God for it," said the older woman vigorously. Her friend managed to silence her, however, as Julian and Simone came closer.

Regina closed her eyes. She couldn't bear it! Her suspicions were true. He had had an affair with Simone, and from the looks of things he might still be carrying on with her. She had heard about the amorous Frenchmen and the way they kept mistresses, but had discounted it. Julian did not seem the type. But what did she know of men? She had been shielded from them all her life.

"Regina?" Julian was standing at the foot of her deck chair. "Are you asleep? Shall I take you below? The wind is rising."

"Oh—yes. Perhaps I had best retire to change for dinner." She managed to speak naturally, but she could not smile at him and Simone. The woman still clung to him as though for support, but her catlike smile was cool and superior as she stared down at Regina. Regina unwound the deck robe and moved to stand up. To assist her, Julian had to shake off Simone's insistent grasp.

Vicky stirred, sat up. "Oh—I was asleep," she said. "What a hectic time in New York! Oh, Ken, do let us go below. It has turned cold."

Ken was yawning and stretching. Vicky moved to whisper to Regina. "We change for dinner the second night. Do wear something spectacular, my dear, and knock them off their feet!"

"Thank you," Regina said gratefully.

Julian supported her as they moved across the windy deck to the doors. An officer opened the door for them, and they escaped into the warm interior of the ship.

"Do you like Vicky and Ken?" he asked casually as they wound along the corridors.

"Oh, yes, they seem quite nice."

"They are. They gossip a bit, but don't pay much atten-

tion to that," he said. "Otherwise, they are amusing, and
they know so much about the arts. We must get Ken to
show you his jewelry collection. He is quite a gem expert."

"I noticed his rings, and hers," Regina said, trying to
sound natural. But how could she erase Simone from her
mind? She wished she could be alone, to think it over and
calm herself. But Julian stayed close at hand as they
changed for dinner, and then Ninette came in to help
Regina dress.

Regina chose a smart outfit that night, heeding Vicky's
advice. Her gown was of rose silk, with ruffles to the knees,
then pleats to her ankles. With it she wore her diamonds, a
tiara, a choker, bracelet, and rings. Julian raised his eyebrows.

"Am I overdressed for the evening?" asked Regina
coolly as Ninette fastened the safety clasp on her bracelet.

"Not at all. You look . . . splendid," he said soberly.

When they entered the dining room, Regina on Julian's
arm, her chin was raised, her gaze steady. Then she saw
Simone.

The woman was in scarlet, a scarlet that would kill dead
any rose or pink within fifty yards. The gown was daringly
low-cut, showing the tops of her fine breasts, and the jet
necklace laced with pearls was two inches wide on her
throat. She waved a fan of black feathers, and on her dark
hair was a black lace mantilla fastened with a pearl pin.
Her skin was like ivory, skillfully powdered, and her eyes
were outlined in kohl. Regina looked—and felt—like a
young innocent in comparison.

The dinner was long. Simone seemed to dominate the
conversation, speaking of Julian's mother, his vineyards,
their friends, people they both knew and Regina did not.
She grew more and more silent, quietly furious, but unable
to figure out what to do about it.

As they rose to go to the lounge, Simone moved over to
her with the grace of a cat, the train of her long gown
swishing on the parquet floors.

"My dear, you must learn the art of smart conversation,"
she said, just loud enough for Julian to overhear. "I shall
be happy to assist you any time you wish. Perhaps some
French lessons also. I want to help you—"

Regina burned in silence. She could not even smile at the
woman's arrogance. And she hated it when Julian said,

"That is most kind of you, Simone. I know Regina will be grateful for your assistance. This is all so new to her."

"Forgive me," Regina said clearly, loudly, in English, "but I have been out for some time now. And I have had no difficulty holding my own in New York society. It must be the topics of conversation that are introduced here! I know nothing yet about vineyards or the château—but I shall learn—when I arrive *home*," she said deliberately.

Claude chuckled audaciously in the silence that followed. Simone flushed with fury, sparks flying from her dark eyes.

"Come along, Simone, you may speak to me," said Claude, and took her arm to lead her into the lounge ahead of Julian and Regina.

Julian said in a low voice, "Must you be rude?"

"When necessary," Regina said frostily, and she swept before him but he gripped her arm and forced her to walk more slowly.

In the lounge, she sat quietly. Someone poured coffee and tea, and relatives and friends began to chat again. Claude and Simone were talking, heads together; Julian sent them worried looks while Regina raged inwardly. She was relieved when Vicky and Ken Longstreth came up to sit with her on the couch. Julian had left her momentarily and was surprised to find his place taken by Ken when he returned. He leaned against a post, drinking his coffee, gazing into space as they talked. It was late when the little crowd broke up and Regina stood to leave the room.

Julian came to her to take her arm and escort her to their rooms. He too was quiet, and she stole uneasy glances at him. Was he still angry with her?

Ninette was waiting to undress her while Julian changed in the small room off the bedroom. Another night. Regina's hand moved to her face in a weary gesture. She would have to endure it, and many thousands more.

It seemed that a new lifetime had been born with her marriage, one in which she was uneasy and uncomfortable, and often vulnerable and hurt. Would it go on forever? Probably, she thought bitterly. She had been bought and sold. Why should she expect happiness?

She got into bed. Ninette whispered good night and departed. When Julian came in, he brushed his hair slowly in front of the mirror before turning down the lights. She lay tensely, waiting to see what he would do.

He came to her bed, took off his robe, and lay down with her. She froze. He put his arms about her and said quietly, against her shoulder, "I shall not hurt you tonight, Regina. Please do not be afraid of me."

She could not believe it, but he meant well, she supposed. Even with her eyes closed she saw Simone holding him possessively, and Julian smiling at her smart remarks. She could not relax.

Was Simone his mistress? Had she been? Was she now? Regina knew little of such matters. She had only heard her brothers joke and laugh about things, but it was not a subject discussed openly in her presence.

What did an affair involve? Would Julian continue his affair, if indeed Simone was his mistress? Did everyone know about them? Why hadn't her father learned of it when he had had Julian investigated?

Julian's hand moved gently over her shoulders, and he bent to kiss her white throat. "So beautiful," he whispered. *"Belle—ma belle—"*

His lips moved over her throat, nipping gently at her shoulder and bared arm, under the silk nightdress. But she was stiff and unyielding, and he lay back with a sigh.

"Tonight, I will just hold you," he said quietly. "Do not be afraid, *ma belle.*"

"I am not afraid!" she blurted out angrily. Courage was a trait she much admired, and no one called her a coward.

"Of course not, not really," he soothed. His hand moved over her back, drawing her closer to him. "It is just all strange to you. It will take time for us to be close and comfortable with each other. But I wish most of all for you to be happy in your new life with me."

"Happy?"

"Yes, of course," he said. "When we are at home in the château, we may be alone often to talk of our own thoughts. I look forward to that time with you, Regina."

She was silent. Her eyes closed and she realized she was sleepy. She moved her head against his shoulder, smelled the masculine scent of his body and the shaving lotion he used.

"Yes, sleep, my darling," he whispered in her ear, and kissed it gently. "We have all of our lives together."

His hand was still on her back, not moving. Tonight he was not grabbing her or lying on her or being hurtful. A long sigh escaped her lips, and her thoughts ran together, into sleep.

She awakened a couple of times in the night, to the strange feeling of a man in bed with her. Julian's face was turned toward her, tranquil in the moonlight that streamed in through the porthole. She studied it sleepily. It had strength, firmness, the cheekbones jutting out. Was he too thin? Did he work too hard? Tenderness overcame her as she saw him so vulnerable and defenseless.

She lifted her hand cautiously to touch his face. He stirred, murmured, but she could not catch any words. In the silence of the night, he seemed all hers, close to her; her husband, her lover.

CHAPTER FIVE

Aboard ship, Regina continued to feel in two worlds. During the day, Julian paid much attention to his relatives and friends, and she often wandered the deck alone. Sometimes Vicky joined her, and they strolled and chatted in English.

Regina felt that Vicky understood the situation, and her unspoken sympathy was heart-warming. Over and over, Regina was stung to anger by Simone and her possessiveness of Julian. She heard the whispers and saw the reproving looks at Simone and at Julian. Did all the world know of his affairs? It seemed so. She wondered bitterly how she would endure it.

When Ken joined Regina and Vicky, the conversation often became lighthearted. It was hard to be cold and aloof and unhappy when Ken Longstreth was around. He had a buoyant humor and an unquenchable gaiety that she much admired. Yet he had not had an easy life, she learned from Vicky, who adored her husband.

"Ken was the youngest of three sons. His father was a wealthy railroad magnate," explained Vicky during one of their solitary strolls. "The eldest inherited most of the stock and bossed them all unmercifully. I suppose he had to, to carry on the business. But Ken rebelled, turned to politics, and then became a diplomat. He has done well, but he fought hard to get where he is."

They seemed to have plenty of money. But they had had no children, and when Vicky spoke of it once, briefly, her mouth was sad. They had been married eight years and they still hoped, but Ken had spoken recently of adopting the son of one of his cousins, who had eight children. "I suppose it would work out," Vicky said, "but, oh, I did want to give him a child."

Regina did not know what to say. She was so newly married that she could hardly believe she was a wife, much less a possible mother. What would Julian do if she did not have his son? Divorce her, probably. But, no; he was a

Catholic. He could not divorce—or could he? If she didn't
bear a child, could he have the marriage annulled?

These were hardly thoughts for a new bride, she knew,
but she felt raw and wounded by his treatment of her. So
devoted at night, so cool in the daytime. He was very proper and formal, and made sure each relative and friend had
a share of his attention. But Simone demanded more, and
she received it. She often walked the deck with him, snug-
gling close to him and clutching her frivolous hat, often
shrieking with enjoyment and feigned alarm at each gust of
wind.

"He should be strolling with you!" Vicky muttered, between tight lips, as they passed the two of them one afternoon.

"He seems to be very much amused by her," Regina said
colorlessly, passing them without a glance in their direction. She sensed Julian looking at her, but she gazed off at
the turbulent blue-green sea.

Vicky gave her an odd look as they paused to lean on
the deck railing. "You must assert yourself, Regina," she
said. "God forbid I should hand out advice so soon, but
don't let yourself be trampled on!"

There was no time for more. Julian and Simone paused
beside them, and soon Simone was rattling on brightly
about how much she was enjoying the journey.

"Such a marvelous holiday for us!" she purred. "I can't
thank you enough, Julian, for arranging all this!"

Regina gave Julian a wide-eyed stare. He had arranged
for Simone to come? Had he paid for her trip? By his rising
color and rare confusion, she guessed that he had.

"You deserved a holiday," he said brusquely, "as you
have been working so hard on the estate. She now manages it alone," he explained to Regina.

"How very . . . clever of her," murmured Regina.
Julian shot her a hard look. It had sounded catty, she decided, but she didn't feel like being complimentary.

She half expected Julian to scold her about the incident
when they were alone that night, but he did not speak of it.
He's afraid to bring it up, she thought angrily, and lay
stiffly in his arms though he caressed her warmly. Finally
he got up and went to his own bed without a word.

She was happy to arrive in France. She was weary of the
ship, of wearing different clothes morning, noon, and night.

She was tired of being forced to witness his closeness to
Simone and to endure Claude's joking remarks. She was
tired of straining to understand the rapidly spoken conver-
sations. She wanted to be home! But that was impossible.

The ship docked at Le Havre, and Julian and Claude
arranged for their departure. They rounded up the multi-
tude of trunks, suitcases, hatboxes, crates of wedding presents and purchases from New York City. Julian spoke to
the officials, managed to reserve a fine parlor car in which
they would proceed to Paris, and ushered Regina and the
other ladies into it.

"How long is the journey?" asked Regina. They had
risen at five o'clock in the morning, and she was still quite
sleepy.

"Only three hours," said Julian encouragingly, and sat
down beside her on the red plush seat next to hers. Simone
looked longingly toward him and smiled, dimpling. But for
once he turned away from her. "I want to point out the
sights to you along the way. I hope you are not too weary
to enjoy them."

He was as good as his word, pointing out little fishing
villages along the way, glimpses of the sea and the sailing
vessels, the towers of Rouen. By the time they reached
Paris, Regina too was craning her neck and exclaiming
over the sight of the Eiffel Tower.

To her surprise, and quiet relief, the relatives and friends
began to disperse at the railroad station in Paris. Some
took trains to the north while others took carriages to a
train station in the south. Claude managed the crates and
trunks and boxes, and saw them into carriages.

"See you at the château!" he said cheerfully, waving to
Julian and Regina. Simone was in the carriage with him as
the driver picked up the reins and started off.

"They are not staying in Paris?" Regina asked as casually as she could.

Julian gave her one of his quick enigmatic looks, which
she was beginning to realize meant that he saw much more
than he said.

"No. Not on our honeymoon," he said definitely. "Simone has an apartment here, and so does Claude. But I
gave him orders to take everything home at once. He is
inclined to remain longer and play around, forgetting his
duties."

"His—duties?"

"He is manager of the Verlaine estate," Julian explained. "He is my first cousin, but inherited nothing from his father. He has worked for us more than ten years now. I cannot do everything, and he has been invaluable."

Regina was silent, digesting that news. Claude seemed so dashing, so charming, not like the manager of an estate. She wondered how well he did; he did not seem as responsible as one of her father's managers or clerks or foremen. The French were truly different.

The ride to the townhouse was rather long but thoroughly enjoyable. Away from the train station, the avenues opened out, and she saw the chestnut trees in blossom.

"April—and in Paris," said Julian softly. "Smell the fragrance, Regina! There is nothing like it."

Obediently she drew a deep breath and smiled joyously, turning toward him to touch his hand spontaneously. "Oh, they smell as lovely as they look! Just look at those flowers!"

She pointed to a charming park tucked unexpectedly between two streets. She craned forward to look at the daffodils, blazing red tulips, lilac bushes bursting with lavender and white blossoms. Then they were past it, and trotting into a wide boulevard. Julian showed her the home of a friend, and she studied the houses against the hills of Montmartre.

"Shall we go up there?" she asked timidly, indicating the hills. "I've heard it is charming."

"Yes, of course, I shall take you there. You will never go there alone, however. It is quite dangerous for a woman," he said.

"Dangerous? Among artists and writers and musicians?"

"Among those who hang on the fringes of the art world," he said firmly, his chin jutting forward stubbornly. "Promise me you will not go out alone."

She was silent, troubled. She had ridden alone except for a coachman in New York, and been fearless. Julian's fingers closed over her gray-gloved hand. "Promise, Regina!" he insisted. "It is truly not safe."

"I do promise then," she said in a low voice. "But I am accustomed to going where I please, to shop and ride about—"

"Not now," he said. "You belong to me now, and I shall

not allow you to run into danger. Remember, you are in unfamiliar surroundings."

He seemed truly concerned, and she felt warmed by it as well as irritated. A married woman seemed to be bound by so many strings!

"Do you mean just in Paris? Surely I can go about alone at Verlaine."

"Well . . . perhaps there. But I would prefer to have you go with me," he said.

The coachman was pulling up the horses. Startled, she looked about. They were in a large square formed by three sides of a stone building, capped with a slanting red roof. The fourth side was the street, edged by a handsome grassy park. A butler, in green and gold livery matching that of the coachman, approached the carriage. Julian smiled down and greeted him as he reached to hand Regina down.

The other servants were formal, but undeniably welcoming. It was their great pleasure to serve Madame la Baronne, they said warmly. They hoped she would enjoy her new home, and Paris, it was so beautiful in the spring!

After she had rested for a day, Regina began to explore her new home. The center of the townhouse was three stories tall, while the wings on either side were two stories. It had been built in the seventeenth century and the furnishings were from the seventeenth and eighteenth centuries, formal, gilded, stiff, yet of luxurious fabrics and design.

The entry hall was of sandalwood, gilded and ornately carved yet somehow as warm and welcoming as the servants. Flowers were arranged, fresh daily, in porcelain vases of blue and white, and there was even a stunning golden vase that usually held white lilacs.

The drawing rooms, four in all, displayed precious Persian carpets of blues, greens, reds, and gold. Regina noted that many of the velvet chairs and sofas were faded and even torn, though neatly mended. She longed to order fresh fabrics for them, and wallpapers for the handsome walls where they were peeling or stained.

Cautiously, she brought it up to Julian. "Do you not think, Julian, that while we are here I might begin to refurnish the rooms? The blue drawing room needs draperies—"

He looked embarrassed and defensive at once. "It would cost a great deal, Regina. You do not realize how much material would be required. And I wish to spend our time here seeing Paris, becoming close, not redecorating."

"But I could have them measured, we could look about for fabrics, and see—"

"No," he said, frowning. "I do not wish to put any money into this—not at this time. After the harvest there may be some things we can do at Verlaine."

She meant to suggest that she had money of her own, but the look on his face dissuaded her. He was sensitive about the money.

The day after their arrival in Paris, Julian had gone to his bank, and he had been away the entire day. She had not thought much about it, but she had noticed that he'd returned with a portfolio of notes and papers. He spent the entire next day in his study going over them, and when she wandered in to discuss their plans for the evening, he looked up guiltily. She caught the word "paid" in French on several of the papers.

He saw that she had noticed and was looking at him questioningly. Finally he nodded.

"Your father was most generous, Regina," he said, biting his lips. "I have been able to pay debts that were outstanding for many years, since the death of my father."

"Oh!" Regina was stunned. She sank down into the shabby chair opposite his handsome mahogany desk and bent her head. "I am glad—that is over, Julian. You must feel very . . . relieved. To have debts hanging over one— that is terrible."

He studied her face as though unsure of her meaning, then he nodded. "Yes, and the interest here is very high. I kept sinking more and more into debt. Last year I had such hopes for the harvest. I could have paid off much of this—" He waved at the mass of papers before him. "But it failed—" He stopped abruptly.

The unspoken words were there. He had had to come to America to choose a wealthy heiress as a bride. How stinging to his pride, how galling to someone of his temperament, proud and independent as he wished to be.

It was then that Regina began to understand him. She smiled gently and said, "About this evening, Julian. Ken and Vicky wanted to go to Montmartre. Would that fit into your plans, or shall we postpone it? You must be weary, with all the work."

He smiled back at her. "I should like to go out with you, my dear, and celebrate! I feel as light as a feather, now that all this is paid off. I can begin again, with your help. I am . . . most grateful to you, and to your father for his generosity."

"Father said that you were a good investment," she managed to reply lightly. "He has great faith in you, that you will make the vineyards prosper again, as in the old days."

His eyes lightened, changing from green to gold. "He said that? It is very kind of you to tell me. I am very proud of his trust, and I hope it will soon be rewarded."

He rose and picked up a velvet box from the desk, where it lay among the papers. "I was able to have some family gems mounted in new settings for you. I hope you will like them and will wear them tonight."

He snapped open the case. She gasped and took the box carefully in her hand. On the white velvet inside lay a necklace of glowing emeralds set in gold and dotted with small diamonds. There were matching earrings, and a slim bracelet of emeralds and diamonds. The crowning jewel was a huge emerald ring surrounded by diamonds. Regina was speechless.

"Don't you like them?" he asked anxiously.

She let out a long sigh and shook her head slowly. "I have never seen such a splendid set of jewels. I was wondering how to thank you. What gown I could possibly wear to show them off? Can I do justice to them?" She looked up at him smilingly.

He touched her cheek with his long fingers, and his gaze lingered on her. "You will be most beautiful," he said softly. "But people will gaze at you—not at the gems."

He stood back and she said quickly, "I must send a note to Vicky and Ken. What time shall we meet, and where?"

"I'll take care of that. You go and consult with little Ninette about which gown will dazzle us!"

Regina and Ninette chose a soft gray chiffon and velvet gown, which set off the emeralds and diamonds to perfection. Regina's hair was dressed high, and the emeralds circled her slim throat. Ken whistled when he saw her, and insisted on examining the jewelry closely.

"They're marvelous, Julian!" he said admiringly. "And from the old cut of the stones, I'd say they go back several hundred years. About 1550?"

"About right." Julian smiled. "One of my fire-eating ancestors returned with them from a raid into Spain. These probably came from the emerald mines of Brazil, stolen by a Spanish grandee, or maybe pirates," he joked.

Julian was in high spirits that night, boyish and charming as Regina had never seen him. The relief of paying off the old family debts acted like an elixir. They took two carriages up the winding streets into Montmartre, early enough to enjoy the misty blue that stole over the city as the sunset faded into night.

They enjoyed champagne and an amusing revue in a café, and then moved on to a splendid restaurant decorated with Tiffany lamps that cast blue and green and yellow reflections on their faces. Throughout the evening, Ken pointed out the well-known patrons of the restaurant as they came in the door.

"That is the artist Pissarro. Some say he will be the greatest of the great! And there is Monet. I like his work, with its beautiful colors. You must meet him. There, he is looking this way. He sees you, Regina!"

She saw the keen eyes studying her. Every artist, she thought, has that penetrating gaze. She felt as if he could see her very soul.

Later Monet came over to their table. Ken and Julian stood, and Ken introduced them all. Monsieur Monet bowed over Vicky's hand and then Regina's; his eyes lingered on Regina's face.

"I should like to paint you," he said curtly.

She started, her lovely brown eyes wide. "Me? But I— I—am not pretty enough," she stammered.

"Pretty? Hah! You have glorious coloring. No, you are not pretty. You are beautiful," he said, scowling. "I see you in rose, in blue. Come to my studio tomorrow."

"She cannot come," said Julian definitely.

The sharp gaze swung to him. "Why not? I will paint her well!"

"Because we are on our honeymoon, and I want her with me," said Julian seriously.

Someone at a nearby table laughed; everyone was staring at them. Regina put her hands to her cheeks in embarrassment.

"Hah! I can understand that," said the artist, softening. "Very well, another time. You come to me, eh?"

"Perhaps," said Julian. The man walked away, after another assessing look at Regina. Sometime later they saw him sketching at his table, waving off the waiters, stealing glances at Regina and then drawing rapidly.

"The fellow is sketching you anyway, Regina," Ken told her, quite pleased.

"The gall of him. I did not give him permission," Julian grumbled. But he smiled at Regina. He stood and drew her into his arms, guiding her to the dance floor, to the soothing strains of a waltz.

As he swung her close to him, Regina felt his lips on her forehead. "You are *très belle* tonight."

"Thank you, Monsieur," she said demurely. She felt rather intoxicated. A painter had called her beautiful, and Julian had been jealous! And best of all, Simone had gone away. She was quite happy.

He laughed against her hair. "Ah, this is one of the happiest days of my life!"

"Not our wedding day?" she dared to say.

"I was happy then, but not like this. I was terrified of the crowds, worried you might refuse me at the last moment, unable to believe it was happening to me," he said with his old seriousness. "I could not believe you were truly my bride until that night."

She blushed brightly and ducked her head against his black coat. He pulled her close, leading her around the dance floor and back to their table.

The evening was long and gay. They finished their dinner, ending with flaming crêpes soaked in brandy, and more champagne. Then they moved on to a nightspot Ken knew. Regina looked with amazed fascination at the Apache dancers who performed magnificently. The male dancers tossed their female partner between them, high into the air. Every time the girl showed her scarlet pantaloons, the men in the audience cheered!

Next, a woman in a long black shapeless dress came out on stage, the spotlight shining on her gaunt face. She began to sing in a husky, almost haunting voice, and the crowd became silent, paying her the tribute of complete attention. She sang of love lost, of empty days and nights, her fluttering hands emphasizing the loneliness.

Julian took Regina's hand under the table. He squeezed

her fingers and she squeezed back, caught in the spell of the night, the music, the odd thought that if she lost Julian she also would be lost. What a strange idea, she mused, caught again in the sadness of the woman's singing.

The next performer was a comedian. Ken whispered, "This one gets a bit risqué. Shall we go on?"

They moved out of the crowded smoky room to their carriages. Ken knew another place not far away, and they headed in that direction. Regina caught sight of her tiny gold watch, and was shocked to see it was three in the morning, and they were still going strong. So was Montmartre; music poured from behind closed doors, lights shone in the windows, laughter spilled from the very streets. Chilly as it was, people even sat outdoors under bright red umbrellas, drinking great steins of beer and singing, as they held hands and swayed back and forth.

"It is spring," said Julian, in Regina's ear, and managed to kiss it. "Everyone is in love, in the springtime!" His teasing words did not sting; his voice was low, intimate, and significant.

When they arrived at the café Ken had chosen, Vicky and Regina went to the powder room to repair their makeup and straighten their gowns. Vicky studied the pretty flushed face next to hers in the mirror. "Love, in the springtime," she said, and Regina realized she had overheard Julian. "Very pretty. The trouble is, most Frenchmen are out of love by the autumn!"

Regina's brown eyes widened, she stared. "What do you mean by that, Vicky?" She powdered her nose from the small powder box in her golden mesh bag.

"Oh—just that the French aristocrats today seem to be more loose and promiscuous than ever," said Vicky, unusually bitter. "You don't see under the surface yet, Regina. Maybe you never will, but I am afraid you are too smart to remain blind."

Regina's hand was stilled. "Say what you mean to say," she demanded with her father's bluntness. "Do you mean—Julian?"

Vicky hesitated, straightening her skirts. "I think he has settled down. Certainly he seems devoted," she said earnestly. "I was just warning you—in general. French society today is very loose, some men are quite promiscuous, certainly out for all the pleasure they can find, no matter who gets hurt. Keep your dignity and your distance, Regina. You won't be sorry."

"In Paris?" Regina persisted. "Do you mean, just in Paris? I know Julian warned me never to go out alone."

"Absolutely not! A Frenchman would take that as an open invitation. But at Verlaine as well. Remember that French country estates are societies in miniature," Vicky warned, more gravely. "You will be continually on view. Everyone will be watching you, the men who might wish to seduce you, and the women you will despise who could lead you into situations— Oh, I am making too much of this. We must get back to the men." She started out the door before Regina could question her further.

"We must talk again," said Regina as they reached her table.

"Any time," said Vicky, smiling as she seated herself beside her husband.

Julian ordered crème de menthe this time, which must have been potent. Regina felt her eyelids drooping. Julian leaned toward her, laughing a little. "My poor darling, I must get you home. You are not accustomed to these late hours."

She slept on Julian's shoulder on the way home, waking only briefly to see the dimming gas lights as the dawn began to creep pink-fingered in the eastern sky.

Ninette was in her bedroom. "Oh, did you wait for me?" murmured Regina, too sleepy to speak in French.

"Non, non, non, non, non, Madame! I get up an hour ago." Ninette giggled. "I am so 'appy that you enjoy Paris!"

She helped Regina undress and returned the jewels to the velvet box as Regina tumbled into bed. She was asleep within seconds and did not wake up until evening. When she opened her eyes, Julian was standing over the bed, his robe on, stretching and yawning.

"What a night! I have not done that and enjoyed it so much for years," he said. He lay down beside her and took her into his arms. "Hello, darling, my lovely," he said softly, covering her face with kisses.

He ordered a little dinner brought to them both, a delicious omelette with bits of ham in it, hot coffee, toasted rolls, and butter and honey. They ate in the sitting room, talking idly of the evening and of their plans for the next few days.

"What would you like to do tonight?" Regina asked innocently as they finished the coffee and rolls.

He grinned, looking younger and more relaxed than she had ever seen him. The worry lines seemed to have smoothed away from his forehead and around his eyes.

"I should like to go back to bed—with you."

"Oh—Julian," she said, swallowing the roll the wrong way. She began to cough. He got up and pounded her back efficiently until the crumb was swallowed.

"Sorry, love, I didn't mean to shock you!" he teased, and drew her into his arms. "Are you . . . shocked?" he whispered into her ear.

She struggled a little, embarrassed. "I think—Ninette will—I ought to get dressed—"

"Why? We shall only get undressed right away," Julian said, and he drew her into the massive bedroom. He kissed her as he removed the rose negligee, ran his fingers through her loose thick curls. He pulled her down on the rumpled bed from which she had risen only two hours before.

The draperies were half-drawn and she could see out into the misty blue Paris night. Julian's arms were close and tight; his kisses grew more urgent.

Soon she forgot the outside world. She could dimly see the gentle blooming of the gas lights on the street outside the huge French windows, but Julian was so close, so strong, his arms moving about her, his hands caressing her slim body. Gently he removed her nightdress and tossed off his robe. His head bent down to her round breasts; he kissed and fondled them. "You are so lovely—so warm and soft and sweet—" he whispered against her, and somehow tonight she enjoyed what he said.

She felt heat within her body, and a softness that welcomed him. He must have known it, because he went on and on, kissing her, holding her until her arms came up and closed about him, and her hands went shyly to the thick hair on the back of his neck.

He entered her slowly and this time there was little pain, only a quick twinge that barely made her wince. He was gentle with her and thoughtful as well, helping her to feel the pleasure of their lovemaking. As his hard thighs moved against her soft ones, he whispered love words to her, and she began to enjoy it shyly, lying still as he moved.

"Oh, darling," he breathed, and she felt the throbbing of his body as he spent himself inside her.

He lay back to relieve her of his weight, and curled her up against his moist body. He drew the covers over them and held her quietly. She stirred and put her head on his shoulder, his strong hard shoulder, and felt his arms move more tightly about her. One hand moved up and down her spine, thrilling her.

"My love," he said softly, "my beautiful love."

And she was content. It had not been bad for her, and Julian had been pleased. She forgot about Vicky's warnings. She had not understood them anyway.

All she knew was that her husband had made love to her, had wanted her urgently, and this time she had enjoyed his caresses. Maybe her life with Julian would not be so bad after all. She let out a long sigh of relief and felt quite giddy as she watched Julian sleep, his dark head on the pillow beside hers.

CHAPTER SIX

By the end of two weeks in Paris, Julian became restive. Regina knew it by his impatience, his occasional curtness, the eagerness with which he scanned letters from his mother and sister and Claude. He was eager to return to his vines, she thought.

But Regina was reluctant to go. She had been so happy in Paris. Julian had been thoughtful and considerate. They had wandered through the Louvre, studied the paintings and sculpture there. They had walked along the beautiful gardens of the Tuileries. They had strolled, hand in hand, along the banks of the Seine and watched the fishing boats. On Sunday they had gone to the bird markets and the flower markets, and attended the service at Notre Dame.

Julian was a Roman Catholic. He had followed the service of the mass devotedly, and afterward had gone to light a candle at one of the altars. She had wondered about it, but he only explained briefly, "It is the custom, after a journey, or with a happy event, to give thanks in this manner."

"But you agreed to our wedding in a Protestant Church," she said thoughtfully.

"Your parents would not agree to a service in a Catholic parish hall, and as you are not a Catholic, we could not have had a Catholic mass," he said briefly.

"Is everyone in your family Catholic?" she ventured.

He nodded. "Yes, but you needn't worry about it. You won't be required to become a Catholic. You signed papers that any children would be raised as Roman Catholics, though, and that is all that's necessary."

She gasped. "When did I do that?"

Julian stared at her. "Why—in New York, two weeks before the wedding. Don't you remember?"

"I signed some papers my father wished me to sign. He did not say what they were."

He put his hand to his forehead. "My God," he said. "Did they explain nothing to you?"

"Mother was so busy, and Father gets cross when I ask too many questions. I thought—well, I thought it was about . . . my dowry."

"Oh, Regina," he groaned. "I must speak to the priest. He will explain things to you." And Julian said no more about that.

Did he think she was a fool? She did indeed feel foolish, and disturbed, that papers had been put under her nose and she had signed without reading them. What had her father said to her? "It's just business, Gina. Go ahead and sign, and don't trouble yourself about them." And trustingly, she had signed. Well, it was done. Another piece of her life taken out of her hands.

But everyone else in her new household would be Roman Catholic, and it would be another thing to make her feel like an outsider, she realized. She tried not to think about it, but as they ate luncheon at a charming restaurant on the island behind Notre Dame, she kept remembering the candle he had lit and the way he had knelt before an image of the Virgin. What had it meant? she wondered. There were so many new things in her life, and now this.

She left Paris reluctantly. She did not feel ready to take up the reins of yet another life, and Julian seemed to have become distant these past few days. He still made love to her and seemed to enjoy it, as she did at times. But she could tell he was anxious to leave for the château. It was time to move on.

The carriages were prepared and stacked full of boxes and trunks. She and Julian entered their carriage early that morning, toward the middle of April, and Ninette beamed from another carriage where she guarded the jewel and hat boxes. Three coachmen and six footmen as outriders accompanied them to guard against bandits and robbers, for there were hungry and desperate people on the roads. Julian had not told Regina this; Ninette had.

Their journey was without incident, however. Julian pointed out the sights, the chestnut trees, the winding silver rivers, the fruit trees. It was past their blossoming time, which he said was a beautiful sight, especially in Normandy where the apple trees bloomed pink and white. She looked about her with great interest as the carriages rolled along the roads to the south.

It was not a very long trip. Julian explained that in the

fifteenth and sixteenth centuries, the nobles at court followed the example of their kings, setting up country houses close enough to court and to Paris so they could attend court sessions, yet far enough away so that they could hunt and enjoy the coolness of the summers in the country.

"They were built as summer homes, and as fortresses against invaders, especially the English," he told her. "You will find many of stone, with towers and narrow windows to prevent arrows from coming through. Some still even have moats. Verlaine was built about 1200, even before this period, as a fortress for one of my ancestors. It's been remodeled and rebuilt from time to time, but the old towers remain. The moat is now filled in and the gardens are beautiful."

Julian would lean forward eagerly to peer out the windows of the coach, pointing to a château on a distant hill, or a church tower, or a small village perched high for protection. And then he began to point out vineyards.

"You see? That one is of special white grapes, which make the white wines. The next one is purple. The rows are set far apart, and the vines are fastened to wires to keep them high, so the sun can reach the grapes and make them ripe and sweet." He eyed them keenly, and said they were coming along well. They looked like so many dried sticks and vines to her.

"Dry, sandy soil is best for grapes. Along the Loire River, where we live, there is excellent clay soil. Also our storage cellars are built into the limestone cliffs at Verlaine to keep the wines cool and at a constant temperature. That is necessary for the sleeping of the wines."

She listened eagerly. Julian spoke with such enthusiasm that she realized what his friends had said was true. Julian loved his wines and his vines. They were his heritage, his work, his passion. She would learn all about them, she vowed, so she would be able to understand her husband.

When they reached a certain bridge crossing the Loire, Julian almost fell out of the coach window in his eagerness. He studied the river eagerly. "Ah, it is high," he said. "Good! There will be ample water to enrich the fields. In the winter and spring, the river should be high and overflow its banks to give life to the soil. In the summer and autumn, the river is usually so low that one can see the sandbars in the middle of the river."

It looked rather dangerous to her, the gray waters swirl-ing, and she was glad to be across the bridge and on the winding road that curled up the hill on the other side. Then Julian pointed proudly. "There is Verlaine."

In the distance, the towers stood out like so many turrets of a fairy castle from one of her childhood books. As the carriage continued up the hill, the building was lost from sight, only to reappear from time to time. She watched ea-gerly as they came closer.

"Our vineyards," Julian said, pointing. "These are the south fields. They yield the best growths, and I have excel-lent grapes planted there now. They will yield my new rosé wine, if all goes well. We shall have the whites, they are dependable. But this year, I count heavily on the rosé."

"Why is that?" she asked eagerly.

"Oh, the whites are popular enough, but not distinctive. If I can make a good rosé, with a bit of sparkle, what we call *petillant,* ah—then I will have something unique. It will sell well, and if it can travel, they will want it in Amer-ica. I have planted many hectares of these grapes." He fell silent, frowning, thinking.

"What is a hectare?" she finally ventured to ask.

"Oh—it is a metric measurement. It means about ten thousand square meters. That is almost two and a half acres per hectare."

He sounded cross with her, and she asked no further questions. Didn't he want her to understand, or did he think she was too stupid to learn? She resolved to ask oth-ers if she had to. It was important for her to understand his work.

Dusk was falling quickly over the flat land of the Loire Valley as they approached a lighted castle. They had been traveling uphill for some time now, and alongside a wind-ing creek. Julian was silent, his face in darkness. Regina clasped her hands tightly inside her warm fur muff. She was cold, chilled by the thought of meeting her new family. She was a stranger, an outsider.

Then the carriage ahead of them seemed to disappear. She wondered where it had gone. Their own carriage rat-tled across a wooden drawbridge and under a tunnellike entrance. She gazed in awe and amazement at the sight before them.

They stopped in an open lighted courtyard, so large it

looked almost like the one at the Louvre. On all sides rose
tall golden stone walls. The grooms ran to take care of the
tired horses while servants poured out of the building.

"Home," Julian said with a deep sigh of satisfaction.
"Ah, it is good to be home. Welcome to Verlaine, my
dear!"

She managed to smile as a groom appeared to help her
down from the carriage. She stepped out, stiff from the long
jolting journey, and gazed about. A tall maid in black uniform and cap came to her side.

"If Madame la Baronne will accompany me?" she murmured in French. Regina followed her inside, and Julian
was just behind her. She blinked at the torches and the
candles and lamps inside, lighting the mellow wooden
paneling of the rooms. The maid led her on.

"The Dowager Baroness awaits you in the drawing
room, Madame la Baronne," she said respectfully. Regina
followed her past a room with a piano and harp, golden in
the dimness. The opposite room seemed to be a study, with
a huge desk and deep comfortable chairs. But they went
on.

Regina and Julian were led into a huge drawing room,
so big the one in her parents' home on Fifth Avenue could
have been tucked into one corner of it. A fire crackled in
the fireplace under a white marble mantel. A lady in black
gown and white widow cap rose unsteadily from a rose da-
mask armchair, leaning on her cane.

As Regina approached her, the woman sank into a curtsey. She was white-haired, tall and slim, with frail shoulders and slender, sensitive hands. Regina sank into a deep
curtsey, as her mother had taught her.

The woman stood erect and a smile creased her cheeks,
so like Julian's smile that Regina felt reassured. "My dear
daughter," said Madame Diane Herriot, the Dowager Baroness. Regina was relieved that her French was clear and
easy to understand. "How beautiful you are! Julian wrote
that you were lovely—" Her approving look traveled over
Regina, from the proud tilt of the chestnut haloed head, to
the fur coat and muff, to the long legs and dainty feet in
small gray boots. "Was the journey difficult? Julian should
have done it in two days!"

"I was eager to be home, mother." Julian approached,
took her in his arms, and kissed both cheeks with evident

affection. "How are you, Maman? You look well, and there is color in your cheeks. Thérèse must have taken good care of you."

"Of course, what else did I have to do?" said a petulant voice from behind Regina. She swung around to see a tall woman in her late twenties with light-brown hair and dark eyes wearing a shabby gown of blue silk. "I am Thérèse," she said more calmly, and held out her hand to Regina.

Behind her stood a tanned husky man. He smiled, shook her hand, and murmured his name: "Marcus Bazaine."

"My husband," Thérèse explained. "Jeannette wished to wait up to see you, but I sent her to bed. She gets naughtier by the day!" Regina detected pride and affection in her tone.

"I am anxious to see her." Julian smiled. "Ah, here is Aunt Agnes and Uncle Oliver—" A warning look went quickly to the bride.

Aunt Agnes was in her late fifties, plump, with spectacles. She was chic, somehow, in a French manner. Uncle Oliver was older and white-haired. He peered at Regina in a puzzled way.

"Who did you say you are? A cousin? Henri's girl?"

Thérèse sighed and shook her head behind his back. By this Regina deduced the old man was probably senile. She contented herself by shaking his thin quivering hand.

"Where is Eric?" she asked shyly, still testing her French.

"Here I am," said a shy voice from the doorway. A footman guided the wheelchair in, and Regina saw the thin young man, the light-brown hair, the green eyes so like Julian's. She tried not to look at the blanket that covered his motionless legs. He cocked his head to look up at her and gave her a vague smile. "How do you do . . . Regina? Welcome . . . to Verlaine." He cleared his throat nervously.

"I am glad to meet you, Eric," said Regina self-consciously. "We had such a good time, Julian and I, choosing some books for you in New York. I do hope you will like them."

"Claude brought them, I am reading them already. Yes, they are—splendid." He remained for a short time, but then with a furtive smile at her, he was wheeled from the room.

Julian explained, briefly. "He has a large room, on the ground floor, the Hunt Collection room. It saves going up and down the stairs."

"Thérèse shall show you around tomorrow," said the Dowager, sinking gladly into her rose chair and indicating the chair next to her for Regina. "I fear—I cannot walk so well now. My legs do not always do what I tell them to do!"

Regina was later showed to the suite she and Julian were to share. It occupied most of one wing of the château. There was an immense blue and rose drawing room, with sofas, chairs, desks, and bookcases. Next was her huge bedroom, and across from it the dressing room for the baron. Next was the master bedroom, occupying the entire length of that wing, with enormous windows overlooking the woods and fields.

Regina was rather shocked to see what they called the "bathroom." It held a large tin tub, into which hot water was poured from large kettles brought from the kitchens below. There was no toilet. Instead a white-painted stand held a discreet porcelain chamberpot painted with roses. On top of the stand was a basin and a pitcher with hot water.

Regina tried not to show her amazement and unfamiliarity with chamberpots. Out West they had gone outdoors to a wooden privy, or even into the bushes when out hunting. But for this—this *castle* with all its luxury—not to have indoor facilities of better quality than this was amazing to her. She imagined her stepmother in such a setting, and her lips twitched as she saw the humor of it.

The Paris townhouse had had indoor plumbing, but the château had obviously not been renovated. It remained as it had been when restored some two hundred years ago.

Ninette was already unpacking for Regina in the rose bedroom. She had the assistance of two other maids in black uniforms, while a footman wearing the Verlaine green and gold carried in the last trunks and cases. Fortunately there were three large wardrobes for her clothes, as well as tall dressers for her undergarments. The maids whispered with admiration over the dresses, caressing the silks and velvets.

She and Julian went down to dinner. "These stairs are over the carriage entrance," he said absently. "Thérèse will

show you about soon. Tomorrow I should like you to ride
out with me over the estate. I want you to see the land, the
vineyards. And I am anxious to see the vines."

She glowed, knowing that he wanted her to come with
him, and it helped her to get through the evening. Claude
dominated the conversation, speaking so rapidly in French
that Regina missed most of what he said. Marcus Bazaine
seemed very silent, frowning into his plate. Eric had not
come down; he ate in his rooms, the Dowager said.
Thérèse kept gazing at Regina in her stunning silk dress
trimmed with petitpoint lace, making her feel overdressed.
She resolved not to wear anything so ostentatious. The
Herriots were evidently landpoor, with little money to
spare for refinishing the shabby elegant sofas and chairs,
installing modern plumbing, purchasing gowns for the ladies, suits for the men. She wondered if Julian would
change all this now, or if he truly did not notice it. Would
all her father's money be used to repay debts and improve
the vines?

Regina wondered how they managed to afford the large
staff that ran the château. There seemed to be dozens of
servants. A footman stood behind each place at dinner.
Maids scurried about in the halls. Even her stepmother had
less hired help.

Julian's mother spoke to Regina during dinner, ignoring
Claude's business talk. "I fear we will be dull for you, my
dear Regina," she said. "Most days we do little but embroidery and needlepoint. I am refinishing the chairs in the
rose drawing room. However—there is so much to do!"
She sighed.

Regina longed to say she would send for decorators, plan
new draperies and chair covers, and oversee it all. But after
Julian's reaction, she did not want to say anything yet.
However, Regina had her own fortune and now that she
was married, she could draw on it. Her father had said so.
Perhaps she could tactfully manage some changes.

"This is the small dining room," said the Dowager, indicating the room with a bend of her head. "It is always
done in gold and white. The large drawing room next is
opened for grand occasions, the hunt balls, the harvest dinners, holidays. It is always in silver and white."

Regina had glimpsed its grandeur under dust sheets as
they had passed by. A huge piano stood to one side, and

there was a table long enough to seat at least twenty-four
guests on each side, she guessed.

"The table there opens for fifty," said the Dowager Baroness. "We also open this room and the next one behind
me. Then we can have a hundred to one hundred and fifty
guests."

Regina restrained a gasp. No wonder it took so much
money to run the château. One hundred and fifty guests!
Her father was wealthy beyond dreams, but even he would
not be equipped to have such a dinner at home. The Dowager spoke as though these events were not uncommon.

Julian overheard them and said, "Such things are part of
our lives, Regina. It is our duty and obligation, as heirs of
Verlaine."

"And that comes first of all, one's duties and obliga-
tions." Claude laughed, leaning back in his chair and picking up his wine glass. He tossed his drink off in one swallow and grinned at Regina. "You will soon find, my dear
Regina, that duty is all, work is the highest joy, and one's
rewards are *all* in heaven."

Julian was about to intervene, sternly. Regina could see
the anger in his face.

"You sound like my father!" she said swiftly. "That is
what he believes. Work is a sacred duty to him. He would
no more think of staying home from the office than of—of
flying in the air! He has worked hard all his life, and he
believes that hard work keeps one out of mischief, and is its
own reward."

"It made him plenty of money, that's sure," muttered
Claude.

"Hard work never hurts," said the Dowager.

Marcus muttered, "A new philosophy!"

As if to end the conversation, Julian's mother stood up
and led her family across the drafty room and down a hallway to the cozy drawing room on the other side of the
building. As she passed one door, a valet was moving to
close it, but Regina saw inside briefly. The walls were hung
with antlers, hunting prints, and rifles. At a large desk,
Eric sat, bent over a book.

She moved on thoughtfully. Poor Eric, to sit among trophies of the hunt, when he himself was crippled. It must be
a sad mockery to him. Would he not prefer another room?
The bed she had glimpsed was narrow and spartan. Per-

haps the hunt trophies could be removed and the room
decorated more to Eric's liking.

Her first night in the château, and she was already
changing it about! I must be wary of any such suggestions,
she scolded herself.

It was so late, they did not linger long over coffee. Julian
excused himself and Regina, and they went upstairs.
Claude turned to leave, and Julian, seeing her surprise explained, "Claude lives out in the lodge. Mother, my aunt
and uncle, all have rooms in the wing opposite ours. Also
there are several guest rooms. Thérèse and Marcus have a
suite over ours, with the nursery for Jeannette," Julian explained.

She went to bed thoughtfully, alone. Julian led her to her
bedroom and kissed her good night but did not come in.
She did not know where he slept, in the master bedroom or
in the smaller neat room opposite hers. She lay awake for a
time after Ninette had left her, gazing at the shabby blue
canopy over her own bed, at the faded wallpaper of dainty
roses and white vines. Everything was so worn, probably
fifty to a hundred years old—except the furnishings, which
were two or three hundred years old! The dresser was in
the Louis XVI style, a little plainer and more handsome
than the flamboyant Louis XV but, she began to realize,
they *liked* it this way! They were proud of their heritage. If
she tried to change anything, she would meet with more
than Julian's resistance.

Yet—they could not be proud of threadbare rugs and
sofas or fraying draperies. What should she do? It would
not cost a fortune to replace some paper, some fabric. She
would have to find the right way to approach them with
her ideas.

Regina wakened when Ninette brought in a tray and
smiled down at her. "I have brought you an omelette," the
girl announced.

"Oh, how lovely!"

Regina sat up against the lace-edged linen pillows and
stretched. She felt worlds better. She'd slept well and was
no longer the least bit tired, but more than that she had
overcome her nervousness. She had met Julian's relatives
and they had not bitten her!

"You work miracles, Ninette!"

"*Oui,* Madame!" said Ninette, and poured out the hot

tea for her. "Monsieur le Baron wishes that Madame should wear a gown for riding, as he wishes to ride out with her in one hour."

"Is he in his room?" she asked diffidently, cutting into the delicate omelette with its bits of ham and greens.

"Oh, *non, non,* Madame. He is up these two hours, and dines in the breakfast room with Madame the Dowager Baroness, and then goes over the papers in his study."

Ninette rattled cheerfully on, taking out the dramatic black riding habit with the long divided skirt and plumed hat. Regina finished eating, washed hastily in the porcelain basin in her small bathroom, shivering in the unheated room, and donned the riding habit. She walked down the long winding stairs, her boots striking the marble floor very loudly, she thought.

"Monsieur le Baron is in the courtyard," announced the butler at the front door. Regina went out to find Julian with two splendid black horses.

The first ride was an ordeal. Regina went bravely, gritting her teeth over her aching thighs. The second day was better, but even if it was not, she would not have stopped riding with him. Julian was so busy in the vineyards during the rest of the day that this was really their only chance to be together.

The villagers were nice, shy with her and doubtful of her French, but quick to smile, hand her flowers, and urge her to try a piece of fresh-baked bread. Some of the men and women seemed the same rough, good-hearted type she had known in the Rockies during her childhood. She could relate to them, she could smile and speak to them of their work, pick up a child and play with him. She found herself going to the village after her rides, to talk to some of the people there. She liked them. She wanted them to like her.

One morning, Regina came down a little late, only to find that Julian had gone off alone and left word she would not need to ride today. Somehow she resented that; she was useless, but he did not need to emphasize it! She smiled stiffly and accepted a piece of embroidery from her mother-in-law.

Julian did not return until almost one o'clock, for luncheon, and with him was Simone de Lamartine. Smart in black riding habit, with a scarlet stock to set off her fair skin, she smirked at Regina.

"I met Julian and we have had such a splendid conversation! He is such a help and comfort to me," she said to them all. "We have been good friends—oh, such a long time! And since the death of my poor Hilaire, how he has helped me! I never would have been able to harvest my grapes! Julian does it all for me. Such a fine man!"

Regina seethed. Claude did not seem very happy either and kept glaring at Simone. The Dowager did not answer, only welcomed Simone formally to luncheon and remarked that it had been a long time since they had had the pleasure of her company.

This was not the last time she came. Julian went out earlier and earlier each morning and if Regina did not rise at seven, she could not hope to go with him. Often Simone encountered him on the estate—by design or by chance?— and came home with him, her hand confidently in his arm, hanging on his every word, seated at his right hand at luncheon. The Dowager had insisted on Regina taking the end of the table; Julian was at the head. Regina could not even speak to him at meals. They were so far apart! She hated the situation, and hated even more the way Simone confided her problems to him. Julian seemed eager to help her. Often Regina could not understand the quickly spoken French, and now Julian was not nearby to translate for her.

After one luncheon, Simone went off to the study with Julian, to discuss her finances, they said. Claude went up to Regina as she rose from the table and patted her arm.

"Never mind," he said in a low tone, smiling down at her gently, not in his usual challenging, mocking manner. "It is *you* he married, not her! You have nothing to fear. He will honor his marriage vows."

She could not answer that. She could not confide in Claude, and she was not sure of her answer anyway. What she had overheard on the ship came back to her, along with Vicky's vague warnings. Was Julian making Simone his mistress? Or had she been all along? They were close, that much was certain, and Regina did not like it at all.

With a vague notion of asserting her rights, Regina decided to join Julian and Simone in the study. The door stood slightly ajar, and she hesitated, hearing the voices within. She noticed that Simone's voice was husky and broken.

Determined, she pushed the door open. She would go in and sit with them. It was not right that Julian should be alone with another woman. She could imagine his rage if she, his wife, sat alone with another man! But as she stepped into the doorway, Regina's eyes widened with shock. Simone was standing in Julian's arms, his hand was on her dark head, pressing her face against her shoulder. There was a look of suffering in his eyes as he gazed blindly toward the far wall.

"Simone, Simone, you have been so brave. Do not give way now. All will be well one day. You must be patient—"

"I have been patient—for so many years!" came the broken voice. "But to be parted so often from the one I love—it is killing me, Julian! How can I continue to endure it?"

"Patience. My dear Simone, it will not be forever. Your love is strong, you are young and lovely. I will continue to help you all I can. You know I have promised, no matter what happens—"

Regina recovered enough to withdraw silently, drawing the door slowly back to its original position. She fled from the scene, her cheeks stinging hot, her hands cold. She went upstairs, but Ninette was in the bedroom, and looked at her questioningly.

"Madame is not well?"

Regina shook her head. "I must lie down," she said wretchedly. She took off her shoes and stretched out on the day couch. Ninette covered her with a plump down coverlet and put her hand briefly to Regina's forehead.

Regina closed her eyes, pretending to rest, but her heart was pounding furiously. Simone was Julian's mistress! And they hoped one day to make their relationship legitimate! What would happen to her?

Her shock became fury and then cold hurt, and finally resignation. Vicky had tried to warn her. Julian, like many Frenchmen, kept a mistress. He desired Simone, and one day if Regina did not produce an heir, he might even marry her in order to have that heir. By then Julian's precious vineyards would be producing well, his fortunes would be restored, and he could afford to discard Regina. . . .

She put her hand over her mouth to stifle a cry. She could not weep, for she was too upset for the relief of tears.

Julian was no better than the others. She would have to face that fact and endure it.

Unless . . . she could win his love. Could she compete with Simone? Did she want to compete with a Frenchman's mistress? Could she smother her pride and try to win him away from a cunning woman like Simone? She knew that Simone's husband had died two years ago. If it had not been for the need of a wealthy wife, Julian would probably have married her.

Regina's eyes opened. She did have that one weapon, distasteful though it was. She had *money*. After all, that was why Julian had married her. As long as he needed money, he would still need her.

She thought then of Julian's responsibilities: the expense of the château and the estate, his invalid mother and brother, his sister and brother-in-law, the host of servants. Julian was responsible for all of them, and he was not one to take his responsibilities lightly. No, he would take care of them, even if it meant keeping his mistress hidden and marrying a wealthy woman from America.

Julian saw honor in a different light than she did. Yet perhaps her father was not so unlike Julian. He did things he might personally dislike because they were necessary to his business. Perhaps all men were like that, if they had ambition, and if people depended on them.

Well, she could not lie here all day, brooding. She didn't want to return to Julian's mother and the embroidery. His mother might be frail, but her eyes were keen and she was intuitive enough to detect a hidden problem.

Finally she went up to the nursery to play with four-year-old Jeanette. The lovely dark-haired, dark-eyed child already adored her. Nobody played with her as Regina did. Nobody knew such charming fairy stories, and such strange tales of ranchers and bears and Indians. They had a fine time together on afternoons when Regina felt she could not endure the adults any longer. Jeanette would hug her doll named Regina and show her the dollhouse, or talk to her in lisping baby fashion, and it was a great comfort to the lonely American girl in a strange country.

CHAPTER SEVEN

"Regina? Regina?" A feathery kiss brushed gently across her eyelids. She yawned, struggled to awaken, and opened her eyes to find Julian sitting, fully dressed, on the side of her bed. "Regina? I want you to ride with me today."

He smiled down at her as she blinked. "Oh—Julian! Of course, I'll get up at once."

It was very early. The sunshine scarcely skimmed through the lace curtains, with the faded blue velvet draperies drawn back. Regina sat up and yawned widely. "I'll only be a few minutes."

"I'll call Ninette—or let me help you," he suggested. He did seem eager this morning, striding to one of her wardrobes, to frown over the full gauzy dresses there.

"My riding habit is in this one," she indicated timidly. She slid from bed, caught up her robe, and went to wash hastily in the adjoining bathroom. When she returned, Julian and Ninette were laying out her new blue velvet habit with the tall blue hat and light-blue plume. Julian retreated as Ninette began to prepare to dress Regina.

"Do hurry, Ninette," Regina said, sitting down to pull on her boots. "I don't want him to go without me—" She stopped and blushed. Ninette smiled knowingly.

"We shall hurry, Madame!"

Regina was dressed and ready in twenty minutes. She longed for a cup of tea or coffee, but Julian was waiting impatiently.

The splendid black horses were stamping in the courtyard as she descended the wide stairs. Julian tested the saddle girths for her, instead of waiting for a footman. She felt easier about riding now that she had been at Verlaine for three weeks.

The early May sunshine was warm on their faces as they headed southeast. "It's a long ride and I wanted an early start," Julian said. "I'm going to inspect the south fields, where my prize red grapes are planted."

"Do please explain to me about the grapes, Julian. I want to understand everything."

He frowned a little, but not in anger, rather in thought. "Well . . . Regina, it all started almost two thousand years ago. Vines were flourishing in early Christian times and must have begun in the Mediterranean lands long before then. You know the story of Noah and his drunkenness. And Cato the Elder, of Rome, wrote a book on farming and vine growing two hundred years before Christ. When the Romans came up into Gaul—that is, France, now, they brought knowledge of vine growing with them, only to find that some vines were here already, along the Rhine and Rhone and up into this area."

"So long ago!" she breathed. She was continually stunned at the ease with which the French spoke of a thousand or two thousand years past. In America a hundred years was a long time, but it was just a moment to the French.

"Yes. The Romans encouraged the growing of vines. Their wines might seem crude to us, but they were undoubtedly good ones for that time. Later on, when the Vandals came to drive out the Romans and only the monks in their monasteries were left to carry on Latin culture in the Dark Ages, the vine growing continued. As the monks were the centers of learning, so were they of vine growing and winemaking also. By the Middle Ages, the wines were a large business. Some monasteries grew their own vines, made wines, stored them in casks, fermented them, bottled them, and shipped them as well. That is how they made money for their orders."

Regina listened in fascination as he spoke, and they cantered easily along the dusty paths toward the south. She was looking around as he talked, noting the long wires hung through the fields, the vines strung on them about a yard apart, with plenty of room for the leaves and the thick clusters of grapes to come through. She looked up at the vivid blue sky, with its little feathery clouds, and at the long straight line of poplars lining the banks of a thin stream. The sun glistened on them, making them shine like golden trees in a fairy tale.

Julian smiled at her and went on with his story. "When my grandfather began to have troubles, so did the other growers around us. A disease called oidium, or mildew,

came in. This ruined some vines and then another called
black rot came, and the grapes turned to hard black stones.
My grandfather died and my father took over. He tried
new methods of coping with the problems we were having.
I remember as a boy helping to oversee the spraying of
chemicals over the vineyards. Then came the worst blow
of all. An insect called phylloxera. It came from North
America, on the new swift ships. It seems that in the old
days, when the ships came more slowly, the insects on
fruits and flowers would die before they reached Europe.
Now the swiftness defeated us." He smiled sadly.

"From North America?" asked Regina. "From—us?"

"Yes." He nodded, seeming not to see her embarrassment and anguish. He was gazing ahead of him, toward the
vineyards. "It seemed that the North American insects
came and feasted on the fine fat rootstocks of the French
and English and German grape vines. The American vines
were thin, tough, and wiry, otherwise they would not have
grown wild on the riverbanks when the settlers came to
America. Men went to study this, and finally they recommended to us that American rootstocks be used in France."

"But what happened to the French vines?" asked Regina.
"Were they ruined completely?" She could not imagine it;
the fields were full of vines.

"Yes, completely. Whole villages were wiped out, their
vineyards gone. Many people lost their livelihood, and
moved away, some as far as the north of Spain, where they
began again in different soil. But we could not leave, we
are Verlaine," he said simply. "So we joined with others to
try to find a solution. Many roots were brought from
America, and various vines of our area grafted onto them,
as experiments. We worked for almost twenty years. Some
efforts failed, some succeeded, but the wines from them
were rough and bad. The ones that did best were kept, and
improved. So there"—he waved his riding crop toward the
fields they were riding past—"there are my Chinon blanc
grapes, sometimes called Pinot de la Loire. They yield a
white sparkling wine, a young wine that must be bottled
within six months and is drunk soon. It does not travel
well, however. Not yet."

She longed to ask one question after another, but was
afraid she might discourage him with stupid questions.

"My experiment now," he went on, "is with a Cabernet

franc. This Cabernet franc grape yields a red wine if pressed in that manner. That is, pressed, fermented for a month or longer, with must—that is basically the skin of the grape—and seeds and pulp all fermenting together. It makes a delicious red wine, but my dream is of a fine rosé, a little sparkling, light, delicate. To do this, I grow the Cabernet franc grapes, let them ripen to the right moment in late autumn, then pick, crush, and press immediately, as though making white wine. The color gives a pale rosé that has much of the character of the whites, with the lightest most beautiful rose color in the world! It has the light fragrance of a violet and oh, the delicacy!"

He speaks with the air of a lover about his mistress, thought Regina, both amused and annoyed. Julian did love his grapes! More than Simone, she thought bitterly. But she was soon caught up in his enthusiasm, as he pointed out the south slopes. The air was brisk, that early May morning, and the fields were gleaming in the morning sunlight. These vines were planted a little farther apart than the white grapes, she realized. Julian scanned the fields eagerly and waved to a man tending them.

"They need more water. It is being hauled up to the top of the slope, then allowed to trickle down into the channels between the rows. Just enough to give them a taste of water," he explained. "The weather must be just right for our vines. We need a long summer of sunshine, then a clear warm autumn with no rain. The grapes should ripen in the sunshine on this south slope, facing the autumn sun. Then—if all goes well—the grapes grow very ripe and full, dark red, almost black. We pick them at the right moment, then press and hope."

"But, Julian—so many things can go wrong," she murmured, appalled. "The rains, at the right time, the sunshine just right. The water—it all must go right."

"Exactly," he said quietly. "All must go exactly right. Sometimes they are not right for three or four years. In 1893, two years ago, conditions were gloriously right—but I had only just begun my south vineyard. I experimented with only a few hectares. If only—" He stopped abruptly. "But it is as God wills," he murmured with a shrug.

"And last year, the rains came," she added.

"Yes. This year—who knows? Perhaps it will be a good harvest year." He slid off his stallion, absently handed the reins to Regina to hold, and strode off among the vines, holding them tenderly, inspecting one after another.

She watched him soberly. If the harvest had been bountiful last year or the year before, she would probably not be here now. She would be at home in New York—perhaps preparing herself for marriage to a German graf or an English viscount. Not here, married to Julian, a stranger in a strange land. It struck her that somehow she was contented at times, often happy at night in Julian's arms. She was actually coming to love him, to lean on him, and need him, and she wondered how he truly felt about her.

Marriage. How mixed up she felt about marriage. There was so much pain and confusion at first, and then with her growing understanding and knowledge came urges and desires she had never dreamed of. She wanted more and more from Julian, his love as well as his passion. Was it completely hopeless? Would Simone always stand between them?

Julian returned, took the reins, and swung up into the saddle, where he seemed as much at home as on his feet. "Bon," he said briefly, but contentment was in his tanned face.

As he turned the horses, she wondered if they were going home. But no, he struck off across a narrow path through the fields. He gave her one of his whimsical grins.

"I sent word to the wife of one of my workers," he said. "Breakfast is being prepared for us there by Madame Michaux. I thought that you would enjoy it."

They raced the eager horses across the land and pulled up only when they had reached the farmyard with its neat chicken run, some shade trees, a bit of a stream running off through the back of the property. The house was made of stone and red brick, with a red slate roof and a red brick chimney. The woman who came out to greet them was plump and smiling.

"*Bonjour, bonjour!*" she called out. "All is prepared! Ah, Monsieur le Baron, it is very good to see you once more!"

She gave a curious, assessing look to Regina as the girl dismounted, her eyes lingering on the slim body, the rounded breasts and thighs. Then she nodded, as though satisfied. Julian introduced her gravely. The woman curtseyed and led the way inside.

There was one large room with a few small bedrooms

leading off from it. The floor was packed dirt, the walls red brick like the immense fireplace. A well-scrubbed wooden plank table was the center of activity, and several neatly made wood chairs were set around it.

Regina sat at the table while Julian wandered toward the fireplace, with the blackened irons in front, ledges full of copperware shining above it. A huge pot of soup bubbled on an iron support.

Madame Michaux brought an immense coffee pot and huge white mugs to the table. She poured out the coffee and smiled as she gave Regina a cup. "So, you have ridden long and are cold! This will warm you. The omelettes will be ready soon."

Julian had picked up the wooden tray of hot bread and brought it over, as though accustomed to helping himself. A small pot of fresh butter was set before them. As Regina sipped the steaming black coffee, he tore into the bread and buttered her a slice. It was dark bread, coarse and indescribably delicious. The woman set the table with plates and silverware, then quickly brought the copper pan from the stove and turned out half the omelette onto Regina's plate. The eggs were steaming hot and smelled of ham and herbs.

Madame Michaux served Julian next, and he cut into his omelette hungrily, eating and drinking with gusto. The woman watched over them like a mother over her children, hands on her hips. "So, it is good, eh? More coffee?" And she poured out more of the steaming brew.

"It is the best coffee I have had since I left America," said Regina bluntly, and Julian laughed. The woman grinned down at her.

"Ah, you like it strong and black and hearty, eh? So do I! And my good man!"

A child cried out sleepily, and the woman left them. Regina reached for the coffee pot to refill their cups. Julian said quickly, "Careful! It will be hot."

Regina smiled. She took her napkin, held the handle with it, and poured. "It reminds me of our coffee pot at home, in the cabin," she said absently in English. "We always made a huge pot in the morning, it was so cold in the Rockies. I made it as soon as I got up, and drank cups of it while I fixed ham and eggs for breakfast. Father got up early to feed the chickens, and the boys were always starved—"

Julian was staring at her. She paused abruptly, blushing. "You lived—in the Rocky Mountains?"

She nodded, uncomfortably shifting in the wooden chair. She had promised not to talk about it! "I—um—I did for a time," she said.

"And when did you come east to New York?"

"I was young," she murmured. "Mother . . . didn't want me to talk about it," she added.

"But you lived out there, in a cabin?"

She nodded. "The people here, the farmers, those who work in the vineyards—they remind me of the miners and the men who drove the mules. I feel at home with them," she admitted. "Father made his money in the gold fields, you may know of that."

"I had heard it, but I thought it was only an investment. I never imagined he worked in the mines."

Regina nodded and quickly changed the subject. "Yes. You know, he was very curious about your work. I should like to write to him and explain the vineyards to him. I worked for him until we were married."

Julian gazed at her, his light-green eyes glowing yellow in the firelight. "I did not know that. You worked?"

She grimaced. Her mother would be furious! But Regina was married now, and she saw no reason to keep secrets from her husband. If she was not honest with him, how could she expect him to be honest with her? "Yes. I went to college, but on holidays and in summers, I lived at home. Father would have secret projects he didn't want even his secretary to know about. So he would dictate letters to me, and I wrote them out. I even helped him with the bookkeeping. He liked to discuss business with me because he said I had a head like his. If I had been a boy, he would have trained me for banking." She gave a sigh, unconsciously.

"Thank God you are not a boy," Julian said with a little grin and a slow look down her rounded body. She flushed and put her hands to her cheeks. "That outfit you wore this morning—that white nightdress with the rose ribbons at your throat and waist—I could hardly think of going out to the vineyards!"

"Julian!" He laughed at her reddened cheeks, but his eyes were not at all cruel. They were gentle on her.

"What—what grapes did you say were on the south slopes?" she asked hurriedly.

"Cabernet franc," he said, and spelled it for her. "The white wines will carry us, if we have a good harvest. But the rosé from the Cabernet franc could make a fortune! I bottled some from 1893 and we shall sample it when we have the big dinner next week. Winegrowers from all around are coming, and also some brokers from Paris. It is always a grand occasion, and I bring out our best wines. It is strange—" He frowned slightly over the last of his omelette, spearing it and putting into his mouth. "I really thought we would earn more from the 1893 wines than we did."

He talked more about this, seeming surprised at her interest and her understanding. Yet she had comprehended far more difficult matters with her father.

Julian seemed pleased with Regina, however, and that was the most important thing to her now. She wanted to please him; she wanted to be closer to him. She wanted—fiercely—to hold him so he would not turn back to Simone. Simone had lived here in the valley all her days, and they had a shared interest in the vineyards. But Regina had married Julian, and she wanted to be a part of his life, a vital part.

Could she hold on to Julian? The scene with Simone had badly undermined her confidence, had shaken her belief in Julian. Yet in New York she had felt so close to him. They had shared so many interests and concerns.

It could be that way again, she told herself. He had married her, and since he was Catholic he would surely think twice about divorcing her! If she had the courage and the love, she could make their marriage work.

Yes—love. She loved Julian; she knew that now. She wanted to remain with him, to be his wife, to share his interests, to bear his children, to help him always. If she showed sympathy, patience, compassion for his troubles, wouldn't that help?

I'm no coward who would give up quickly, she mused as she finished the hot coffee. Julian was chatting with Madame Michaux, bringing a burst of laughter to her lips as she rocked her youngest child. He could be so charming, so lovable.

Regina hoped Julian would turn to her with his troubles.

She wanted him to hold her in his bed, to come to her when he felt desire for a woman, to want her, to need her, to see her as his wife, the mother of his children, his partner. She loved him, even though she knew he had married her because she was wealthy. Yes, he had frankly admitted he needed the money. However, he had turned away from other wealthy women because they did not interest him. He had *liked* Regina; he desired her now. Couldn't that liking and desire turn to love for her?

Still, Regina could not erase the scene in the study from her mind. Did he love Simone de Lamartine? Perhaps. Yet Regina was the one married to him.

And Regina did admire him. He had courage, he had determination. Year after year, he worked with his grapes, hopefully, intelligently. He took his responsibilities to his family, his heritage, and his vineyards seriously. She respected him deeply for that. He was a good man with many fine qualities. She knew he would not insult her openly by flaunting his mistress before her. Perhaps he would recover from this obsession with Simone. Or maybe Simone would tire of waiting and look for a husband elsewhere! She was young and beautiful. Surely she could find a man of her own.

Regina would fight with quiet determination for Julian's love. She would make him respect her, honor her, want to keep her as his wife. The French were practical; she could help him a great deal.

Maybe all this would outweigh his love for his mistress. Regina meant to try hard.

They arrived home about eleven o'clock. Julian disappeared, and Regina went up to the bedroom suite to change to a more appropriate gown of ultramarine blue silk taffeta with a black embroidered pattern before the midday meal. The vivid blue set off her chestnut hair and made her appearance more striking. I want to look outstanding, she thought, to compete with Simone.

But she only succeeded in competing with her sister-in-law. Every time Regina appeared in a new gown, it seemed to arouse Thérèse's jealousy and antagonism. Yet Regina had her whole wardrobe of trousseau gowns to wear. Most of her plainer and more youthful dresses had been given away by her mother.

Thérèse glared at her across the dinner table, then pointedly ignored her. Eric had come in his wheelchair; sometimes he did if there were no guests. He was intensely shy in public, hating curious stares. Regina had him seated beside her, at her right.

"I wanted to ask you, Eric, how you are enjoying the books. I am writing to Papa, and he can arrange to send more of whatever pleases you," she said.

Eric's wistful brown eyes lit up. "Oh, they all please me," he said softly. "I have read and reread all those in our library. Such riches, to have a hundred new books to read!"

He confessed to a liking for Emerson, and they discussed several of his essays. Regina's opinion that Eric had a bright, unusual mind was confirmed. It bothered her that his intelligence was going to waste.

"I had a glimpse of your rooms, Eric," she dared to say. "Do you sleep well with all those heads above you?"

A shadow crossed his thin, sensitive face. "I used to have nightmares when I was a child," he answered simply. "After my—illness—I was moved from the nursery to the hunt room, for convenience. I would wake up in the night and want to scream at those horns looming over me. But now, I sleep rather well." He shrugged his shoulders, smiled, in a faint echo of Julian's smile.

"You know, I was wishing I could redecorate the room," she ventured boldly. She was aware that Julian's mother was listening to her, and Julian had grown silent also, straining to hear her at the other end of the table. "I would move out all those heads and antlers, and redecorate the room as your bedroom and study. We could bring in bookcases, a bigger more comfortable bed, and a nicer desk. Don't you think so, Julian?"

His mouth was compressed into a straight line, the sweetness of the morning long gone. "The Hunt Collection is famous, Regina. When the hunts are held, we always use that room as a trophy room for the kills. It is traditional."

"But what about Eric?" Regina's dark eyes were flashing. "Isn't he more important than the hunts?"

There was an awkward silence. Julian looked cautiously at Eric. The young man was flushed, and he put his hand impulsively over Regina's on the table.

"Don't trouble yourself, my sister. During the hunts, I am moved upstairs to one of the guest bedrooms. I am quite comfortable, I assure you."

"But then you can't get around in the chair!" she said. "Honestly, I don't understand the sacredness of the hunts! It is barbaric anyway, to go hunting, except for food," she went on recklessly, despite the worried look on the Dowager's face and Julian's growing chill. "I shall never understand it! The only times we went hunting in the Rockies was for food, or when a grizzly bear was bothering the horses!"

There was a long pause then. Everyone was staring at her. I've done it again, she thought. Now they would all know about her own crude upbringing!

"I'm sorry," she muttered. "I don't understand the customs here."

There was a stir at the table. Marcus Bazaine began asking about some plowing to be done and Julian answered him, their conversation turning to work. Then Eric looked at Regina, his eyes alight.

"I hope one day you will tell me some of the stories that you tell to Jeannette. She is most fascinated, but cannot repeat them to make sense. I should enjoy hearing of your life in the mountains."

"Sometime," she said ruefully. "My mother—my stepmother, that is—she warned me not to talk about that life. She wishes to believe that my life began in New York City. But I was in my teens when we moved. I loved it out West; it was so free, so open, so wild. I liked the people. I never saw them again."

He looked interested and understanding. But she changed the topic. "Tell me about the dinner we give for the winegrowers."

"Ah, the dinner for the *vignerons* and the brokers," said Eric with a smile. "Another of our fine traditions. In the spring we gather to discuss the prospects for the coming year, and the successes and failures of the past. Then in the autumn, after the harvest, we gather also to talk of that, and of how much money can be expected. It is always less than we had hoped," he added with a sigh. "We see the great casks of wine, the barrels filling, the bottles to be filled. It looks so immense. We send to the brokers in the spring, after the six months of fermenting, and the bottling. Then we get the accounts—and it does not seem like so much."

Regina was puzzled and thoughtful. She wondered, Are the brokers honest? How much commission do they get for selling? She wished she could see the books. But Julian was looking rather formidable this afternoon. The friendly mood of the morning was quite gone. She had blundered by asking to remodel Eric's rooms, and even more by suggesting they toss out the motheaten antlers and heads! Well, she must keep control of herself, and try again. It was hard to repress her frank nature and say only what was expected of her.

Only with Jeannette could she be open. And with Eric, she was beginning to learn. He welcomed her when she ventured into his formidable Hunt Collection room. His sturdy valet came to greet her with a smile, for she made his master smile. With Eric she could relax and talk about the old days in the mountains, how a grizzly bear had caught one of their horses and Regina had been forced to shoot it; how Regina had ridden a donkey many a time, down the trail to the gold works; how she and one of her brothers had guarded a pack of gold from drunken visitors when her father and older brother were away. Eric and the valet listened, with open mouths and complete attention as Regina talked. It was good practice for her French also.

And Eric talked to her, in his shy sweet fashion. He never complained, though sometimes he was in such pain that white lines were carved around his mouth. He told her stories about the Herriot family, about Julian and how he had had to take over the estate when his father had died. Julian had been only twenty, and in the university. He had come home and plunged into the work of cleansing the vineyards with fire and water to rid it of the louse, then worked with chemists to try to come up with a hybrid vine that would yield good grapes.

Eric explained patiently, with words and drawings, how the vineyards were restocked and how the vines were grafted onto the American rootstocks. He told her about the process of crushing and fermenting the grapes and she realized that he had as thorough grasp of the subject as Julian. She wondered how he got out into the vineyards and to the winery.

"When the harvest is brought in, I make them take me out in my wheelchair to watch everything. As a boy, it was my one amusement, my one passion, the one time of the year I could go out and join in the work. I could direct that, when Julian was busy bringing in the harvest. It does not take physical strength to tell the men when to stop crushing and begin to pour the masc into the pipes to go into the barrels. Or to time it all, and make sure the masc, that is, the pulp and juice, was separated at the right moment from the stems and seeds and skins, so that the wines will not be too red."

She listened in fascination and asked a thousand questions, which he answered with patience and much knowledge. She came away from their talk feeling that she was learning at last about Julian's work. And more than that, she had a new friend in this household: Eric.

CHAPTER EIGHT

Regina could not decide whether to wear the blue velvet, the silver chiffon, or some other gown for the grand dinner for the visiting brokers and neighboring *vignerons*. Ninette, with her shrewd French sense of dress, had no such qualms or puzzles.

"It shall be the gold lamé, Madame," she said firmly, drawing it from its cotton sheath and laying it lovingly across the bed. She gazed down proudly at the gown.

It was close-fitting with a swirling train at her feet. Over it was sewn a loose sheer gown of gold chiffon, softening the rich metallic color and creating an effect of such elegance that Regina had never worn it before.

"But it's so sophisticated," Regina murmured thoughtfully.

Ninette nodded, very sure of her decision. "This dinner is the biggest occasion of the year, except for the harvest dinner, Madame. This dress is perfect for it. You shall be the grandest lady there, which is fitting, as you are Madame la Baronne."

Regina wore it, and Julian gave a nod of approval as he came in from his dressing room. He was wearing a formal black suit, white frilled shirt, studs of gold set with rubies. "They belonged to my father, and to my grandfather," he told Regina when she commented on them.

"You must be very proud of your father and grandfather," she said, studying the rubies. "How handsome! They are *en cabochon*, the old way. It brings out the beauty of the rubies."

He seemed pleased at her praise. "What jewels are you wearing, Regina?"

He went over to her dressing table, where she had set out the boxes of velvet and of satin that held her jewels. He had brought them up from his safe in the office.

"I cannot decide. This dress is so ornate—"

Ninette came to join in the crucial decision. "I believe

just the emerald earrings and ring, Madame," she said respectfully. "The dress is a jewel in itself."

Julian nodded in satisfaction and watched as she set the earrings in her ears and the ring on her finger. On her left hand was her diamond and her wedding ring. "Yes, you look elegant but not overdressed. Very suave," he praised her.

She wondered briefly if she would outshine Simone, but then pushed the thought from her mind. She was happy now in her marriage. Julian slept with her almost every night; he talked to her about his work. She was gradually taking over the household from the Dowager Baroness, who was evidently relieved to work less. The older woman was much more frail than she would admit.

Julian and Ninette went to return the other boxes to the safe in his study. Julian alone held the combination to it, as it contained his most precious papers, deeds, checkbooks, and jewels. Regina had heard Claude complaining one day that he could not get into it for papers he needed, but Julian had said nothing, only looked annoyed.

As Regina descended the curving stairway to the ground floor, she considered how handsome her husband looked tonight. She watched him proudly as he came from his study. In the black formal suit, he looked taller than his five feet ten. The lights from the candles in the hall chandeliers struck his light-brown hair and made his green eyes almost yellow. He was gazing up at her as she came down the last steps, and he came and held out his hand to help her.

"You are gloriously beautiful tonight, my dear," he said. "I am very proud of you." He smiled at her, his whimsical, gentle smile that tugged at her heart. He could have resented her for the money she represented, but he did not, it seemed.

No, thought Regina as they proceeded to the hallway. No, Julian had never taunted her about money. He never spoke of the matter if he could help it. He did not remind her that he had married her because of her father's wealth.

In fact, she thought curiously, Julian did not seem to think about money, except as a worry, a necessity with which to pay bills. He was never reckless in spending for jewels, clothes, or gambling. It never seemed to occur to him that with the money she had brought to their marriage, he could have relaxed and spent his life in leisure.

No, he did not think of money, and he did not resent her. He seemed to be genuinely pleased with her.

She pressed his fingers fiercely for a moment. "Oh, Julian, I want you to be proud of me always!" she said passionately. "I never want to let you down. I know I talk out without thinking, and I'm too blunt, my stepmother says—"

"Always be honest, my dear wife," he said quietly. "That way, we shall be comfortable with each other. You may not always like what I say, but I shall tell you the truth. And if you do so also, then our marriage will grow and ripen and last. Like the grapes, with the honest rain and the sun."

She managed a quick smile behind the tears at his dearness and understanding. Feeling closer to him than ever before, she crossed the hall, kicked back at her train impatiently with her golden-shod feet, and then stood proudly in the doorway of the grand drawing room to greet their guests with him.

Several brokers staying with them came down first from the guests' chambers on the first floor. Monsieur François Lepine came down with Monsieur Souriau. Regina did not care for either of them. Maybe brokers were always cold and calculating. They seemed to look about at the furniture, the Ming vases, the Persian rugs, as though figuring to the last sou what they might cost.

Next came two others, not much better, and she smiled and bowed as they cast speculative looks over her gold gown and jewels. Julian greeted them formally, as though he too did not care much for them.

Thérèse and Marcus Bazaine brought the brokers into the salon to talk with the Dowager Baroness. Thérèse was dressed in a blue velvet gown that Regina was sure was not new, and she felt sorry for Thérèse. When the harvest came in, she would urge Julian to let Thérèse and Marcus take a trip to Paris to buy some new clothes. It wasn't their fault that the vines had failed and that one disaster after another had struck Verlaine.

Marcus was stocky, more like a farmer, rather uneasily running his finger around his tight white collar. He wore a tight-fitting black suit, and looked quite different from Julian, somehow, as if he had forced himself into something appropriate for the occasion. Julian was an aristocrat to his heels, thought Regina. He even looked splendid in a shabby brown riding habit that had seen years of wear.

The carriages began to roll up into the courtyard. The butler opened the great doors to let in the neighboring *vignerons*. One of the first to come was Madame Tillemont. A white-haired widow in her late sixties, she ran her own lands with a sure though fragile hand.

Eric had warned Regina about the old woman. "Don't mind what she says. She is very outspoken, but she has a good heart. And she is partly deaf, which is why she shouts."

Madame Tillemont stomped into the room, leaning on her cane and the arm of a green-and-gold-clad footman. She eyed Regina, after bowing to Julian. "Handsome woman!" she shouted in French. "Should have big babies!"

Regina blushed crimson. Julian managed a smile and bowed over Madame Tillemont's hand. "How are your vines, Madame?" he said in a loud clear voice.

"Splendid, splendid. But they look so every year, until August or September! Then they show their stuff! What do you think, Monsieur?" Her eyes peered up at him anxiously.

"They look good," he said positively. She beamed at him and tapped his tanned cheek with her fingers.

"Good boy," she said more mildly. She looked again at Regina. "Golden girl!" she shouted. "Are there more in America like you?"

Regina did not know what to say. Julian was shaking his head.

"No, Madame," he said. "Regina is unique. I know, I had to look for a year to find her! She is musical, she is intelligent, she has a good heart. Unique!"

"*Très bien,*" said Madame Tillemont, and went on to the drawing room where she was soon shouting good-humoredly at the Dowager Baroness.

Regina drew a deep breath. Julian gave her a slight wink, and a grin creased his cheeks, but he had no time for reassuring words before the next guests arrived. Regina had known there would be thirty at the table, but it seemed that there were already that many people in the drawing room and more were still arriving.

She liked Monsieur Gustave Carnot and his son Oscar.

She could tell Julian liked them also, by his relaxed informality with them and the warmth of his greeting. He clasped their hands, exchanged warm greetings, talked of their vines quickly before they went on into the drawing room.

Monsieur Vital Feuillet, in his forties, came with his buxom, handsome wife. He seemed cool and intelligent, with a gleam in his sharp gray eyes. Soon after came Monsieur and Madame Mangin, both in their sixties. He seemed cautious, placing a finger to his lip as he spoke of his vineyards.

It was all they seemed to care about, Regina thought later when they were seated at the table. Oh, they asked about Paris and painters, they spoke of music and briefly touched on world affairs and French politics. But the talk always returned to the vineyards, and their eyes lit up. Their tones became louder, and their hands waved with more expression. With all the sea of waving hands, Regina feared for the footmen waiting on them, but they were well trained and skillful. Impassively, they ignored the effusive gestures and managed to set the hot dishes before the guests without burning them.

"The harvest of 1893—"

"Ah—so good. Now, if only the sun will shine through September—"

"On the south slopes—"

"The whites of Monsieur Carnot looked so good last year—the rains, ah the rains—"

The brokers sat and listened intently, shrewdly assessing the *vignerons'* speculations about their harvests. All had had a bad year in '94; the rains had come wrong, they mourned. But this year, ah, this year might be quite good.

How they live in hope, Regina thought, gazing at Claude who sat halfway down the table, and at Madame Simone de Lamartine who was next to him. She looked splendid in crimson velvet and jet beads, but even her elegance and sparkling radiance was ignored as the talk turned to wine. She tried to attract attention to herself, Regina noted with secret glee. She would stare into Claude's eyes or those of the man on her other side, Oscar Carnot. But when the talk turned to wine, their eyes glazed over. They saw no woman, only wine, wine, wine, in bottles, with their labels on the beautiful casks, wine flowing into tall glasses, wine tasted by critical judges to be the best, to win the grand cru or the premier cru. Simone did not have a chance, although she looked a bit like a superior red wine, thought Regina, amused.

If only Eric were here, to share in her quiet amusement. But he was safely hidden away in his Hunt Collection bedroom, with dinner on a tray. Guests wearied him, and he felt very self-conscious about his infirmities. He never attended these dinners, Julian had told Regina. She thought it wrong; however, Julian was accustomed to overprotecting his younger brother.

Monsieur Mangin, an old friend of the Herriot family, leaned over to Monsieur Feuillet and said, "You know, I am still bewildered by the reports from the 1893 sales. They should have been higher. It was a splendid year."

The entire table of thirty fell silent as the *vignerons* instinctively turned toward the brokers. Monsieur Lepine waved his hands.

"The same story! You always expect the money to be higher," he said offhandedly. Somehow he reminded Regina of a banker who had tried to cheat her father.

Absorbed in her thoughts, she missed the next exchanges. But Monsieur Carnot was saying gravely, "We must go over the books again, Monsieur Souriau. I cannot understand either why I received so little for my wines. I sent all the bottles you requested—I have little left of the 1893 wines. You said they were splendid."

The broker held out his hands, palms up. "Monsieur, we have gone over this again and again! The wines were rather good, but many are wary of French wines now. The reputation must be built up once more. Who knows of the Carnot wines? No one in America! *Non, non,* we must pay for advertising them. I had to give away many bottles to promote the wines. I explained all this to you."

Julian made no attempt to stop the arguing that broke out. Instead, he listened intently, as though he too were gravely concerned. His intent look was one Regina had seen on her father's face, or her brother's, when one of them was thinking shrewdly and wanted to hear all the sides of the arguments.

Are the brokers charging too much? Or even cheating

their clients, the *vignerons*? Regina wondered. And why
does every *vigneron* have his own broker? She counted.
There were almost as many brokers present as *vignerons*.

"And there is the expense of coming to this area, of cart-
ing the bottles back to Paris," one broker was continuing.
"I must make a special trip here, you know. Most of my
clients are in the Burgundy area. And the Rhine wines are
competition for you. You must produce an even better
wine."

"That is what we are going to do," Regina heard herself
interrupting with some amazement. "Our rosé is going to
be very special. Then the price will be high, we warn you,
Monsieur!" She smiled to take the sting from the words.

Julian smiled at her from the head of the table. Her clear
voice had rung along the length of the long table. He raised
his glass of rosé wine to her.

"This is the wine of which my wife speaks," he said
proudly. "Our rosé. The 1893 rosé was good. The 1895
one will be greater, and we will have more of it. To the
next harvest!"

As one, the *vignerons* stood, and the brokers soon followed. They drank to the coming harvest. It was evidently
a ceremony that ended each spring dinner. Regina was
touched by their solemn, hopeful faces. What a gamble it
was, this business! And how rewarding it could be.

She rose then, after the toast, and led the ladies into the
rose drawing room. The Dowager Baroness moved nearer
to her, touched her arm, and smiled at her sweetly. "That
was excellent, what you said, my dear daughter."

Regina glowed. Her mother-in-law was so proper, so formal, that Regina sometimes did not know how she felt. But
this time the Dowager had spoken and the approval in her
voice and eyes was appreciated by the American girl.
"Thank you, Maman," she whispered.

The footmen and maids served the hot coffee and tea
that Regina had ordered. She poured the coffee from the
beautiful silver service that had been a wedding gift to her,
and Thérèse poured out tea to the ladies. The gentlemen
were lingering with their cigars and port and brandy.

They did not join the ladies for almost an hour. The
ladies could hear the hum of voices from the dining room
across the great hall. Madame Tillemont was frowning in
thought, and finally boomed to the Dowager Baroness:

"One hopes they are not making decisions that will affect me! Just because I am a lady does not mean I can be left out of decisions!"

"Of course not, Madame," soothed the Dowager, but she also looked concerned. Simone, on the other hand, looked bored. She disliked the company of women and made no secret of it.

Finally the gentlemen came in. Julian was cordial as always, but Regina sensed an unease in him. Marcus was grave, so was Claude. Had matters gone badly? She thought the brokers seemed very satisfied with themselves.

The talk turned to lighter matters. Some spoke of the hunt that would be held at the end of May, and the dinner that would follow. It was evidently an all-day affair, with buffet luncheons in the fields and a formal dinner that evening, with the gentlemen still in their hunting outfits. Regina thought of the heads in Eric's room and shuddered.

Finally it was midnight. Old Madame Tillemont was the first to rise and prepare to depart. She shook Regina's hand cordially and said in a loud voice, "And you will come and visit this old lady one day soon, eh?"

"I know no *old* ladies, Madame," said Regina demurely, a twinkle in her eyes. "But there is a young one with a vineyard she manages very well, and I should like to call upon her."

Madame Tillemont burst out laughing. "So you will come, eh? You will come soon?"

The other *vignerons* left soon as well, with some of the brokers. Footmen showed the Verlaine guests to their rooms, while others began to extinguish the candles in the tall chandeliers.

Regina went up the stairs, and soon heard Julian's footsteps behind her. He caught up with her and tucked his hand in her arm.

"You were wonderful tonight, my dear," he said approvingly. "You looked so magnificent, and you were most poised. I am glad you got on well with Madame Tillemont. She is a good soul."

"I liked her. She speaks her mind."

"Ah—yes," he said, and looked thoughtful. "I wish she had been with us after dinner." He frowned and fell silent.

Julian went to change in his dressing room, aided by his

valet. Ninette had waited up and was bright-eyed, asking how the guests had enjoyed the evening.

"And your gown, Madame? It was admired, yes?"

"Yes, Ninette. It was a good choice. I had not realized how splendid the occasion would be. Your advice was right."

Ninette beamed happily. She helped Regina take off the golden dress and hung it to air. She brought the white satin nightdress and the matching robe edged with swan's down. Regina slipped into them and sat to have her hair brushed the required one hundred strokes.

Julian came in as this was going on. He sat down nearby, in his dark-red brocade robe, and watched absently, his chin in one hand. Regina gazed at him in the mirror. His green eyes were very dark tonight, as though he were troubled.

After Ninette had been dismissed, Regina asked, "What worries you, Julian? Sometimes I think you worry very much."

He sighed and nodded. "Tonight showed me something. I thought I was the only one who overestimated the harvest two years ago. Now I realize we all did. How could that be? Is the commission to the brokers too high? Yet they will not handle our small quantities for less than fifty percent."

"Fifty percent!" Regina breathed, shocked. She swung around on the bench to face him. "Julian—so much?"

He nodded. "They say the expense of handling such a small bottling operation is too great. Yet we are all small vintners. I do not wish to handle great areas. I do not have the land. And no one would sell. The work would be immense. Regina, I do not know what to do. In the old days, it was not so. Grandfather had good harvests, and the money from them kept us going for years."

Regina was thinking of the exorbitant cost of that great dinner tonight. Her practical mind, inherited from her father, had been appalled at the preparations. The great quantities of paté, made in their own kitchens, served with fine white wine, the best in their cellars. Then the rabbit stews, prepared in red wine, and the beef steaks. The huge platters of fresh new peas and potatoes had not cost much, as they were from their own gardens. But the strawberries and ice creams had been brought from Paris at great expense. The cakes were made with the best creams and butter and white flour. And the cases of their best rosé to end the meal, the cigars imported from Spain, like the cognac and sherry and port—she shuddered just thinking of the expense.

Her father would have gone up in a terrible uproar if her mother had planned such a dinner. He would have insisted on more practical planning, with local wines, local produce.

"What are you thinking about, my dear?" Julian stood to remove his robe.

"Oh, the hunt dinner," she said. "I think—Julian, I shall plan better next time. We can use all foodstuffs prepared here at Verlaine, I am sure of it. I shall plan better—"

"My dear," he teased, bending over her, to kiss her long shining chestnut hair. "I am thinking romantic thoughts, and you are thinking of the next dinner! I thought you more romantic than that!"

"Oh, Julian!" Her cheeks glowed pink as he drew her into his arms. "Oh—Julian—" He unfastened her white robe and slipped it off her arms to gaze at her slim body outlined by the silky white nightdress.

He led her to the huge bed, and lay down with her. Within moments she forgot all about the dinners, the brokers, the distress on the face of Madame Tillemont as she spoke of her poor vineyards. She forgot the troubles of the estate, forgot all but Julian.

"You are so beautiful. Each time I look at you it is a fresh delight to see your glorious red hair—your soft brown eyes—"

"My hair is not red," she murmured feebly.

His hands went through her hair, caressing it. He had not blown out the last candles as he usually did before getting into bed with her.

"In the candlelight tonight, it was red," he said. "I was watching you at the dinnertable—the lights were in your hair, you seemed enveloped in a golden haze, and your smile—it was so sweet. I can scarcely believe you belong to me." His words made her warm all over as he stroked her hair, touching the nape of her neck and smoothing his hand over her shoulders.

She thrilled to his touch. They seemed so close now that she could scarcely remember their wedding day, when she had been so uncertain, even terrified, of the future. He would confide in her now. They could talk frankly about the estate, about everything—except money.

She had spoken again about remodeling the rooms, buying fresh velvets to make window hangings, ordering bright new wallpaper. But Julian would not discuss it. "After the harvest, we will speak of it," he had said. "I cannot afford to think of it now." From the proud lift of his head, she knew she could not mention her own money.

Julian felt that he had been given a dowry from her father, and that was all the money he had. He would use it to help get Verlaine back on its feet but only the necessities would be purchased.

Her thoughts drifted as he kissed and caressed her. She shivered as he nibbled at her earlobe. He knew now the caresses she reacted to, and his hand went to her bared breast, to cup it and smooth his thumb over the nipple. His strong hard fingers, a little rough from long hours of work in the vineyards, lingered over her silky thighs, to her knees, and back up slowly along the inside of her thighs.

He bent over her and held her nipples in his lips, kissing one and then the other. He was frank in his lovemaking. He made no secret of the fact that he desired her body, that he enjoyed arousing her, that his own body reacted swiftly to her closeness. He pressed himself to her.

"My love, my darling, I long for you."

Her hands went shyly to his muscled back as he entered her, and her fingers played curiously down his spine, and to his hips. He shuddered with pleasure as she rose to meet him.

"Regina," he groaned. "Dear—Gina—"

Teasingly, she pulled at his hips, getting a greater reaction than she had counted on. Her whole body seemed on fire, as he moved so quickly. His arms went under her body and he pulled at her, fiercely, so that she moved with him, her arms locked tightly about him. She came up to him, and they moved as one, wildly, on the bed. Regina had never forgotten herself so completely. He moved faster and faster, and she moved with him. Suddenly something seemed to spin inside her. She almost fainted with the violence of her reaction. She seemed to be floating, held up to his body, feeling him in her, and over her, and around her.

Heat built up inside her, and she felt as though her body

contracted about him, refusing to let him go. Her very center held him, and he moaned softly, coming to completion as she did. Still she felt the thrills, over and over, fading a little then, finally spinning out into nothingness.

She was limp. He rolled to the side, but his arms were still close about her.

"My God—" She heard him sigh. "Gina—Gina—"

She wondered what had happened to her. She had never felt like this before, such rapture that she had almost blacked out. Her head still felt dizzy, and she did not want to move. Her arms were flung out on the bed. He bent and kissed her elbow, up to her shoulder, down to her breast.

"You are—glorious," he whispered. "Never so much as now. Oh, darling—Gina—"

"Um—Julian—" She could barely say his name.

"Are you all right?"

"Yes. I felt—I felt—"

"How, darling?" he asked urgently, his arms about her. He nuzzled his chin against her breasts, intimately, down to her arm, back to her waist. "Tell me how you felt. I know you felt something tonight."

"I never felt—like that—before—"

He laughed a little, triumphantly. "I know. You gave yourself completely, my dearest! It was magnificent. I had hoped you would be so warm, so loving—and you are!"

"I don't understand," she complained sleepily. He laughed against her throat, and kissed the pulse beat there.

"It will happen again, my love," he said, and that was all she remembered. She must have gone right off to sleep, held tightly in his strong arms.

All she knew was that they were somehow closer than ever. She was closer to Julian than to any person in the world, and it was . . . glorious.

CHAPTER NINE

Regina rose late the next morning. It was almost noon before Ninette came in with the silver tray and porcelain cup of hot chocolate. Regina rolled over sleepily, felt automatically for Julian beside her.

Ninette smiled knowingly. For such a young girl, she seems to know a great deal, Regina thought as she sat up, blushing.

"Monsieur left two hours ago for the vineyards, Madame," said Ninette, bustling about to lay out a fresh muslin gown for the day, one with green ribbons at the wrists and waist. Regina spared a thought for her former maid, Giulia. She hoped the girl was content with Sally, who could be very kind or very difficult. Giulia would be far from her family in New York, and that would not be good. She wondered if she should write to Sally and suggest that the maid be allowed a vacation week with her Italian family.

After eating, Regina bathed and dressed in the muslin gown, then went downstairs to see what work there was to be done. Julian's mother had slept late; she was still in her rooms, a maid informed her. But Thérèse was up, directing the clearing of the dining room and drawing room, making the preparations for luncheon. The broker guests would be departing soon afterward, to return in their carriages to Paris.

Thérèse seemed quiet and sullen this morning. She answered curtly when Regina spoke. Regina gave up trying to cheer her up, and concentrated on the table arrangements for the luncheon. I will have the most senior broker at my right, she thought.

"Madame de Lamartine will be at Julian's right," said Thérèse abruptly, entering the dining room at Regina's back. Regina turned around, her pad and pencil in hand, surprise on her face.

"Madame—de Lamartine?" Why should Simone be here today?

"Yes, she went riding with Julian early this morning."
Thérèse seemed to take pleasure in telling her this. She
looked sour, Regina thought, as though life had gone
wrong for her. Yet she had Marcus, an adoring and attentive husband, and she had darling Jeannette, a sweet-
tempered, beautiful child.

She wished Thérèse liked her, but if not—she shrugged,
and tried to forget the incident. Julian mattered most, and
next to him the Dowager, his mother. Regina enjoyed Eric
so much, and she endured Claude although she despised his
indolence and pretense of working hard. But Thérèse—the
woman worked hard and deserved more than she had. Why
did she hate Regina so? Probably the money, thought the
American girl with a sigh.

The luncheon went well. The brokers were pleased.
When it was over, Julian saw them off, standing in a chill
wind for nearly an hour to be sure they were sent off royally in the carriages to Paris. Then he came inside, looking
almost blue with cold.

Regina brought him a glass of brandy. "Julian, you will
take cold," she urged quietly. "Do stand near the fire.
There is such a wind today."

He smiled gratefully, and bent to kiss her cheek. She led
him over to the fire in the rose drawing room. As they
stood there, it began to rain, and the raindrops struck
forcefully against the long French windows. Regina noticed
that the water seeped in under the windows.

"We really must repair these windows, Julian. Look at
the water coming in! Can we get a carpenter and some
good cedar wood to replace—"

He frowned, shook his head impatiently. "Regina, I told
you before! No work is to be done until after the harvest.
And if the harvest is not good—no work then! I cannot
afford it!" His tone was so harsh that his mother looked at
him in reproof, and Regina bent her head.

Thérèse spoke up angrily. "She would replace everything! Our velvet curtains are too shabby. Our rugs are
worn, even though they are valued Persians! She would
turn us inside out, Julian! Americans always want everything new and fresh—and expensive!"

Regina reacted sharply. "Yes, I would! I'd like to replace
the wallpaper also! It is so torn and faded that in places the
pattern is no longer visible! But most of all I would like to

toss out every antler head and moth-eaten animal in the Hunt Collection, and give Eric a bright, cheerful room! I think it's a shame he has to live with those horrible things, when he cannot even go out hunting—"

She came to an abrupt stop when she saw Julian's face. Incredulous, furious, hurt. His mouth was set as he leaned to place the brandy glass on a nearby table. "I am sorry, Regina. It cannot be done," he said flatly, and strode from the room.

She drew a deep unsteady breath. She had done it again, spoken out without thinking. Thérèse had goaded her— and the girl knew it. She flung a triumphant look at Regina, as though she had scored a point.

The Dowager rose from her chair, leaning on her cane. "I must—go to my rooms," she murmured. "Excuse me." She left the room, walking shakily like an old woman.

Regina could only be thankful that Simone had gone home after the luncheon. She would have hated to have her witness her humiliation. Marcus murmured an excuse and left also, hurried, to go back to the study. Only Regina and Thérèse remained, with the coffee tray between them.

Regina picked up her cup and drank the coffee without realizing it was cold, until she had drained the cup. She set it down unsteadily.

Thérèse said, "You are very foolish, Regina," she began. "Julian loves these old things, his old way of life. Do you not realize you cannot change what has been?"

"No, I do not realize that," said Regina stubbornly. "This is my home also. And I have the money to buy fresh materials for draperies. Oh, Thérèse, I don't want to change it all and make it look American! But I would like to make it look fresh and clean and bright. It could be so beautiful—"

"Yes, you have money," said Thérèse, staring angrily at Regina, looking her up and down in the white muslin gown with the lace at her throat, the pearls in her ears. "You have the money to purchase gowns that make us all look drab, even Simone."

"Thérèse, I wanted to suggest," said Regina carefully, "if you don't mind, I should like to help you purchase some new gowns. You would look stunning in the new styles, you have such a lovely figure—something in the new velvet brocades—"

An angry flush came into Thérèse's face and swept down her long throat. "Am I supposed to thank you for your charity? Well, no, thank you! Julian has promised me new gowns when the harvest comes in! Until then I am quite satisfied! Keep your—your money! You will need it to compete with—"

She halted herself with an effort.

"Pray continue," Regina invited evenly. Heat throbbed in her pulses and she felt almost sick with the heavy beating of her heart. "With what—or whom?"

"With Simone, of course!" Thérèse flung the words at her as if delighting in the torment of her sister-in-law. "Julian had an affair with Simone—even while she was married. Hilaire de Lamartine was elderly, ill. He did not understand her. Julian had known Simone all her life, and he was often over there, helping with the farm and the vineyards. It was not easy for her. She is gallant, strong, brave, and she does not complain! But Julian wanted to help her—and it happened. They are still most fond of each other. I think they meet often."

Regina sat as still as a statue, gazing at the shabby Persian rug at her feet. The thing she had most feared and dreaded was confirmed. Julian and Simone—an affair—

Thérèse went on drearily. "After Simone's husband died, she and Julian argued bitterly. I heard them. He wanted to marry her, I am sure, and she begged him—but he refused. She had no money, you see. Maman said he must marry money, we could not continue this way. He went to visit many good families in France, looking at the girls with big dowries. But so many of them—the war ruined many of them, with the titles. So he went to America."

"Please—don't go on," whispered Regina, her hands to her cheeks.

"Why not? You might as well hear it all," Thérèse stated coldly. "Maman said, 'Julian, go to America. Look at the girls there, the wealthy ones. Many Frenchmen have married well, and the newly rich want titles. Well, our title is as good as any in France, in all Europe.' So Julian went."

Regina swallowed the sour bile in her throat. She could not be sick. She kept her hands on her cheeks; she knew Thérèse was studying her expression with bitter satisfaction. How she must have bottled up all this anger and hatred!

"Julian came back, not married. Maman said to him, 'Why not? Have you not met anyone you can marry?' And Julian said, 'No, many of the girls were crude and vulgar and their families impossible!' But the harvest failed, he had to return and try again."

"And he married . . . me," said Regina slowly. It all fell into place: Julian's first visit; his later trip when he was tired and discouraged as he came to see her; his talks with her father about a dowry. Julian needed money, not just for himself and Verlaine, but for the rest of his family as well.

Julian and his responsibilities! And his beloved vineyards!

"He should have married Simone," said Thérèse. "The lands would have been joined. And one day we will have a good harvest! You'll see it—we shall be wealthy again one day, and then we won't need your money!"

She stood up unsteadily. Regina raised her head and looked up at her husband's sister. Thérèse's eyes were dark brown, not like Julian's, but her face, her hands—so like Julian's, large and capable.

"Maman would be furious if she knew I had spoken to you." Thérèse looked unsure of herself then, as her anger died. She rubbed one large hand against her hip, looking about uneasily. "No, I suppose I should not have spoken. You are married to Julian, and it is final. Though it was not in our church," she added.

"What does that mean?" Regina hardly recognized her own voice. It was cold and controlled.

Thérèse looked distinctly uncomfortable. Finally she muttered, "When the marriage is not in our church, and one is Catholic and one Protestant, the marriage can be annulled. It takes time, but it can be done. Especially if there is no child."

Her mouth trembled and she raced from the room, leaving Regina with bitter, horrible thoughts. Was this why Julian had not had their marriage in church, in his church? Was this why he had not sent for the priest to talk to her, as he had suggested he would? Was he waiting for the harvest, to discard her if he did not need her—and her money—any longer?

After the days and nights of harmony and understanding, and yes, love and desire, it was a bitter blow. Regina stood up, feeling old and wretched, scarcely able to move.

The rainwater spilled over the precious Persian carpets. She looked at it, and then rang for a footman.

"Will you bring cloths and a pail, and wipe up the water?" she managed to say.

"*Oui*, Madame. At once!" He returned with a pile of cloths and two maids who giggled as they worked. But Regina scarcely heard them. She was numb with the shock of all that had happened.

Throughout the day she felt chilled and unhappy. It was one thing to speculate but quite another to have her fears confirmed by Julian's own sister. Everyone must have known about his affair with Simone, and that he would have married her if she had had money.

Aunt Agnes eyed her shrewdly that day, and shook her head. The Dowager Baroness fussed about her a little. "I fear you have caught a cold, dear Regina," she said later that evening.

"No, Maman. I don't think so. I am just a little weary from getting to bed so late last night." Regina managed to speak with composure but Thérèse looked distinctly guilty and shaken. She probably regretted what she had said, but it was too late for that.

Eric had wheeled himself into the rose drawing room. "Do let us have some music tonight. It's so dreary outside," he urged. "Marcus, will you play? And you, Thérèse?"

Thérèse went at once to the large old piano in the corner, and Marcus went to open the velvet box where his flute was kept. After a few preliminary notes, they began to play, and it was soothing. Uncle Oliver wandered in from his room and lit up a cigar, puffing contentedly. Julian's mother took up her needlepoint and worked slowly, tapping her small foot in time to the music. Regina leaned back in the shabby but comfortable old chair and tried to relax. But her mind raced, the fury and the hurt welling up inside her. She felt that she could hate them all for encouraging Julian to marry her for her money— and then despising her for the very money they wanted. She was confused, wary, chilled to the bone by more than the rainy weather that persisted outside the windows.

"That was lovely," murmured the Dowager as Marcus finally laid down his flute. Thérèse rose and closed the piano lid. "Regina, my dear, do you play?"

Regina shook her head. "No, Maman," she said. It was

just about the truth. Years ago, as a child, she had played
the fiddle, but she had not attempted it for years. "I just
enjoy music. That was beautiful," she added politely to
Thérèse.

"Thank you." She kept looking guiltily toward Regina.
Too late to be sorry, thought the American girl, much too
late. It had been said. And perhaps it was better to know
the truth.

Julian came to Regina and helped her to her feet. "An
early night for us, my dear," he said. "I think you are half
asleep already. This was a strenuous week for you."

"Yes, yes, most strenuous, though Regina managed very
well," the Dowager said, folding up her work, neatly setting
the threads into her sewing box.

Regina went up to bed with Julian, but she felt ill at ease
with him. How could she yield tonight, knowing he had
spent much of the day with Simone? Knowing that Simone
had been his mistress, and still was? He probably wanted a
child, and that was the only reason he came to Regina at
all. After he had a child, would he still want her? Or would
he consider his duty done once an heir was produced?

And if the vineyards produced well this year, would he
discard her and get an annulment? These painful thoughts
did not help her relax. By the time Julian came to bed,
Regina was lying still and hopeless in the wide bed.

He lay beside her, caressing her gently. "You are tired,"
he said when she did not respond. "Regina, dearest, I'll
stay in the other room tonight. Sleep late tomorrow, you
must not weary yourself so much."

When he left, she wanted to weep, but she gazed into the
darkness instead, drawing slow painful breaths to keep
from sobbing.

Matters grew no better between them. She could not relax with Julian. More and more often he slept in the other
bedroom. Regina lay awake night after night, and soon
blue shadows appeared around her eyes, and she became
thinner and pale. She rarely went riding, discouraged by
the steady hard rains. Nothing seemed to matter anymore.

Julian watched her worriedly, and so did the Dowager.
Something was obviously wrong. Regina knew she should
put on an act for them, but she could not. She had always
been frank and open, even in New York society, as her
stepmother had fretted. She couldn't conceal her feelings. It

seemed to her that her future was hanging in the balance, for if the harvest was good and if she did not conceive a child, there would probably be an annulment. And in the meantime, Julian disappeared all day, every day. He said he went to the vineyards, but Regina thought he often went to Simone.

Even Jeannette was not much help. Regina would go up to the nursery to play with her, to read to her. But the sight of the lovely dark-haired child with the wide flashing dark eyes, the sparkling smile, even the way she hugged her doll and demanded, "Tell Regina and me a story, Aunt Regina!" would make Regina aware that perhaps she would never have such a child. It was painful to be with her.

Julian grew restless, observing her with keen eyes. He sighed often. And one dark and stormy day he did not ride out. He remained in his study to work.

At luncheon, he said tersely, "I would like to speak with you after we've eaten, Regina. If you will?"

"Of course," she murmured.

She could barely taste the food, and set down her fork after a few mouthfuls of the delicious veal. She wanted no wine. Her mind must be clear if Julian wanted a confrontation. The Dowager looked from one to the other, her soft eyes troubled.

Regina went with Julian to his study, and he closed the door after them. As she sat in the chair opposite his desk, she noted his shabby red velvet draperies, the torn rug. The desk was handsome, mahogany inlaid with gold and silver. The bookcases were filled with leather-bound volumes that looked well used. She gazed at the titles, most of which had to do with farming and vineyards.

"Regina, you are not happy here," he said abruptly, sitting behind his desk. "I feel there is something wrong."

She started. "Why—it is the weather." She averted her gaze from his. He shook his head.

"No, I have not been kind," he said simply. "I have thought only of my pride. Forgive me. You wished to make some changes here at Verlaine and I wanted to wait until the harvest—but it is discourteous to you. And you are accustomed to being active. Also, you are used to having beautiful surroundings."

She waited, her eyes lowered.

"What I am trying to say is, if you wish to make some

changes you may go ahead," he said slowly. "You would like to change the Hunt Collection room. I have spoken with Eric, and was amazed to hear that he disliked the room intensely, that he'd even had nightmares about the heads."

She looked up, finally nodded. Julian did not look hurt, but rather puzzled. "Yes, he told me, Julian. I thought—if the heads could be moved somewhere else, the room could be decorated in any colors he wished, with beautiful paintings. He likes the Impressionist painters. Perhaps we could find some lovely scenes for him."

"Hmm. I always thought that Eric—but never mind, I understand. He is confined to the wheelchair, he cannot hunt. It must seem like a bitter mockery to him, to be confined to the hunt room. I find it hard to forgive myself for my lack of understanding. I love Eric—but I did not know this about him."

Regina cleared her throat, touched by his simple admission. "Sometimes a stranger, an onlooker, sees things more quickly than—the family," she managed to say.

"But you are one of the family, Regina! However, I know what you're saying. You have come here only recently. We have grown up together, and did not realize it. And Eric has a gentle way of accepting all that fate has dealt to him. He has never protested at the unfairness of his life."

"No. He has a gallant spirit."

"So—I thought perhaps you might wish to begin with Eric's rooms. To remodel them as you like. The heads could be put into the lodge, since no one lives there now. I thought one day that Thérèse and Marcus might wish to live there, but they have said nothing of it. For now, the heads, the prints, all the heavy furniture could go there. I understand that in the attics there are sets of furniture. We can look at them and decide on some for Eric. Do you know how to measure rooms and windows for rugs and draperies?"

Regina's eyes widened. She nodded. "Oh, yes, I helped my stepmother to furnish the house on Fifth Avenue."

"You did? And it is in excellent taste," Julian commented with a smile. "Then perhaps you and Thérèse could arrange it. And you will want to get fresh wallpaper for his room—and for yours and mine," he added, with an evident effort. "I think you would be happier with papers and draperies of your own choosing. The rugs could be put elsewhere if you wish."

"Thank you, Julian. I—I should like to plan for this," she said, feeling a little spurt of pleasure. Perhaps he really did care for her, after all! If she could just endure his affair with Simone— She felt the bitterness rise in her again, and firmly suppressed it. She would have to get accustomed to this—if she remained.

"Good, that is splendid. Perhaps Thérèse—"

A knock came at the door, a timid little tapping. Julian went to answer.

"Maman! Come in, if you will."

The Dowager entered, the little black shawl slipping from her thin shoulders. Julian gently replaced it and saw her to a chair. Her anxious gaze went from one face to the other.

"I thought perhaps you might be—that is, you are not quarreling?" she asked haltingly.

"No, no, Maman," Julian assured her. "I have just given Regina freedom to change the rooms that she wishes. Eric also wants a new decor. You do not mind?"

"Of course not! She is the Baronne, after all," said the Dowager with gentle dignity. "I have feared that our daughter was becoming bored with us. After all, she is accustomed to lavish parties and lots of activities, I'm sure."

"No, I am not bored, Maman," Regina assured her hastily. "I like the country."

"But you have been confined by the bad weather. Julian, I have been considering the matter. You must take Regina to Paris, for some gay times together. After all, you are newly married and Regina is used to much more excitement—the music, the opera, the social life. We cannot have her disliking our Verlaine because it is so remote."

"I do not dislike Verlaine," Regina protested again. "It is—just—oh, the weather, I suppose."

"The summer will be better. But Julian, really, do please think of going away with Regina for a few weeks, before the heavy work of the harvest begins. A bit of time in Paris would be splendid for you both."

"Yes, we can manage it," said Julian after a slight hesitation. Regina wondered if he was reluctant to leave Simone. "Regina will measure for draperies and rugs and all that, and then while we're in Paris she can order just what she needs."

"It will be expensive," said the Dowager, frowning a little.

"I have some money of my own," Regina said, braving Julian's look. "I should like so much to go ahead on these projects. No matter what the harvest is, I should like to help make Verlaine shine, the way it must have once."

"You are a sweet girl," Julian's mother said, patting Regina's hand. Julian was looking flushed, and his generous mouth had set in a thin line. He stared down at his desk, one hand clenching a sheaf of papers.

He finally looked up. "Yes, good. If you really wish to make a start, Regina, we shall do it. Of course, I do not wish you to spend much of your money on this." His head lifted. "I can obtain money. We can use some—"

"Please, Julian, I should like to do it. My father has provided for me," she urged quietly. "If Verlaine is to be my home as well—" She let the words hang in the air, watching him closely.

"Of course, it is your home," Julian said decisively, and Regina let out a breath in relief. "You must feel quite at home here, and do as you please. Maman, I think Thérèse will help with the measurements—"

"And Ninette," said the Dowager. "Such a bright quick girl! I sensed in her at once that she has potential. A good seamstress also."

"She is a good girl, very kind and efficient," said Regina. "I am so glad that you trained her, Maman. I do not know what I would do without Ninette." The Dowager looked intensely pleased.

They talked for a short while about color schemes. "I should like to keep the same colors," Regina said quickly. "I like them so much. My rooms are beautiful, in rose and blue."

"They were chosen by Julian's grandmother," the Dowager said. "How artistic she was! I remember her matching the wallpapers and the velvet when she remodeled all of it about fifty years ago. I was living on the next estate, and I visited often to watch as she worked. Little did I think I would marry Julian's father and come to live here, and have such fine children!" she mused, lost in fond memories.

"And Eric's rooms—we must ask him what colors he

would prefer," said Julian, his mouth softening. He seemed reconciled to the loss of the hunt room. "I think he likes yellow very much, and perhaps red."

As they talked, they became more enthusiastic about fixing up the rooms. Regina took a pad and a pencil and began to sketch out some ideas, indicating the colors beside the rooms.

Julian watched her with a smile. "And now you will be happier, Regina," he said hopefully. "I had forgotten how you like to be busy."

"Yes . . . I like to be busy," she said, trying to match his smile. "I want to be useful."

"My dear child! But you do so much now," protested the Dowager. "A weight is off my poor shoulders," she added, touching her arthritic shoulders a little painfully. "You and Thérèse, you manage it all! I live in luxury and peace, with no worries!"

Julian gave her an affectionate look. "You have always worked hard, Maman. You deserve a rest and some peace." He helped her up and she patted his lean brown cheek with a thin hand. He turned the hand to his lips, and kissed the palm.

"Dearest boy," she said softly, and tears stung Regina's eyes. One day, would she have a fine strong son—like Julian? Or would they never get that far together?

CHAPTER TEN

Perhaps because Thérèse was ashamed of what she had told Regina, she was very helpful as Regina and Ninette measured the rooms, discussed colors, and planned the changes. Only once was Thérèse difficult and obstinate. When it came to deciding where to put the Hunt Collection and Regina suggested the lodge, Thérèse objected bitterly.

"But the lodge was for Marcus and me! Julian promised! He always said that when there was enough money, we could move into the lodge—" She stopped hastily at Ninette's stare.

"Oh, I am sorry, Thérèse. Of course, the heads can be put elsewhere. I wish we could toss them all out." Régina glared at the big glazed eyes of the nearest buck.

Ninette cleared her throat. "I have the idea maybe?"

"What is it, Ninette?"

"One of my uncles—he has an inn where the men drink, you know? Where the hunters come in. If you wish to be rid of some of the heads, he would be glad to have some. To decorate the walls, and to brag a little, the way men do, you know? To say they were given to him by the Baron of Verlaine."

Regina consulted Julian and he agreed, but the collection would only be on loan.

So Ninette's uncle came with a wagon, to carry away the heads and clear them out of the room. Marks were left on the great paneled walls. Eric eyed them ruefully.

"Whatever will we do with the walls, Regina? But I am glad to have those gross monsters out of here." He made a comical face with his thin lips and expressive eyes.

She studied the walls, her hands brushing over the pale marks. "I think those could be rubbed down by a carpenter and finished with varnish and stain," she said thoughtfully. "What about the hunt prints? I think some of them are good."

"Those could go into the lodge," said Thérèse. "Marcus

likes them. Even if we do not live there—" She flushed at
Regina's look. "Well, we might not," she said hazily, and
she turned to lift a print off the wall.

Regina wondered about her. Thérèse seemed so moody
and difficult at times. And sometimes she and Marcus
seemed so sad and quiet. What could be wrong? Julian did
not speak much to Marcus; he consulted mostly with
Claude, and sent Marcus out to the vegetable farms to take
charge there. Wasn't Marcus smart enough? Or was he
lazy? Regina didn't think so. He seemed to work hard at
any task he was given, and came in tired and covered with
mud late in the afternoon.

Regina found herself looking for work to do. It had not
taken long to measure the rooms and choose the color
schemes. Eric was pleased with the removal of the heads
and was waiting patiently for her to order draperies and
rugs. Ninette had helped her select the furnishings, which
the footmen brought down from the attic. There was even a
large wide bed with a good firm mattress. The old beds
were taken to the lodge. They would do as beds for children later, and so they were set in a second-floor bedroom.

"The master is more cheerful already, Madame," said
Eric's valet Joseph. "He disliked the room as it was, but he
is not the kind to complain."

"You must tell me if he is happy with his new bed," she
said gently. "We want him to be very comfortable. And
yours is fine, is it?"

"*Oui*, Madame, it does very well," he said happily. He
had a larger bed also, on the other side of the room, so he
could help Eric if the young man needed him during the
night.

There was little more for Regina to do. She did not want
to order draperies and rugs sight unseen, so they would
have to wait until Julian felt he could take time to escort
her to Paris. In the meantime Regina hunted for something
else to occupy her time.

One day she wandered into Julian's study. She longed to
fix it up, but Julian insisted that the red draperies and old
rugs were what he liked. Claude was out on the estate that
morning, and the account books were piled in stacks on the
desk Claude used on the far side of the room. More stood
in the bookcase behind his desk. Regina sat down and lifted
the top one to study it.

She glanced over the books with curiosity. There were separate books for the farm produce, the wages, and the wines. These latter books were of most interest to her and she began to study the entries, starting with the 1890 harvest. She was good with accounts, as her father had relied on her to keep his books, and she found Claude's methods quite similar to her own.

She examined one record after another, of money poured into the harvest, wages paid, grapes crushed, number of bottles purchased, number of casks—but the end result was poor. The same in 1891, and in 1892. The entries of 1893 were higher, but still at the end there was little money in the balance. Regina frowned and went back to the earlier pages. What had she missed? There were the broker commissions, which seemed much too high, but even so—

She was so absorbed in the figures before her that she did not even hear when Claude and Julian came in, tired and muddy. Claude stared at her, aghast, almost white under his tan. Julian frowned stonily.

"Regina, what are you doing?" he snapped.

Embarrassed, she shrugged lightly. "Going over the books. I want to understand everything about Verlaine," she said, setting down the last one on the pile.

"But darling, you don't know bookkeeping," Julian said with a sigh. "I know you want to work, but my love, don't bother about these dull figures! I don't understand them myself!"

Her father had believed firmly that everyone should do his share of the work, even a small girl. But before she even had a chance to explain, Claude broke in coldly.

"If you could do this work, you would take my job away from me," he said tightly. She looked to see if he were joking, he was not. He was truly angry, his hands shaking as he moved to his chair.

She rose quickly. "I'm sorry, Claude . . . Julian," she muttered. "I just—wanted to understand."

"Leave this work to us," Claude said curtly, and Julian did not protest.

Regina left the study without another word. She was furious. They had treated her like an idiot!

* * *

Julian rose earlier and earlier as the days lengthened toward summer. He was long gone by the time Regina awakened. Well, she decided, she would go out riding by herself.
She refused the groom curtly, and Julian was angry and
concerned when he found out about it.

"Regina, you must not ride alone! It is not proper!"

"I don't care about that," she snapped. "I want some
fresh air. And I want to be alone."

He looked as though he was holding his temper on a
short leash. "It could be dangerous," he said with contained calm. "You could fall and be hurt, and no one
would know. Or some scoundrel might stop you and—
Regina, it is not safe!"

"So I should stay indoors all day and night, then?" she
said with false sweetness, her eyes flashing.

"I suggest that you take the carriage, have the head
groom drive you. And take Ninette, she has sense."

"And I don't?" she asked. But the look on Julian's face
made her relent. "Forgive me, Julian. I am unreasonably
cross. It's just that I am accustomed to driving and riding
out by myself—"

"In New York?" he asked shrewdly. "Or out West, when
you were a child?"

She scowled, and he laughed gently and kissed her
cheek.

"Regina, my dear, just take care, that's all I ask. I do not
want anything to happen to you."

So she sighed and gave in. She drove out with Ninette,
sitting properly in an open carriage to enjoy the fine
weather. They couldn't drive through the country lanes,
which were too rough and narrow, so the only place to go
was along the main highway, out to the village that lay at
the gates of Verlaine, or a little farther to the inns beyond.

The ride out and back did not take much time so Regina
decided to stop in the village and walk about with Ninette.
By noon she felt hungry and rebellious. She had no desire
to return to the château, to Thérèse's silent disapproval
and her mother-in-law's sweet meaningless chatter. The
men never came home until late afternoon.

"Is there some place we can have luncheon?" she asked
Ninette, looking curiously at the inn signs. There was a

Sign of the Dragon, a Sign of the Goose, a Sign of the Green Vine.

"*Oui*, Madame, if you wish. The Green Vine has good meals," Ninette said. She understood that her mistress was given to impulses.

"Let's go there, then."

Once inside, Ninette spoke to the inn host, who wore a long white apron. He bowed and went to get his plump wife from the kitchen.

Regina had some trouble understanding the patois the innkeeper spoke, but she managed to order a slice of roast beef, a green salad, and coffee for Ninette and herself. She insisted that the maid sit with her at the rough-hewn clean table.

Regina remembered wistfully the one breakfast she had shared with Julian at a country home, seated at a rough table, eating the delicious food. She remembered the closeness they had felt and wondered if it was gone forever.

She was leaning back in her armed chair drinking coffee, when she realized she was being closely observed. She looked about, to see a tiny woman in black staring at her. The woman had gray hair and sparkling black eyes. When the woman saw Regina meet her gaze, she rose quickly and came to the table, bowing rapidly several times.

"Madame la Baronne, out of the goodness of your kind heart, I would have you listen to my pleas," she began swiftly.

She spoke in the patois, but Regina could understand her fairly well. The innkeeper started over to her, frowning, but Regina waved him back.

"Yes, I will listen. What is the trouble?" she said very slowly and precisely. Ninette did not seem surprised, only alert, her eyes wary.

The woman pressed her worn hands together. "It is the roof, Madame la Baronne. It leaks so much. I sent a message to the château, but nothing has been done."

Regina looked at Ninette. "Is this house owned by Verlaine?"

"*Oui*, Madame. Everything here is owned by Verlaine," said Ninette.

"All the village, all the houses?"

"*Oui*, Madame. The church, the inns, the streets—everything."

"Good heavens." It's feudal, she thought. She rubbed her head. "I want to see this house," she decided abruptly. This surprised even Ninette.

"Oh, Madame, you need only speak to the Baron," Ninette advised. "It is not done—"

"We will go now," said Regina, and beckoned to the woman. First she paid the innkeeper, who did not want to take the money, glancing uneasily at his wife. Regina had to estimate the amount, since he refused to discuss it. She set coins on the table and smiled charmingly. "The meal was delicious. I shall come again," she said firmly, and swept out.

The coachman was waiting. "Wait here for me," she told him. "I will be back soon."

It felt good to walk about. She followed the elderly woman as she trotted down the cobblestone street and around the corner.

They entered a small wooden house that was immaculately clean. The woman pointed to one corner of the room where a pail had been set out on the floor, apparently to catch the rain as it dripped from the roof.

"When it rains, it is terrible, Madame! I am up all night to empty the pail." She pointed dramatically to the roof. "Open to the sky, it is!"

Regina walked over for a closer look. "What is that?" she asked Ninette. "It is not wood, not brick—"

"It is of thatch, Madame," said Ninette.

Regina frowned. "Thatch? It does not look like it would last one winter!" she said. It looked like dark straw to her.

"Oh, but Madame, it does," Ninette said, enthusiastically. "A good thatcher will make the roof to last twenty years, thirty, forty. I know it. My family lives in such a house, in this village."

"And where is a good thatcher?" Regina asked.

"My uncle is such a good thatcher," Ninette said modestly.

"Well, ask him to do the work, then, Ninette, and send the bill to me. Can he do it today?"

Ninette stared at her, at the woman, back at Regina. "But the permission of the Baron de Verlaine," she whispered. "Do you not need to have his permission—"

"He is too busy," Regina said bitterly. "It must be done,

and he hasn't the time to look. So I will order it done. Today, before it rains."

"*Oui*, Madame. I will go to my mother, and ask her to speak to my uncle—if you wish?"

Regina went with Ninette to her parents' home. The young maid spoke to her mother and uncle privately first, and then introduced them to Madame La Baronne.

Ninette's mother was slim and looked much like her daughter. Behind them was a tall man swinging a basket of tools. Regina talked to them and told the man she wished to have the cottage roof repaired.

"It should be completely redone," she said. "I saw other worn places, so the entire roof could go soon."

"*Oui*, Madame, I will do it," Ninette's uncle said. "I suggested it to Monsieur, but he said it could not be done now."

"No, it must be done," she said firmly. Then she paused. "Monsieur—you mean the Baron?"

"No, Madame. Monsieur Claude Herriot, the manager. He told me no." They were all waiting for her reaction.

"Well, go ahead on the work."

"Madame? There are five other cottages where the roofs are also leaking," he said with respectful firmness. "If you approve this one, the other tenants will complain. They have asked over and over for the repairs."

She flung out her hands. "Do them also," she said recklessly, refusing to consider what Julian's reaction would be. "Do all that need fixing! Send a bill to me directly, and I will see that it is paid."

On the way home, Ninette said shyly, "It was very good of you, Madame. Monsieur le Baron has much on his mind."

"Monsieur Claude has little on his mind," Regina said tartly. She touched Ninette's hand. "Let me know of any other problems, Ninette. Between the two of us, we should be able to take care of these things that the men are too busy to handle, don't you think?" Ninette had to grin at the mischief in her eyes.

"*Mais, oui*, Madame! We will take care of it!"

When Regina confronted Claude on the matter, he protested vigorously that there was no money for new roofs.

"Doctor's bills would come higher!" Regina said. "They could catch terrible colds."

She went to look over the work on the roofs, and approve it. She was invited into cottages for tea or coffee, and she listened to what the women said. The men were more wary. The priest, robed in black, stopped her one day and introduced himself. "You have done good work here, Madame. God will surely bless you."

She wondered if he would speak of instruction for her, but he did not. Instead he told her of a sick widow and her child who needed to be taken care of, and Regina saw to it that money and food were made available and that the doctor would treat the woman and send the bill to Verlaine.

Regina found some pleasure in the work. At last she was doing something useful. Soon she would have to begin preparations for the hunt and ball, and she found she resented taking time away from her work in the village.

Many entertainment events were arranged for the hunt. Thérèse helped Regina silently to prepare for the buffet luncheons to be sent out in wagons, and the huge dinner to end the day, with dancing to follow.

The hunt began early in the morning, with horns calling the horsemen and dogs. Regina peered sleepily out her window, to see the group gathered in the courtyard, looking splendid in their hunting outfits.

The dogs were yapping and howling, the men shouting to each other. "What a din," Regina complained, and decided she might as well wash and dress.

The ladies assembled in the two large drawing rooms. They were given breakfast, over which they gossiped until it was time to take lunch out into the fields to the men. The wagons were loaded with food; it took more than twenty men to load them and drive them out. In the fields, Regina felt sick. Men were bringing in bags of game, rabbits whose white fur was matted with blood, birds hanging still and lifeless.

Even Julian had a bagful of pheasants in his hand, his rifle over his shoulder. Regina found she could not eat anything, but the men ate heartily, drank more, and boasted of their kills.

They returned to the hunt in midafternoon. With compressed lips, Regina helped clear up, and then returned with the ladies to the château. She was seething with rage at the killing and the waste. Some of the men had tossed the rabbits they did not want to the dogs, and the sight of it turned Regina's stomach.

Surprisingly, Thérèse understood Regina's feelings. She put her hand timidly under Regina's arm as the girl got down from the carriage. "It is something men do that women cannot understand," she said in a low tone. "And the rabbits and game must be kept under control, or they would eat all the vegetables."

"It is so—so bloody!" Regina breathed. "I feel sick!"

"Go inside and lie down. I will take care of matters for now. I am used to it," And Thérèse urged her gently toward her rooms. "You need not come down until dinner. Shall I send up a tray of tea?"

Regina shook her head. She felt nauseated and wanted nothing. How could she make it through an entire dinner?

She rested for a while, then rose and dressed. Ninette had prepared an ice-blue satin gown with a lace stole. She put it on wearily, wishing she could skip the dinner. Instead, she would have to smile at the ladies, ignore the drunken men who bragged about their "kills," and be a polite hostess.

She sat silently through the dinner, as platters of food were carried around to the eighty guests. Five footmen were kept busy filling the wine glasses. Watching it all, the banker's daughter began to count up in her head all that it cost—the day of entertainment, the wagons, the luncheon and the dinner, the wines, the brandy and cigars. It was appalling—and all to kill some rabbits and pheasants!

A ball followed the meal, but some of the men were too much in their cups to do anything but sprawl out in front of the fire in one of the drawing rooms and talk of kills past and present. Regina, however, was expected to dance, and she did so with a false smile set on her lips.

"Well, well, a splendid hunt today," one man greeted her, his fat red face even ruddier from the wine he had drunk. He held her too closely, and she found him disgusting. She thought she could smell blood on all of them.

"I think hunting is appalling and brutal," she said in a clear voice. Several couples stopped to stare at her. Had they heard Madame la Baronne correctly?

"Brutal! My dear Baroness, you do not understand our customs!" her dance partner exclaimed. "It is a splendid thing to shoot and shoot well. The sport of kings! It is why these châteaus were built, to take advantage of the hunting." He laughed at her.

Her cheeks were flushed with anger. "Indeed? Then I think kings have bad taste! They should have come here for rest and fresh air," she said. "And they—and *we*—should let the rabbits and pheasants be hunted by the villagers and farmers who need them for food!"

"An American radical," said the man, and the couples dancing around them frowned uneasily. One woman giggled, fanning Regina's fury.

"I believe in killing animals and birds only when absolutely necessary, for food. How much of the game today will go for food? The whole idea of a hunt is primitive and barbaric. We should be more civilized than—"

Julian appearing out of the crowd, jerked her away from her partner and swung her into the dance. "Be quiet, Regina," he hissed. "My God, they love hunting! Say no more!"

"What have I said that's wrong? The poor rabbits and birds are hanging in the game room in the lodge to rot! Why shouldn't the peasants have the fun of the hunting and then eat the game? I think this whole idea is rotten—"

"Another time, Regina! For the love of God," he groaned. "I will explain the customs some other time—not tonight!"

"Don't bother. I am sure you will find some excellent explanation for men to continue being ruthless and brutal," she snapped.

She saw Simone laughing quietly with Claude, both of them sending amused looks at her. She burned all the more. But she kept quiet, as Julian's arm tightened warningly about her waist.

At midnight, a game pie was served, an immense one made of many of the rabbits and pheasants shot that day. She could not touch it. She thought only of those limp bloody objects hanging from the rough brown bloody bags.

"I would think you would be pleased," Claude taunted softly in her ear, taking a large forkful of the pie and grinning at her. "We are eating the game, are we not?"

"Oh, if you could have seen the faces of your guests!" Simone sneered. "What a disaster! It will be a long time before they forgive you for slighting their cherished institution of hunting."

Regina gave her a long stare. "I can imagine that you longed to participate," she said, and turned away abruptly.

"What do you mean by that?" cried Simone after her. "What did she mean, Claude?" The plaintive cry followed Regina as she walked away.

The ball went on, but Regina had had enough. She slipped away, up the back stairs to her rooms, and went to bed. Ninette helped her out of her gown and listened to Regina's exasperated remarks.

"They will have their pleasures, Madame," Ninette said at last. "Our ways are not the same as those of the Americans. Though I have heard that the English hunt for foxes as well."

"Cruel, brutal, stupid!" stormed Regina.

"*Oui,* Madame."

"And foolish as well!"

"*Oui,* Madame."

The brush stroked soothingly through Regina's long chestnut hair. Finally she relaxed, but she wished she could shut out the sounds of hearty laughter and the breaking of bottles that floated up the stairs.

Regina sighed. "I'm sorry, Ninette, for taking it out on you."

Ninette smiled knowingly. "I am sorry, Madame, that you are unhappy at times. It is hard to live in another place and to feel at home there. But things are changing, I believe. You are finding your place here."

Regina looked questioningly into the mirror, at Ninette's thin young face with the wise old eyes. "What do you mean?"

"Your place, Madame, the place of la Baronne. You will make a fine Baronne for us. You have the sympathy, the feeling, and the will to do what must be done. One day, God will reward you with the happiness only He can bring."

"I do not understand," said Regina. But Ninette only smiled.

"The women of the village say this, Madame, and I know it is so. The trust will come, and you will learn the truth."

"Ninette," said Regina fretfully, "you talk in riddles to-night, and my brain is too fuzzy to comprehend. Please speak more plainly."

"The time is not yet, Madame," was all Ninette would say.

CHAPTER ELEVEN

Several weeks passed before Julian finally felt able to get away and take Regina to Paris. Regina thought his mother had been urging him, for he still seemed reluctant to leave. But once in the huge carriage and on their way, Julian began to relax.

"Ah, my darling, it will be good to be alone with you," he said, and reached out to clasp her hand. "I feel I have scarcely seen you these weeks."

It was true. He was gone from morning to night, and she wondered if he spent much of that time with Simone. But she had to admit that he came back with his boots muddy, his hands grimy. Surely Simone did not receive him like that. But then again—perhaps it was all an act. Perhaps everyone was laughing at her behind her back.

"What are you thinking, my dear?" His troubled green eyes studied her face. "You are thinner. I think you are working too hard. And I hear you toss and turn at night. You need a rest as much as I do. Thérèse could do more, and Aunt Agnes too."

"No, no, they do so much already," she hastened to assure him. "I only fret that—that I cannot do more."

"I did not bring you to Verlaine to slave for us," he chided gently. "You do so much, you drive yourself too hard, I think."

"Perhaps it's an American trait. My father is the same way. But he hates to waste time in what he calls foolish pleasures. If mother gets him to an opera, he soon falls asleep in the box! I think she has given up making him go."

Julian chuckled and squeezed her fingers. "Do you remember when you first invited me to the opera? It was the first time I thought you might be at all attracted to me. And the sweet way you smuggled me into your father's study, to get me warm and comfortable! I think it was then I began to realize you were different from the others."

"What others?"

"The American society girls. The giggling overdressed jewelry-hung girls whose mothers forced them at my head!" he said. "All I could see was the emptiness of their minds, the vacant expressions when I spoke of anything serious. You were different. You had read, listened to music, you cared about what happened in the world."

So that *was* why he had chosen her! A warm glow spread through her, and she let him hold her hand, banishing thoughts of Simone from her mind. It was important to her to think Julian had chosen her for herself, not for the dowry her father could give.

After a pause, she said, "And it was that day I first began to know you and appreciate you. Do you remember? You walked to our house so that the horses would not have to travel the icy streets. I felt the same way, that it was cruel to let them be treated so."

Their reminiscences shortened the long journey to Paris, and by the time they had arrived at the townhouse, Regina was feeling like a new woman. Julian was anxious to please her, he was concerned for her. He must have some feeling for her!

They retired early after the long ride, and he did not come to her bed. But she rested, content, and wakened early to see the sunshine coming through the drawn draperies. She rang for Ninette, who brought hot chocolate. "Ah, Madame, you are up early this morning," the maid said, beaming.

"It's such a lovely day!"

"Monsieur wakes up early also. He is already down at breakfast. He will be pleased that you are ready to go out with him. I shall set out your gown."

Julian was pleased when Regina joined him at the table wearing a dress of dark blue wool with white piping. He jumped up, smiling at her. "Ah, my dear, the Paris air agrees with you," he teased. "Do you smell the delicious aromas of the shops and the cafés?"

She giggled. "Now, Julian! I just want to go out walking! I want to walk and walk—and go to the Louvre. If I were only a child, I should run in the parks!"

"Hmm, I wonder if we could get away with that." He pretended to consider it seriously.

They went out to stroll along the avenues, peering in the shop windows and talking amiably. The sun was so bright

and warm that day, they decided not to go into any mu-
seums. That could wait for a rainy day. They did leave a
card at the Longstreths', and when they returned in late
afternoon, they found a gay message from the couple, inviting them to go out the next evening. The Longstreths pro-
posed a visit to Montmartre as before, if they had no objec-
tions. Julian sent a footman with their acceptance at once.

"And about tonight," Julian said. "Let's go dancing, Regina. We shall find some out-of-the-way place where no
one knows us, and I shall have you all to myself! If any
stranger comes up and asks you to dance, I shall knock
him down!" He furrowed his brow and looked quite fierce.

Regina laughed out loud; he was so silly and sweet.
When they went out, they had a lovely time, all by themselves. Julian found a dancehall frequented by middle-class
women, shop girls, young gentlemen in striped trousers,
and artists with bright red bowties under their bearded
chins.

The lights in the hall were Japanese lanterns, which cast
a pretty pink glow. Regina wore such a demure dress that
she thought she blended well into the crowd. But Julian,
even in plain gray suit, looked so distinguished that all the
women stared at him.

"You have made a conquest," Regina whispered to him
teasingly, as one girl at a nearby table winked at him bra-
zenly.

Julian winced. "My dear, I already have the prettiest girl
in Paris on my arm!" He bent over and brushed a quick
kiss across her forehead.

"You flatter me, Monsieur. What are your intentions?"
she asked playfully. He chuckled and leered at her.

"The worst, *ma petite* rose! To seduce you, that is what I
wish!"

"You are very frank, Monsieur. I think I should fear
you! I am most strictly brought up! My papa would not
like this!"

"No, but I would," he whispered, and kissed her earlobe,
knowing it would make her shiver. Just at that moment the
lights dimmed, and everyone squealed. In the darkness,
Julian drew her closer and kissed her passionately on the
mouth.

Later, as they sat to watch the dancing, a man strolled
up to Regina and bowed.

"Will the lovely lady care to dance this one with me?" he asked.

His eyes were bold, black, inviting. She stared up at him wide-eyed, stunned. Julian stood up, lithe as a panther.

"The lady is my wife, and she dances with no one but me."

"*Ah—pardon!*" The man bowed regretfully and walked away.

"Impudent!" Julian muttered, sitting down again.

"I suppose . . . in this place," Regina said timidly, "it is done. Perhaps we should leave," she added, but she really didn't want to go. She felt delightfully anonymous there, not Madame la Baronne on her best behavior but a woman with her lover.

"Not if you are enjoying it," Julian said. "I can deal with your admirers, I suppose."

But they left about midnight, as the crowd became a bit wild. Regina noticed that many of the girls had slipped away also, two or three together. They came to dance, it seemed, and that was all.

At the townhouse, she went to bed, and Julian came into her room after Ninette had left. The moon was shining brightly through the parted draperies, and a delicate breeze wandered in, flirting with the light white curtains.

He discarded his robe and slid into the bed with her. "My darling, I have come here to seduce you," he said dramatically.

She began to giggle, having expected anything but that. "But, Monsieur, you have to ask the permission of my papa!"

Julian began to laugh. "I have the permission of your papa! Now I need only your own—" He turned to her and drew her into his arms. "How beautiful you are, my sweet Regina," he said softly, their jesting forgotten.

He drew aside the soft folds of her nightdress and began to kiss her throat and white shoulders. She raised her arms and put them around his neck, her fingers caressing the strong muscles at his shoulders and the thick hair at the nape of his neck. His lips roamed over her, his kisses growing hotter on her arms, her breasts, her stomach. He pushed back the sheet that covered them, and a gentle breeze blew over her. She shivered.

"Are you cold, love?" He moved on top of her, drawing

the covers over the two of them with one hand while stroking her rounded thigh with the other.

He was such a skillful lover that she could not help wondering about the women he must have known before her. She could not imagine him making love to Simone but the very idea of it upset her, and she felt her muscles tense. He brushed his lips across her breasts, teased at the nipples, took the time to make her relax again. She must forget Simone—she must forget her—

Julian murmured to her lovingly, in French and in English, his voice husky with passion. But he is so considerate of me, she thought. He was so dear—so wonderful a lover—and she wanted him to love her. She wanted to show her love.

She drew him closer and made herself relax in his arms. Deliberately, she shut out all thoughts of anyone else. They were alone in the world, they were alone in this room, he wanted her. . . .

Oh, he wanted her very much. She knew it by his quickened breathing, the tautness of his body pressed to hers. His kisses became demanding, his tongue teasing her tongue intimately. She was absorbed in that sensation when he slowly moved between her thighs. They clung to each other, closer and closer, rocking back and forth as one. She squirmed to get closer still, and now it was Julian who held back. He held himself above her and made her come to meet him. Her hips rose up to his, ardently, impatiently, wanting to feel the power of him within her. Desire blotted out all resentment, all pride. It was all that existed.

She felt the rush of ecstasy and moaned helplessly, hanging on to him as he skillfully completed the embrace and came with her. She trembled, quivering as each wave went over her.

When it was over, she fell back helplessly onto the pillows. Julian held her, kissing her tenderly, praising her. "Ah, you are so sweet and giving, my darling! You are the most generous lover in the world, you give so of yourself—I adore you—I adore you. . . ."

She fell asleep with his words still ringing in her ears, the imprint of his kiss fresh on her cheek, his arms about her warmly. When she awakened his arms still circled her, and she felt gloriously in love. The sun shone brightly, so high in the sky she knew they had slept late.

He smiled at her and kissed her lazily. "I've been studying your beautiful face for the past hour," he said. "I think
I will keep you. No one else has such a sweet nose"—and
he kissed the tip. "No one else has such long eyelashes on
such pretty brown eyes"—and he kissed each eyelid softly
shut. "And no one such a rosebud of a mouth. Yes, I shall
keep you, all to myself. I think we will stay in bed all day
today, and tomorrow—"

She giggled, pulling away as he teased her with a shower
of kisses. "But, Monsieur, what about the guests this evening? We have promised to go out," she said.

"Mon Dieu." He sighed. "The world, it presses in on us.
Regina, what would you like to do today?"

"Do—what?" she asked dreamily.

"Would you like to go out to the drapery shops today
and choose some material?" he asked practically. "It might
take several days to find the right fabrics. And the wallpapers and rugs. How about doing some shopping this
afternoon?"

"We could go this morning." She sighed reluctantly.

"My dear one." He chuckled. "It is already past morning! By the charming clock in the corner, it is twelve-
thirty."

She shot up, but then remembered she was naked and
pulled the sheet up to her chin. He grinned and traced a
lazy finger down her spine.

"Or since the day is so far gone, we could remain in
bed?" he suggested seductively.

"I really must—oh, Julian, there's so much to do!" she
complained.

"And the Longstreths will be here at five. If we hurry we
can get in about two hours of shopping," he said, and when
she moved to get up, he did also.

They visited two stores, but Regina felt too hurried to
make any decision. She resolved to make an early start another morning, and take Ninette with her. Julian distracted
her!

Ninette had a lovely gown laid out for her when they
returned in midafternoon. There was just time to wash and
dress in the filmy silver and black chiffon gown, which
made Regina look more mature and sophisticated.

"Ummm," Julian said in appreciation. "I adore you in

rose, you seduce my heart in blue, but in black—*mon Dieu!*" He rolled his eyes teasingly.

Ninette suppressed a giggle. It was a delight to see Julian so charming and gay, as though he had thrown off all his worries. Regina responded to his moods, and when the Longstreths arrived, they did also. It was a happy party that roamed the hills of Montmartre.

They were sitting in a lovely café, chosen by Ken, when a young artist approached their table and introduced himself as Armand. He had a portfolio of sketches with him, and Julian looked through them intently.

"I would like very much to paint Madame," he said, nodding respectfully toward Regina. "I could sketch this evening, and have something ready to show you tomorrow," the artist added hopefully. His face was eager and gaunt.

Julian nodded, to Regina's surprise. "Yes, do that. You may come along with us this evening to do some sketches. But if you do her portrait in color, I wish her in rose or blue," he said.

Armand nodded, and his smile told of his relief. "*Mais oui*, Monsieur! It shall be done in rose—and in sunlight, I believe," he added, studying Regina more closely. "I think she is a lady of sunlight. Roses and daylight."

"You are quite right," Julian told him. "Could you come to my townhouse tomorrow afternoon and sketch her there? Or must you work in a studio?"

The artist hung his head a little. "My studio is up many stairs. I would not ask a lady to climb them," he said frankly.

"Then come to us." Julian gave him the address. "Shall we say, at three o'clock?"

The appointment was made, to the amazement of the other three. When the artist left to sit at a nearby table and quietly sketch Regina, the others expressed their surprise.

"But we could have had a famous artist," said Kenneth Longstreth. "I know a dozen or more—"

"I like his sketches," Julian said. "He makes people look like people. He has a gift of capturing an expression. I like his work." Apparently it was settled.

When they went on to a nightclub, the artist came with them in their carriage. He was quite pleasant, intoxicated by the hope of a commission. He ate with them, and over dinner, he revealed something of his work, his hopes and dreams. His gentle brown eyes glowed as he talked.

After dinner, Regina danced with Julian and gazed up into his eyes with wonder. She had never seen him so quietly happy. She felt his contentment in the way he held her, the way he danced, his laughter, his tenderness.

When they returned to the table, the artist was sketching busily. Julian glanced over at him, and he showed them the sketch. It was of Regina's face, glowing with her love, looking up at Julian.

"Yes." Julian nodded. "Yes, it's perfect!"

The artist continued to fill his pad with hasty drawings. Regina felt self-conscious at times, very much aware of the sharp dark eyes so intent on her face. For a while it was difficult for her to relax, but eventually she was laughing and joking with her friends.

They left reluctantly at about two in the morning. It had been a delightful evening. When the carriage finally pulled up to the townhouse, Julian helped Regina out and led her to her room. She stumbled into bed and slept soundly. Julian did not stay beside her, but she was too sleepy to have enjoyed his attentions.

The next morning they went shopping, looking more closely at velvets and wools, trying to select from the many exotic colors. Regina finally found a yellow velvet for Eric's rooms, and then they returned to the townhouse, to find the artist Armand waiting for them. They asked him to join them for luncheon, and then Regina and the artist went out into the back courtyard, near the rosebushes, to work on some sketches in color. Julian went in and out, too curious to be able to stay away for long.

About six o'clock, as the evening was turning a misty blue, young Armand was triumphant. "I think I have it, Madame!" he said, and brought the sketch to show her.

Julian appeared so promptly he might have been listening. He also looked at the sketch. Regina was shown from waist up, wearing the rose dress. She held a yellow rose in her fingers, and was gazing into the distance as though listening to a bird singing. There was a look of enchantment on her face, the sunlight on her right side casting part of her face in shadow. Her hair was tinged with red and her eyes were a wistful dark brown.

"Yes," Julian mused. "I have seen this very look on her face. It is Regina."

Armand looked anxiously at his model. She nodded appreciatively. "*Bon!* Then tomorrow I come at this same time. It is important for the light to be the same, at the same moment. I will bring canvas and easel, and my paints. You will pose for me again?"

"Yes, she will," said Julian. "We have not set upon a price. Suppose you come into my study with me."

They must have settled on a healthy sum, for the artist was dazed with happiness when he arrived the next day. He had paid the rent on his studio for a month, he confided in Regina. The monsieur was most generous! He began to paint at once, to capture the effect of the light on her skin and hair. It was important for him to work on her face, arms, and hands first. "The rest I can fill in in the studio from my sketches. Or I can work on it when it is dark and rainy. But today I must take advantage of the light."

After he had left, Regina stretched and twisted her lithe young body. Sitting still for almost three hours had been hard work!

Julian watched her anxiously. "You are weary?"

"Not too tired, Julian. I just need to walk about."

"What about dancing? There is a new place near Pigalle."

She smiled. "I should love to go!"

"*Bon!* Would you wear one of your blue dresses? The blue and gold is enchanting."

She wore the blue and gold gown because he wanted it, and she wanted to please him. She wondered a little cynically, when she had time to think, with Julian always wooing her, and making love to her, was he trying to get in her good graces in the event she found out about Simone?

She set the gold jewels in her ears, around her throat. She wanted to look beautiful for Julian so he would continue to desire her. Was that all he wanted from her now that he had the money? She wondered if he wanted a son. If they remained married—if she stayed in France—if she had a son—would that reconcile her to being second in his life? Or would he someday give up Simone? Regina wanted to be first with him.

* * *

"You are very quiet this evening, my Regina," Julian said later as they watched the Apache dancers. "Are you too tired? Perhaps we should have stayed in."

"No, no, I am enjoying this," she assured him, and managed a bright smile. She watched the lithe figure of the man as he tossed his partner about his shoulders and up into the air. "You would not dance like that with me, Julian, would you?"

"*Non, non,* not unless Madame wishes to be tossed up to the ceiling," he assured her solemnly, in his teasing voice. "Does Madame wish to be—*mon Dieu!*" he cried as the dancer flung his partner around and around in a wild circle.

They met each other's eyes as the dance ended, and Regina burst out into little giggles, which she tried to suppress. He laughed and ordered another bottle of wine. He is so charming, so amusing when he is free from worry and work, she thought.

They went on to another nightspot and watched a colorful display of Russian dancing, while eating caviar and drinking vodka served by Russian waiters in black and gold tunics. It was fascinating, and she enjoyed the singing that followed, the full, rich voices and the sad melodies. They went home about two o'clock in the morning.

"This is getting to be a habit," said Julian as they slowly climbed the stairs.

"We won't know how to act when we return to Verlaine. We shall demand caviar and wild dances in the drawing room. What will Maman say?" Regina laughed.

"She will probably say, 'My, is this the way the young people dance these days?' and go on with her embroidery," Julian said with a wry twist to his lips. "She used to be quite frivolous and gay, Regina," he told her, more seriously. "The years of poor harvests, Father's desperately hard work and his death changed her from a happy matron to an old woman." His fingers caressed her cheek. "I do not want that to happen to you. I want you always happy and without cares."

"Life always has cares, Julian," she said gently.

They went on into her bedroom. Ninette had gone to bed, on Regina's orders. She didn't want the girl to stay up to all hours. Absently, she began to unfasten the buttons on her gown. "I do not know of any life without cares. My own mother—I saw her die, took care of her as she lay—" She stopped abruptly, self-consciously.

"Tell me, Regina," he urged gently. "You speak so little of yourself. I think you had many sad experiences in your youth."

She placed the jewels on the dressing table thoughtfully. "Well—it is long past," she evaded. "I suppose it helped harden me. I am tougher than I look."

He smiled. "You look about as tough as a rose in bloom, as a kitten sunning itself on a ledge. Please tell me, Regina."

"Not tonight, Julian." She shook her head. "Perhaps sometime—when we are not so tired, when you have time to listen. It is a long story." She tried to smile, but her eyes were shadowed.

"Very well, sometime soon."

They went to bed. He made love to her tenderly, before they slept, wrapped in each other's arms.

Armand came again the next afternoon. Julian worked in his study while Regina sat on the white bench in the sunshine and thought of what they had said the night before. Did he truly want to hear all about the old days?

She thought of the hard work, the freezing cold mornings when she had risen to find sixteen inches of snow at both doors and no way to get out but by shoveling. She remembered the frozen hunks of meat she had to saw in order to cook and the scrawny vegetables. But there were happy memories too: the pleasure of an unexpected guest, a miner dropping in, a traveling peddler, or even an entire family traveling west, willing to stay over for a week or so to rest.

"Your eyes are different, today, Madame," Armand said, laying down his brush. "Each day, you are different. How can I capture you on canvas, when your face and eyes change with your thoughts?"

"I am sorry, Armand, I will try harder," Regina apologized. "How shall I look?"

He sighed. "I should like to paint all your various faces. But if you will look—dreamy, happy, as you were the first day? If you will, Madame?"

She tried, by thinking of Julian and his embraces, and

Armand made a little sound of satisfaction as he picked up his brush and began again.

He returned the third afternoon and the fourth, and had accomplished enough so that by the time some rainy days came, he was satisfied. "I shall finish it in my studio, Madame," he told her as the first clouds appeared. "It shall be done in just a few more days. My best work! My most glorious work!"

Julian said, "I'm very happy with it." He gave the canvas a long, careful look. "It looks finished now."

"*Non, non*, Monsieur. It needs more work on the background, and on the gown. You will see. But the main work is done, Madame's face and her hands. They are most important, you see."

After Armand had left, Julian said, "You know, I think that young man will be famous one day. He brings you alive on the canvas."

"Is that why you chose him? Because he will be famous one day?" she asked curiously.

"No. I liked his sketches, I thought they showed promise. But I did not expect him to do as well as he has."

"Then why, Julian? Why choose him?"

"Because he looked like he needed the work," said Julian, so abashed that she had to hug him.

"You are the nicest man in the whole world, Julian," she declared, and kissed his cheek. She was surprised that he had noticed the man's gaunt face and shabby clothes, and she wondered how he let his own tenants go hungry and without good roofs over their heads. It was not consistent.

There was something odd there, and she stored it in the back of her mind to ponder over later.

CHAPTER TWELVE

Regina felt as if she were in a dream. She had never been so happy. The weather in Paris was pleasant, and Armand was finishing his painting. She and Julian were quite happy with him.

During the days they often shopped for the materials they would need to redecorate. Ninette came with them, and they searched diligently until they found what they wanted. The shop, located on a side street, was owned by a Russian Jew with a full beard and a skullcap perched upon his head. He brought out beautiful lengths of fabric. Regina gasped again and again as he showed them the velvet brocades, the cut velvets, the fine satins.

"Where did you find such beautiful material?" Julian asked him incredulously.

"My cousins travel abroad," he said matter-of-factly. "They go to the Middle East, to Italy, to the Baltic countries, even back to the old country, Russia. They find the small places where hand work is still done, the workshops where the pieces are fashioned on hand looms with loving care. You see, Monsieur?" He laid out a length of thick carpet to demonstrate his point. "Hand work. Look at those knots! So close is the work. This rug will last you two hundred years, three hundred."

Regina bent to examine the knots tied on the wrong side, and nodded at the careful work. "How strange and humbling," she said thoughtfully, "when one thinks that this rug will outlast us all. And our children and grandchildren as well. It makes you wonder. . . ." She paused, fingering the rug.

The shopkeeper squinted at her approvingly with his sharp eyes. "Madame speaks the truth. She is wise. Yes, yes, it is to inspire awe in one. And to think of the many works of man that outlast him! The paintings, the sculpture in ivory and marble and gold. Yes, yes, it is to wonder."

He went into the workshop behind him, and Regina heard him issue orders in Russian. As they sat in small

velvet chairs beside the long table in his showroom, he
brought out to them lengths of even more exquisite velvets
and silks, magnificent huge carpets from Persia and Turkey
and India. Ninette was wide-eyed, rubbing the carpets with
gentle fingers, unable to keep from touching them.

"Ah, Madame, never have I seen such beautiful ones!
Oh, Madame, but look at this one! You must have it for
your own living room, Madame la Baronne!"

"Madame la Baronne!" the old man repeated, eyeing
them keenly. "Monsieur is le Baron? May I have your
name, Monsieur?"

"Monsieur Julian Herriot, Baron de Verlaine." Julian
held out his hand to the old man.

The shopkeeper looked amazed, but finally he put his
own fragile hand into Julian's and murmured his name,
"Judah Silver, Monsieur le Baron. You honor me," he
added. "I know that name, Verlaine. It is an old and honorable one."

Julian bowed his head briefly. "Some eight hundred
years, Monsieur Silver. And I imagine yours is quite old
also."

The man grinned, showing gold-capped teeth. "Two
thousand or more, Monsieur, if legend is to be believed!"

He turned to Regina. "And you, Madame? You are not
French?"

"I am an American," she said. Julian looked displeased.
"That is—I was, until my marriage."

"Ah—America! The Land of Promise, the land of gold
in the streets! You know such stories, Madame?"

She was impelled to say, "I have heard them, Monsieur.
However, we did not find gold in the streets. My father
mined gold in the Rocky Mountains, and that was the basis
of his fortune."

Judah Silver looked stunned. "Truly?" He turned to
Julian, to see his smiling nod. "Amazing! It is true then!
Gold in America!"

"America is a land of rich promise, my father always
said," Regina told him, a bit shyly.

"Yes, promise, promise, the new country," he said with
the enthusiasm of a much younger man. "My sons have
said, 'Papa, why do we not go also to America?' I tell them
France is their country now, and we travel to many lands
of our people. Still they want to go to America. They say

there a man can be free, truly free. Is this so, Madame?"

Regina looked thoughtful. "I believe," she began slowly, "there are many opportunities because America is still a wild and untamed land. Men can leave poor farms and go west to find farmland for very little money. There they can grow rich crops. Also there are the mines and forests."

"Truly a marvelous country!" breathed the elderly merchant. "One hears of such things but cannot believe them. A land of such riches for the taking! All we know is hard work, the effort of making a living and passing on what little we have to our sons. What does your father do now, if I may inquire? He still mines the gold?"

"No, not for a long while. Now he is a banker."

"But if there is more gold for the finding? It is easy to find?"

Somehow Regina felt she must go on. The old man with his curious eager face, his hungry eyes—not hungry for food, but for knowledge of the world, made her want to tell him more. "It was not easy, Monsieur. You see, I grew up in the West. My father was out mining for gold in the mountains, sometimes chipping away at rocks for days and weeks and months without finding a thing. Often he stood in streams up to his hips from early morning until the sun set, to pan the gold. He would take a pan with holes in the bottom and sift the dirt from the river, and find maybe a few grains in the bottom of the pan when he was done. For years he worked until he finally located a vein of gold, and then he was able to buy more equipment, hire miners we knew and trusted to help mine the ore."

They were all listening eagerly, the Jewish merchant, his assistants peering from the back rooms, Julian and Ninette. Julian's gaze was intent on his wife.

"Truly a marvelous story," Silver said, absently setting out another glorious Persian rug with flowers of rose and blue, and a border of the most beautiful celestial blue she had ever seen. "Look at this one, Madame, I beg you. But your father—he worked for many years, Madame? And your mother approved?"

"Many years. My mother died of a fever," she went on impulsively, feeling somehow that these people would understand. "My brothers went on working with my father. I cooked, did the laundry, nursed their colds, even pneumonia! I drew water from the well, or in winter melted snow in pans for fresh water. My lessons were from a few books we had to read. My father taught us all our sums, and Mother had taught us to read. I did most of the writing and the accounts."

"And Jeannette said you shot a bear once—" Julian said quietly, not to disturb her thoughts.

"Yes, that's true. I had a pet horse, and one night I was alone in the cabin, when the boys slept out near the mine because some claim jumpers were about. I heard my horse whinnying madly, so I took a rifle and went out the back door. I saw a big shadow in the corral, terrorizing my horse. My horse was running about madly, trying to get away. I just shot at the big thing, and it went down after three shots. It thrashed about horribly—" She shivered. "I thought it would break through the corral fence, but it did not have the strength to climb back over the fence to attack me. In the morning, I found the bear there, dead. My horse was half crazed with fear. It took days to calm him down."

The merchant muttered in admiration, and Julian was studying her gravely.

"There—I am talking too much," said Regina, embarrassed. "Forgive me! When I start on the old days, I become boring."

"But it was most fascinating," the merchant said. "I see you are a most unusual lady. Monsieur le Baron is most fortunate to have such a courageous lady for his Baronne. Please allow me to give you this fine rug as a gift. I think you will enjoy it."

Regina protested, but he insisted and the rug was wrapped up for her. Then they proceeded to choose from the magnificent velvets and satins for draperies and curtains. Ninette efficiently helped to work out the amount of fabric they would need. When they had made their choices for Regina's bedroom, she turned to Julian a bit timidly.

"Now your bedroom, Julian. And the master bedroom. I looked at the materials there, and they are so dusty and worn—" She looked at him worriedly. Would he be offended?

"I think we should take advantage of this magnificent material. We shall choose fabrics for the bedrooms and also for the chairs in the rose drawing room. They are getting quite shabby."

Eventually they decided on beautiful red velvet for Julian's smaller dressing room-bedroom. Then they chose a reddish purple—the color of grapes, Julian said—for the master bedroom, with satins to match for the chairs.

They were quite tired. "We must stop for today," Julian said firmly. "Regina, this is supposed to be a vacation for you."

Regina would have protested, but the merchant agreed with Julian. "It is difficult to choose wisely when one is weary, Madame. I will have those you have picked out sent to your townhouse, and you may return another day. Meanwhile, I shall send word to my cousins, to see what else they may have. I have a cousin in Montparnasse who can easily send some of his more special materials to me."

"It would be very kind of you, Monsieur Silver," Regina said. "Yes, I think we must stop for today. Oh, dear, is it four o'clock?" she gasped, looking at the little watch on the golden chain about her neck.

The merchant bid them good day and they went on their way. But Ninette was still worrying over the list of measurements.

"Madame, we have not measured the lengths we will need for the rose drawing room," she said.

"No matter," Julian replied. "Why don't we choose a material, then write to Monsieur Silver from Verlaine with the measurements? I am sure he will not make a mistake. And while we're at it, we might request that he look out for some fine Persian rugs for us, to use in both drawing rooms."

Regina drew a deep breath of pleasure. "Really, Julian, you will allow me to change the brown drawing room also? I should so much like to get a bright color, perhaps a gold or amber, to lighten that room."

She could scarcely believe that Julian was letting her make so many changes without a look of regret. He smiled at her.

"If it will make you happy, we shall make it purple and gold," he said good-naturedly.

She giggled, and even in front of Ninette, she put her head on his shoulder. "Oh, Julian, you are so sweet! I promise not to make it too gaudy. I am sure Thérèse would be—"

She paused; she must not say it. He put his hand gently on her hands, which were folded in her lap. "Thérèse is foolish at times, and jealous of your youth and beauty, and yes, of your money too. Marcus is a good man, but weak, I think. He will always be just a worker at the farm, I fear. Do not let Thérèse disturb you."

"I should like to get some dresses for her while we are here, Julian," she said hesitantly.

"If you know the size, we shall do so. Do you know what colors she would like?"

"I think so. A pale yellow muslin would look lovely with her hair. A bright gold evening dress in velvet. Perhaps a blue satin too," she said eagerly, looking to Ninette, who nodded in agreement.

"*Oui*, Madame. And once I heard Madame Thérèse say she would like so much one day to have a bright red velvet gown. I think she looks at those of . . . another lady," she said discreetly.

Regina's face shadowed. She had almost forgotten Simone. Must that woman ruin everything?

Ninette hastened on. "I have been a maid to Madame Thérèse and the Dowager Baroness. I know their sizes. If Madame wishes to purchase dresses, I could be of help. Or perhaps it would be better to purchase lengths of material. There is a good dressmaker in a village near Verlaine. She used to work in Paris before her marriage five years ago. She would work well with the fabrics?" Her voice ended in a question.

It was agreed upon. Regina, Julian, and Ninette went back to Monsieur Silver's shop several times. His cousins came and went, bringing lengths of fabric, precious rugs, and ideas for what they might find on their next journeys.

Regina praised Monsieur Silver. "You all work so well together. Is it your custom to manage the shops while they journey?"

"Ah, *mais oui*, Madame." He smiled. "We cooperate on these ventures. When one is out of a certain article, we send to the other's shop. If business is good in one and poor in another, we close one and all of us work in the other. And we take turns traveling. If one is expecting a child or if a member of the family is ill, perhaps the others take his turn."

"That is an excellent idea," she said thoughtfully. The word "cooperate" had struck home to her. She began turning it over and over in her mind.

Julian and Regina had one final night out with the Longstreths before they left Paris. They started out at sunset and rode in a carriage along the Seine, quiet in their appreciation of the way the setting sun shone on the buildings and the river. The last orange rays seemed to accent the details of the sculptured stone of the buildings, the ironwork, so delicate yet so firm, the chimneys, the lampposts.

They spent part of the night in one of the finest Parisian restaurants, then went to a nightclub, and ended up at a charming club up in the hills at about three o'clock in the morning. Vicky sighed when it was over.

"When will you come again? It was such fun," she said.

"Not until after the harvest, I'm afraid," Julian said, a faraway look coming into his eyes.

"But that means September or October," Vicky protested.

"*Oui.* I must be there at Verlaine from now on. The blossoms are on the vines, and soon the grapes will appear. I must supervise everything, watch the growth closely to make sure the watering is done. Then the harvest comes about mid-September, ending in early October, and after that, the pressing of the grapes. I must be everywhere at once." He frowned, mocking himself with a grimace. "The rosé is so important to me—to us. If it does well—ah—"

"Julian, come back from your grapes for a few more minutes," chided Ken laughingly, "and help me choose a wine for us now."

Julian laughed and obeyed. It was a happy evening, even though it was their last time together for a while.

Julian woke Regina early the next morning, in order to make the trip back to Verlaine in one day. Ninette had supervised the packing of the new rugs, the fabrics, all their luggage, and the new painting. She rode in one huge carriage with the trunks and hat boxes while Julian and Regina took the smaller coach.

"She is a gem of a maid," said Regina, as Julian settled into his seat.

"She certainly is. Her mother is just like her, hardworking and a good soul. I am glad you approve of Ninette," Julian said.

Julian kept glancing at her as they drove out into the countryside, the outriders splendid in green and gold. They rode along the river for a time, and Regina noted the lines of poplar trees, so straight and slim, their leaves gloriously green with the morning sun shining through them.

"Regina, are you sleepy?" he asked, noticing her silence.

"Oh—no, no, not really."

A little later he asked, "Regina, are you sad about leaving Paris? We shall try to come back soon, whenever I can possibly manage it. I promise you."

She roused herself, to see his worried green eyes. "Oh, no, Julian! I am looking forward to returning home, to Verlaine. There is so much to do—the remodeling, making draperies, covering the chairs, and so on. But I was thinking about something else. About what Monsieur Silver said."

He frowned slightly, puzzled. "What was that?"

"About the way he and his cousins and relatives cooperated in their business. Julian, do you know what cooperatives are?"

He stared at her. "Why—some sort of socialist venture, I believe. Why?"

"Well, I know Papa started a cooperative out West, with the gold mines," she explained. "He could not remain there to handle everything. So he and the other miners formed a cooperative. They elected a treasurer and several directors. Whenever a decision had to be made, they wrote to each other, and sometimes they all came to New York to discuss matters."

"That is a very serious topic to think about on this beautiful spring morning," he answered, beginning to smile. "I am happy to learn more about your adventures in the Wild West, Regina. Will you tell me about them?"

"Oh, Julian, I am serious! I was thinking about all the brokers you *vignerons* hire. Why do you all have different brokers?"

"Because we always have, I suppose," he said. "My father and grandfather hired the same firm year after year. And others in our valley did the same."

"What if you all had the same broker to handle your work? And only one man had to come to Verlaine to work with you? Then he wouldn't have an excuse to charge fifty-percent commission, would he?"

Julian studied her eager face, evidently bewildered. "But

Regina, how would we ever work together? Imagine Madame Tillemont working with Monsieur Feuillet and with Monsieur Carnot. No, no, we would all disagree on whom to choose."

"Disagreement can be very costly, Julian," she said quietly. "If you had a cooperative broker, and a bank to tide you over the rough times, money to draw on at low interest rates when you needed, a common treasurer for your firm—"

"Come, come, you are going too fast for me!" He gazed into her eager face. "Regina, what exactly are you talking about?"

"Well—Julian—I should like to write to Papa to ask him if I am right about this," she said, taking a deep breath. "But I have been thinking for some time that the brokers charge excessively, and that is why you make so little on your wines. In bad years, so much money goes for interest on bank loans. In good years, why don't all the *vignerons* set aside money in a common bank account? When one has a bad year, he can draw out enough money to keep him going, at low interest. Or if one is ill and cannot work, the others can help him in his fields and charge low rates."

"We already help each other out, Regina," he said shortly. "We all help Madame Tillemont. I loan her workers, Monsieur Carnot checks the vineyard to see when it is ready for harvest, Monsieur Mangin handles her bottling—"

"And Madame Tillemont is overwhelmed with your generosity and humiliated with your charity, which she feels she cannot repay."

He stared at her, biting his lip. She wondered if she had offended him, but he was thinking.

"I do not understand it all," he said finally. "Begin again, and explain to me how a cooperative works. I fear I have never studied the matter."

Much of the journey back to Verlaine was spent talking. Regina told Julian how a cooperative would be formed, how each member would have stock in the corporation, how they could buy casks together and obtain a cheaper bulk rate. They would select a treasurer and do all the bookkeeping for the vineyards together. They could even market their produce together. The better wines could be bottled by each vineyard under its own label. The cheaper wines could be combined, to bring out the best of the *vin ordinaire*. That could be sold locally, as Chenin Blanc wine.

They could form a credit union to help them obtain loans more easily, and they could share equipment and workers as well. As the grapes ripened on various hills at different times, the workers could move smoothly from one vineyard to another.

Julian asked questions from time to time, and Regina admitted she did not know all the answers. "But if I might write to my father about this, he could explain it all. Or perhaps there is some firm in Paris that might know how to go about it. Legal papers would have to be drawn up."

He ran his hand through his hair. "This is something I have never considered," he said frankly. "I don't know what to think. But it sounds good, Regina. I think you must have inherited your father's business sense!"

"Oh, I wish he were here to explain this. He could do it so much better, I am sure."

"No, it is I who am stupid about this," he said. "I have never handled the finances of Verlaine. I left them to Claude, who is clever with figures. I can work in the fields, test the grapes, study how to make better wine. But the accounts—this idea—it is something I will have to study. If it could cut expenses and raise our profits, I would be a fool not to take advantage of it."

She smiled then and leaned back to rest and enjoy the remainder of the journey. She began to recognize a few landmarks as they neared Verlaine. "There are Madame Tillemont's fields," she remarked, pointing out the window. "And look, there is her château. And the cathedral—" She moved closer to the window to get a better view. "Oh, Julian, there is home. I see Verlaine!" she exclaimed presently. It rose on the hillside, the glowing golden stone surrounded by acres of pleasant green trees.

Soon they were traveling over the cobblestoned streets of the village leading to the gates of Verlaine. Someone recognized the carriages and waved to them, crying out, "Welcome home, Monsieur le Baron. Welcome, Madame la Baronne!"

Regina waved back at the old man and to her surprise, Julian waved also, craning to see his face.

"Old Nicolas, one of our best vineyard workers," he told her. "His sharp old thumbnail can pick a bunch of grapes so that not a grape is bruised. It is an art, to cut the stem just so."

The carriages rolled into the estate and up the hill into the courtyard in front of the château. The butler came out, and the grooms ran from the stables. Candles were lit in the rooms bordering the courtyard to welcome them.

Julian jumped out of the coach and helped Regina down. "Welcome home, my darling," he said as he lifted her in his arms. She smiled at him, and clung to his arm as they went into the château. She could not help thinking of that time months before when she had fearfully entered her new home for the first time.

Julian's mother tottered into the hallway to greet them. Even Thérèse was smiling, and Jeannette had been allowed to remain up for their arrival. Regina knelt to take the small girl in her arms.

"How is my little darling?"

"Oh, I'm fine, Aunt Regina. I'm not allowed to ask if you brought me anything," she said, beaming.

Her parents groaned, but Regina laughed and pressed her cool pink cheek to Jeannette's warm one. "I did, darling, a beautiful new doll, and some material for a new wardrobe for her. I may even have some fabrics for my favorite little girl too."

"Me?" whispered Jeannette.

"Who else?"

Ninette had packed the doll at the top of a small trunk, and it was soon produced for the girl's ecstasy. Regina turned to Jeannette's mother. "We couldn't resist the fabrics there, Thérèse. We brought some back for all of us. Ninette said there was a fine *modiste* nearby."

Conflicting emotions raced over Thérèse's face, but she could not reject a gift. "Most kind of you," she mumbled, but her skeptical look went to the many trunks and boxes being carried up the wide stairs.

Regina hugged Aunt Agnes and kissed Uncle Oliver's cheek, smiled at Claude and shook Marcus's hand. It was good to be home.

There was just time to wash before they went to dinner. There was chatter and gossip, news of the estate, and tales of the wonders of Paris. The Dowager looked from Regina to Julian and back again several times during the meal, and finally nodded, satisfied. It had worked; there was harmony between them again.

Ninette began to unpack everything the next day. But before Regina started in on the new draperies or directed the placing of the glorious new rugs, she sat down and wrote a long letter to her father, asking his opinion on the cooperative idea and begging for suggestions.

Then she sent it off to Paris with the coachman, who was bringing them more fabrics from Monsieur Silver. She had taken measurements also, and sent those along. Then, satisfied, she settled down to oversee Verlaine once more. She wanted to see the books too, and try to figure out how much had been paid to the brokers, the gross income, the expenses of cooperage and bottles, and so on. It would be a satisfying job, to help Julian in this way.

CHAPTER THIRTEEN

The next days and weeks were busy and happy ones for Regina. She felt useful; she felt that she was fitting into the routine of the Verlaine household. The Dowager had gladly turned over the reins of management to her, yet she was there to help with decisions and advice whenever Regina needed her.

Thérèse was reluctantly won over by Regina's persistent friendliness. She consulted with Regina over her duties, and they began to work better together.

One noon, Claude found her coming to the study and shook his head at her. "No, no, my cousin! Not the books, not for you! You have enough work to do!"

"But I want to understand everything, Claude," she protested. She had said nothing to him about the cooperative idea. She did not know if Julian had.

"Be off!" he teased, shooing her away. "Go find Julian! Why don't you take his lunch to him in the vineyards? I am not going out that way today and would have to make a special trip to do it."

"Oh—very well, then. It sounds like a good idea." Regina was puzzled, thoughtful, but she went away.

Regina changed into her riding costume of navy blue with the blue plumed hat, and then went out to the kitchens. The cooks and maids were becoming accustomed to her sudden appearances and no longer dropped pans and knives in agitation when she came in. "Ah, Madame, you wish something, yes?" The chief cook beamed at her.

"I should like to have Monsieur's luncheon. I shall ride out to take it to him," Regina explained.

"But of course, Madame! Should Madame like enough food for herself as well?"

"That would be very pleasant," said Regina, a little dubiously. She was not sure she would be welcome in the vineyards. Did Julian usually relax over his lunch or would she be disturbing his work?

The cooks efficiently put together a basket of food, a

bottle of wine, two plates and glasses, and handed her the basket. She thanked them, told Thérèse where she was going, and set out.

The stablehand cleverly set the basket on the saddle before her, tying it on so all she had to do was ride and keep a cautious eye on it. He told her where Julian had gone to work that day, on the north slopes with the white grapes. She headed in that direction.

She rode for about half an hour, enjoying the woods and the open vegetable fields. People waved to her as she rode past, the farmers working in the fields, the women with them, enjoying their luncheon in the shade of the trees. Even the young children were there, playing, nibbling at their bread and meat, and drinking from cups of watered wine.

She found the north slopes and paused, bewildered, at the sight of so many men at work. They wore great straw hats for protection against the sun as they carried water up the hills, up the steep slopes, to pour it very slowly into the trenches cut between the rows. Others were busy tying up vines on the wire fences.

One man came over to her and doffed his huge hat. "Madame wishes to visit Monsieur? He works up there. Shall I call to him, Madame?"

"Yes, thank you. It is better not to try to take the horse up there."

"*Oui*, Madame, that is correct. I will tell him Madame has brought his luncheon. It is time to stop. There comes our wagon." He nodded toward a lumbering cart approaching along the dusty road from the village.

Soon Julian came down the hill, wiping his dusty face with a mud-stained handkerchief. "Regina! What are you doing here?" There was pleasure in his green eyes as he gazed up at her.

"I brought your luncheon, Julian. Claude said he had to ride in another direction this morning," she said lightly. "Cook fixed up enough for us both. May I lunch with you?"

He laughed aloud with delight. "But this is splendid! Come, there is a brook nearby where I can wash. It is shaded from the sun. This way, my dear." He led the way from the fields, walking lightly in his sturdy brown boots. He was shabbily dressed, in worn jodhpurs of dark brown

and matching leather jacket. The inevitable broad hat was
on his head yet he looked so handsome, so aristocratic, that
one would never mistake him for an ordinary man, his wife
thought proudly.

He led the way along the paths and into the trees. It was
suddenly shady and cool, and a small brook twinkled in the
bits of sunlight that gleamed through the leaves of the
poplar and oak trees. Julian helped her out of the saddle,
then tied the horse where it could take a drink at the
brook.

Regina busied herself with the picnic basket, taking out
the food and spreading it on the grass. Then she took out
the bottles of white wine and the glasses, and placed them
on the checkered cloth beside the cooked chicken pieces,
the jar of carrots and other raw vegetables, several pastry
tarts and two cooked potatoes with a little packet of salt.

Julian, his face shining with water and beaming with a
smile, came to sit beside her. "This is glorious, Regina!" he
said. "Are you sure you do not mind eating out here?"

Regina smiled up at him rather shyly. "I'm enjoying this,
Julian. I only hope I am not disturbing your work," she
added worriedly.

"Non, non, non," he said. "My word, I am hungry! This
looks marvelous." He reached for a piece of chicken and
took an enormous bite.

Seeing his informality, she felt more relaxed. She helped
herself to a potato and salt, and found that it tasted quite
good in the fresh air, with the delicate breeze rustling
through her hair. She added some chicken to her plate, and
some carrots. Julian was pouring the white wine.

"To your health, Madame," he said ceremoniously, lifting his glass to her.

"And to yours, Monsieur," she said. "And to the grapes
of 1895!"

"Ah, yes, the grapes," he said, sobering. "They do look
good, Regina. The blossoms are in good shape. And the
soil has been watered well by the recent rains. We have
had to water only a little on the north slopes. Tomorrow I
will start watering on the south slopes, among the reds."

"And do they look good?" Regina asked timidly.

He nodded, and ate for a few moments in silence. "They
look very good. Ah, how I get my hopes up every year!" he
said a bit wistfully. "It takes four or five years for the vines

to begin bearing fruit. Imagine, Regina, soon we will be growing grapes that wil produce wines in the next century! It is an amazing thought."

"Rather like children," said Regina, though she blushed at saying it. "You bear them—hope, watch them grow, train them as well as you can—but it is years before you know how they will turn out."

"Exactly," said Julian seriously. "Just like children. I remember my father speaking of his vines and the new grafts before he died. I thought, he speaks of them like his own children. And that is how he thought of them. He left them to me in his will, you know. I will show it to you sometime. He said to look after Thérèse and Eric and the vines—" He sighed a little, looking absently into the distance toward the slopes.

"And you do, Julian. You look after them all," Regina said gently. "You have so many responsibilities."

He looked at her oddly, sharply. "Yes," he said, and reached for his wine glass. "Many responsibilities. All of Verlaine—all that is Verlaine." His voice was terribly solemn, but the next moment, he was gay again, teasing Regina playfully.

Before she rode back to Verlaine, he walked with her among the vines, showing her the delicate blossoms and explaining how the berries would form. Then a delicate bloom would appear that helped in the fermenting.

It was Louis Pasteur who had discovered that this bloom was very important in the fermenting of the wine. The bloom had something to do with what Julian called wine yeasts, and their presence made the wine bubble up and yield its gases. When the process stopped, the grapes had become alcoholic.

With the red wines, the process was allowed to go for many days, even weeks or months, to give the deep-red color and stronger alcoholic content. With the whites, the process was stopped after about eight hours, and the must (the pulp and juice) went immediately into oak casks for much slower fermenting for about six months.

"I test it all the time," Julian said. "It must be just right. And it will vary by the coolness of the air, the ripeness of the grapes—the white grapes must be overripe when they are picked, did I tell you that? Yes, I watch the fields carefully, and the grapes must be more than ripe before I decide to begin the harvest. The sugar content of the grapes must be at its peak—"

She did not understand it all, but she was content. Julian's face glowed as he talked, and Regina was happy to be a part of his work, his life.

The workers had not yet returned to the fields. They relaxed, eating and drinking wine in the heat of the afternoon, and would not return to the fields until they had had two hours of rest. That was Verlaine's unofficial rule.

"It is better for them to rest. Then they will work later when the day is cooler. It is better for their health, and better for the work."

She wondered again how he could be so considerate of his workers while he seemed unconcerned about the villagers' problems—the leaking roofs, the illnesses. Perhaps Julian did not have time to worry about the villagers because he had to concentrate on the vineyards. Well, she would have to make up for that.

Reluctantly she returned to her patient mount. Julian's arm tightened about her waist as they came to the horse.

"Regina, I'm so happy that you came today, to share in my obsession, as Claude calls it," he said, with a smile. "I hope I did not bore you. Claude says I eat, drink, and sleep wines."

"I enjoyed hearing about it, Julian," she said earnestly. "I want to share your interests, I want to know as much as I can about all this. And—perhaps you'll let me come again with your luncheon?"

"Every day," he said promptly, smiling into her dark eyes. "I want you to come every day that you can—except when it rains, of course. I found this most delightful."

He bent to press his lips gently to hers. His mouth was warm, with a taste of wine, a touch of sunshine on his cheeks. She put her hand to his shoulder, clinging to him for a moment, until she finally drew back.

"I—I must get back," she said breathlessly.

"I will see you this evening, my darling! Did you get the measurements done to your satisfaction?"

"Oh, yes, I will tell you tonight!" She knew his mind was on his beloved grapes, and forgave him. "Good-bye, Julian."

She rode back happily, with the empty basket before her. The cook took the basket with a significant smile at her flushed cheeks and sparkling eyes. "Madame enjoyed her luncheon, yes?"

"Oh, yes, the food was wonderful, and the day was so beautiful—"

"You would like it tomorrow again, yes?"

"Yes, please. Unless it rains."

"Oh, tomorrow it will not rain," the cook said confidently. "Not until the weekend, Madame. The weather has been perfect for the grapes. The end of June will be fine, then the rains will come in July and August, then good sunshine in September."

Regina went up to her rooms to wash and change into a thin muslin gown. The heat of the day was making the cool château a little warmer than usual. Often the cold stones kept out the heat, but the draperies were drawn back and sunshine streamed in the long French windows.

Finally she went down to Julian's study on the ground floor, passing the rose drawing room where her mother-in-law was working on her needlepoint and listening to Thérèse at the piano. She would not join them for tea just yet. She had something on her mind.

Claude was usually out at this hour, leaving early for his own amusements. Sometimes he returned for dinner, often not. Yes, the study was empty. The books were put neatly away. Regina closed the door softly and sat down at the big desk. She took out the books for 1893.

She took a pencil and pad and began to copy out figures. She checked the big ledger as well as the preliminary books with the workers' wages and the costs of the materials written in Julian's neat hand. She compared the figures in the ledger with the accounts as Julian had written them, and long before she was done she was frowning. Even before she got to the broker's fifty-percent commission, she was upset.

Claude had altered the accounts. She was sure of it, but she could not see what he had done, or how he had accomplished it. Yet there was an alarming difference between the two sets of figures. She finished copying the numbers, and heard horses in the courtyard outside the windows. She peered out to see Julian getting down from his stallion, pausing to talk to a stablehand.

Regina closed the books and gathered up her scribbled notes, looking about to make sure everything was back in place. She could not talk to Julian about this until she had more proof, more evidence.

And she needed to think. She could not confront Claude until she was absolutely sure. But Frederick Pierce's daughter had a tight line about her pretty mouth as she put the notes carefully into a large workbasket of embroidery, shoving them down under the fabrics before leaving the study to greet Julian at the doorway.

She would return again tomorrow, and the next day, and the next, working in the study when she knew Claude would not be around. She didn't want to raise his suspicions. The longer he thought Regina was a fool, the better.

In the days that followed, Claude's duplicity became increasingly evident to Regina. Painstakingly, she compared Julian's figures with Claude's. She noticed that sometimes items that were not in Julian's workbooks, appeared suddenly in Claude's. "Repair of a roof," she noted, and frowned. She was practically certain that the roof in question had never been fixed, but the entry listed the expense for a year ago.

Still she kept silent. She wanted to be very sure.

On a Sunday afternoon in June, the nearby *vignerons* gathered at Verlaine, at Julian's invitation. He had spoken informally to each one about Regina's idea for a cooperative; now he would talk to them all.

Regina greeted them in the hallway and showed them to the large brown drawing room. The Dowager was not present, as she had caught a cold, but Thérèse and Marcus were there, and Claude. Eric had been curious but, feeling uncomfortable, he backed out.

By the time Julian was ready to begin, about fifteen people were gathered in the drawing room. Regina saw the men giving her and Thérèse curious looks, as though questioning what women were doing there. But Madame Tillemont seemed glad of their presence. She settled herself firmly in the front row of chairs, not wanting to miss a single word.

Julian stood at the mantelpiece, his foot on an andiron, and began to speak with poise. Regina thought how handsome and assured he looked, how much the Baron de Verlaine. So might one of his ancestors have stood, greeting his esteemed guests. She half smiled at her own fancies.

"Good day to you all. It is a pleasure to have you here

at Verlaine. I have spoken briefly to each of you about this matter of a cooperative. Today we shall have some preliminary discussion about it. I am sure you have many questions, and I do not have all the answers.

"I am consulting with a lawyer in Paris who has some experience with cooperatives and how they work. My wife, the Baronne, has also written to her father, an eminent American banker, who is on the board of directors of a cooperative. We hope to hear soon of his reaction to these matters."

Julian went on to outline what he understood of cooperatives, and what he hoped they would gain by forming one.

"We could hire a broker together. That alone should save us money. I don't think we should continue to pay fifty-percent commissions. What are your thoughts on that matter?"

He addressed his question directly to Madame Tillemont.

She cleared her throat, then spoke up bravely. "As for me, my dear Baron, I *must* reduce my commission. I told Monsieur Lepine so when he was here. I am continually in debt, and it is ridiculous. I do not have a large vineyard, yet it produces well. I work hard all year, and so do my workers. Yet when my bills are paid, I have but a few bottles of wine to show for my labors. I cannot continue in this manner."

There were murmured words from the others. Monsieur Carnot nodded to his son Oscar. Monsieur Mangin patted Madame Tillemont's wrinkled hand. "Bravely spoken, Madame. I feel the same way. I have worked hard all my life, and for what? I earn money every third or fourth year, which goes only to pay my debts, and then I start again."

"I do not understand about this cooperative," said Monsieur Feuillet, with his cool gray eyes fixed on Julian. "Does this mean that we combine all our finances and keep books in common? I am not sure I should wish to go along on that. My finances are a private matter."

"Of course they are!" said Claude Herriot vigorously, looking a little pale. "They should be. I think we are being too hasty, jumping into such a venture."

"It sounds interesting to me," said Oscar Carnot, with a glance at his father. "My father and I have discussed it. Why not combine some of our operations? The *vin ordi-*

naire could certainly be combined and bottled under one label. Only our *crus*, our higher quality wines, would be
separate. That makes sense to me."

"Who said anything about combining our wines?" asked
another man, looking bewildered. "I thought we were just
going to get a broker in common."

"This is all preliminary," Julian said quietly, yet in such
a commanding voice that all the murmuring stopped, and
they turned to listen to him. "I am not a financial wizard,
you know that. My feeling is that we must explore all the
avenues, find out about cooperatives, and discuss which operations we wish to combine. We may choose to sell in
common, through one broker. Or we may wish to combine
harvesting operations. A credit union would be of help to
us, combining a banking operation. In fact, we may set up
our own bank, to place money in it in good times and borrow from it at low interest rates in bad times. There are
many possibilities. Today I wish to explore some of them
with you and decide how we wish to continue."

"I have heard of such cooperatives," said Marcus Bazaine unexpectedly, from the back of the room, sitting on
a sofa next to Thérèse. "There are farming cooperatives
in which they set up banks, work together in the fields,
and market their produce together. It could work here, I
think."

Julian frowned slightly. "This is not a farming cooperative, Marcus," he said. "This will involve only the vineyards. *Oui*, Madame Tillemont, you wish to speak?"

Marcus leaned back, his mouth tight, his face bright red
with embarrassment. Regina scarcely heard Madame Tillemont's quavering question in her loud voice. How slighted
Marcus was! Yet she had been noting recently that he was
intelligent rather than stupid or weak. Why did Julian
think so little of him? Marcus ran the vegetable and fruit
gardens single-handedly and quietly managed it without
having to refer to Julian, now that she thought of it.

He must be brighter than Julian thought! Thérèse was
angry at the slight also, and sent glaring looks toward her
brother.

Regina forgot the matter as the men argued about the
various possibilities of the cooperative. Some were reluctant
to get involved in anything that sounded risky. The wines

were enough of a risk, they said. Others resented the brokers' high commissions, yet what could they do?

"My father dealt with him for years. He's handled my wines for forty years," said Monsieur Mangin. "Am I to tell him now I no longer want him? And what if the new broker cheats us?"

Julian finally appointed one man to investigate the reputations of brokers, to see which one might do the best work for them. Oscar Carnot was going to Paris, and he would talk to a lawyer about possible contracts and how much each *vigneron* would be involved. Another man was to investigate credit unions and find out how they worked. They all admitted they knew little about these matters, but were desperate to find solutions to their financial problems.

"Combining our ignorance will do little good," Julian said with a charming smile. "I think we need to learn much more before we meet again."

"What about Madame's father?" Monsieur Mangin turned to Regina. "When you hear from your father, with advice, might we have another meeting to discuss this?"

"Of course. I will let you know as soon as I hear," said Regina quickly.

"You will all be notified," Julian assured them.

Marcus leaned forward and spoke up again. "I know some of you are planning to buy more oak barrels against the harvest. Would it not be wise to put off the purchases until we find out if we can obtain a better price for a large quantity?"

"We may not be able to wait. The harvest does not wait," Julian said. "Well, we will let you know when the next meeting is to be held," he told the group. "I thank you for coming. I believe coffee and wines are being prepared. Regina?"

She rose, with a set smile. She did not like the way he had humiliated Marcus again. That suggestion had been valid. "At once, Julian," she said, and went out to have the trolleys brought into the drawing room.

Some drank their wine or coffee and left; a few stayed on for dinner. Marcus did not remain. Thérèse was at the dinner, but she said little.

Regina was rather quiet also, a little angry at Julian for ignoring his brother-in-law's suggestions. When the dinner was over, the gentlemen remained with their port and brandy, while the ladies adjourned to the rose drawing room for coffee. Madame Tillemont made a little grimace at Regina.

"Again I am sent to the drawing room, though I too am a *vigneron*," she said ruefully.

Regina patted her hand. "I understand, Madame. Women are not supposed to think," she said, the corners of her mouth turned down.

Madame Tillemont laughed and began a conversation with Thérèse about cooking. But the old woman left early, and Regina knew she had felt slighted.

Thérèse and Regina saw her to her carriage. When the door closed, Thérèse burst out, "I know how she feels. But it is worse for Marcus!"

"Come in here with me," Regina said, and drew her into the unoccupied music room opposite Julian's study. "Tell me—what is there between Marcus and Julian? I never thought Julian rude before tonight, but I could have—I could have hit him!"

"He has never thought much of Marcus," Thérèse admitted, twisting her handkerchief and looking as though she held back tears. "When Marcus was courting me, he could easily talk to me. But when it came to talking to Julian, he stammered and stuttered, until Julian must have thought him a fool. Julian said he could make a much better match for me, but I loved Marcus, I *still* love Marcus. He is a smart man—oh, Regina, it hurts me to see how Marcus is ignored and his suggestions treated with contempt! He works so hard."

"I know he does," Regina said thoughtfully. "At first, I thought he was not—intelligent, because he spoke so little. But now I realize he is shy in our company. Why is that?"

"He is from a farming family. Julian is—Verlaine!" said Thérèse. "The difference galls him. We may not stay."

Regina gazed at her in the dim room. "May not stay? Oh, Thérèse!"

"I know. I refused to go before. I could not leave, I was needed. Maman was often ill. Julian was gone all day. But now . . . you have taken over, Regina—"

"I do not mean to make you feel unneeded," said Regina, in evident distress. "We *do* need you here, Thérèse—

I would háte to have you go. And Julian! He believes all the Herriots should live here—"

"Marcus has had a fine offer from a distant relative, an old fellow who lives in Normandy. He wants Marcus to come and manage his apple trees. He makes fine cider and apple brandy. Calvados, it is called. He has offered Marcus a lot of money, and will make him his heir if he comes. Marcus is ready to do it—and I will hardly ever see my family!" She was about to burst into tears, and her mouth quivered. "Maman is so old—What if—"

Regina was thinking quickly. It was a splendid offer for Marcus, but Thérèse did not want to leave. And if they left—and only Claude remained. . . . That situation did not bear contemplating.

"Put him off, Thérèse, coax him to wait. I think things will be happening soon, about the cooperative. I will speak to Julian when I can. He doesn't realize how much he needs Marcus. Who would do all the farming? I know the offer is good for him but—"

"Marcus does not really want to go, even for the promise of the land. The old man is mean, he cut off his own son. But Marcus will go, and hope for the future, if things are not better at Verlaine," said Thérèse, shaking her light-brown head gloomily.

Regina dared to put her hand on her sister-in-law's arm. "Plead with him to wait, and let me talk to Julian, if you will, Thérèse. Marcus will have more responsibility and appreciation for his work. And something else may happen— I cannot tell you now," she added hurriedly, as she listened to the heavy boots of the gentlemen coming from the dining room and the rumbling of their voices. "We must get back and serve coffee. But let me talk to Marcus and encourage him to wait—for what will come."

Thérèse glanced curiously at Regina as they walked back toward the rose drawing room. In a low tone, she remarked, a little more cheerfully, "You sound as though some roof was about to blow off, as we say here."

"Yes—a roof might blow off," Regina agreed grimly, thinking of the poor villagers. She managed a bright smile as the gentlemen approached them, and she and Thérèse went into the drawing room.

"Coffee? Brandy?" she offered. But her mind was busy, busy with other matters.

CHAPTER FOURTEEN

Regina was working in the study the following afternoon when a timid knock came at the door. Worried that it might be Claude—yet it did not sound like him—she hurried to the door, and opened it, to find Marcus standing there uneasily in his farm jacket and muddy trousers.

"Madame—" The hat was being turned round and round in his large capable brown hands. "My wife, Thérèse, she says you might—speak to me?"

"Come in, Marcus." She drew him hastily into the room and shut the door. If she had not been so preoccupied, she might have smiled at his look of amazement that she would bring him into a room to speak alone with him.

"Madame? Thérèse said she spoke of the other—offer—to you. I wish to say I have not made up my mind. I have another month to decide—"

"I shall say nothing to Julian," she said, cutting through his nervous sentences. "I hope to persuade you to stay. You are much needed here, Marcus." She sat down at the desk, where the opened books and ledgers spoke of what she was doing. He eyed them with surprise, then sat down awkwardly opposite her.

"Madame is kind, but I am not needed here," he said, and she saw the hurt behind his reserve. "Monsieur le Baron and his cousin handle all the matters of importance. Anyone can handle the vegetables and fruits—"

"Marcus, pray call me Regina. I am, after all, your sister-in-law. And you *are* needed here. I want to tell you something," she said, studying him thoughtfully. How long could he keep an important secret? She was not willing to say much until she was sure of her facts. Julian would never forgive her for spreading gossip about his cousin, if her fears should prove unfounded. That was the crux of the matter—*if unfounded.*

"About the cooperatives?" He twisted the hat around and around, his dark eyes troubled. "I have studied about them, I have spoken with farmers about them. Indeed, I had hoped to speak to Monsieur le Baron—" At her look, he smiled faintly, and said, "To Julian—about the matter. But he is very distant and cool with me. Sometimes when I speak, I think he does not hear me. He thinks I am an idiot!"

She did not deny that. "But I don't think so," she said firmly. "Marcus, I want to talk to you about the cooperatives first. I think you would fit well into this. Julian is too absorbed in the actual work in the vineyards to manage the finances also. He must be out there, supervising the work. I am beginning to realize how much he is needed there. Every phase of the work with the wines is so important, from the grafting to the testing of the grapes, to determining just when the harvest shall start. And then there is the work of transferring the wines from barrels to smaller casks, and then to bottles."

He nodded gravely. "*Oui*, Madame—Regina," he added with an unexpectedly charming smile. He was tanned, husky, with tired lines about his eyes. He worked hard, she knew, and did not resent the work. What he resented was the offhand way he was treated. "However, Claude takes care of the finances. And even if he is . . . light of morals and spends much time with the ladies, he does work hard."

Regina stared at him thoughtfully. She had never heard anyone say that about Claude. She knew he disappeared many evenings, and was often late to work in the morning. But never had Julian or Thérèse or Maman said that Claude was loose. It was strange, however, that the handsome man of thirty-six was not married. Until now she had not thought much about it.

"Let us leave Claude for the moment," she said. She tapped the desk thoughtfully with a pencil, glancing at the books. "Marcus, the cooperative will entail much work that Julian has no time to handle. I hope to arrange matters for him, to help him, when he realizes I can do so! My father trained me in many bookkeeping matters, to understand accounts and finances. I shall study the cooperative scheme and hope to help with it. But I know the men about here will not readily accept a woman's voice and suggestions. However, if you also study the matters, and have ideas, we can discuss them and you can speak for Verlaine."

"I—Madame! You flatter me!" Color had come up in his tanned cheeks. "I am but a farmer! I am not of Verlaine!" he said bitterly. "No, I am sure—"

"Marcus, we need you here, more than you know," she said gravely. "I have something important to tell you but I beg you not to tell even Thérèse as yet, it is so very secret. I have not told Julian, I am not yet ready. I must have proof."

"What is it, Madame?"

"Regina," she said firmly.

"*Oui*—Regina."

"I have been studying the accounts, Marcus. These books here are kept by Julian. He entered the wages, the costs of barrels and bottles and casks, the money he paid out or authorized to be paid. Here"—and she tapped the ledgers—"are Claude's accounts. According to the way my father taught me, the rough figures should be entered *exactly* into the final ledgers. The accounts should agree."

"And—they do not?" he asked softly. His face was grave, but not very surprised, she noted keenly.

She shook her chestnut head. "No, Marcus. Some costs have been doubled, even tripled. The final account for the months of June and July, which I have just finished checking, make a triple expense for each month. Marcus, if what I suspect is true, Claude is padding the books. That is, he enters far more expenses than Verlaine has, and I must suspect he is pocketing the rest."

"Ah—so that is it!" he breathed, nodding.

"You suspected it?"

He nodded, his big hands now flat on his hard thighs. He leaned forward earnestly. "Regina, I suspected it, but I dared say nothing. It was one of the reasons I was going to leave Verlaine. The money came in from the wines, I saw the figures once. I was bitter. My wife had old clothes on her back, while Claude bought jewels in Paris! Yes, he has fine rubies and diamonds, and new velvet jackets, while Thérèse wears dresses of her mother's that have been altered! I did not complain. Julian had said that no new expenses could be met until this harvest, if it was good. Yet I wondered—I worried—I thought about it at night—"

"I don't have enough proof yet. I need help. I wish I could get a professional accountant to check all the figures—"

"Eric would help," Marcus said eagerly.

She stared. "Eric?" She thought of the poor boy in his wheelchair, his bright eager eyes. "Eric? Does he know—"

"When I first came, Eric was studying all sorts of subjects, to help pass the time, you know. His mind is very bright, yet Julian always wanted to protect him from any work. Eric offered to help with the books. He did some work, entering figures. Then Claude stopped it. He said Eric got too tired and made mistakes. He complained to Julian, and Julian told Eric to stop. He thought it was too much for him." Marcus shook his head. "How it hurt Eric! He withdrew even more, remaining in his rooms, reading or just sitting to stare out the window."

Regina put her finger to her lip, her father's old gesture, as her eyes narrowed in deep thought. If she enlisted Eric's help and he was really too frail to endure work, she would earn the enmity of all the Herriots, including Julian. Yet if Marcus was right and Claude kept the boy from helping because of Claude's own criminal motives, that was another story!

She looked at Marcus's honest face, the face of a man who did not use deceit or guile, who worked hard and well. She thought of Claude's charm and facile gallantries—no, she did not like him. But trust? That had to be a more detached matter. One did not smear a man's reputation lightly.

"I must work further on this, Marcus. And I want you to help me. I don't know how we will manage it, but we must manage to be alone in this study when Claude is not here. However, you work long hours—"

"We will do it, Regina!" he said, his eyes sparkling. "I wish I could tell Thérèse, she is so unhappy. Nevertheless, I will keep my word and tell my wife nothing. I will say only that we have had this talk, and that you feel I provide a service to Verlaine—"

"A valuable service, a dedicated and honest service, Marcus."

His face glowed. "You are . . . very kind. You give me heart," he said.

Just then they heard hoofbeats in the courtyard; Julian was coming in.

"Oh—the books! I must put them away," Regina said.

She scrambled to put the ledgers in order and set the work-books in the drawers.

Marcus jumped up to help her, dropping two of the books in his haste. He picked them up, tucked them away, and shut the drawers. Regina stood up, looked over the desk to make sure all was in order. She stumbled as she turned, and Marcus caught her, to hold her upright.

Just then the door opened, and Julian stood there, some-how ominous in his jacket and brown jodhpurs. He stared at them, at Marcus still holding Regina.

"What are you doing?" he asked them both. Marcus dropped his hands hastily.

"Why—we were talking, Julian," said Regina uneasily.

Marcus beamed at him, too honest to hide his feelings. "Yes, we have had a very good talk," he said, and walked out smiling.

Julian glared at Regina. "You were alone in this room with him?" he asked slowly. "For a long time?"

Her spine stiffened. "Yes, we were talking, Julian," she repeated patiently. "How—how did your day go?"

"We will discuss it in our rooms!" he said, and stood back so she could precede him. They went out of the room and up the stairs. In the master suite, she turned to face him. She had never seen him so angry, his nostrils flared, his green eyes yellow with rage, his fists clenched.

Nevertheless, he seemed to hold onto his control with a great effort. "Regina, in France one is more careful of one's reputation than you seem to be," he said tersely. "I realize that American women are less traditional, some seem even reckless. However, here I wish you to observe our customs. It can make for much loose talk if—"

Her shoulders arched back and her chin went up. "I am not ashamed of being an American!"

"You are not an American now, you are French! I have said I wish you to observe our customs, our mores. My mother would be offended if you—"

"She has no reason to take offense at what I do!"

Julian tried again. He seemed to spit the words between his teeth. "I beg you, do not make me furious! You are my wife, you must be respected! The few scandals in our fam-ily have caused much grief. I shall not endure having the reputation of my wife stained. I'm telling you again, do not see Marcus alone. If there is business to discuss, I will take care of it. Marcus is a fool about business anyway. There's no need to talk of the workers with him."

"You do not understand or appreciate him!" Regina cried. "He is an intelligent man. I cannot tell you now what we discussed; we must work on a private matter—"

Julian took a step closer to her. He seemed somehow ominous.

"Now, tell me again. What were you and Marcus doing alone in my study?"

Her head went back. "Talking," she said briefly.

"Marcus is usually in the fields until dark. He comes home about seven," he said sternly. "It is but five."

"So he came home early."

"On a bright summer day? With the work not completed? Oh, Regina, Regina, do not lie to me!" His face was taut with emotion.

"Do not accuse me—"

"What else can I think? Have you no feeling for me, for my sister Thérèse? I had heard of the loose ways of American women, but I did not think you—"

She gasped. "Julian, do not insult me! I shall not endure it," she blazed. "I am an honorable woman—"

"Are you? Are you? Yet you let yourself be sold for a title," he accused wildly. "I should have known—you seemed so sad when we married— Why *did* you marry me, Regina? Did you think you would have a gay time in France? Are you bored so soon? Must you entice everyone into your silken net? Had I not watched you, would you have had an affair with Armand?"

Regina had gone completely white. She felt as though the blood had drained from her body. She swayed and put a hand on the bedpost to steady herself. He could not be saying these things.

"Well? Well?" Julian had come close to her. She smelled the dust of the fields on him, the honest sweat of his hard-working body, and the heat of his anger. He caught hold of her as she did not answer. His tanned face was tight with emotion.

"Let me go!" She pulled herself away from him. "You—you insult me—grossly!"

"Do I? Then tell me what you did with Marcus," he demanded. "Why was he holding you? I should keep you

too busy to fool with other men! I should have started a
child in you, to occupy your time!"

Was Julian saying all the things he had been thinking
these past months? Did he truly think of her as a reckless
American wanton? Or was his anger speaking for him?

Before Regina could think about it, he had pushed her
down across the wide bed and sprawled on her, holding her
down. His hard kisses roamed over her face, her throat,
tearing apart the fragile muslin material to press on her
breasts. She cried out, frightened.

He paid no attention. His face was set and hard. He
ripped her dress apart, yanked down his trousers, and
pressed himself to her. He had never treated her like this,
so brutally, with such contempt for her feelings.

She could not move. He held her passionately beneath
his hard body, his long legs forcing hers still. When he took
her, it was with force, hurting her, and she cried out again.
"Julian—do not—not like this—oh, God, Julian—"

He held her, forcing her to receive his hard body. While
he did so, he studied her delicate face. She turned away but
still he kissed her cheeks, her ear. It was a travesty of all he
had done to her, so tenderly, so gently, in the past.

She felt his passion, and his derision. He wanted her—
like a harlot, she thought, with fury. She did not relax and
was hurt all the more, but she endured his thrusting, his
insistent kisses on her breasts, his hands digging into her
flesh.

He finished and rolled over, breathing hard. She was
trembling with fury and with pain. Pain seared her thighs
and her bruised body. Pain tore at her heart, for all the
loving words he had uttered in the past months had meant
nothing. He did not love her; he felt only contempt for the
wealthy American girl who had married him—so he
thought—for his title and the amusements France could offer.

He did not understand her at all! They were not close in
mind as well as body, as she had hoped. The marriage was
as false as their relationship. She felt as though her future
had died.

She lay still as he got up. He flung the sheet over her,
carelessly, she thought. She gazed from the bed toward the
window, refusing to look at him as he gathered his clothes

and went to the door. The hollow slam was like the closing of her life.

The sheet over her thighs was red. Dully she realized she was bleeding. She got up, went to her bathroom, washed. The dress was in shreds. She left it on the floor and put on her nightdress and robe, and went to sit in the window seat.

I'll leave him! she thought furiously. She hated him, she despised him, more than he had despised her! How could he treat her so and accuse her with such contempt when he was carrying on with Simone de Lamartine?

Eventually Julian returned to the room. He had washed and dressed, in a black formal suit with white ruffled shirt.

"You will dress and come down to dinner," he said abruptly, standing in the doorway.

"No, I am not hungry," she said tonelessly, not looking at him. She continued to gaze out at the dusky evening, out toward the gardens she could see only dimly now.

"Come down anyway. Appearances must be kept up."

"You keep them up!"

"Well," he said, more gently. "Perhaps not . . . tonight. I shall send Ninette with a tray for you."

If he had apologized, said he felt sorry for his treatment of her, she might have given in. As it was, she stiffened.

"Verlaine food would choke me!" she told him. "I want nothing from you!"

He didn't reply. The door closed softly after him. She sat on for a time, growing chilly but feeling so numb it did not matter.

Ninette entered softly, carrying a tray. "Monsieur sends your dinner, Madame," she said, setting the tray on a table nearby.

Regina could hear a burst of laughter from the dining room below. Her throat constricted.

"I want nothing," she said.

"But Madame must eat—"

Regina finally turned from the window seat. "Ninette, either you take that tray away or I shall fling it out the window!"

Ninette's eyes went wide. She saw the torn dress on the floor, the rage in Regina's face. "*Oui*, Madame," she said, and took out the tray.

Regina blew out the candles and went to bed. She lay

stiffly in the darkness, seething. She would never forgive
him for this! The insult to her body, the insult to herself.
And she was innocent, innocent!

She lay awake for a long while, heard Julian go to his
room after midnight. Still she could not sleep. She thought
of leaving—but how could she do that? In spite of everything, she was needed here. The Dowager Baroness needed
her, she was so frail. Thérèse had come to depend on Regina. Marcus would leave if he was not prevented—

Whatever I am, I am not a quitter, she decided with a
sigh, as she wakened late the next morning. Frederick
Pierce had never let any of his children grow up as quitters.
They must see a job through, no matter how tough it became.

She went for a long ride by herself and felt better. The
June air was sparkling, the sky was blue and clear. She
avoided the vineyards, and went to the village, riding along
the highway. She turned off onto a small country lane leading to Madame Tillemont's property. The older woman
was gallant. She had not quit in the face of obstacles—her
husband's early death, the death of her son, the hard work
of the land.

Regina returned to Verlaine at about three, ate a quick
lunch and had a cup of tea in her room. Ninette served her
silently. She helped Regina change to the navy-blue dress
with white piping.

Finally she said timidly, "Madame remembers the dinner
this evening? Guests come about seven, twenty of them."

Regina had forgotten. She sighed, leaned her head on
her hands. "What shall I wear, Ninette?" she asked sadly.

"I thought the blue satin, Madame. With the lace collar
and your diamonds."

"Very well. I will dress about six."

"*Oui*, Madame."

Regina had planned to work on the books again, but
there was no time. She went down to the kitchens to find
Thérèse going over the menu with the cooks. She consulted
with her, and they planned the table arrangements. She put
Simone de Lamartine at Julian's right, her mouth curling in
contempt. Let them enjoy each other's company!

Thérèse kept looking at her oddly, but Regina refused to
be drawn into any conversation. She had had enough of the
Verlaine problems for a time.

She changed just in time to come down and greet the
guests. Simone was among the first, her carriage rolling up
the drive promptly at seven. She looked splendid in one of
her many gowns of crimson satin, her dark eyes sparkling,
her skin untouched by the sun. Her black hair was piled
high, set off by a jeweled comb.

Regina eyed her with open dislike and avoided speaking
to her. She saw Julian frown at her but if he said one word,
she vowed silently, she would let him have it! He would
learn what she thought of him!

Claude came, merry and splendid in a blue velvet suit
with sapphire cufflinks. Regina studied him with new curiosity. Yes, he does live well, she thought. His own lodge
house, jewels, extravagant clothes. Julian did not pay him a
high salary, he could not afford it. So . . .

But she could not think of that tonight. She was the hostess. The Dowager was still ill and would not appear this
evening.

She noticed that Simone was standing beside Julian, her
arm linked possessively in his. Regina did not look directly
at them, though she was conscious of the keen look from
Monsieur Carnot and his son Oscar. Monsieur Feuillet
with his cool all-seeing gaze took in their closeness, and his
lip curled. His buxom wife pretended to see nothing.

The dinner went well. Regina saw to it automatically,
gesturing to the footmen to serve, murmuring to a new
maid when she needed help. Marcus was there, his face
shining, with a new assurance radiating from him. Thérèse
was eyeing him in puzzled fashion; Julian glared at him.

Surely Julian could not really believe Regina had had an
affair with Marcus! But no, his green eyes blazed at Regina
when he saw her smile and speak to Marcus.

The dinner dragged for her. She sat through the appetiz-
ers, pushing the paté and bread cubes around her plate.
She had not touched her wine. The beefsteak was well accepted, *à la Americaine,* one person called it, with a laughing look at Regina. With it, they had new potatoes and
fresh green peas from the cottage gardens. The next course
was fruit, fresh red raspberries in thick cream. Then the
pastry course, delicate meringues filled with almond pud-
ding.

Regina led the ladies to the rose drawing room for coffee. She found Simone at her side.

"A little light for a French dinner, Madame," Simone said. "If you like, I will teach you something about the French styles."

Her tone was solicitous, but the look on her face was of pure malice. Regina smiled frostily.

"Thank you, Madame de Lamartine. I shall manage my household as I choose. If the food does not please you, do not come!"

Simone gasped as Regina walked away. She would probably report to Julian, Regina thought, but she was too angry to care.

In the drawing room, Madame Tillemont boomed, "Excellent dinner, Madame Herriot! I am glad you omitted a fish course. I see no reason to serve both meat and fish. It is much too heavy! I shall imitate you in my next dinner."

"You are most kind, Madame."

Simone sat sullenly near the fire, waiting impatiently for the gentlemen to join them. Thérèse served tea, and Regina the coffee. It was almost an hour before the gentlemen returned to the ladies.

Simone beckoned lazily to Julian. He glanced at Regina, then moved deliberately to sit next to Simone. She smiled—like a satisfied cat, thought Regina, moving to sit near Madame Tillemont.

It so happened that Marcus was on the old woman's other side, earnestly discussing Madame Tillemont's fruit trees. "They should have been sprayed in early spring, Madame. I fear it is too late now, the worms are at them."

"Ah, I should have asked you before, Monsieur Bazaine. Another crop failure. I do feel like a foolish old woman." She grimaced and made light of it, but Regina saw the look in her watery eyes and the way her hands trembled.

"If you wish, I will come over early tomorrow," Marcus said. "I will look at the trees and see if anything can be done. Sometimes washing down the blossoms lightly can help. The blooms should not be damaged."

"It would be very good of you, if you can spare the time, my dear Monsieur Bazaine." She patted his bronzed hand.

Regina gave him a grateful smile also, and when she lifted her eyes she met Julian's stare from across the room. He had intercepted the smile, and the burning glare of his green eyes blazed at Regina. She returned his look with cool indifference.

He turned to Simone. She moved her head and almost leaned against him, murmuring something so softly that he had to bend his head to listen.

Regina burned. So did Thérèse, eyeing her brother scornfully, then giving Regina a sympathetic look.

The evening went on and on. When Marcus lingered near to Madame Tillemont and Regina, Julian said, rather loudly, "Why don't you and Thérèse play for us, Marcus?"

His tone made it clear that his request was an order. To the surprise of all, Marcus sat still. "Not tonight, Julian," he said pleasantly. "Some of the guests do not care for classical music." His gaze went deliberately to Simone, then to Claude.

Julian flushed, but turned to Simone again and began a quiet conversation with her.

Marcus turned to Madame Tillemont and to Regina. "The last time we played for guests," he said with a grimace, "Simone yawned again and again, and finally coaxed Claude to take her for a walk in the gardens, 'away from the noise.' I have decided not to be insulted so again."

"You're quite right," said Madame Tillemont. "Though why you regard the opinion of such a—such a—" Words seemed to fail her. "All the world knows what she is!"

Regina was startled. Was Julian's affair with her so widely known? He really should be more discreet. He had a position to uphold! Or didn't it matter, since he was the Baron de Verlaine? Could he do anything he chose?

Men could do anything. Only women had to be careful—or willing to give up their reputations. Was Julian paying Simone? Regina wondered. There had been some odd items in the ledgers. She thought he had purchased some land from Simone, but was it land he had bought—or something else? She resolved to study those entries more closely.

Monsieur Mangin came over to speak to Madame Tillemont, and Marcus jumped up to give his seat to the older man. Then he wandered off, filling teacups, bringing cushions to some of the women, talking to a couple of men about their fields. Marcus did show more assurance tonight, and Regina sensed that Julian was watching his brother-in-law, wondering about that new air of confidence.

Well, let him wonder, Regina thought. Let him worry!

CHAPTER FIFTEEN

Regina decided to avoid Julian until she could present him with proof of Claude's deceit. She went out riding each morning, but not toward the vineyards. She went alone, defying Julian's frown and Ninette's concern, after a brief visit with her mother-in-law, who was slowly recovering her health. Regina would start out on her favorite mare and head toward the village.

Sometimes she rode through at a gallop, then turned back to talk to her friends there; for they were becoming her friends, greeting her with a shy smile and a bow of formality at first. She was coming to know them now. One morning, she rode into the village, tied up the horse, and then went to speak to the tavern owner's wife.

She sat in the tavern, with a cool drink of apple juice beside her, and the woman came to sit with her. Regina had learned that the woman was shrewd. She and her husband knew just about everything that went on, probably from listening to the gossip at their bar.

"Madame Galande," Regina began cautiously, "I know you are a friend of many in the village, and know of their problems."

"*Oui*, Madame, one hears a great deal here," said the woman, her keen dark eyes watching Regina's.

"There is the matter of the roofs," said Regina. "As you know, I have ordered them repaired. However, I am puzzled that the work was not done earlier."

"*Oui*, Madame la Baronne. Your good husband, the Baron de Verlaine, he comes through and sees the roofs, and says the work must be done. *Mais*, Monsieur Claude—he comes and says there is no money for the work, it must wait. So it waits. One year it waits, until Madame la Baronne comes, and it is ordered and done."

"Ah," Regina said. "So Monsieur le Baron ordered it done one year ago? And it was not done."

"That is the truth of it, Madame."

Regina gazed directly at the woman. "And—the rents? I

have heard some words said, and some grumbling, about
the high rents. When were they raised and by whom, do
you know this?"

The woman hesitated, glanced uneasily at her husband
who was wiping the bar and pretending to ignore them. He
gave a little curt nod and went to draw some beer for an
elderly man who had wandered in on uncertain feet, his
cane holding him steady.

"Well, Madame—it goes back many years."

"How many years?" Regina felt her way cautiously, but
she must know.

"Well, Madame—you see, the old monsieur—the father
of your husband—he was kind and good, but absentminded. He kept the rents the same for many years, so said
Monsieur Claude. When the old monsieur died, and the
young monsieur takes over, Monsieur Claude is caring for
the books. He comes around and says it has been too long
since the rents were raised. They must go up, up and up."
Her hands lifted dramatically, palms to the roof.

"So it was Monsieur Claude," Regina said slowly.

"*Oui*, Madame. And he comes again the next year and
raises the rents again. And two years later, again. And
again but a year ago. We try to complain to Monsieur le
Baron, but he says that Monsieur Claude takes care of it
all. So—" Another prodigious shrug of the wide shoulders,
the heavy bosom heaved in a sigh. Regina nodded to her in
understanding.

"So the rents go up. But the wages did not go up?" Regina asked in the patois she was coming to learn.

"*Oui*, Madame, that is so."

"Are there others who will speak with me honestly,
Madame Galande, and tell me the truth of it?"

The woman was silent for a time, gazing absently out the
opened door of the tavern. It was a green place, hung with
vines and cool against the summer sun.

"Madame, I do not know. Monsieur Claude says if any
complain, it is out with them. They lose their house, their
job. 'I will not have Monsieur le Baron disturbed in his
hard work with your stupid complaints,' he says to us."

Regina's eyes opened wide, and indignation flared in her
brown eyes. "He said that? That Julian did not want to be
disturbed?"

"*Oui*, Madame. However, I wonder if he wished more to

keep the complaints to himself? Eh?" The wise dark eyes met Regina's gaze.

"Oh, I want so much to know the truth." Regina sighed, her hand brushing over her eyes wearily. "I have gone over the accounts—" She stopped abruptly. She had not meant to say that.

The woman had caught it and looked satisfied. "Ah, the madame is kind and honest, eh? And she knows about finances? I keep my husband's books, he trusts me because we are both in the business. It was my dowry which made us able to buy this tavern; we are both in this. But Monsieur Claude, he owns no part of Verlaine, eh?"

"You are correct, Madame Galande. I beg you to keep my confidence for now," said Regina soberly. "Can you tell me which of the women of the village might speak to me as honestly as you have?"

"Hmmm," said Madame Galande, frowning. "There is Madame Bonnet, she fears not the devil himself. But her husband is dead and without the little pay from Monsieur le Baron, she would not eat, Madame. And there is Madame Darlas, who lives next door to me. She has four small children. She has a blunt tongue, but her husband works in the fields with Monsieur Bazaine, and works hard, mind you. However, the pay comes from Monsieur Claude. You comprehend?"

"Only too well. Where may I find Madame Darlas?"

"I shall go with you, Madame." She stood up, seeing Regina had finished her apple juice. "It is good, eh? From last year, kept in the cool cellars, no fermenting there. We make a bit of cider and serve it in the autumn. It is most refreshing. This way, Madame, if you please."

She walked with Regina a short distance along the dusty road and turned in to the house next to the tavern. All was confusion. A child was wailing, Madame Darlas was rocking another one in her arms. The smaller one was choking and gasping, his face turning from red to purple.

"*Mon Dieu!* What is the matter?" Madame Galande asked sharply.

Madame Darlas was young and pretty, apple-cheeked, obviously a farm girl. "I do not know," she gasped. "He was all right a few moments ago—"

Regina snatched the small boy from his mother's arms.

"Give him to me," she said sharply. She turned the boy upside down and smacked him sharply between the shoulder blades. Madame Darlas cried out in shock.

"You are hurting him!"

Regina hit him again, holding him up by the legs a little awkwardly. Madame Galande helped her by catching hold of the boy by the waist and holding him up. Regina hit again, a little desperately.

Amid his mother's wails and the other child's, Regina could scarcely think. She had treated a child before like this, years ago, when he had swallowed a coin. But what if that was not the cause of this child's choking?

The boy gasped, choked, and vomited. Along with the vomit came a small hard object, a nail.

"Ah, there it is," said Madame Galande calmly. "He ate a nail, Madame Darlas. Thank you, Madame la Baronne, I will soothe him now." She sat down, the boy in her ample lap, and stroked him as she spoke to him gently.

Madame Darlas flung her apron over her head and wept. She was so embarrassed, and thankful, and shaken, that Regina was hard put to calm her.

"Sit down, Madame," she said. "Let me pour some coffee—" She found the pot, a heavy cup, and poured it out for the distraught woman. "There, now, a taste of this—" And she patted the woman's shoulders as Madame Galande patted the little boy.

The small girl was watching wide-eyed, tears still streaming down her cheeks. Regina sat down at the table and beckoned to her. She came forward timidly.

"Ah, *petite*, what a mischief your brother made, no?" she said, smiling at the girl. The child leaned against her knee, watched her soberly. "Little ones have to be watched every moment, or they would swallow everything in sight!"

That made the girl give a weak smile. Madame Darlas sniffed and finally began to compose herself. She drank some of the hot coffee, the red flush began to recede.

"How—how did Madame—know what to do?" the young woman asked finally, looking at Regina with respect.

"I grew up in the country, far from a doctor, Madame Darlas," said Regina. "We had to take care of ourselves and the small ones. I remembered a young boy who had swallowed a coin. I saw him put it in his mouth, fortu-

nately, so when he began to choke, I knew what was wrong.
I turned him upside down and hit him until it came out his
mouth."

She spoke a little more about that, and of the life in the
Rockies, as the others listened with rapt attention. When
she told of riding a donkey, all of them smiled and shook
their heads. To think of Madame la Baronne riding a donkey!

"Like the mother of Jesus," said the little girl softly. "She
rode a donkey."

"Ah, out of the mouths of babes," said Madame Galande. She put the little boy down on the floor again, and
he crawled over to some wooden toys, his unhappiness forgotten. The little girl followed to play with him soberly, as
though she watched over him.

"If they live to grow up," said Madame Darlas, "I will
give thanks to *le bon Dieu*. They make such trouble—I am
almost frantic at times."

"With four small ones, it is hard," said the tavern owner's wife, nodding. "But when they grow up, it is good to
see them sturdy and working hard, and going to church on
Sunday. Madame does not attend our church?" She turned
unexpectedly to Regina. "Monsieur le Baron, he comes,
but no Madame."

Regina put her hand to her cheeks, in the old gesture.
"I—was raised as a Protestant, Madame. My—husband
mentioned that I might have instruction from the priest,
but—it has not been arranged—not yet."

And perhaps never would be, she thought bitterly. If
Julian decided to divorce her, it would be much easier if
she never became a Catholic. Was that why he did not
arrange for visits by the priest?

Seeing the shadow that crossed her face, Madame Galande dared to pat Regina's hand. "All will be well one
day, Madame," she soothed. "But to the other matter.
Madame Darlas, Madame la Baronne wishes to know
about the rents and the wages. She is uneasy about what
Monsieur Claude does—as we know." She gave the woman
a significant look.

Madame Darlas looked very uneasy and shifted in her
chair. "Madame knows I am very grateful to her—but
what can one say? I do not complain. I have a good roof
over my head, my children are fed—"

"But your rent is very high, and your husband has low wages, though he works hard," said Madame Galande encouragingly.

"That is true?" asked Regina.

Madame Darlas nodded and finally burst out, "It has made us bitter. My Jean-Paul works so hard, and Monsieur Bazaine praises him and says his wages will be higher. But never are they higher. Indeed, no one received the Christmas bonus last year. No one in the village. It was a scandal."

Regina distinctly remembered seeing a large amount listed in the ledgers for Christmas bonuses last year. She had been gratified by this evidence of Julian's generosity.

"No one received it, Madame?"

Both women shook their heads. "The priest was going to speak to Monsieur le Baron about it, but Monsieur was busy preparing for his journey to America and could not be disturbed. And Monsieur Claude said the harvest had been poor. We knew it, the rains came too soon."

Had Julian stopped the bonuses, or had Claude? And if so—why were they entered in the ledgers?

"I shall see about this," she said. "But I want to hear more. Will Madame Bonnet speak to me, or some other women?"

"Perhaps tomorrow," said Madame Galande. "I shall speak to some of them. You will come tomorrow, yes?"

"Yes, I shall come again tomorrow." She looked at the watch on its tiny gold chain and started. "So late! I must go home!"

"It is late, Madame. Will you have some luncheon here first?" offered Madame Darlas eagerly. "I was preparing our meal when our small one choked—" And she looked pale again.

"If it will not be an inconvenience, Madame, I shall be pleased to remain," said Regina. It was important for her to build a rapport with these people if they were to trust her.

Madame Darlas was pleased and flew about to finish the meal. The soup had been boiling for hours on the stove, a meat bone with some beef still on it, with leeks, onions, carrots, tomatoes, and potatoes added. It was delicious, served with thick warm brown bread and butter and soft cheese. Regina ate as though famished, which she was. She had not eaten well for days.

The children lost some of their shyness and clamored for more stories. Regina told the one about the bear and her horse, and the older women—Madame Galande had remained also—were equally fascinated.

"Well, there was the time my brother George and I were caught out in a snowstorm," said Regina, recalling that time with a shiver. "Up in the mountains the storms could come up suddenly. George is ten years older; at that time he was seventeen and I was seven. We had gone out to cut some branches for a Christmas tree. Father was away, Mother did not want us to go out, but we were very stubborn."

"Ah, the naughty children," said Madame Galande with a smile. She munched on her bread hungrily, listening to the story eagerly. All the French, from one to one hundred, loved stories, thought Regina.

"Well, the trees near to our cabin were scrawny, not filled out. We wandered farther and farther, looking for the right tree and some fine branches. Finally we found some pines with thick branches, and we started to cut. George had a saw for the higher branches, and I had a bag to keep some cones and needles in, to decorate the trees. We put flour on the needles," she added, "and covered the cones with paint. We were working when the snow started. We went on cutting, and collecting, thinking nothing of it."

"What happened, Madame? The snow, it came down hard?" asked Madame Darlas, leaning her capable arms on the rough-hewn table.

"Oh, did it ever!" said Regina in English, with a grimace. She repeated it in French, then went on, searching for the words. "We were caught in the wind and swirling snow. A blizzard had come up quickly. George was always calm and very smart. He is now a fine banker. Anyway, he found a thick fallen pine, and we crawled into the shelter of it, dragging the branches George had cut after us. I made a pillow of the needles and cones, and lay down to sleep. The snow came and came, filling up around us. I slept, but George, forcing himself to remain awake, kept making holes in the snow, so air would come in and we could breathe. We were there for two days and three nights."

"And your parents," breathed Madame Galande compassionately. "They thought you had died in the storm, yes?"

"I suppose so. I didn't think much of it then." Regina laughed ruefully. "All I knew was that George would protect me, and he did. When I wakened, we ate snow. When the snow finally stopped, and we crawled out, we walked back home to the cabin, dragging the branches for the Christmas tree. Father spanked George and Mother spanked me. Then they hugged us and we set up the tree and painted the pine cones."

Madame Darlas was shaking her head in wonder. "And you thanked your elder brother, yes?"

"Well, I had received some coins for Christmas. I bought some red flannel and made George a shirt. I was just learning to sew, and it took me three months to cut it out and sew it properly. I think I took out the seams three times! And when it was done, it was too large. He wore it anyway and declared it was the warmest shirt he had ever had, and he would grow into it. He really did; by the time he was twenty it fit just right!" And she had to laugh, remembering.

Regina finally realized she must go home. She thanked the two women and went to find her patient mare. She arrived home after four o'clock.

Eric's door was open when she passed by. On impulse, she went to the door. As she entered, she saw Eric sitting in his wheelchair, gazing absently out the window. How patient he looked, his hands idle in his lap, his withered shoulders bent. He turned his head and saw her, his face lighting up.

"Regina! I have not spoken with you for days!" he said.

She felt guilty at her neglect. How the time must drag for him. Surely he could get out, in the carriage or somehow. She must arrange for it.

Joseph, his valet, was smiling, holding a chair for her.

"Good afternoon," she said cheerfully. "Please close the door. I want to talk secrets with Eric!"

His eyes, so wistful, grew large with wonder, like those of a child. "Secrets? What?"

Joseph was about to leave, but Regina motioned him to stay. "I know you can keep a secret," she said, her eyes sparkling. "Eric, Marcus told me you used to help Claude with the books. Do you remember about the accounts? When was this?"

His face fell. "Oh—some years ago," he said with reserve. "Claude said I—I bungled it."

"I don't think that was why he wanted you to stop," said Regina bluntly. "Eric, I have been checking the accounts. I think I have uncovered some stealing by Claude, embezzling of Verlaine funds."

Eric stared but did not seem as much surprised as intrigued. "You have? How did you discover it? I suspected as much, but could not do anything before Claude dismissed me. What has happened?"

"Nothing has happened yet. I need time to compare the accounts in Julian's workbooks against Claude's ledgers. I talked to Marcus about it. He has suspected much also but said nothing. Julian did not seem to value Marcus's opinions, he said."

"No, Julian does not realize what Marcus has done," said Eric quietly. "He lives for the vines; everything else is a sideline for him. I have been worried—"

"But you also felt you could do nothing against Julian. He is stubbornly loyal to Claude, I believe. Well, I shall have to work harder to reveal the facts, and then I'll tell Julian," Regina said thoughtfully. "Eric, when you worked with the accounts, did you see the actual ledgers?"

He nodded, his light-brown eyes shining with interest. "Yes, I entered the numbers in the ledgers from Julian's books. I checked them again and again, the way my accounting books said to do. When Claude returned from his journey and said I had added wrong and was bungling the matter, I could not believe it. I wanted Julian to check the accounts, but he believed Claude. And I got too excited and screamed—that upset everyone. So—" He sighed deeply. "I decided to retreat. After all, it is peaceful here."

"Eric, you said, 'when Claude returned from his journey.' Was that when you worked, while he was gone?"

"Yes. Julian let me try it. I was restless, and the work was piling up, the bills unpaid. I made out checks, I entered them so carefully—then Claude came back."

"And found that his little schemes were about to be uncovered," said Regina. "How he must have sweated!"

"I think he must have been afraid, yes. But Claude made Julian think I was working too hard. I rested one hour, worked one hour, rested another hour. How could I be working too hard?" asked Eric with resignation, not bitterness. "But nobody talks against Claude; he twists the words cleverly, he makes one feel a fool. That is why Marcus dislikes him so much. He talks to Julian about Marcus, calls the man a fool, and Julian believes him."

"I think Claude has been too clever," said Regina finally. "He is too secure. Have you noticed his velvet suits, his sapphires and diamonds and rubies? Well, I think he has bought his last jewels at the Verlaine's expense!"

"Truly?" asked Eric. "Regina"—he hesitated—"I do not want you to arouse Julian's anger. He is not often angry, but when he gets angry—he is very unforgiving and hard. He has the Verlaine temper, though one does not often see it. Perhaps it would be best not to go further. Let Marcus do it, or Thérèse—or me," he added dubiously.

Regina thought of Julian's anger and the results. Her mouth hardened. "He will find he is not the only person who can get angry," she said decisively. "Claude is not going to tangle me up in his clever words. Not when I get final proof of his deceptions! Eric, I have talked to some of the village women. Some have told me of very high rents, very low wages. They said the Christmas bonus last year was never given. Yet it is entered on Claude's ledgers!"

"Ahhh," said Eric, nodding. "So that is it! The anger at Christmas last year. Thérèse told me about the priest's sermon. It must have gone right above Julian's head. I truly do not believe Julian knows what Claude is doing."

"Oh, I wish I had all the proof right now," Regina fumed. "I would throw it at Julian's thick head!"

Eric looked startled, the valet shocked.

Joseph said tentatively, "I believe Monsieur Claude, he goes to Paris soon, Madame."

Regina stared up at the impassive face. "He does?" she breathed. "When, do you know?"

"I do not know. It may be next week, Madame. May I make very discreet inquiries from his valet? I shall be most careful."

"Oh, please do that! Then I can work—Eric, you must help me! And Marcus! As soon as Claude leaves, we will start in on the books. We will read the entries back and forth, study to make sure whether it is correct or a false entry. With the three of us checking, we won't miss anything!"

Spots of color stained Eric's pale thin cheeks. "I must study up on this! Where are my accounting books? I will work all this week, and try to remember all I had learned about it. I will be ready when you need me, Regina!"

"Good! With you and Marcus helping me, we'll find out," she said confidently. She rose to leave. "And not a word to anyone, either of you! I don't want Claude to find out and burn the books!"

"No, no, it is our secret!" Eric said, wheeling around to follow her as she went to the door. She opened the door, turned to smile back at him. "Thank you, Regina, for coming to me!" he added. "You will not regret confiding in me! I shall do my best!"

"I know you will. I am counting on you, Eric," she said, closing the door with a smile. She turned to see Julian coming along the hall to her. His face was grim.

"Where have you been all the day? What were you saying to Eric?" he demanded.

She went up the stairs without a word. He followed her. In her living room, she turned on him. "Well, Julian?" she asked coolly, her flashing eyes belying her calm. "What is it now?"

"I want to know where you were all the day! Even Ninette did not know where you had gone!"

"I went for a ride on my mare," she said, her chin up.

"All day? And alone? I have forbidden you to go out alone!"

"Nobody forbids me anything, Julian! You have yet to learn that," she defied him. "I shall ride where I please, when I please. And you may do the same!" she snapped, thinking furiously of Simone.

He frowned. "I am a man, it is different."

"You think so, you and all Frenchmen!"

"And what did you say to Eric? I will not have him troubled!"

Regina could not help it. She laughed out loud, tauntingly. "Why, I am having a mad affair with Eric! Too bad you discovered it so soon! The wild American harlot you married must have many about her—didn't you say so? I must have my fun!"

His hand lifted. Her eyes dared him to strike her. He

went out, turning on his heel. Regina went to the door and
slammed it after him, slammed it hard, so the sound
echoed through the second floor of the château.

There. Let him brood about that! She would not be dic-
tated to, she would not be ordered about—especially by a
hypocrite!

Regina continued to be cold and aloof with Julian. She
continued to go to the village and encouraged the women
to talk to her and tell her of what had been happening.

Julian did not come to her bed. But she felt his gaze on
her thoughtfully, in the evenings, as they sat at dinner, at
the opposite ends of the long table.

He was puzzled, no longer angry. I have him wondering,
she thought in bitter triumph. She would pay him back for
that evening he had taken her so brutally. She thought she
could never forgive him for that.

The Dowager came down again for meals and was troubled at the coldness again between them. She sighed and
picked at her needlepoint, but did not offer any more
advice. The young people would have to work out their
own differences. She spoke of the June days, the loveliness of the new rugs that had been laid down, the beauty
of the new satin covers on the rose-room chairs. The
maids and Thérèse had been working hard, cutting, sewing, fitting.

And Thérèse had new dresses, a new blue muslin, a yellow muslin, and was looking over patterns for some fall
and winter dresses. Regina wrote again to Monsieur Silver
in Paris and asked him to watch for more fabrics for them,
giving him the measurements for the draperies in several
more rooms. She might have to leave Verlaine, she might
get kicked out, but she would have it all bright and shining
new before she did, she vowed stormily to herself.

She had another conference with Eric and Marcus, in
Eric's rooms, and they laid their plans. They would be
ready to go to work as soon as Claude left. Marcus borrowed an accounting book to study at night. Regina
warned them against talking about it. Claude must not
learn what they were up to before he left.

So they waited, anxiously, for Claude to leave.

CHAPTER SIXTEEN

July came, with warmer days and nights. The sun shone brightly on the vineyards, and the grapes grew in thick bunches. Julian went out early in the morning and stayed late, brooding anxiously over his vines, testing one field after another to make sure the soil was moist.

He also went over to Simone's and spent long hours there. His mother thought he worked in her fields and instructed her men. Regina thought he did nothing of the sort. What a chance for him, an opportunity to be alone with the white-skinned beauty with her mocking dark eyes!

Regina rode out daily, and the sight of Madame la Baronne on her fine mare, her riding habit of black or navy blue, and the fine plumed hat became accepted. She always had a smile for the workers and the townspeople, and a wave. Many a time she stopped in the village for a drink of hot coffee or cold juice, or for luncheon with one or more of the women.

The men were more reserved, but the women welcomed her. She was interested in them, in their children, in their houses, in their wages, in their problems. Encouraged by Madame Galande, they talked more openly to her. And Regina stored up all they told her and kept track of the figures they mentioned, the wages that were paid. At home, she wrote down notes and locked them away in a jewel box in the bottom drawer of her desk.

One early July morning, Eric's valet was waiting for her at the bottom of the steps as she came down, ready for riding. She was about to draw down her veil when he beckoned to her anxiously.

She went along the corridor with him toward Eric's room. "Anything wrong?" she whispered, looking anxiously toward the opened door.

"Monsieur Eric, he wishes to speak to you," murmured Joseph.

She nodded and followed him. Eric had been studying and studying, perhaps he had overworked and become ill!

It would be her fault. She entered the room and was vastly relieved to find Eric sitting up, face glowing with excitement.

The valet shut the door. Servants were always passing through the hallway, and sometimes Claude came in from the stables to go to the study through the courtyard.

"Regina, such news!" Eric whispered excitedly.

"What is it?"

"Joseph has discovered Claude goes to Paris tomorrow!"

Regina looked at the valet, who nodded, his eyes shining.

"What happened?" she asked him.

"Well, Madame, yesterday evening, I heard voices from the study, and much quarreling. I wait, I listen—discreetly—Madame. I go out to the courtyard. Monsieur Claude, he comes out, he says to Monsieur le Baron that he goes to Paris on Wednesday and will remain for a week. Monsieur le Baron nods, as though he is very unhappy."

"Ah—Julian did not want him to go?"

"No, Madame. Last night, I talked to Monsieur Claude's valet. He is upset. He has orders to pack the trunks and be all ready to go Wednesday morning, with a carriage and two outriders. Monsieur Claude goes to his Paris flat and means to be gone two weeks! That is what he says. I think—" The valet laid his finger alongside his nose and nodded wisely. "I think Monsieur Claude wanted two weeks all along, but Monsieur le Baron told him he might go for one, and Monsieur Claude says all right. But he will remain for two! He is sly, that one."

"Even one week would be enough, if we work hard," mused Regina. "He might come back on time. Well, that is it. Eric, tomorrow you and Marcus and I will take action! Are you ready?"

He saluted gaily, lifting his arm with an effort. "Ready, *mon generale!*"

They all laughed softly, even Joseph, his eyes sparkling.

Regina went out on her ride, but she kept it a short one, returning at luncheon. She was churning with apprehension, so many doubts. But she had to finish what she had started. If Eric showed signs of tiring, she would tactfully send him away, and she and Marcus would go on.

How to tell Marcus? she wondered to herself.

She talked casually with the Dowager and with Thérèse

at luncheon. Only the three women were at the table. Aunt
Agnes had gone to visit a friend for several days. Uncle
Oliver had not been well, and had kept to his rooms.

"Claude is coming for dinner," said her sister-in-law. "He
goes to Paris for a week, for fun, a holiday." Thérèse
sighed. "He has had two holidays already this year, and my
dear Marcus has not had any vacation at all!"

"Encourage Marcus to come to dinner, Thérèse," Regina said thoughtfully. The Dowager looked at her
shrewdly. Thérèse seemed surprised. "I think Julian may
be surprised to find Marcus has many interesting things to
say!"

"Not in front of Claude." Thérèse grimaced. "Claude always makes fun of Marcus."

"Tell Marcus I want him especially to come, and tell
him the occasion, that Claude is going to Paris."

"Regina, do you have something planned?" Thérèse
asked bluntly. "You have been acting so oddly these
weeks."

Regina only smiled. "Just say nothing to Claude," she
finally said, more seriously. "I want him out of the way for
a time."

"Well, so do I, but not just for a time," Thérèse said
gloomily. "He makes me feel—like a—a country bump-
kin!"

"He's not so smart," said Regina, but that was all she
dared to say. She patted her mother-in-law's hand. "Dear
Maman, do not worry, all will turn out well. Bear with us!"

"My dear daughter, I trust you," said her mother-in-law
gently. "Do whatever you must, only do not hurt Julian.
My poor boy works so hard, and so does Marcus. If only
all might go well with Verlaine, that is all I ask for my last
years."

"Don't be gloomy, Maman," Regina said. "I think things
are about to go up in fireworks!"

"Fireworks?" Thérèse repeated.

"Yes, at home we have fireworks on the Fourth of July,
our Independence Day," Regina said glibly, as a servant
brought in fresh hot coffee. She elaborated on that for the
rest of the meal, refusing to return to the subject of Claude
or Julian.

Dinner that evening was pleasant. Marcus did come, and
Regina found a moment to talk to him. "Claude leaves to-

morrow morning. Come as soon as you can. Eric and I will be in the study!"

She saw Julian studying her from across the room, his face cold and set. She resisted the impulse to make a face at him and heard Marcus say, "I shall come about nine o'clock. The men can work in the fields for a few days without direction. *Bon?*"

"Bon," she agreed, and poured out his coffee for him with a dazzling smile.

Julian came over to them. "Marcus, will you play for us? Thérèse is at the piano."

"I would hate to bore Claude on his last evening with us," said Marcus pleasantly, and he remained in the seat next to Regina.

Julian looked thunderous but Claude laughed. "Marcus must be out of practice, he is so timid about performing!" he murmured.

"No, Thérèse and I have been practicing each night after work," said Marcus. "We enjoy music, especially classical. However, since Claude's preference is for can-can dancers, I am sure we would not amuse him. And Claude loves to be amused, don't you, Claude?"

From the amazed expressions on all the faces in the room, Regina concluded it was the first time Marcus had ever struck back. She was pleased, but she did not want to give anything away.

"When Julian and I were in Paris, we enjoyed both," she said quickly, giving Marcus a little nudge of the arm, which was not missed by the sharp-eyed Julian. "We went to nightclubs in Montmartre, and also to concerts. I find both most interesting."

Marcus leaned back, a half smile on his face as he drank his coffee. Thérèse left the piano and came to sit beside him. He took her hand affectionately.

"Ah, those lovebirds, after all these years of marriage," sneered Claude, who seemed determined to give pinpricks tonight.

"You should marry, Claude," said Marcus unexpectedly. "It might settle you down. Instead you flit from one girl to another. There is nothing so satisfying as a fine wife and good children. You should know the pleasure of it."

An odd look came over Claude's face. He seemed to wince and did not remain long afterward, saying he had much to do and wished to retire early before the journey.

Julian went to the door with him, and Regina caught his words. "Be sure to return in one week, Claude! We cannot spare you so long—"

"It is good to know I am so needed," said Claude, laughing.

As soon as the carriage had clattered away, Marcus rose and drew up Thérèse with him. "Now we will have music, eh?"

She went willingly to the piano with him. The Dowager Baroness said mildly, "Marcus, you were naughty to tease Claude so. He is sensitive about his age, thirty-six and not married!"

"I have not prevented him from marrying, Maman," Marcus said, mildly. "The remedy is in his hands— perhaps." He turned to his flute, took it from the case, and began to play.

Soon they heard Eric's wheelchair, and Julian went to the door to help him enter. Eric looked about quickly, seemed satisfied with the company there, and indicated he would like his chair wheeled next to Regina and the coffee tray.

"Some cakes, Eric?" Regina asked softly, as Thérèse was playing.

"*Oui,* Regina, *merci.*" He selected two and sat back to eat them with enjoyment. She poured a cup of coffee for him, and set it carefully on the tray so he could reach for it easily. Julian was watching them curiously, a puzzled frown on his brow.

Let him wonder, let him worry, let him puzzle! thought Regina, remembering his accusations with fury. He would be sorry soon! Then she saw the weariness on his face, as he leaned back in the rose-covered overstuffed chair and closed his eyes. He did work so hard with all the responsibilities of Verlaine on his shoulders. He had always worked hard. Should she begrudge him his amusements with Simone?

Yes, I should, she thought stormily. If he wanted Simone, he should have married her! But since he had married Regina, he should have given up Simone!

The music caught them all up in its spell, and Regina began to feel calmer. How beautiful it was, the sound of the piano and the flute, played so skillfully and with such feeling. She watched Thérèse, her tired face transformed into ecstasy as she played the Mozart melodies, and Marcus, looking so serious and intent and happy, as he waited for his part to come in.

Eric looked at Regina, smiled at a particularly beautiful passage. She nodded. When she looked across at Julian, the lines were smoothing out of his face. If only their lives might be this peaceful and beautiful!

They enjoyed the music until almost eleven o'clock, when the Dowager, stirring, said, "I must retire. Marcus and Thérèse, thank you for such a beautiful evening."

Marcus bowed low, Julian gazing at him in wonder. "Our pleasure was increased by your pleasure, Maman," said Marcus.

"A graceful speech, Marcus." The Dowager smiled. He came to help her up, escorted her to the hallway where a footman waited to help her up the stairs to her room.

The others soon went to their rooms as well. Eric gave Regina a bright wink as he departed, and Julian caught it.

Regina did not explain as she went to her bedroom, where Ninette waited. In bed, she lay with hands folded behind her head, thinking of tomorrow. They would start to work first thing in the morning, and break at lunchtime so Eric would not get too weary, and Marcus could go the the fields without causing comment. Anxiously, she willed herself to sleep.

Julian had gone off to his beloved vineyards before nine o'clock. Regina ate her rolls hastily, drank her hot chocolate, and was dressed and ready by nine. She went hurriedly down the stairs to the study, and found Marcus and Eric there before her.

"Ah, I am the late one," she joked as she shut the door. They were excited.

"These drawers are locked, Regina," Marcus said gravely, motioning toward the desk.

"Then we will get them open," she said. She found a penknife, and Marcus worked at the locks, opening one drawer after another. He took out the ledgers while Regina took the workbooks from the shelves behind them.

"Let's start with the present and work back," she suggested. "I know the entries were larger and larger as Claude grew bolder. Let's start with 1894 and work back as far as we can."

"*Bon,*" they agreed. Eric took Julian's workbooks and scanned the entries. Marcus took the matching ledger for 1894. Regina sat ready with paper and pen.

They worked all morning. In three hours, they had done about half a year of the work, checking back and forth with utmost care. Eric worked as steadily as the other two, and did not seem to tire. He read on and on, pointing out changes in Julian's workbook cleverly made in a similar handwriting.

"Here, there is another change. See how the pencil was erased? That is not Julian's hand. He does not make his fives that way."

At twelve, she stopped them, pleased with their progress. "We must stop. If Eric gets too tired Julian will have my head!"

"Oh, no, Regina, we have just this week," Eric urged. "I am not tired, really I am not!"

"We could work on it this afternoon," suggested Marcus. "Let us stop for luncheon and then continue. I want to get this straight! Perhaps it is sinful of me, but I have wanted to smash Claude's face since I first met him!"

Eric laughed aloud, and so did Regina. "Oh, I feel the same way," said Regina. "Well—let us stop for two hours, then. Eric, you get some rest and have lunch in your room, and be terribly good! For my sake! Marcus, you and I had better go our separate ways and then come down for lunch."

"There is a horse that needs attention," he said. "I'll see to it, then come in. I often work in the stables so Thérèse will not think anything of it."

Regina ate lunch, abstractedly pondering what to do next. She had the figures down on paper, but would Julian believe them and understand what they proved?

Thérèse seemed surprised when Marcus came in, but ordered another place set.

"How good to see you at luncheon," his mother-in-law said. "Recently we have just had feminine chatter about nothing."

"Thank you very much!" said Regina, her nose in the air.

"My dear child, I did not mean—" her mother-in-law stammered.

Thérèse and Marcus began to laugh, and so did Regina. She leaned over to pat the Dowager's hand.

"There, I know what you mean! I am being silly. It does bother me, though, to have the gentlemen talk seriously about the vineyards, while the ladies chatter about needlepoint in the drawing room," Regina admitted.

"Well," said the Dowager, "there is chatter about children and babies, household tasks, that men find boring. And they need to speak without watching their language, or so it seems to me."

"But women are kept too much away from making decisions," said Marcus thoughtfully, spearing his fruit. "I think Madame Tillemont is very hurt that decisions are made about her harvest and she does not even know about them until later. Julian is good to help her, but she is not an idiot."

"One day women will not be satisfied to sit back and let men make all the decisions about their lives and their properties," Regina said decisively. "One day women will revolt! After all, we have minds and can use them."

"Dear me, Regina, how fierce you sound," said Thérèse, a line of worry between her eyebrows. "I am content to let Marcus make the decisions."

He grinned at her. "Such as the one about living in the lodge?" he asked.

"What is this?" asked the Dowager. Marcus turned to her casually.

"Thérèse is thinking that perhaps one day soon we will clean out the lodge and move in there. We will be close yet have a home of our own. If God blesses us with other children, we will need more space, Maman."

"Why—yes, you will," she said. "Have you spoken to Julian about this?"

"Not yet. There are other matters to settle first," said Marcus.

Luncheon finished, Regina went quietly back to the study, and soon Marcus came in. Eric was wheeled in by the valet. He looked a little tired, yet still excited.

They started to work again and managed to get through the remainder of 1894 accounts. The biggest discovery was that in Julian's workbooks, a large Christmas bonus was listed among the expenses, but on Claude's books the bonus was not listed. Instead, there was a huge entry for farm machinery.

"Hmm," said Marcus, studying the entries. "There is no farm machinery maker by that name that I know of. That is some amount! And with the other entries for farm machinery—that adds up to about thirty thousand American dollars, Regina."

"All in one year?" she gasped. He nodded. "And Claude withdrew that for expenses?"

"Yes, it must have gone into his pockets. I wondered how he could afford sapphire studs and all those suits on his salary. And rumor has it that he keeps a woman—" Marcus stopped, embarrassed.

"Go on, Marcus, you can't shock me," said Regina impatiently. "A woman—where?"

"In Paris. I think that is why he is so anxious to go there several times a year. You know, he stayed over four days after you returned on the ship. He didn't go straight home to Verlaine with your trunks. Julian was furious when he learned of it later."

"I heard some of the arguments," Eric contributed. "Claude said there was no worry about the delay, nothing was urgent. But Julian said he had his orders to go, and why couldn't he obey orders? It was quite an uproar, but Claude managed to talk his way out of it, as usual."

Eric was looking weary. Regina checked her watch and exclaimed, "Good heavens, it is almost five o'clock. We have to clear this up before Julian comes in and catches us. You go ahead, Eric, and Marcus and I will stuff these things in the drawers."

He grinned and wheeled himself away.

Julian came home about five-thirty, tired and dusty. Regina was safely in her bedroom, changing for dinner. She went downstairs, demurely gowned in blue lace, with pearls around her neck, and was pouring out sherry when Julian came down in his evening wear of gray striped trousers and crimson velvet smoking jacket.

He looked so handsome, her heart quite turned over. But she still felt hotly angry at him, and could scarcely speak to him naturally. He would eat his words, she vowed.

* * *

Eric, Marcus, and Regina worked again the next day, getting through the crucial year of 1893. They found that Claude had withdrawn huge sums and sent them to Paris banks. "Probably under his own name. No wonder we made no money from the fine wines that year," said Marcus, savagely bitter. "We could have done so well! Thérèse would have had new dresses, we could have purchased good machinery for the fruit trees—and the men could have had higher wages. When I think how I promised the men good wages—and Claude stopped it!"

"Regina, look at this item." Eric pointed out some figures in Julian's notebooks. "Look—higher pay for all these men. Let's compare them with the ledger."

They looked carefully but found no such higher pay. Apparently Julian had authorized raises but Claude had diverted the money to his own use.

They worked a third day, and a fourth. Thérèse had caught on that all three were working in the study, but Marcus had asked her to keep their secret. Her eyes were bright with excitement as the week went on. The Dowager saw nothing since she kept to her rooms much of the time during the heat of the day.

Aunt Agnes, however, was curious. She said once to Regina, "My dear child, are you trying to do the accounts while Claude is gone? He won't like it, you know."

Her bright eyes speculated. She always looked like a trim pouter pigeon in her dark blues with white lace at the throat, a picture of a chic mature Frenchwoman. She never went out, even to inspect the garden, without donning an immense navy-blue straw hat.

"No, we are not doing the accounts, Aunt Agnes," said Regina. "I beg you to say nothing to Julian for now. It is—a surprise."

"Umm. You have my word," said Aunt Agnes, who always saw more than the others thought she did. In the way of spinster aunts living in other people's houses, she saw much and talked little. She saw her life as that of smoothing the way for others, and she did what she could to do so.

On Thursday, Julian returned to the château at three o'clock. He strode into the study, to find the three of them working at the accounts. Regina jumped up guiltily. The others remained frozen where they were.

"What in the world are you doing?" Julian asked in shock.

"I'll tell you later," said Regina. "We haven't quite finished. If you please, Julian, will you wait?"

His puzzled gaze went from the three of them to the ledgers and workbooks and papers scattered over two desks and a table. He went over and picked up one workbook. frowned over it. "Eighteen ninety-two," he said, and frowned again. "What the devil—"

Regina said, a little desperately, "Julian, we must get this finished soon! Please, I will explain it all later."

He looked at Marcus, with red pencil in hand marking a ledger, at Eric, with a flushed face and sparkling eyes. His hand brushed tenderly over the light-blond hair of his brother. "Don't work too long, Eric, will you?" he said. He hesitated, then finally left the room.

"Whew." Marcus sighed. "What does he think, I wonder?"

But Regina did not know. Perhaps he thought they were keeping the bills and accounts up to date. The workers were usually paid on Friday, and Claude had left the pay in little envelopes with the names on them.

Nothing was said at dinner, though Marcus was nervous and laughed too much. Eric came to join them, and managed very well, though his hand shook at times. His bright gaze took them all in, watching his family with affection.

"Dear Eric," said his mother. "How well you look. Joseph tells me you are eating much better."

"*Oui*, Maman," said Eric. "I am—enjoying life so much, you see. Regina has brightened our lives, has she not?"

Mischief sparkled in his light-brown eyes. Regina shook her head warningly at him, and he laughed aloud.

"I have not heard you laugh for some time, Eric," Julian added. "I am glad you are happier. Are you enjoying the books we brought you?"

"Oh, yes, Julian, thank you. And Regina's kind brother George sent some good books, all about the Wild West of the United States. I cannot believe them all, but they are very interesting. All about cowboys and Indians, and a postal service by fast ponies through Indian territory. There's a man called Buffalo Bill Cody who had such amazing adventures!"

"Regina, you must tell us more of your stories of the

West," said Julian mildly. "They must rival those of this—er—Buffalo Bill."

Regina's cheeks reddened. "Sometime," she said evasively. Did he mean he did not believe her stories? Did he think she made them up?

They all retired early. Marcus had told Regina that the accounts wearied him more than hard work on the fruit trees. She had undressed and sent Ninette away, and was sitting in her gown and negligee before the mirrored dresser when Julian tapped at her door.

Julian had not come to her rooms since his angry accusations and attack on her. She stiffened.

"Come in," she said finally, coldly.

Julian came in and shut the door. He was in his nightdress and light summer dressing gown of brown silk. He sat down a careful distance from her, as she picked up the brush to continue brushing her long curly chestnut hair.

"Regina, I am very puzzled," he said quietly. "Some strange things are going on, and I do not understand them. Will you tell me now?"

She hesitated, then nodded. "I might as well tell you tonight, Julian. Claude could come back anytime, and I want you to have these figures first."

She went over to the desk, unlocked a small drawer, and took out the notes she had made so carefully. She set them on a small table beside him, then sat down on the rose sofa.

Julian frowned at them, picked them up, fingered through the pages. "I don't understand. You know I have no head for finance," he said defensively.

"Well, I do," she said coolly. "And what I, and Marcus, and Eric are discovering and proving is the extent of what Claude has been doing. Julian, he has been embezzling funds from Verlaine for more than ten years. The last year's amount alone is about thirty thousand dollars, American. The year of 1893, your good harvest, was more than that, about sixty thousand dollars in all."

The color seemed to drain from Julian's tanned face. His hand shook as he picked up the pages again and stared at them blindly. "What? Regina, what are you saying?"

"I'll begin at the beginning," she said, and began to speak, telling him of her suspicions when she first saw the books. "Then I went to the village. I soon found that Claude made no repairs, he raised the rents, he kept the wages low—all in the name of your poor harvests. Monsieur le Baron must not be disturbed, he told them. Julian, he even kept all of the Christmas bonuses last year. The priest was going to talk to you about that and protest for the men, but you could not see him."

Julian ran his hand through his hair, leaving it standing up in light-brown peaks. "Regina, I swear I knew nothing of that. I did not know he wished to see me—"

She softened at his broken voice. "I thought not, Julian. Claude is very clever. But he has overreached himself. By the purchase of all these new clothes and his jewels, he roused suspicion. The women finally told me willingly about the matters."

She told him about her visits, what Madame Galande, Madame Darlas, Madame Bonnet, and the others had said. "The men would not speak to me. They are suspicious and shy. But they will talk to you, Julian, if you go to them."

"I will go to them, of course. But I must look at the ledgers—or get an accountant from Paris," he said, shaking his head. "I do not understand that—it will have to be handled by an accountant—"

"That isn't all, Julian," she said. She might as well plunge and tell him the whole story. "There is Marcus and there is Thérèse, and there is Eric."

"What do you mean?" He flushed a little. "Regina, forgive me for saying what I did that night," he said simply. "I was wild with jealousy. I had no right to say those—horrible things. You would be right to keep on treating me coldly. I accused you falsely and then treated you—in such a manner that makes me sick with shame. I hurt you—I cannot expect you to forgive."

She swallowed and looked away. It was hard to resist his appeal. "I was talking to Marcus, Julian, because Thérèse told me he was thinking of leaving. He has had an offer from a distant relative, to go to Normandy and manage an apple farm. He would help with the harvest, supervise the making of cider and Calvados. And when the old man dies, he promised to make him his heir. It was a good offer, except that Thérèse would have to leave Maman, and Marcus thought the old man mean and cold. But he would have left—because Claude has always made trouble for him."

Julian was looking more and more amazed. "Marcus—leaving? But how could Claude affect that?"

"Claude always mocks Marcus. His slick tongue can trip up anybody, and Marcus was made to feel like a dunce in front of everyone, especially you. You think him a fool," said Regina bluntly. "You told me he was. Well, he isn't! He is a smart and a kind man, very much in love with his wife. Enough to slave for her for years, with low wages, no appreciation, left out of conferences, treated with contempt because he is a farmer, not a son of Verlaine." .

Julian was still staring at her. "But it was not because he was a farmer. I mean, Marcus is a good man, but not very bright, Regina. He has no sense."

"He has sense enough to know a cheat when he sees one! Sense enough to go through the ledgers with me and Eric, and find where Claude has altered the accounts, and sense enough to know that Claude paid out large sums to imaginary makers of farm machinery. Sense enough to know that Claude has sent money to Paris, into his own bank account. Sense enough to help Madame Tillemont rescue her fruit trees. Sense enough to manage fifty men and keep them on the job, even when their promised wages are not delivered and no raises are given." She paused for breath.

"No raises?" Julian caught at the last words. "But I authorized wage raises every two years, all I could afford."

"Madame Darlas told me her Jean-Paul has had no raise for ten years. They have four children and can scarcely make enough to eat and clothe their children."

Julian was shocked and silent, turning over the pages in a dazed manner that told Regina he was not taking in the meaning of her neat figures.

When he remained silent, she went on. "One final thing. About Eric. Years ago he wanted to help with the accounts. He worked while Claude was away. Claude returned, found fault with his work, and told you Eric was too stupid, too much an invalid to work. But he wasn't, Julian. Eric knew even then that Claude was doing something to the books. With only the little training Eric had acquired from reading accounting books, he knew that! Your brother is a smart man, and I suggest you let him handle the books from now on."

"My God, Regina!" Julian whispered. "I am in shock. Give me time to recover, can't you? I cannot take all this in. Eric, do the books? But he must be protected. He would work too hard—"

"Claude worked less than four hours a day, I figure, five days a week, less his many vacations. Eric could do that easily."

He ran his hands over his face. "I must think this over."

"I'll show you the books tomorrow. We have gone back four years," she said. "Then you will realize what Claude has been doing. We can continue, go back the next six—"

Julian shook his head. "Claude must go. This is the final blow," he said. "No, Claude must leave. I can never trust him again."

Regina was puzzled by his words. But he persisted. "Then do you believe me, Julian?"

He stood up, letting the pages fall to the precious Persian carpet given to her by Monsieur Silver. He went over to Regina, ran his hands slowly down her shining chestnut hair to her shoulders, and held her steadily.

"Whenever I did not believe you, Regina, I was a fool. I hope I am never a fool again. I believe you, and trust you, with my life. Forgive me. I have gone through hell without you. I lay awake, wishing I could wipe out that horrible night and those dreadful lies I said. Can you ever forgive and forget?"

"Oh—Julian!" Suddenly she was crying. He was humbled, and he believed her. She had her revenge, but it was not sweet. "Oh, Julian, I love you, and it has been horrible—"

She was in his arms, and he was holding her tightly against him, and he was whispering, "I love you, my own, so much. My darling beautiful Regina. I missed you so much! The nights have been so lonely and dark without you. Never condemn me to such nights again, my sweet. I do not think I could bear it. I love you—I love you—I love you—"

And that night, when they lay together in her wide bed, he held her close to him, as though he never wanted to let her go.

Yet some part of her still held back. Julian was still con-tinuing his long affair with Simone. How could Regina forget that? Could she become indifferent and manage to ignore Julian's indiscretions?

She loved him and wanted his kisses and caresses. She wanted to be closer to him in body and mind. She loved lying beside him in bed, feeling his sleeping warmth against her. Yet—yet—Simone also knew him intimately. She knew him sleeping and waking, making passionate love to her. Regina winced, her teeth clenched at the thought of sharing Julian with the spiteful, triumphant Simone.

Must she always share him? Dared she hope that one day she, as his wife, would become all to Julian? She wanted desperately to believe it. However, she was a practical woman. Perhaps she must settle for second best. If Regina made herself indispensable to Julian, he might keep her as his wife even though he would continue to see Simone, visiting her, keeping her as his mistress. He might be pragmatic enough to keep his useful and wealthy American wife as well.

It was sad, but it might be enough for Regina if she could learn to endure this situation. He turned in bed, sleepily, and drew her against him again, and she pressed her face against his broad chest.

CHAPTER SEVENTEEN

Julian remained home the next day. He and Marcus, Eric and Regina went to the study at nine in the morning, and except for luncheon, remained there for the entire day.

Regina and Marcus tried to explain to Julian what Claude had done, patiently showing him the workbooks and ledgers, marked in red where they had found major changes. Eric pointed out the wages of the men, the actual amounts paid.

Julian kept shaking his head, not in disbelief, but in sadness. "And to think the men were faithful to Verlaine, and kept on working these past ten years, even with no raise in wages."

"They love Verlaine," said Eric quietly. "And they would work for nothing if they could. In the old days they did, you know, when the lord of the manor provided the peasants with food and shelter and nothing else. But those days are past, Julian. The men should be paid decent wages. Even though they still feel they belong to Verlaine, they should be paid."

"I know, I know," said Julian. "Have you figured what wages they do receive?"

Regina showed them her notes and they discussed them.

"I will speak frankly to the men who work in the fruit trees and the vegetable gardens, and the stablehands," said Marcus. "Julian, I think everyone will have to know that Claude suppressed the raises that were authorized by you."

"Claude is part of Verlaine," said Julian dejectedly. "Must they all know?"

"They already know," said Regina bluntly. "And they thought you knew and condoned it. I think it is better for them to know the truth, that Claude was deceiving all of us."

"Deceiving me, you mean," said Julian, sighing deeply. "I was the blind one." He rubbed his hand over his eyes.

Eric looked with gentle eyes at his elder brother. "You were always so busy with the vineyards, Julian. They were your chief concern. We cannot blame you for not seeing what Claude did. The vineyards occupied you and took up all your time and energies. And you trusted Marcus to do his job, and Thérèse, so why not Claude also?"

"I should never have trusted Claude," said Julian. "He is—not worthy of trust. But because he was part of the family—" He shook his head, and Regina was puzzled by what he said. Had something happened in the past to make him suspicious? Something he had forgiven and forgotten?

"What should I do first?" asked Julian after a time. It was late afternoon, and the books lay strewn about them. "Where do we start to unravel this mess? I do not even know how much money is in the bank, how much the men are paid—"

"I have thought about this," Marcus said. Julian turned to him, a little startled, but Marcus did not see the questioning in his face. "First I think we should hold these books as they are, pack them away somewhere that Claude can't get his hands on them. We should start with fresh books. If I handle them, or Regina, or Eric, we should start over. Julian, you start with a fresh notebook today. We shall start fresh ledgers."

Regina was nodding. "Yes, an excellent idea! Leave the old ones to be checked by an auditor. I think you should get an accountant from a good firm in Paris to go over them all, find out where we stand and how much Claude has embezzled."

"But I cannot prosecute him in court," Julian said simply. "I cannot drag the name of Verlaine through the courts."

Regina compressed her lips. "Julian, he took over one hundred thousand dollars from you and Verlaine!"

"What hope is there of getting it back?" he asked. "He has probably spent it on jewels, clothes and women."

"I'm afraid Julian is correct about that," said Marcus. "But at least we should know, for evidence, if Claude ever tries anything more. It doesn't have to go to court, but it should be known, if Claude tries to say he was fired unjustly."

Julian finally agreed to have an outside accountant come and sort out the books. "But about the current books," he added. "Who should we hire to do them? I cannot ask Marcus to do them, he has so much to do already."

"I could," said Regina. "But I have other duties. I think Eric should become treasurer—with a salary," she added.

"Eric?" Julian turned to his younger brother. "But Eric is—I mean—he is not trained—"

"And I am supposed to be an invalid," said Eric. "Pooh. This week since I have had work to do, I have eaten better, slept better, felt better than I have for years. Do let me work, Julian! I have felt like a—a leech for so many years. Let me do something for Verlaine."

"But the work is long and hard, Eric," said Julian gently. "I would never forgive myself if it damaged your health."

"I want to do it, Julian. Please! I promise to try hard to do the work just right. Regina can teach me more about accounting than I learned from my books. She knows. And the accountant from Paris can remain a time, and make sure we set up the books right. Let me! If I tire, I will rest, I promise! Only let me do something to—to justify my existence here!" he ended passionately.

Julian went over to him and put his hand tenderly on Eric's eager face. "My dear brother, you shall do whatever you choose. Your place here is justified, however, by the joy you have brought to our hearts, by the patience and goodness you have shown through all your pain, by the example you set."

Eric put his hand on Julian's and pressed it to his cheek, his eyes filling with tears. Regina bit her lips to keep from weeping herself, and Marcus's eyes were suspiciously bright.

"Thank you. But do let me do something for Verlaine! Please, Julian."

"If you wish to do this, I will not prevent you." Julian sighed. "I am at sixes and sevens, however. What next?"

"Next—to fire Claude when he returns," said Marcus practically. "And tell him why. He must not be allowed to go unscathed. Even if you do not choose to prosecute him, he must know he cannot work here at Verlaine."

"No, never again, or live here," said Julian. "He has always caused too much mischief. So—Eric will do the books. An auditor will come from Paris and help us. We must find out what the true wages of the men are and raise them, set up new books, and what else?"

"The meeting this Sunday of the *vignerons*," said Marcus. "Have you had time to find out about banking? For I have investigated quietly at some banks about this."

Julian looked startled. "The meeting? I had forgotten—"

"Madame Tillemont is ready with her report on cooperatives in Scandinavia," said Marcus. "She told me when I saw her yesterday that she had received letters from nine of the groups. She was most proud."

"She should be in on the meeting, not just have her report presented," said Regina impulsively. "She resents not being included because she is a woman. After all, she is also a *vigneron*."

Marcus and Julian looked at each other and nodded.

"And you also must come, Regina," said Julian. "After all, it was your idea. And your knowledge of banking is greater than mine—or even of Marcus's, for all his recent studies!" He grinned teasingly at Marcus, dazzling them with his smile that had not been seen much lately.

"That is a good thought, Julian," said Marcus. "But you know how the men will feel about it. They will oppose having women in our meetings. Yet Madame Tillemont and certainly Regina know as much if not more than any of them."

"They will have to accustom themselves to the new order of business," said Julian decisively, throwing back his head. His green eyes flashed. "If they say anything, I shall tell them I let my cousin cheat me for years—until Regina discovered the matter. Aren't women shrewd housewives? Don't many of them manage the books for their husbands? Are they not shopkeepers and managers of taverns when their husbands are away? It is time we recognized the fact!"

"Here, here!" said Eric, pounding the desk before him. When they all looked at him in surprise, he added sheepishly, "That is what they do in the British parliament when one agrees with the speaker."

Marcus leaned over and pounded also. "Here, here," he said solemnly, and they all began to laugh.

Claude returned to Verlaine on Saturday evening. He entered the château about six in the evening, ready for cocktails and armed with an array of excuses for being gone eleven days rather than seven.

Julian had been forewarned by Joseph, Eric's valet. He had come down early, and so did Regina. "I dislike doing this on the weekend, but I cannot have him go into the study, or start to work again," he said gravely.

She nodded. "I am glad the books and ledgers are all packed up and safely away," she said.

Footmen had brought down three small trunks from the attics, and they had packed away the workbooks and ledgers. The trunks were locked in Julian's dressing room, awaiting the accountant from Paris who had been sent for at once from a reputable firm Julian had dealt with before. They did his bank accounts, and had rendered a statement to Regina's father when marriage between them had been suggested.

Regina wondered how Claude had managed to remain out of their reckoning. Julian had explained that his Verlaine accounts and his family accounts had been kept separately, and only his family accounts had been audited. He had thought the Verlaine accounts contained only debts.

"And to think of those debts piled high, the notes I held, and the high interest I had to pay—when all the time Claude was taking funds," said Julian bitterly.

Regina had added in her mind, "And to think you might not have been *driven* to marrying me!" but she did not say it.

They had been close these past nights; she did not want to rend the delicate fabric of their lives together. They had started badly enough.

"Claude, I wish you to come to the study with me."

Julian stood stern and tall near the doorway. His mother had not yet come down; Regina was grateful for that. Thérèse looked with some excitement from Claude to Julian. Marcus was on his feet.

"Without a drink? Julian, do not drive me to the books tonight!" Claude laughed and turned to the small silver trolley of drinks.

"You will think better without a drink," Julian said. "Come, Claude. And Marcus, Regina, and Eric, you will come also."

Claude opened his handsome eyes wide. "Come now, what is this? Has Marcus been complaining about his men?

Oh, let it wait until tomorrow, Julian! I am weary from traveling."

"Now, if you will, Claude." Julian held the door open. Regina went out first, toward the study. Marcus waited for the other two men, something in the manner of a constable guarding his prisoner, thought Regina.

Regina had wanted to be present. She was secretly afraid that Julian would be soft with Claude or weaken in the face of his denials. After all, Julian did not know finances, he admitted that. She was relieved that Julian wanted her and Marcus to be present.

In her violet muslin gown, with the deeper purple ribbons at her waist and in her hair, she walked into the now-familiar study and sat down near the desk. The room had been swept clear of workbooks and ledgers. Eric had taken them to his room to enter figures from Julian's fresh workbook into the new ledger.

Claude looked about in confusion. The cupboard doors hung loosely; two were opened showing the locks had been forced.

"Robbery?" he gasped. "Are the wages missing? The wage envelopes? How much was taken?"

"No robbery, Claude. Sit down." Julian took a seat at the desk to which Claude had headed automatically, and indicated another chair. Behind the desk he eyed Claude steadily, and the man shifted uneasily in his chair.

"What is this? I hope you realize I've had a long journey from Paris today, rushing back to be ready for work tomorrow," Claude began petulantly. "I suppose Marcus has made some fool complaint—"

"No. Not a fool complaint. We have discovered, Claude, that you have been embezzling funds from Verlaine for many years." The words dropped into the silence of the somber brown study.

Claude's face turned red, then the blood drained from it, leaving him a greenish color under his tan. "What—are you—saying? Who dares to accuse me?"

"We all do," said Julian. "We have been working on the ledgers, comparing them with my workbooks. Not only have you cheated Verlaine, taking more than one hundred thousand dollars from the estate over the years, but you have—"

"Dollars?" repeated Claude, and turned to look at Regina. "So? It is your work! You would snoop and pry, you bitch! I should have known you would make trouble!"

Marcus leaped from his chair as though he would strangle Claude. Julian had stood too, but he had more control. "Enough! Do not dare speak to my wife like that! I repeat, not only have you cheated Verlaine. You have dared to cheat the men who work for Verlaine, who trust Verlaine. You are a disgrace to our name."

Claude flopped back in his chair. "So? What do you plan to do about it?" He shrugged. "Let all the world know?"

"I think the world already knows about you, Claude," said Julian slowly. "Only I had blind trust in you, trust you betrayed more than once. This is the final blow to me. You will go."

"Go? Where? This is my home, after all!" Claude grinned, crossing his legs. "You want the world to know— *everything?*"

"By God, you have the gall—" Marcus sputtered, outraged. "How dare you—"

"Enough," said Julian. "I am head of Verlaine. I will handle this. Claude, you will leave Verlaine tomorrow, never to return. You have money to live on—"

"No, I don't. I have spent it," said Claude, turning sullen. "Your meager salary—"

"And the amounts you took?" Julian asked.

"Spent," he said, his eyes gleaming under his half-closed lids. "I had a splendid time with it!"

Marcus looked as though he would like nothing so much as to put his hands around Claude's throat. Eric listened, his eyes shining with the excitement. Regina felt a cold disgust.

Julian sat down again and moved a pencil slowly on the desk. "Very well. I will send you a small allowance twice a year, enough to live on modestly," he said quietly. "Because you are family, because Father would have wished it, in memory of your father. But no more. You will never return to Verlaine. You will move out all your possessions tomorrow. And I will personally see to it that you do not take possessions which belong to Verlaine. That small lodge will be empty and you will be gone by noon. That is all, Claude."

"Oh, no it isn't!" raged Claude, jumping up. "I have

some rights. I worked for you and your father for years, slaving here—"

"Slaving? You scarcely worked a full day any day of the year," said Julian dryly. "No, Claude. By rights I should take from you the diamonds you wear. And those sapphires you bought last winter. Are those the men's Christmas bonuses which you stole? We owe you *nothing*."

"You pompous fool!" Claude snarled, all charm gone. His face twisted with rage as he leaned on the chair back and pointed at Regina. "And it's your doing, you filthy bitch! Snooping and prying around! Well, you haven't heard the last of me! By God, I'll have my revenge!"

"That is enough! Go!" Julian stood and went to the door, holding it open. Marcus followed, as though to push Claude out.

Claude said something in French that must have been filthy. Fortunately for Regina, her vocabulary did not include the words. Eric's eyes opened wide, and he gasped. It was the last straw for Marcus. He took Claude by the coat collar and pushed him out.

Claude screamed back, "I'll get you for this! All of you! You will be sorry—you will be sorry!"

Marcus rushed him out to the courtyard and into his carriage. He ordered the groom to drive him to the lodge. Then Julian sent two footmen after him to help him pack. "And make sure he takes no vases, no paintings, no valuables with him. I will come later to make sure. Leave all trunks and valises open for my inspection."

It was a silent dinner. Julian seemed drained, shaken by the disagreeable scene with Claude. Regina felt rather sick herself. She did not know what more Claude could do to them, but she kept remembering his twisted ugly face as he had pointed at her.

The Dowager chatted lightly, eyeing them keenly. Thérèse was subdued, but kept close to Marcus, catching hold of his hand from time to time.

After dinner, Julian went to Claude's lodge and did not return until midnight. The next day, Regina heard that Claude had packed and left that night, after an inspection sternly carried out by Julian to make sure he had taken no Verlaine treasures with him. Julian had locked up the lodge after him.

* * *

The meeting of the *vignerons* was scheduled for two o'clock on Sunday afternoon. Regina wondered if Julian would continue with it, he seemed so weary and disheartened. But he did.

The company assembled in the gentlemen's drawing room. Madame Tillemont came in somewhat timidly, at Regina's insistence, and Regina and she sat on a sofa near the door. The men eyed them curiously and made small talk for a time.

Then Julian sat down at a small desk. "I believe everyone is here now. We shall begin."

"The ladies will wish to withdraw." Monsieur Feuillet smiled, his gray eyes cool as usual.

"No, they do not," said Julian definitely. He seemed changed somehow, calmer and more assured than ever. Regina studied him. His face is harder, she thought. She hoped he would not be embittered by Claude and the embezzling.

"But—ladies in a business discussion?" Monsieur Feuillet waved his hands expressively. "It will tire their minds! Let them withdraw to their embroidery, Monsieur le Baron."

"No, Monsieur Feuillet," Julian said. "Before we begin to speak of the cooperatives, I have a small announcement to make. As you may have heard, it has been discovered that my cousin, Claude Herriot, has been embezzling funds from Verlaine for many years. I have dismissed him. He has left and will never return to Verlaine. And the person who discovered this and worked hard to win the confidence of our people, to find the errors in the books, was my wife, Regina, of whom I am very proud."

All turned to stare at Regina, who blushed. She put her hands to her cheeks.

Julian continued. "I am most unhappy about this, that a man in whom I put such trust has betrayed all of us here. Yet I am proud of my wife, and of my brother Eric, and my brother-in-law, Marcus Bazaine, who worked tirelessly to uncover Claude's deception and prove to me what he had done. I feel that Regina has earned the right to remain here. Besides—" and he sent a beautiful smile toward her—"I feel that she probably knows more about banking than any of us! Her father has taught her much."

There were murmurs and whispers and frowns of displeasure. Julian waited serenely until the talk calmed down.

"As for Madame Tillemont, she is an eminent *vigneron,* and as a property owner, she certainly has the right to help decide what is to be done with her lands. So we will begin with the report of Madame Tillemont. She has heard from many cooperatives, and will share her findings with us at this time. Madame Tillemont, you have the floor."

The good Madame Tillemont cast a startled look at the faded Persian rugs. Regina whispered to her, "That means it is your turn to speak!"

"Oh—*oui,* Madame. *Merci!* Well, gentlemen and Madame la Baronne, I wish to make this report. From the various letters sent to me, I have compiled a list of the important elements in a good working cooperative."

A little breathlessly, her old hands shaking a bit, she went through her information, a model of conciseness and order, Regina thought proudly. The men listened, heads cocked a little dubiously, and looked at the letters she had brought along.

Then Julian said, "Thank you, Madame, for the excellent work. You will follow up the suggestions of the gentleman from Denmark, and continue to correspond with him, since he is so kind with his advice. Perhaps we could invite him to come here when we are a little further along, to give us the benefit of his counsel."

There was a strong murmur of approval. Madame Tillemont sank back in the sofa. Her hand squeezed Regina's.

Then Julian motioned to Marcus. "My brother-in-law has made a study of the banks involved in cooperatives. He will make the report that was assigned to me—which I was too busy to pursue. I have asked Marcus to continue his work, as he is much interested in this project and has studied cooperatives for several years."

Again, there was a mumbling of surprise at this gracious speech from Julian. They all knew how he had treated Marcus; indeed, they themselves had thought little of the husky young farmer in the past. But they listened respectfully as Marcus stood up and gave a brief report on the banks.

Two others spoke after Marcus, and three said they had not completed their work. When the meeting was opened for discussion, there was spirited, eager discussion of the best ways to proceed.

"I believe," said Marcus, standing again, "that it would be well to go ahead with one project at once. I understand that several of you are planning to buy oak casks before the harvest. I have heard of a place where we can buy one thousand casks for a lower price—good material, mind you. If we go together to purchase them and send wagons together to pick them up, we will all save money. Verlaine needs at least two hundred. Do any of the rest of you wish to buy some with us?"

"We need two hundred fifty," said Oscar Carnot thoughtfully. "But have you examined the casks? We want the best quality. Just because they are cheap is no reason to purchase them."

"They are well made," said Marcus slowly, and looked to Julian, who nodded. "I will go and look at them and perhaps one or two of you will come with me to examine the casks, before we order them?"

"My son will go with you," said Monsieur Gustave Carnot.

"And I would like to go," said the cautious Monsieur Feuillet. "I shall need five hundred, and I want to be sure they are good ones. What if we need more than one thousand?"

"Then we order as many as we need," said Julian. "The more we order, the better the price, especially since they will not have to deliver, as Marcus said. It saves them money if we go to pick them up. And we have the wagons and the workers."

"But who will pay for so many? I order and have my broker advance me the money," said Monsieur Mangin.

Julian looked at Regina, who nodded firmly. Regina spoke up. "Verlaine will pay for them this time. Later a cooperative would have its own funds to pay for them. The price we pay is the price we charge—no discounts, no higher price. It is not a chance for profit among us; it is to buy at the best price for the highest quality. That is what an organization like this is meant to do."

Monsieur Mangin drew in his lip as Regina spoke out so boldly in the meeting. Monsieur Feuillet gave her a cool look. Only Madame Tillemont nodded in agreement, and Julian smiled at her.

"Madame speaks truly," Oscar Carnot said at length. "It will take us a time to comprehend all we can do with this cooperative. Should we not send for a lawyer from Paris, to begin arranging formal agreements?"

"Not so fast, not so fast," said Monsieur Feuillet. "I wish to buy the oak casks this way, if they are good. However, I am not ready to sign contracts! Not until I know much more."

"That is wise, Monsieur Feuillet," said Regina. "None of us should sign until we have explored all aspects of this matter. We do not want to go blindly into business agreements. That would be unwise. Let us continue to explore matters. However, I do think we should consider soon the matter of having one broker to handle all our wines."

This caused argument and much discussion. It was late before the meeting broke up, but it was with amiability and good feeling. Oscar Carnot had reported that a lawyer he had consulted with had strongly advised them to go ahead, and would investigate the reputations and business abilities of various brokers. He expected to have a full report in two weeks.

"That was a good meeting," Julian said later that evening, as they relaxed in the rose drawing room. The tired lines were smoothing out of his bronzed face. "Regina, you spoke well. I am glad you were not offended by their comments. It will take us French farmers a bit of a time to accustom ourselves to wisdom in business matters coming from ladies—especially one so lovely as yourself!"

"Yes, they will be slow to change their ways," Marcus agreed. "Yet I know each depends on his wife for advice. And many a farmer has his wife keep the books, when she has a smarter head for figures than himself. It is the speaking up in public that bothers them. Well, why not? Why not speak in public as they speak in private?"

Julian nodded, giving Marcus a long grave look, as though revising his opinions of the man.

"Well, now, my curiosity has not been satisfied," said Aunt Agnes over her embroidery. She smoothed her neat blue dress. "What happened to Claude? Why did he leave in such haste?"

Julian explained quietly, and they listened. The Dowager expressed horror and shock, but Aunt Agnes just shook her head. "He spent so much, I wondered where he got the money," said the spinster. "He was either betting on the horses and being very lucky, or getting the money from someone."

"He has such charming manners." The Dowager sighed over her needlework. "However, one heard rumors about him."

Julian shot her a look, and she said no more. Thérèse slipped her hand contentedly into her husband's and said, "Well, I for one am glad he has gone. He could say such spiteful things with a smile, I quite longed to wipe his smirk off his face with a cream puff!"

"A cream puff, my dear?" said Marcus, as though shocked. "No, no, quite too good for him! I had other—stuff—in mind!"

Eric chuckled. He had joined them again, eagerly, his face flushed with pleasure. "Well, perhaps now no one will think I am such an invalid and idiot that I can do nothing for Verlaine! He made me angry!"

"Dear boy, did he? Then I am glad he has departed," said the Dowager fondly.

And that seemed to sum up how they all felt.

CHAPTER EIGHTEEN

Eric had taken over the bookkeeping and began to work long hours in the study. The family and servants became accustomed to seeing the young man sitting in his wheelchair in the large room, bent over the books, comparing the notes in Julian's neat handwriting with the ledger accounts.

Julian worried about him. At breakfast one morning, he said to Regina, "He's working too hard. I shall have the doctor come to see him, and if it is too much for him, he must stop. I will not have his health on my conscience."

Regina winced. She too worried about Eric. But he was so much brighter and happier, wasn't it worth the risk? She did not say that to Julian.

"I will watch over him. I work with him daily, Julian. If I see him becoming weary, I will find some reason for him to stop. I promise you."

Julian put his arm gently about her waist and drew her to him. "I worry just as much about you, my dear. You are also working hard, and I had meant for you to enjoy Verlaine and live a happy life here."

Regina was more sure of her ground there. "Oh, Julian, I would be bored with nothing to do! I was raised to work for a living! That probably sounds like a—like a peasant! But my father didn't hold with idleness; he felt it made one seek out foolish pleasures and squander the rich life God meant for us to have on earth."

Julian listened to her thoughtfully, then nodded. "I think he was right. I know many people think I am mad—or at the very least undignified—to work in the fields. Yet I enjoy it, working under the beautiful sky in the light of the sun, holding the vines in my hands, seeing the grapes that I have helped to graft and grow. When the grapes are harvested and I see the rich bulk of them slide into the presses, I feel like bursting with pride. And when I drink the wine I helped to make, the taste is very sweet indeed."

Regina smiled at him tenderly. How Julian did love his

grapes! "I know, Julian. Well, all of us feel that way here about work. Even your mother wishes to feel useful, though she could easily rest and do nothing the remainder of her days. Still she works at the needlepoint for the chair covers and helps the maids measure the lengths of velvet and satin for the sofas and other chairs."

"She feels, since you came, that she may relax and do whatever work she pleases. Before, she worried too much over the household." He bent and kissed her cheek, his lips lingering on the rose-petal softness. "That is due to you, Regina, that she no longer worries, and her sleep is good, she tells me. You and Thérèse manage everything between you."

His words of praise were as sweet to her as his wines were to him. She rested against him for a moment, and he held her more tightly; they were much closer now, emotionally and mentally, than they had ever been.

She felt a part of Verlaine. She had worked here, she had helped save Verlaine from Claude, who would surely have bankrupted them and forced them to sell out. If Julian had not married her, Claude might have gotten his hands on most of the rest of the money.

"Well—I must go back to the fields, my dear," Julian said reluctantly. He left the breakfast room with a smile and wave for her.

She went thoughtfully to the study. Eric and the auditor from Paris were already working there, separately yet companionably. The older man was not only going over the old accounts and making note of the sums that Claude had taken; he was also setting up the new books for Eric, showing him double-entry bookkeeping, explaining the finer points of the work. Regina wanted to listen to them, work with them, and learn all she could. She found her father's methods were excellent, and this was a refresher course for her in accounting.

She left them after a while and went out for a ride in the village. After an hour of good riding, she stopped at the tavern, where the boy took her mare and gave her a rubdown. Regina went into the tavern and was greeted by Madame Galande with a beaming smile.

"Ah, Madame la Baronne, you honor us again!"

"*Bonjour*, Madame Galande. How are you today?"

"Very well, I thank you. All goes well?"

All the village knew about Claude, and many were frank in expressing their approval that he had departed. The wages had been raised, a bonus had been given for good work, and thanks expressed by Julian to his men, and Marcus to his, for their many years of faithful service.

"All goes well, thank you," Regina answered. She sat down at the well-scrubbed pine table. Monsieur Galande brought over a cool lime drink without being asked. She smiled her thanks. Madame Galande sat down to chat with her.

After exchanging news, Madame Galande then told Regina a few of her concerns. A baby was due, and the husband was an idler and drunkard. Everyone was worried. Could Monsieur Marcus, who was so sensible and practical, speak to him? As for the young mother-to-be, if Madame la Baronne thought best, several would help to make clothes for the little one, and a cradle.

Regina took out her small pad and pencil, which went everywhere with her now, wrote down the names and "baby" beside them. They talked about who would make the cradle and sew the small garments. The cloth would be available to them from the general store, and the bill would go to Verlaine. That was understood.

Then there was an old woman whose husband had recently died. She mourned too much, she should have work to do, said Madame Galande.

"For work and being useful makes one's heart lighter, no, Madame la Baronne? I myself feel better if I can scrub a floor and take out my anger on the poor pine!" And she laughed heartily.

"Yes, indeed, work is a salvation," said Regina thoughtfully. "Let me see. What work can she do?"

"She sews well, Madame. Her stitches are so tiny one can scarcely see them."

"Good. That is the solution. More materials have come from Paris to replace the worn ones at Verlaine. I will ask her to come and help, and tell her she is much needed, not only to sew, but to help teach the new maids how to sew those fine stitches."

"Ah—*bon, bon!*" Madame Galande beamed at that.

Together they went to see the poor widow, and Regina

asked her to help out at Verlaine. She brightened amazingly and called down blessings on their heads as they departed.

Regina returned home before luncheon and paused to
look into the study before going up to her room to change.
She was worried about Eric. If anything happened to him,
Julian would be terribly upset.

She was relieved to find him listening alertly to some
story the auditor was telling, of how he had uncovered a
very clever embezzlement in Paris. She listened also, then
interrupted their work.

"Now it is time for lunch, and Eric must rest for two
hours before coming back to work," she said with a smile.

"Oh, Regina, but I am enjoying this so much!" he protested.

"I know. But you can't play all the time," she said with
pretended severity. "You must rest. Eric, please do as the
doctor asked."

"Very well, I will. But I will be back here at three, Monsieur," he said to the auditor.

"Fine. We will continue with the lesson about balances,"
the older man said.

Eric wheeled himself away.

"He is so eager to work and please his brother," the auditor said gently. "Do not worry about him, Madame. He is
useful, he told me, for the first time in his life. That is the
best medicine he can have."

"I know. The change in him is amazing. But I do not
want to jeopardize his health. If he collapses—" Regina
shuddered.

"He has a good mind, an excellent mind," said the auditor. "It is a pity—it was an illness in childhood, I believe?"

"Yes, a serious fever, and it left him like this. But he has
kept up his reading and studies."

"He is a good man. I will teach him to the best of my
ability. And I believe you know much about bookkeeping,
Madame, and can continue to help him when I depart."

"We can both learn from you," she said.

He bowed, and she left the room. She changed to a
practical dark-blue dress with white trim, for this afternoon
she wanted to oversee the making of the draperies. The two
carriages conveying Claude to Paris had returned laden

with goods from Monsieur Silver. Thérèse and the footmen
had unpacked it joyously.

What glorious silver fabrics, what elegant satin brocades,
what lush amber velvets for the men's drawing room. Regina finally had the chance to look over the materials that
afternoon. The maids spread them out, reverently unwrap-
ping them from the fine China papers.

Thérèse stroked her work-worn hand over the velvets.
"Ah, Regina, what wonderful colors," she said softly. "The
drab snuff browns will be taken away, and we will put in
these lovely amber colors. It will make all the difference."

"Ah, yes, I like lighter glowing colors, the jewel colors,"
said Regina. "I love color about me, the bright colors of
stained glass windows, of sunlight and the fields, the sky
and the trees. Dark colors depress me so."

Thérèse looked at her with more understanding. "Yes,
you are like the rainbow," she said unexpectedly. "All
about you, you brighten the room, the house, all of us.
When you laugh, we all smile. I notice that Julian smiles so
much more than he did before."

Regina was deeply touched by her remark. Thérèsa was
shy under her roughness. It must have cost her an effort to
say this.

"Thank you, Thérèse. Why—I must have forgotten also
to tell you—" And she spoke of the widow who would
come to help with the sewing.

"Ah, that is good of you. She will feel better, I am sure,
to have some income from the sewing, and to feel useful.
Bon. I will have her to train the new maids also. Ah, look
at this fabric, Regina!" And she held up the end of a length
of blue cut velvet. "Magnificent!"

"Oh, yes, that is for the music room," said Regina. "I
thought blue velvet for the draperies and the chairs there,
and Monsieur Silver promised to send a rug of the right
size, in lighter blue and silver. Did that come?"

"Oh, yes, but I thought that was for the dining room,"
said Thérèse, indicating a roll of carpet at the side of the
room. Regina went over to inspect it.

"I wanted to leave the grand dining room in its silver
and white, and the small dining room in gold and white.
Monsieur Silver is looking for the right fabrics and rugs for
us, but he warned it might be some time before he found
them. He is sending to the Orient for them."

"The Orient," whispered Thérèse, clasping her hands. "How thrilling! Rugs and fabrics from the Orient—in silver and gold!"

Regina smiled. "I think it will be beautiful. I do hope Maman will not mind the changes. I am keeping much the same color schemes, for I think they are beautiful."

"Oh, you could stand on your head in the courtyard and talk Arabic to the duke when he comes, and Maman would think you can do no wrong." Thérèse grinned. "You are keeping Julian happy, and the house of Verlaine has never gone so smoothly. She is contented."

Regina laughed with her, then went to inspect some crates a footman was prying open. "What in the world is this? I don't recall ordering any lamps."

He took out one reverently, cautiously. "Monsieur Silver sent a note with it, Madame," he said, handing it to her as he continued to remove all the papers covering the lamp. The crate held still another lamp, and he dived in for that.

Regina opened the note and read it rapidly. Monsieur Silver's writing was angular and stiff, but very clear.

My dear Madame la Baronne,

   With pride and deep respect I send to you the enclosed lamps of silver. One of our merchants located them in a Middle Eastern country. They are so lovely, I thought of you and of Verlaine at once. Please forgive me for going beyond your orders and instructions. However, I could picture these lamps in your music room, with the rug which I have sent in this shipment to you.

   Madame, I am also looking for some porcelain vases from China of their special famille rose for you, and hope to have them soon. Also I have given much thought to the room for your young brother. May I suggest colors of creamy yellow and amber brown? I enclose samples in a packet for your inspection.

   I hold myself in readiness for any orders you may choose to entrust to me.

                                   Your humble merchant,

                                   Judah Silver.

"How lovely," Regina said, closing the note. The footman was holding up the large silver lamp for their inspection, turning it about in his strong hands. It was huge, and the other was its twin. The overall design was of heavy simplicity, with light scroll work and floral pattern.

"They must cost a fortune!" Thérèse gulped, then swallowed any further remark, looking guiltily toward Regina.

However, Julian said much the same thing later. "They are magnificent, Regina. But I fear—that is, until the accounts are in order and the harvest in—" He paused unhappily, fingering one of the silver lamps.

"I would like to keep them, Julian. May I pay for them myself?" she added rather timidly. She had not told him she was paying for all the new fabrics and rugs out of her bank account. She hoped he did not find out for a long time, perhaps never. "I want so much to make Verlaine as beautiful as I know it can be."

He set down the lamp carefully on the small rosewood table and smiled at her. "I find it difficult to refuse you anything, my dear. I just wish you would not be so generous. It makes it very awkward for me."

"I don't wish to make things awkward for you, Julian! Rather, I want to make things smooth!" she said passionately, clasping her hands together in earnest. "You work so very hard, you have such little pleasure. If some money can smooth the way, why not let it? Do you mind very much—what I am doing?"

He thought about it seriously, studying her appealing face. "My pride minds," he said finally, gently. "But not so much that I shall stop you. I can see how much you are enjoying it and when I remember your early years, and the hardships you endured so gallantly, then I think you too deserve some beautiful objects around you now. No, do what you will, Regina, and enjoy it."

"Oh, Julian—thank you!" she told him gratefully and went over to lift her face for his kiss. He held her waist with his bronzed hands and kissed her cheek, then her lips, lingeringly. Finally she drew back, a little breathless, her face glowing. "Julian—why is this music room unused?"

"Oh, we used to use it. But Thérèse says the piano in the rose drawing room is in better tune. And I never play the cello anymore. So the room is not used. Why, would you like to begin to use it again?"

"You played the cello? Oh, Julian, I used to play the fiddle!"

"The fiddle? What is that?"

"An old name in America for the violin. I would love to try it again."

"I will send to Paris for a fine violin for you, and a cello for me, and we will play again, eh? That will be splendid! We must make time for practice, especially in the winter months," he added. "After the harvest."

But when Thérèse heard of the plans, she insisted they send at once for the fiddle and the cello. "I should like so much for us to have a little music group again. Wouldn't it be lovely, Maman?"

"I adore music," the Dowager agreed. "Do what you will."

Julian came to Regina's room as Ninette was brushing her hair that night. The maid bowed and left. Regina picked up the brush to continue the strokes, as Julian sat down in a nearby chair to stretch his legs and watch.

He gazed at her, in her ivory silk dressing gown, showing bits of the lace nightdress beneath. "You know, Regina, you are like one of those magic boxes in the fairy stories," he said abruptly, as though continuing a thought he had had.

"A magic box? What do you mean?" She gazed into the mirror at his image, in the light-brown silk robe, leaning back in the rose satin chair. Her room had been completed and looked so fresh and pretty, with its rose draperies, blue sofa, the little sandalwood tables and dressing table with the Sèvres inlaid panels of flowered porcelain.

"Why, one opens the box and finds a lovely woman. Then one lifts her out and finds another surprise, that she is intelligent as well." He was beginning to smile, with a twinkle in his green eyes. "One unwraps another layer and finds she loves music. One uncovers the next layer and finds she can decorate and choose fabrics for an entire home. Next, she is compassionate and takes the interests of all people to her warm heart. Next—she plays the violin! What next, Regina? No, do not tell me, I enjoy the surprises!" He flung back his handsome brown head and laughed with pleasure.

"You enjoy teasing me, Julian, I think," she said severely, her face warm. She rose and put the brush down.

Whenever he came into her bedroom, her body felt warmer with anticipation, her heart beat faster, she felt all soft and eager. What it was to be in love! And he could be such a gentle yet demanding lover.

As she moved to pass him, he reached out a long arm and wrapped it around her waist, drawing her back to him.

"Julian!"

He pulled her down to his lap and against his hard body. "Umm?" he said, nuzzling against the ivory of her throat. "You smell good. I like your perfume."

"It is some you bought for me in Paris."

"I have excellent taste, Madame," he said solemnly, in a fake accent that made her giggle. "Ah, Madame, how good you taste! I like your perfume, I like your throat, it is so smooth, ummm. I like your round arms." And he kissed up from her wrist to her elbow under the arm of the robe.

She leaned against him, her eyes half closed with desire. "Does Monsieur have good intentions?" she teased.

"Oh, Madame, the best! I intend to make you very happy tonight! The happiest woman in the world! I will touch you—so—" His hand slid under the robe and cupped one of her round breasts tenderly. Then he opened the robe and bent his head to press his lips against the thin lace covering her breasts. She caught her breath at the delicious feeling that heated her body.

His hand slid down over her waist, down to her thighs, to stroke her over and over, down to her knees, and up again. Leaning against him, she felt her heartbeat increase and the quickened pounding of Julian's. She put her hand inside his robe and stroked the curling hair from his throat to his waist.

"Does—Monsieur—like that?"

"So much—Madame—that we shall soon be in bed."

She giggled, and he kissed the sound from her lips, and their mouths opened and clung hotly. Her hand went on moving shyly over his bared body under the robe. She liked to feel him, the hard chest, the ribs and the waist, the little curl of the hair on him, the muscular arms and shoulders. He opened the belt of the robe to give her free access to him, and she sat on his knees and played with his body as he touched hers.

His eyes were watching her intently, his mouth had a half smile of desire and delight. She rubbed her cheek

against his hard bare shoulder and kissed his throat. He
held her more closely, his hand going through her thick
chestnut curls, to clasp the nape of her neck.

He lifted the hem of her robe and that of her nightdress.
"Regina—I want you a different way," he whispered.

"What?" She wakened from her dreaming daze, as he
lifted and turned her to face him. "Julian—"

"Don't be alarmed, my dear. I have been wanting to try
this, love." And he lifted her hips and set her on his thighs,
carefully, so that his manhood was against her soft body.
He drew her closer, so she felt every bit of him against her,
and he kissed her throat and down her opened nightdress
to her breasts.

She felt so hot, so melting hot, she was feeling boneless
and limp when he raised her and set her down again. She
gasped as she felt him enter her slowly. She clutched him
about the neck and pressed her lips frantically against his
hard brown throat.

"All right?" he murmured.

She managed to nod. He lifted her up and down, gently,
not to hurt her. She felt the passion rising in him, making
him rock-hard.

"There—enough for now," he said, and drew back, looking into her glazed eyes. He smiled at her. "And now to
bed—for more delights, my adored one."

He moved with her to the bed. The lights were still lit;
he made no attempt to blow out the candles or turn down
the lamp. He had removed her robe, the nightdress followed, and he gazed at her white body with pleasure, trac-
ing the curved outlines of it with lips and hands.

She was so deliriously limp that he had no trouble coming into her again. He moved slowly back and forth, then
faster, and faster, and she gave a moan of sheer frustration
when he drew out.

"Wait, my darling," he whispered, and came to her
again, more firmly, swiftly. It set her off, like Roman candles lit inside her, so she convulsed wildly, out of control.
She scarcely knew what went on, the pleasure was so intense. Wave after wave of excitement shivered through her
body. She groaned as he moved away, and pulled him
back, and again she felt the pleasure, more softly this time.

Her body was wet when she finally came to herself.
Julian was drawing up the sheet and blanket about them,

against the cool night air. He snuggled down against her, pressed his lips sleepily to her breast.

"Oh, darling, you are so wonderful, so giving, so loving. How I adore you."

She could not speak, and soon he slept. She lay awake a little while. What if she conceived a child? She had never been so happy in her life. If a child was born of this, he would be a love-child, conceived in the greatest joy she had ever known.

She wanted Julian's child. She wanted to give him a son, for she knew he craved a child. His tenderness with little Jeannette and his wistfulness when he spoke of the many generations that had occupied Verlaine over the centuries spoke of that.

And if that child had been conceived tonight, Regina thought it would be the most perfect way for a child to come that could ever be. A child of this night—this beautiful night when Julian had loved her over and over— And she had responded, because she had wanted to, because she loved him, wanted him, adored him.

She slept, with a smile on her lips.

CHAPTER NINETEEN

Regina's brother George had written a letter saying that they might come to visit Verlaine. Nevertheless, it was a shock to receive a note from him written in Paris, saying, "We have arrived! How do we get to Verlaine?"

Regina flew right up in the air in her excitement. She ran around, quite distracted, until Julian came home from the fields.

"Look, Julian—George and 'the others,' he says, are in Paris! Oh, my heavens! I never dreamed he would come— and who do you think he brought with him? He doesn't even say! For a hard-headed banker, he is very vague!"

She was laughing and crying. Julian hugged her and examined the note. "We must send the carriages for them at once. Ah, they are at the Ritz. Good. Write a note quickly, Regina, and urge them to come to us at once. Do we have rooms ready?"

"They can be prepared quickly. Oh, I do wish I had had time to refashion the guest rooms! I never thought they would come— Oh, do you suppose Sally came, and Bernard? And Betsy? And perhaps Papa? No, for if Papa had come, he would have written. Still, he might have—"

Regina sat down to write a note, adding that if they wished to remain in Paris for a time, they should keep the carriages and come when they would. "However, as it is August, it is warm in Paris, Julian says. You may wish to come to us at once. Verlaine has thick stone walls and is quite cool and comfortable. And there is a river where George can go fishing!"

They came within three days, arriving late in the evening, piling out of the carriages, all talking at once. "Riding in such luxury, Regina! My dear—and four outriders in uniform! We felt so elegant!" This was Betsy, George's wife, rather plump after her two children.

"And the Ritz was so elegant we almost hated to leave, except it was so hot, and everybody had left Paris!" This was Sally, Bernard's wife, blonde and chattering, eyeing everything with a wide curious blue stare.

"Did you bring the children?" Regina asked, peering after them at the carriages in the flare-lit courtyard.

"The children? Absolutely not!" said Betsy. "This is a holiday from the children." Her mouth went down sullenly. "Always screaming and making so much noise, and demanding—how they demand everything!"

Julian was greeting the men, shaking their hands. None of them knew much French, so Julian used his English, which he rarely spoke now that Regina's French had improved. He directed the footmen with the many trunks and valises and hatboxes up to the guest rooms.

Regina went with her relatives to make sure they were comfortable. One room had been Claude's, and was now thoroughly cleaned out. Another was a round tower room, which she gave to Sally and Bernard, thinking it would please them. She wished again she had had time to refurbish the draperies and chairs and beds. But there were fresh linens on the beds, smelling of lavender, and beautiful flowers in the Chinese vases on the rosewood table.

The guests washed, changed, and came downstairs to the rose drawing room. Regina had loaned them Ninette and one of the men trained as a valet.

"But, my dear, no toilets, no hot running water," Betsy drawled in dismay. "Haven't you modernized the place yet?"

Regina could not think what to say. Julian said smoothly, "Not yet. We hope to do it one day. However, it will be a task, bringing lines and pipes up these thick stone walls. We must bring in someone from Paris."

The dinner was served in the grand silver dining room. The visitors were weary but ate heartily of the many courses. They retired early, promising to rise early and breakfast with Regina and Julian. However, only George appeared.

"The others are still snug in their beds." He grinned. "I can't sleep, haven't slept well since I left home. It was the same this June, when I went out to the mining camp."

"Oh, George, you did go! How was it? How is everyone?"

"I have tons of messages for you," he said, squeezing her

hand affectionately. She had not thought she would be so happy to see her brother. He was getting older, looking more than his thirty-two years. He was balding, and a fringe of reddish-gray hair circled his pate. His brown eyes seemed harder and shrewder, in the wrinkles surrounding them, but his smile was the same, as was his quiet concern for her.

"Father says you are thinking about starting a cooperative," he said to Julian.

"Yes, and I have heard you know much about them," said Julian. "We look forward to having a good talk with you, if you will not mind business in the midst of your holidays."

"Mind? Hell, I miss the business like crazy," George said frankly. "It was the girls' idea to come. Betsy said if she didn't get a vacation soon, she would leave me." He laughed heartily. Julian looked rather stunned.

Marcus and Thérèse were trying to follow the conversation in English, but looked rather puzzled as the rapid words confused them. Julian turned to them to translate.

"Perhaps this evening," Marcus said in French, "he would speak of it, and advise us on the bank? I confess I am puzzled by the many pieces of advice which conflict with each other."

Regina translated that, and George nodded happily. "Glad to do it! The gals will be fussy, but we mustn't mind. We'll go in the study and talk, if you like. Father was speaking of it before I left."

"How is Papa? And Mama?" asked Regina wistfully.

"Fine as silk," said George. "Missing you. Mama complains you don't write often enough—"

"I send a letter every month," said Regina.

"Ain't often enough." George grinned. "And she wants to hear more about dukes and kings and all that. She thinks you go to a ball twice a week and entertain royalty all the time. What a laugh!"

Regina scarcely dared look at Julian, but when she did, she found him smiling in amusement. "I fear your mother has a strange idea of us," he said mildly. "We work hard; your sister works from morning to night for us! She has redone the drawing rooms, many of the bedrooms, chosen fabrics and rugs and all. And she rides often to the village to help settle problems there. I don't know how I ever got along without her."

George squeezed Regina's hand again. "Papa will be pleased, I must say. He got the idea that maybe you were playing around all the time. He was grumbling that he thought Julian worked very little in the vineyards, and I half think he encouraged me to come and see what was what!"

Regina was indignant. "You should go to the fields with Julian! You would soon see how he works, George! Six days a week, and so tired and muddy sometimes when he comes home—"

"Do come with me," urged Julian. "If you brought a riding outfit, you might come tomorrow—"

"I'll come today! I've been wanting to get out on a horse. Got one that would hold me?" George laughed and patted his stomach ruefully. "I'll tell you, in the Rockies I almost broke the donkey's back! Couldn't get a horse up those steep slopes, so I had to put myself on a poor little gray donkey."

Marcus was following the story with fascination, straining with his limited command of English. "So, you do ride the donkey out West! I wish to hear more of this. Regina will tell us a bit, but then she stops. How much adventure you have!"

George looked pleased. "Well, we manage," he said, satisfied. "The West is still wild, you know. Ran into a party of hostiles last time out. Good thing we had our repeaters."

Regina had to translate that. "He means hostile Indians. And they had repeating rifles with them."

Julian sighed. "I wish I could stay to hear more, but I must go to the fields. It is past nine."

Marcus jumped up. "And I also. You will tell us more this evening, won't you?"

"If you like," said George. "But I must go up and change to riding gear. I'll follow you out, shall I? Regina, you change also and come along. We can have a natter while we ride."

"I'd love to." She gave her brother a bright, happy smile. Julian and Marcus hurried out while she and George went up to change.

"I'll take care of things here, Regina," Thérèse said as

Regina and George left the château. "Beef for dinner! And
I'll have a good cold luncheon for you. Return when you
will."

Regina and George did have a good talk, riding slowly
along the dry dusty paths, along the shrunken river toward
the fields. She explained how it looked in the spring and
the summer, according to Julian. "In winter, the river gets
quite huge, and iced over at times. And the château is cold,
and damp, Thérèse says. Then they light the fires in the
fireplaces and close off rooms, and we wear woolens, even
to balls. Tell Mama we do have balls, but only in the winter, most of the time, because all the *vignerons* are so busy
during the rest of the year."

"I'll make her a good story," George promised. "She
ain't a bad sort, you know, Regina. She makes Papa happy,
except when she nags him into his monkey suit for some do
he doesn't care about."

She told him about their musical evenings, and how
Julian had sent to Paris for a violin for her and a cello for
him. "And Marcus plays the flute and Thérèse the piano.
Maman does her needlepoint, and I just relax. It is so
lovely, George, you cannot imagine."

"You're happy," he said shrewdly. "That's what I came
to find out. Papa said, 'Find out if the gal is happy.' He
was a bit worried about you at first, living in a strange
country and talking a funny language and all."

"I am happy, George, and I—I love Julian. He is a fine
man, and so—very good to me." She thought of Simone,
and her face shadowed a little. Still, she did not think he
went so often recently to her château.

"Good, good. Papa will be pleased. Now, what is this
about that damn cheat Claude?"

She explained in simple terms what had happened. "Tell
Papa it is all being straightened out. But we cannot hope to
get the money back. Claude spent it. Still, there is now a
belief that Verlaine is in much better financial condition
than Julian had thought. If Claude had not taken the funds,
Verlaine would probably never have been in debt."

George listened attentively, nodding from time to time.
"And young Eric is helping out, eh? Does much good?"

"He's a tremendous help, George," she answered. "Oh,
look, here are the fields of the red grapes, George," she
pointed out proudly. "Julian has these fields of Cabernet

franc. I have tasted the 1893 wines, and they are delicious, a little sparkling, light, delicate. They have the fragrance of a violet, Julian says, and the color is a grayish pink. Cabernet franc should be very popular, if Julian is able to have a good harvest this year."

"Lord, I never thought the fields would be so large," marveled George. "Hey, there, is that Julian?"

The man waved and began to stride toward them down the slopes. "That is Julian," Regina said softly. George glanced at her face and smiled to himself.

Julian reached them and lifted Regina down from her horse. "Here are some of the fields, George," he said with pride. "Today we are watering the slopes. We must be careful to keep the soil just moist."

They went off to inspect the fields. Regina went with them for a time, but finally decided to return.

George came home with Julian in the late afternoon, raving, muddy, happy, with a dozen fish on a string in a wicker basket. He had had a glorious time. He wanted the fish for supper, so Thérèse, laughing, took them to the kitchen and asked the cook to prepare them for the guests.

Bernard was jealous. "You went out fishing without me?" he asked, as the fish were served at dinner, and George told grandly how he had caught them. "You promised to go with me! I missed the West trip, and now this—"

The Dowager intervened gently. "But all of you must go. Marcus knows the most splendid place to fish, where the carp are especially large. Then Thérèse will order for you stuffed Loire carp, garnished with mushrooms, a favorite dish here."

The guests were delighted, and Betsy asked about other regional dishes. The talk went to chicken paté and veal with peaches. The Dowager described the capon, the goose stuffed with apples, and the cheeses, which she pointed out to them, as Thérèse had ordered a large plate of them to be served with the fruit for dessert.

"There is the cream cheese from Gien, the coudrée, the Olivet cheese. They go well with the apple tarts we have this evening."

"Almost like our apple pie with cheese," approved George, munching heartily.

"Save room for the final pastries," warned Regina. Thérèse must have spent most of the day in the kitchens;

the spicy odors had greeted Regina when she went out to inspect the trays.

Footmen wheeled in a silver serving table and brought it to each person in turn, offering almond cake, honey cakes, gingerbread served hot with piles of whipped cream, and finally the pralines of almonds with sugar.

Julian had gone to the wine cellars and brought out bottles of his white wine and several of the few remaining bottles of his beloved rosé from 1893. It was poured carefully into champagne glasses.

George tasted his critically. "Excellent! Julian, you are right. This should go well in the States. Excellent taste, aroma."

Julian smiled in pleasure, but shook his head. "It will be difficult for such a delicate wine to travel well. I shall have to be satisfied with sales here in Europe, should the harvest go well."

"Not export to us? A shame," declared Bernard, drinking his last swallows with enjoyment. "Why doesn't it travel well?"

"There is too much jolting and movement in the ship for a delicate wine," Julian explained. "A hearty robust red can travel, or a sherry, or port, or brandy, of course. But a more delicate wine gets—seasick."

"Just like me," Sally said with a grimace. "The men walked the deck and shouted at the high waves but I could not endure it. Only the thought of the pleasures to come sustained me."

"It is just like that," said Julian gently. "The hearty wines travel well, the more delicate get seasick, and they never recover."

After dinner, they all went to the rose drawing room. The ladies exclaimed in pleasure at the beautiful furnishings, not just the new velvets and satins, but the rosewood tables, the paintings and portraits, the piano, the lamps of bronze and the magnificent chandelier of Austrian crystal.

"Oh, Gina, not much like the old mining camps," George joked. "Remember our battered pewter lamps?"

"They worked well, George," said Regina with a smile. "That was all that mattered then. Light enough to sew and read by, to weigh the gold on the scales, and put it into leather pouches. And Papa reading aloud from the month-old gazettes."

"Oh, do tell us about that," encouraged Thérèse, in her accented English.

Julian looked a little upset. Marcus glanced at him and said, "I think we want to talk to George and Bernard about the banking idea. George said he had some thoughts about that."

"Oh, do please tell us then," said Thérèse. "It is so—important to Verlaine."

George looked at her understandingly. "I know, Madame. Well—here it is, then," and he was about to go on.

"Wait, George, wait a few minutes," said Regina, and left the room. She hurried back to Eric's room and tapped at the closed door. He knew that guests were there, but, sensitive about his appearance, he had not met them at all.

"Come in!" The valet opened the door to her.

"Eric, I want you to come to the drawing room," she said hurriedly, disregarding deliberately the way he shrank back. "George and Bernard are going to give us advice about the banking aspect of the cooperatives. I do want you to hear first hand."

"Regina, I cannot." He indicated himself with a thin hand. "How can I go out there? They will—they will look sick at sight of me. Ladies do, you know."

"I don't, and it is important to me, Eric." She did not waste time in reassurances. "Eric, this is also important to Julian, and to Verlaine. You are going to be handling the bookkeeping and accounts. I want you to know what is going on. Please, Eric, for our sakes. Do come."

He swallowed hard, looking tired and pale. "Very well—all right," he agreed reluctantly. "But I will leave as soon as the topic is completed."

"Yes, yes, as you will," she said, and wheeled his chair out into the hall. She felt a bit guilty, as she did not want to tire him. But she felt he should come out more, to meet people, to get accustomed to being with others outside the family. This would be a good start. One day, she hoped, she would have him riding in her carriage with her! Clear to the village and beyond!

She wheeled him into the rose drawing room. Julian hurried to help her get the wheels over the rugs. Eric seemed to shrink back into his chair as curious looks were directed at him.

Regina ignored them. "This is Eric Herriot, Julian's younger brother. Eric, this is Mrs. Sally Pierce, this is Mrs. Elizabeth Pierce, only we call her Betsy. And my brothers George and Bernard."

The ladies nodded, tried politely not to show their shock at his wizened appearance. The men came over, took his hand gently and shook it, a bit uneasily.

"Eric speaks English so we can all speak English tonight," said Regina gaily, and drew Eric's chair next to her rose chair. "Now, George, you were beginning to talk about the banks. I will translate whenever necessary, just speak slowly."

"Right. I talked a long time to Father about this. And I checked around New York and Connecticut, talked to bankers who have connections with Paris banks."

He paused to collect his thoughts. Regina thought he looked much like their father that night, grave and alert, his eyes shining with interest.

"It seems to me you'll bite off more than you can chew if you go right into banking. None of you is trained in banking, so it would be a problem. Besides, you're all busy with your vineyards. Banking takes a lot of time," he said. "And it is a full-time job, not part-time. Do you know where to invest funds? What would you do if your appointed banker embezzled money, like that skunk Claude did?"

He paused again to look about. Marcus was muttering to Thérèse, who was rapidly translating the words he had not caught.

"I understand you bank in Paris," he said to Julian. Julian nodded, fingering his coffee cup absently, his gaze fixed intently on George. "Well, I hadn't realized how far Paris is. And you have a mighty nice little bank nearby in Angers. There is another one in Tours, with a good reputation. Even closer in Chinon. Right?"

Julian nodded again.

"Well, a big bank can do a lot for you," said George ponderously, declining another cup of coffee from Thérèse. "However, a small bank, preferably in your locale, can do more. Right. More. The local bank takes an interest in your crop, they know the conditions, they know you. I would go to one of them, talk frankly and see if they might

set up a special department in the bank for your cooperative. They would handle just that account separately. It
would be like your own bank, but you would have a professional man handling everything. They would invest the
money when times are good, make loans when times are
poor. And the charge need not be large. Paris is too damn
big, to my taste. Like an Indiana farmer trying to deal with
New York City."

They discussed his idea, which was something new to
them. Julian had never dealt with a local bank. He had
gone to the bank in Paris that had always handled his father's and his grandfather's accounts. "At high rates, I'll be
bound," said George shrewdly.

"I wish you could talk to the other *vignerons*," Eric said,
speaking up for the first time. "They should hear you and
be able to ask questions."

"I was going to invite them all for dinner this weekend,"
said Julian. "It went completely out of my head."

Regina smiled at him. "I'll send a footman around in the
morning, Julian, if you like."

"They should have time for a long meeting," said Marcus in French. "Why not ask them all for the afternoon,
about two o'clock or so, then remain for dinner? We have a
lot to discuss."

Regina translated hastily for her brothers. Julian was
agreeing. They went on discussing the idea, and also that of
a broker. George approved of a single broker and gave
them some intelligent ideas about hiring one in common.

"And not more than twenty-percent commission," he
said firmly. "I talked to some *vignerons*, as you call them,
in upstate New York. They never pay more than twenty,
and usually it is between ten and fifteen percent."

"Madame Tillemont will be overjoyed," Regina said.
"But would a French broker work for so little?"

"He will if he can make a profit, and he can," said
George. "I'll be bound he keeps a number of bottles for
himself and his friends. No more of that, if you take my
advice. He must account for every bottle. Keep it strictly
business. If you want to give him a case for Christmas, do
that, but make it understood that it is not his right to take
a case whenever he pleases. Your profits will fly out the
window."

"Tell that to the *vignerons*," said Thérèse vigorously, a

spark of combat flashing in her eyes. "They think it is not gentlemanly to refuse to let the broker take what he pleases. Well, better to be a shrewd farmer, I say!"

"Right you are, Thérèse," Bernard said easily, grinning approvingly at her. "Now, I understand you and Marcus play a fine tune. How about playing for us?"

Marcus was a bit nervous about playing for them, but Thérèse marched right to the piano. The Americans were different, more easygoing and familiar, but they had enjoyed her food, praised her housekeeping, and the ladies had openly admired the good manners of her daughter, Jeannette. Madame Betsy had even spent a couple hours in the nursery playing with Jeannette, saying she was the best child in the world! Thérèse was afraid of nothing tonight.

Marcus and Thérèse gave them an hour of splendid music, from Mozart to Chopin. Eric remained at Regina's side, relaxing a little. It was a start, she thought in triumph.

The *vignerons* all accepted Julian's invitation on Sunday. The carriages streamed in; both drawing rooms were full before two o'clock. Most of the men went automatically to the gentlemen's drawing room, still decorated in snuff brown but with several of the chairs and the sofa already recovered in amber velvet. Regina was secretly thankful that she had not yet ordered the wallpaper stripped. It would be done as soon as the guests left Verlaine.

The ladies went to the rose drawing room to talk. But Regina excused herself, and she and Madame Tillemont went determinedly to the gentlemen's room to listen and find out what was going on. And to her delighted surprise, Joseph wheeled in Eric and put his chair beside Regina. Several men came up to him, took his hand, and assured him of their pleasure in his presence.

"So you will handle the books for Verlaine, eh?" said the older Monsieur Carnot. "*Bon, bon.* Verlaine is safe in your hands. I hear that Claude makes merry in Paris." He frowned.

The meeting began. George got up and talked slowly in English, then Julian translated clearly for him. Not enough of the Frenchmen understood English, and George's French was very limited. Still, they got along. He told them about banking, explained the problems. "There are the taxes, the laws of the country, many involved matters. If you set up your own bank, you must take all those into account. Far better to deal with a local bank, with knowledge of these, and pay them a small fee for their services. I suggest not more than five percent of the gross income, less if they will accept it. You realize that the larger your account with the bank is, the smaller the fee."

They discussed the broker idea, and when George advised them not to pay more than ten- to twenty-percent commission, Madame Tillemont gasped. "Did he say—twenty?" she quavered.

Regina nodded.

"I could fix the roof of the château," she said dreamily, "rebuild the stable, buy new horses—oh, *mon Dieu*!"

There were many questions. Cool Monsieur Feuillet shot several at George, who admitted he was not familiar enough with French laws of banking, and advised them to get advice from several other sources for that. But he knew his own field and persisted in advising them to go to a local bank, to hire a treasurer.

Bernard got up then and told them what he had learned of vineyard cooperatives in the United States. He had a long statement which he read, then gave to Julian to read. It was involved and complex, and the men said they must read it again and think about it.

"I will take it," offered Oscar Carnot, "and have our secretary translate it and make copies for all."

By that time, it was past six. They adjourned to the rose room for sherry and relaxation. Then, at seven, an excellent dinner was served in the silver dining room.

It was a large group. Eric had joined them, to the delight of Thérèse, who whispered to Regina. "He asked me to set a place for him! Isn't it splendid?"

"Wonderful!" replied Regina. Eric was next to Monsieur Mangin and Madame Tillemont, and was talking to them shyly. He ate little, but seemed to enjoy the stuffed carp and the steak, American style, with mushrooms. Thérèse and the cooks had outdone themselves with the desserts, trays of gorgeous puff pastries stuffed with almond paste, chocolate puddings, whipped cream, and chestnuts in cream.

They retired after dinner to the rose drawing room. To Regina's surprise, the gentlemen came with them, to drink their port and brandy. Julian smiled at her.

"George has promised to tell us of his recent adventures in the West," he said.

Madame Tillemont motioned to Eric as he wheeled himself hesitantly into the large room. "Dear boy, sit with me and tell me what they say," she begged. "My poor ears do not get the English, and I do not want to miss a word if I can help it."

Eric smiled gently at her and wheeled himself beside her. She managed his coffee cup and patted his hand from time to time in motherly fashion. Regina was able to relax and listen to her brother.

George had the floor, and he loved it. Julian stood next to him at the marble mantelpiece and translated quickly as he spoke. They talked in turn, and George's animated face turned often to Julian's thin brown one as they talked.

He told of the trip West in June, how he had found the miners working. "The gold is panning well, and recently a new vein was struck. All would be well, but the hostiles got all upset when one of their women was taken by a miner."

Julian translated, though the ladies opened their eyes in horror.

"We had an attack at the camp about three days after I arrived. The hostiles came in, war paint shining and weapons shaking at us. I got a spear thrown at me, with a message on it. Poor beggars. They told us all to get out, it was their land, and the land of their fathers, and they would fight to the death. The trouble is, they're finished," said George, his face registering his sympathy. "Most are on reservations now. These were renegades trying to revive the old days, with their Ghost Dances and what not, trying to get the young ones to join in."

He had to stop and explain his terms, but that did not faze him. "Oh, and there was Tumbleweed. Remember him, Regina? Well, he showed up, and we had a pow-wow. He talked the Indians into going away, told them where buffalo was running."

"You saw Tumbleweed! I thought he was dead," Regina cried.

"So did I. He is well over seventy, I figure, though he doesn't know his own age," said George. "Remember the blizzard and the winter we were snowed in for two months?

We ran out of meat, except for the rabbits we could catch. We ran out of cornmeal, ran out of beans. When we ran out of flour and sugar, I thought that was the end."

"But Tumbleweed came through the snow on his burro," said Regina, her eyes lighting up. "He brought us flour, sugar—I remember that beautiful box of sugar! And he had killed a deer, and we had fresh meat for the first time in nine weeks."

That really startled them. George, Bernard, and Regina vied for their attention, reminding each other of the Christmases in the snow, the shirts Regina had made for them, the year the horses froze to death. They talked about the men they had known, the tough miners, the pioneer families that had paused briefly before going on. The women and the children. The first school with four pupils. The books they read and reread to each other by the light of a single candle or lamp.

Bernard told about the time he had gone out for meat and was ashamed to return until he caught something. He had been out for a week before he ran into some friendly Indians, and they gave him buffalo meat. "So that was why you brought back buffalo!" George exclaimed. "You never did explain that! I knew you couldn't kill a buffalo all by yourself!"

It was a grand evening, thought Regina afterward. The French seemed genuinely interested in their adventures, completely fascinated by these glimpses into another world of strange wild creatures and hardships.

Sally and Betsy listened also in silence, eyes wide, as though they had never heard about this before. Perhaps they had not, Regina concluded. Well, it would not hurt these two gently bred young women to hear the stories of what their husbands had gone through as children and young men. Maybe they would appreciate them more.

It was past midnight when the carriages finally rolled away. Eric looked white with exhaustion, yet he said, "I have not enjoyed myself so much in years."

"Dear Eric," his mother said affectionately. "How much you pleased me by joining us tonight."

And Regina had been quietly satisfied with it all. Her family had fit in and had entertained the French families, and they had all enjoyed the evening, though they had been raised so differently. Julian had not seemed ashamed of her at all, in spite of her mother's warnings not to speak of her early childhood. It had been quite a lovely night.

CHAPTER TWENTY

Julian threw one big final party for his American guests. They had remained over a week and seemed to enjoy every minute of their visit.

Julian had decided to open the unused ballroom on the second floor, though it was August. The thick walls would keep the room cool, he told Regina. Tall candlesticks of silver were carried up to the room, the footmen and maids scrubbed and polished and waxed the lovely sandlewood floors.

All the *vignerons* and neighbors came to the event. Some were going away for the remainder of August, but stayed until this party, Regina heard. Several women from the village, led by Madame Galande, came to help with the cooking and serving. Monsieur Galande presided over the bar and expertly poured the wines, mixed the drinks, chose the brandy and port.

Regina wore her new gown of white silk shot with gold threads, and wound up her hair to set a diamond tiara in it. Thérèse had a blue silk, of which she was immensely proud, and she looked lovely and stately as she stood in the reception line with Regina, Julian, and Marcus.

"Now I can write to Mama," murmured Betsy, satisfied. "We have gone to a ball in the eight-hundred-year-old château! And I have danced with a baron and a marquis."

A marquis and his wife had come from a neighboring château, some distance away, the first time that summer. They were elderly, gracious, and quite sweet, thought Regina.

The ball began late in the afternoon, with drinks, dancing, introductions to the American guests, more carriages driving up into the courtyard almost by the minute. Men from the village helped with the horses and carriages, and Regina had arranged a meal for them and for the women helping the household.

After several hours of dancing and conversation, an elegant supper was served in the three dining rooms on the ground floor—the silver room, the gold room, and the blue and white. Regina's only regret was that she had not had time to redo them all, though their faded elegance looked quietly lovely in the light of the lamps.

Then all the guests returned upstairs for more festivities. The musicians played on until two in the morning, and everyone seemed to enjoy himself immensely. The Americans certainly did. Betsy and Sally found it hard to choose among the eager partners who came to dance with them. George and Bernard conducted themselves admirably, dressed formally in white dinner jackets with black ties. Their wives had worn their smartest summer ball gowns from New York City, lace gowns with inserts of satin, and their finest jewels: sapphires for Betsy and rubies for Sally. They were quite satisfied with the glances of approval that came their way. They had held their own with the French!

The carriages finally all rattled away by three in the morning. Regina fell into bed and did not awaken until noon. She dressed and went downstairs, to find Thérèse briskly presiding over the immense job of cleaning up, although it was Sunday. It took much of the afternoon to restore everything to order.

In the late afternoon they all had a fine supper together. The next morning the guests would depart for the south of France.

Regina and Julian rose early on Monday to see the guests off. However, Betsy and Sally were not so prompt, as George grumbled. It took several hours to pack the carriages that Julian had insisted on lending them for the next stage of their journey. Later they would pick up a train and proceed.

Practical Thérèse had packed huge baskets of food for them to take for that day, and Marcus had drawn a careful map of the area for George, though the coachmen and outriders knew the way. With many hugs and kisses and admonitions to take care, they finally parted.

"George reminds me so much of Father." Regina sighed, waving a final time before returning indoors.

"You must persuade your father to make us a visit also," said Julian, his arm about her waist. "I think he would enjoy it, and what a pleasure it would be to have him here. Your mother also," he added hastily.

Regina grinned impishly. "It would do Mother good to come! She would get rid of her foolish notions about what the French do! She thinks we dance all night and sleep all day, and entertain kings, I am sure! George and Bernard got an eye opener, seeing you work."

"And you also," said Julian. "I do wish you would not work so hard, Regina," he added gently. "Sometimes I worry about you. There are little lines under your eyes now, and some shadows."

"Those are from dancing all night." She laughed. "Oh, it will be nice to get to bed early tonight and have a peaceful day tomorrow! I mean to go to the village and thank Madame Galande and the other women for all their hard work."

The next days and weeks were peaceful ones for them at Verlaine. Many of the *vignerons* and their families had gone away for August. It was their traditional holiday time, before the final hard work of the harvest. Julian preferred to remain and keep an anxious eye on his fields, to make sure they were well watered.

Thérèse and Marcus finally went away for a short time to visit with some of Marcus's relatives. They returned within a week, well satisfied, glowing from sunshine and fresh air on the sea near Normandy. "Jeannette has a tan," said Thérèse, "and so do I! The family was most pleased with us, they said we seemed so happy. And that's how I feel. With that nasty Claude and his hateful wit—all that gone, I feel fine!"

"We missed you, but I am glad you enjoyed your holiday. This winter you must go to Paris while we manage here," said Regina. "Or perhaps we could all go to the London shows for a time—I understand they are splendid. Then we could go back to the Paris townhouse. I long to redecorate that also, Thérèse." She laughed as her sister-in-law pretended to groan.

"Oh, Regina, you have so many plans and schemes!" Thérèse shook her head, but her brown eyes sparkled. "I would love to go to London and to Paris. It has been years since I went."

The violin and cello had arrived from Paris and Regina had begun to practice again, in a room by herself, for she was very rusty. "Oh, I shall have to have lessons," she moaned to Thérèse. "I have forgotten all I knew."

Julian did not even have time to practice. He was busy in the fields from early morning until dusk now. He was worried about his precious reds. Were they getting enough water? Would the sunshine last, to make them plump and red and very ripe, as they must be? Since no one else nearby had the Cabernet franc grapes, he had to rely on his own judgment as to when to harvest. Some said in September just when they were ripe. Some said in October, when they were overripe. They always waited until the white Chenin blanc grapes were overripe: Should he do the same with his Cabernet franc?

Regina could not advise him. She just listened patiently when he spoke, and encouraged him. "What did you do in 1893?" she finally asked. "Those wines were excellent."

He grimaced. "Rains looked threatening. We picked hurriedly when they became ripe enough to take. I don't know if they might have been better for waiting. We did not dare to wait and ruin all."

"You could pick some when ripe and some when overripe," said Regina. "Though, Julian, you know I do not know much about grapes," she added hurriedly.

Julian looked serious, though. "That is an excellent idea, Regina. The fields are large, and if all goes well—if the sunshine lasts throughout September—it might be well to have two harvests. I could order one picking and one pressing from the ripe Cabernet franc. Then when the grapes are overripe, we could have a second harvest, keeping those grapes and the must separate from the first. Ah, yes, I must speak to Marcus about this! We will need workmen—" And he walked off without saying good-bye!

Regina did not mind. His mind was full of his precious grapes. It was getting to the critical time of year. Julian would be more and more absentminded, Thérèse had warned her. He might not even speak to them at all during harvest!

He had no time or energy for making music. But at night as he relaxed in his favorite chair, he enjoyed hearing the others play, and Regina soon joined Marcus and Thérèse in a trio. Eric came every evening to join them, and she rejoiced in that. He did not seem overtired now;

she watched over him carefully. The auditor had left on his August vacation and promised to return in September. Eric seemed to have no trouble keeping up the present accounts, working just four or five hours per day.

The Dowager was quietly content. It was she who suggested that they read aloud in the evenings. "We used to do this, Regina. And if you wish to increase your French vocabulary, this might help it."

So they began that also. Regina would read aloud, sometimes stumbling over unfamiliar words. Thérèse or the Dowager would help and correct carefully, pronouncing the words until Regina had the accent right. Then they would discuss the meanings of the words. Her use of French increased rapidly.

Rumors of Claude trickled back from Paris. Even Simone de Lamartine had gone away for August, and Regina was pleased about that. Julian went over to her château and directed her workmen, but at least the woman was not there. Julian said she would have a moderate harvest of grapes.

"She has not hired a foreman, as I asked her to," he sighed one evening. "How upset Hilaire de Lamartine would be! Maman, Simone has had an offer to sell the land and château. I do not know what to advise her. It is de Lamartine land. She should keep it, to leave to her children one day."

"But she has no children," said the Dowager.

Julian started and gave her a strange glance. "She is young yet, Maman," he finally said. "The land has been de Lamartine land for two hundred years—"

"She might marry someone with land of his own," said Thérèse thoughtfully. "She is young and certainly beautiful. And if she cannot care for the land, it might be best for her to sell it." Her cheeks colored as she bent over her needlework.

Aunt Agnes contributed a quiet word. "Let her decide what to do. It is her land and her life. If she sells and then squanders all the money—as Julian, I believe, fears she will do—then that is her fate."

"Yes, I do fear that, Aunt Agnes," Julian admitted. "It seems a pity, but money slips through her fingers—"

To Regina's relief, the subject was changed. It upset her

that Julian was worried about Simone. Why couldn't the woman sell out and leave? Why couldn't Julian forget Simone? He seemed to be happy. Or did he still long for his mistress?

That was the only cloud on her horizon, and she deliberately looked away from it. The days were busy, full of work, as she spent some time in the accounting work with Eric and some time riding and going to the village. Julian had no time to see to the villagers' affairs, so she and Madame Galande consulted often, and sometimes the priest joined them, to talk of various needs.

That made Regina wonder. The priest never scolded her for not attending church services, he never spoke of coming to give her instruction. Thinking about it brought back Regina's old fears. If Julian was deliberately preventing her from converting to his faith, did that mean he might still be unsure about their marriage? Perhaps he was waiting to see if Regina had a child. Simone might be waiting also. Perhaps Julian thought that if the finances were now straightening out and Verlaine might be wealthy once more, he would not need Regina. He would be free to marry whomever he chose—and he might choose Simone!

Maybe that was why he hesitated. He might not want Simone to sell the land adjoining Verlaine if she might one day marry him and they could combine their holdings. Frenchmen loved their land, Regina knew that, and Julian would have even more scope for his beloved grapes.

Such thoughts kept her awake some nights, though Julian slept next door and was with her every evening in the drawing room. She wondered what would happen when Simone returned to her own château. Would the torment begin again?

"The hot days are bothering you," Julian said to Regina one day. "There are more shadows under your eyes."

"Oh, I don't mind the heat," she told him hastily. "I feel it only when I ride out into the sunshine. Inside the château, it is quite cool and pleasant. Those thick fortress walls, Julian! Your ancestors built well."

"Yes, but if not that, why are there shadows?" he asked seeming worried. "Are you not sleeping well? I have not come to you often, I have been so weary. But when the harvest is over—"

When the harvest is over—when the harvest is over—
The phrase drummed through Regina's mind, over and
over. How much depended on the harvest. Whether Verlaine would recover its wealth; whether the rosé would
make a reputation for Verlaine; whether Simone would return and claim Julian's attentions once again; whether Simone would come to Verlaine and smile her silky sly smile,
and look up at Julian with her alluring dark eyes—

Regina tossed and turned in bed, and wooed sleep in
vain. She loved Julian, and he said that he loved her. Certainly he treated her with affection, courtesy, and concern.
Was that enough?

It must be, she thought. She worked hard to please him
and to satisfy her own need to be useful. She kept his
mother comfortable, and Eric was much better than he had
been. Thérèse and Marcus and Jeannette were happy, and
talking of fixing up the big lodge for their own home now
that Jeannette was outgrowing the nursery. Thérèse was
even thinking of having another child. She wanted a son for
Marcus.

Yes, Regina was needed there. She had made a place for
herself among them. If only that might be enough to hold
Julian to her and make him forget Simone. How casually
did Julian really feel about Simone? He did not seem to
miss her, except for an occasional word about her land and
the grapes.

The August days slid past, effortlessly. Full of work and
evenings of quiet times together. But Regina enjoyed them
so much, all the more because a little desperate feeling inside her warned it might not last.

After the harvest—*when the harvest was over—*
She looked forward to it, almost in dread. Would Julian
still need her—*after the harvest was over?*

Meantime, she and Thérèse kept the maids busy making
draperies. They finished the gentlemen's drawing room,
beautifully, in amber and gold, and it was so much brighter
that everyone marveled at it.

They decided to use the music room again, for practice.
The walls were stripped, and fresh wallpaper in a cool blue
and white was put up. They hung blue velvet draperies and
the two magnificent silver lamps from Judah Silver. The

Persian rug of blue, silver, and rose completed the color
scheme. The piano tuner came and worked on the music
room's piano and the one in the rose drawing room until
he was completely satisfied. Regina practiced her violin
daily, sometimes alone, sometimes with Thérèse.

They planned the dining rooms, and she measured and
thought about them. As soon as Monsieur Silver notified
her that he had located the right fabrics and rugs, they
would begin to refinish those rooms. Then next winter,
they could entertain royally.

Oh, and the ballroom must be done, so she added that to
her list and went upstairs to measure it. On the way, she
passed the nursery and heard Jeannette chattering to her
nanny.

Regina could not resist going in. She found the four-
year-old playing with her dolls, and dropped down on the
floor to play with her.

Jeannette's dark flashing eyes were like those of Thérèse,
her dark straight hair like Marcus's. Her enchanting smile
was her own, a cherub smile of pink well-shaped lips.

"*Tante* Gina, see my doll. She needs a new dress. She
tore her dress. Look." And the girl stuck a tiny pink finger
in the fabric.

"So she does," Regina agreed gravely. "Let me see.
Should she have a new summer dress of white or blue muslin? Or should we get her ready for winter, with a blue
velvet gown like Mummy's?"

"Dress like Mummy's," Jeannette said promptly, beaming her captivating smile and showing her tiny even teeth.
"You can make it?"

"All right, I'll make it. Let me see. Will you let me borrow your doll tonight, so I can measure the size for her
dress?"

Jeannette entrusted the doll Regina to *Tante* Gina, and
they went on playing with her beautiful dollhouse, with the
little china dolls and miniature tables and chairs, and a tiny
bed with a silver canopy, which was the pride of Jeannette's heart.

Thérèse came along presently. "Oh, there you are, Regina! I thought you had gone up to measure the draperies
for the ballroom."

"I got waylaid by a small bandit," she said. "She has

captured my heart, and I must ransom it back before I can leave."

Jeannette understood enough to dissolve into giggles of pleasure. They decided on a ransom of a half a dozen kisses, and Regina reluctantly left her.

As they went up the small flight of stairs to the ballroom, Thérèse said, "Regina, you should have a child. You would love it, and Julian would go mad with delight."

"Do you . . . think so?" asked Regina, gazing straight ahead of her at the windows.

Thérèse hesitated, embarrassed. "You are thinking about what I told you about Julian—and Simone de Lamartine. I think he has almost forgotten her. You notice what he said about her selling the land."

"He does not want her to sell," said Regina. She walked toward the draperies and took out her tape measure. "I think these should be shorter, don't you, Thérèse? These are dragging on the floor."

"It was the fashion once," said Thérèse absently. She took out her pad and pencil to note down the measurements. "Truly, I do think if you gave Julian a son, he would be the happiest man in the world. The French think highly of a son—an heir, you know. I think he would then forget all about her."

"Perhaps," said Regina. "I must . . . think about it—"

But it upset her to think about it. She tried to put the thought away. But as she cut out the little blue velvet dress for the doll that evening and sewed as they talked in the drawing room, she could not get it out of her mind.

What if she had a child for Julian? A boy, an heir for him? Or a girl—one who would play with dolls like Jeannette? A beautiful child who might hold him, who might clasp Julian with tiny pink fingers. . . .

A child. If she gave Julian a child, *would* that make him forget Simone? Or would he still go to her secretly, regretting that they had never been able to marry?

Regina thought, fiercely, possessively, that she could not endure that. To be his wife, the mother of his child, and have to smile over an aching heart as he showered his attentions on his beautiful mistress would be unbearable. And Simone would smile mysteriously, pityingly, on the American woman he had married because he needed the money for Verlaine.

Julian loved Verlaine; the château, and the land, and his beloved grapes came first with him. Regina understood that.

It was the fact that Simone came second that hurt her. A wife would come third—or even fourth—after a son!

CHAPTER TWENTY-ONE

August ended and some of the *vignerons* began to return. As September came in, with gold and ruby splendor of the trees and flowers and the leaves in the vineyard began to turn also, Julian went out early every day, making the rounds of the fields.

Carefully, he went among the vines, testing a grape here and one there, bending to inspect the plump clusters of fruit resting among the leaves. Marcus began to go with him. When Regina rode out to take their luncheon to them, as she frequently did, she would find the two men deep in discussion. Were the whites ripening early? Would they be able to leave the reds longer on the vines? Were they keeping the soil sufficiently moist?

She returned one afternoon to the château, glad to return to the coolness within the thick walls. A hot sunny September was what they needed. They all kept looking up at the deep blue of the sky, and prayed that the warmth and sunshine would continue. If it did, the harvest would be good, the grapes thick clustered and plump with juice.

One scarcely dared to say it, but this might be a very good harvest indeed. Julian thought they might begin to pick the grapes about the end of September, unless rain threatened, in which case they might have to pick early. But the longer they could wait, the better the wines would be.

Ninette waited for Regina as she went upstairs to change from her riding outfit to a cool muslin dress. The maid looked worried, her forehead wrinkling.

"Madame, a letter has come for you from Paris. The groom who delivered it asked for me and put it into my hand. Oh, Madame, I hope it is not bad news. He waits for your reply below in the courtyard. I do not know the man, he is not from Verlaine."

Regina looked at the bold handwriting on the envelope. Only her name, "Madame, la Baronne de Verlaine, Regina

Herriot," was written there, and there was no return address.

Her heart began to thump unpleasantly. This was not from Monsieur Silver, and she knew only the Longstreths and the artist Armand in Paris.

She sat down at her rosewood desk with the Sèvres porcelain panels in it and tore open the envelope. She stared at the writing inside on the single sheet of notepaper.

> Madame la Baronne: I must urge you to come to Paris at once, and alone. There is something you should know, something I must show to you. Julian would prevent you, but this is important to you, and to me. Simone de Lamartine.

Regina stared at the words, and they danced before her eyes as she felt dizzy and sick. Something important. Something Simone must show to her. What did Simone have to say to her that could not be put in a letter? And why in Paris? Why not in Verlaine? When was Simone returning home? Most of the local residents had returned now to their lands in preparation for the harvest.

Regina would have liked nothing better than to ignore Simone's message, for she knew it could only bring bad news. But how could she help being curious? She wanted this matter between Julian's mistress and herself settled once and for all.

"Where . . . is the groom?" she finally stirred herself to ask.

"Below, Madame, in the courtyard. He returns to Paris tonight." Ninette shifted from one foot to the other. She did not like this, but it was not her place to interfere.

Regina took out a sheet of notepaper, with her new crest on it. She thought carefully, then wrote:

> Madame Simone de Lamartine: I have your note and will come to Paris as soon as I can, probably this week. Will you call upon me at the Verlaine townhouse, and leave your information? Regina, Baronne de Verlaine.

* * *

She put it in an envelope, with Simone's name formally on the outside, and handed it to Ninette. "Please give this to the groom. Has he had something to eat?"

"*Oui*, Madame." Disapproval was etched in every line of Ninette's young face, but she said no more, taking the note below. Regina put her face in her hands, and she began to shake.

What could this matter of importance be? Regina sat so still, she might have been carved in stone. All the insecurity of her marriage, her jealousy of Simone de Lamartine, the scenes she had seen between Simone and Julian, his tenderness with her, his anxiety over her land—all rose up to haunt Regina.

Everything had been so peaceful, deceptively peaceful, this August and September. And now—this thunderbolt.

She felt terrible. Her jealousy and curiosity were like a fever in her. She was dizzy, then hot, then chilled until she shivered. It seemed as if she could see her marriage shattering to pieces before her eyes. Finally she stirred, sighing, as though coming out of a trance.

Regina knew one thing. She had to go to Paris. She would not be satisfied until she knew what it was Simone had to say. She had said she could come this week. Well, she could not wait. She would go at once.

But with what excuse? Her mind began to work again, painfully, slowly. She had to have reasons ready, convincing reasons. What could they be? Why must she go to Paris at once? Ah—Monsieur Silver. . . . He would be her invaluable pretext.

Julian was busy, concerned with the harvest. If she said she must go to talk to Monsieur Silver to order more fabrics, or even some dresses, he might just assent and scarcely notice her absence.

When Ninette returned, she laid out the white muslin dress with the purple ribbons. Regina said, "And a cashmere shawl, Ninette. I have been chilled lately."

"*Oui*, Madame. The château is sometimes cool in the autumn." Ninette set out a fringed cashmere shawl.

Regina changed slowly. When she was ready, she said, "Ninette, I wish you to pack a trunk and two valises for me, and a hatbox. I'll be going to Paris tomorrow. Will you accompany me?"

Ninette's small pink mouth was an "O" of surprise. She struggled with words. "Paris, Madame? Tomorrow? But Monsieur, he is so busy with the harvest—" Her eyes reproached silently.

"I know. He will not be going," Regina said curtly. "Please pack my fur jacket, the blue woolen dress, and some boots, in case of rain."

"*Oui*, Madame." Ninette, schooled to obedience, did not protest again, but went out to order footmen to bring a trunk and several smaller traveling bags to the bedroom.

By the time Julian returned from the fields, tired and satisfied, the trunks were practically packed, for two had become necessary with all Regina thought she might need. She did not even know how long she might be there.

Julian surveyed the scene in total amazement. "Regina! What is this?"

"Oh, Julian, did you have a good day?" she asked. But he ignored that.

"What in the name of heaven? Where are you going?" Looking at her anxiously, he seemed shocked and dismayed.

"Oh, I must go to Paris." She tried to sound light and cool about it. "There is so much to do, Julian. I cannot do it all by letter. I must talk to Monsieur Silver in person."

"Regina, it is not that urgent. I assure you, Verlaine will not fall to pieces if the rooms are not redecorated by this time next year!"

She set her mouth stubbornly. "I want to go now, Julian. Of course, you need not go. It is not necessary. I'll just take one carriage, and Ninette."

"My dear girl, you are mad!" Julian lost his calm. "You cannot ride alone to Paris! You might be attacked, there are always bandits on the road. Why do you suppose we have outriders and I carry a weapon at all times? Absolutely not, I forbid it."

"Then I will take as many outriders as you wish, Julian. Only I must go to Paris! I must—really I must!" She was close to tears. He studied her troubled face and put his hand to his brow.

"Well, I must talk to Marcus," he muttered. "Perhaps he can look after matters for a few days. The grapes are not ready yet. We could go and return in a week—"

She panicked. "No, Julian. I will not take you away

from the vineyard! It is not necessary for you to go also—"

"Of course it is," he said simply. "Haven't I sworn to protect you always? If you must go to Paris, then I will go with you. But I cannot go tomorrow, Regina, there are orders to give. Let it wait one more day. I will try to be ready on Thursday."

Another day of waiting to know what Simone meant! Regina bit her lips. But she could not go unless Julian agreed to it. After all, the carriages would not move, the grooms and the outriders would not go, unless Monsieur le Baron said that they would.

"Very well, Julian," she said coldly. "But I do not wish to take you from the fields. I can very well go with Ninette."

That evening, after dinner, when Thérèse heard the plans, she was loudly disapproving. "Oh, Regina, not now! Not at the harvest! What is so important that cannot wait?"

Julian hushed her, but Marcus also looked troubled, and Eric looked from one to the other of them, with worried gentle brown eyes.

Regina stuck stubbornly to her story, but tried to remain calm so no one would suspect her inner turmoil. "I must talk to Monsieur Silver about the orders. They are very slow right now. If I can talk to him and explain what we need and give him the new measurements, it will go faster. You know I hate to be idle for long." She tried to laugh about it.

Thérèse said, "You do too much, Regina. You have become thinner and there are shadows under your eyes. Try to relax and take things more calmly. Get into the rhythm of French country life. After the harvest you can take a vacation, before the winter sets in. And this winter, you know, I promised to show you how to crochet."

The Dowager intervened gently as Regina looked stormy. "Now, children. I understand how Regina feels. She is missing her own family. And I think our weather is upsetting to her. She is chilled tonight, yes? It takes time to become accustomed to a new country and a different climate."

They all looked at Regina speculatively, and she could hardly endure it. She thought her pain was written on her face.

"I must go," she said simply.

"I can take care of the fields for a week, Julian," said Marcus, his sturdy hands on his knees. His anxious face turned to his brother-in-law. "You may trust me, Julian, truly."

"And I," said Eric, unexpectedly. "If someone can get me into a carriage, I will go out to the vineyards." His cheeks were flushed, and his eyes began to sparkle. "Yes, I know how the grapes should look. And I have been reading up on the process. You know I have helped with the pressing and the bottling in the past, directing the workmen."

Regina was horrified. "But, Eric, you must not work so hard—I would never forgive myself if anything happened to you!" She put her hand on his hot fingers. "Truly, Eric, do not overdo."

"I want to help," he said stubbornly. "If you wish to go to Paris, why not? You work hard, you deserve a holiday."

"I will take Regina to Paris," said Julian finally, passing his hand wearily over his head. "I know—you all think I eat, sleep, and drink nothing but my wines." And he gave his charming smile to them all. "But I do care for my wife, and if she is weary of Verlaine and the quiet country life and longs for Paris, she shall go!"

Regina opened her mouth to protest but shut it again. If he chose to think this, all the better. But how to get away from him in Paris?

Julian gave the answer, innocently. "Besides, I have been thinking. Monsieur Carnot and Monsieur Feuillet are worried that we have not yet chosen a broker in common. Whether or not we form a cooperative eventually, they feel as George suggested, that we should have a common broker, under strict fees. This will give me a chance to interview the men whose names I have obtained. I think we will break with all the others," he added thoughtfully. "A clean break, a new man for the new harvest. Then there can be no debating over which man owns what, and what to do with older vintages. What do you think, Marcus?"

"A very good idea," said Marcus, his face lighting up at being consulted so naturally. "A new broker. And make it understood we will no longer pay the high commissions. You recall that George said no free bottles, no free cases. All must be accounted for."

"And I might speak also to a friend of Monsieur Feuillet, the banker in Paris who might advise us about a bank near to us. That would be a good idea. I have been longing to speak with him and see if his advice agrees with what George told us. Then we can begin at once to make arrangements."

They began to speak of this. The Dowager sewed silently on her embroidery while Thérèse attacked a piece of needlepoint, her mouth drawn into a tight line as she worked. Later she found opportunity to speak to Regina, as they sat on the sofa together.

"Regina, you will forgive my asking, but have you started a child? It sometimes makes a woman nervous and moody, and I cannot but see that you are worried about something. Don't be troubled about having a child—"

Regina blushed. "No, Thérèse, it is not that," she said hastily. "I am sorry to have been moody. Forgive me."

Thérèse patted her hand but kept on looking at her with a disconcerting gaze. "I have wondered, for you seem so on edge. And if you have, it is bad to travel. You could lose the child. Do not be hasty, my dear. Paris is always there, and we can make sure you do not work too hard. Maman is much better, she can help more, and I will employ another woman to help in the house—"

Regina's mouth trembled. She drew the shawl closer about her slim form. "No, Thérèse, really, it is not that. I am . . . restless. I must talk to Monsieur Silver. I am only sorry that Julian feels he must leave the harvest—"

"Don't worry about that. Marcus will manage." Thérèse beamed across at her husband. "Take a vacation, enjoy yourself, and come back with roses in your cheeks again. That will make us all happy."

"You are . . . most kind," said Regina in a low voice. If they all went on being so concerned about her, she would break down and confess why she was going. But she must be silent about it.

By the time Julian was ready to go on Thursday, she was a bundle of nerves. Finally the two carriages were packed. Ninette presided over the one with the trunks and hatboxes and valises, while the outriders pranced out on their splendid horses in their uniforms of green and gold. Julian's mother and sister came out to see them off, and Eric sat somberly in his wheelchair, just inside the door, gazing after them. He was so sensitive; did he perceive it was not mere restlessness that drove her?

Julian's big hand reached out to her bare fingers. "You are cold! Regina, you do not understand the chilliness of our autumns. Let me put the rug about you." He drew up one rug and then another about her shoulders.

"Thank you," she murmured, looking at his dear face with its healthy tan, the thin dark mustache outlining his aristocratic mouth. She loved him, but she did not understand him. How could he be so endearing, so careful of her—and still feel passion for Simone? Would she ever understand Frenchmen and their *amours*, and be able to smile above her pain and jealousy?

She closed her eyes to think and try to rest. Julian said little, musing over his notes before him, obviously thinking of the interviews with the brokers and the banker. She wished it was a normal journey. She would like to have spoken with him about those matters, and listened to his opinions and ideas. But she felt numb, not with cold but with fear.

The journey seemed to take forever. They paused for lunch, eating from the lavish basket Thérèse had prepared. Then they went on, and by the time a blue haze was filling the Paris sky, they were drawing up into the courtyard lit by flares. Julian had sent one man ahead to tell of their coming, and the household was ready for them.

In her bedroom Julian said, "Now, Regina, I cannot help seeing you are not well, and you are most weary. What about a tray in your room, and early to bed tonight? You can see Monsieur Silver sometime tomorrow, if you feel well enough."

Simone might come, might call on them. She went cold and shivered violently. But she had no choice but to agree.

Ninette came and helped Regina prepare for bed. "Madame will feel better in the morning," she soothed. "Do sleep late, Madame. There is no such rush."

Regina smiled wanly. She did feel a little sick. To please Julian, she ate a little, drank some tea, and was able to rest. She kept waking, however, and lay awake as the night wore on. When dawn crept in the windows with its rosy glow, lighting the faded carpets and chairs, her eyes were wide open.

She felt drained, but got up with determination. Ninette peeped in, shook her head. "Madame should sleep longer," she said.

"No, I am fine, Ninette. Please bring some hot water now."

She washed hastily, then dressed in a dark ruby velvet gown. She could not seem to get warm. Julian came in, hearing the stirring in her room. He eyed her gravely.

"Now, do not criticize me, Julian," she said with forced humor. "I know I do not look my best, but I am anxious to see Monsieur Silver. Ninette, you have all the measurements?"

"*Oui,* Madame."

"I shall take you to him, then go off on an appointment," said Julian. "I will come back for you at twelve and we will have luncheon at some gay place. It will make you feel better."

"Yes, that sounds splendid," she said. She had put some rouge on her cheeks and powdered under her eyes where there were dark shadows.

They set off about ten, and were soon at the shop of Monsieur Silver. He hobbled out to greet them, his face beaming. "Ah, you have come yourself! I did not expect you until after the harvest! How does Madame enjoy the carpets, the lamps, eh?"

"They are magnificent, Monsieur Silver," Regina assured him, and she began looking at lengths of material as Julian went off on his appointment with a banker.

She could scarcely concentrate on the fabrics, and the Jewish merchant perceptively felt her distraught condition. "Madame may trust me with the measurements," he reminded her gently. "Permit me to show you some samples which came this week from Persia."

He brought out lengths of silver and gold, of ruby velvet and blue silk, thick carpets as soft as clouds.

"I have ordered some of the silver for Madame. I thought silver draperies for the dining room, with valances of silvery-gray velvet. Eh?" And he showed her samples of the material.

She managed to keep her attention on them for two hours. Ninette remained nearby, to remind her softly of the odd window at the corner of the huge dining room, the

round turret windows in Eric's rooms, for which she was
ordering bright yellow and gold valances.

"I found a rug for the young man." Monsieur Silver
smiled. He sent to the back, and two assistants came in
with it. "It is square, but we can add to the sides—unless
Madame thinks it best to leave bare floorboards for Monsieur's bed? Sometimes a rolling bed is difficult on carpets."

The pattern was of leaves and flowers in golden yellow
and apple green, on a background of deep green that
looked like grass. The border was green, blue, rose, and
yellow. "The Arabs did not want to use so much green,
which is a sacred color for them. However, my agent explained the purpose of the rug, for a young man whose
spirit rises above his physical difficulties, and they made it
as we directed."

"How kind you are," she said spontaneously. "Eric will
enjoy this so much. He likes color, and his room was always so drab and dark, with those dreadful animal heads
looming over him."

Julian came for them promptly at twelve, as they were
still looking with pleasure at the rug. He approved it, and
then they bid Monsieur Silver good-bye. Ninette was sent
home in one carriage with the parcels, and a coachman and
two footmen to guard them. Julian had a light carriage he
was driving himself, to show Regina something of Paris.

They drove around for a time, across the Seine and into
the Left Bank area. He pointed out sights with his whip,
but they did not talk much, enjoying the companionable
silence instead. There was a brisk wind, but Regina was
dressed warmly and did not mind it.

They finished the drive at a small restaurant that looked
like a bar from the outside. The owner came out to help
Regina down, and someone came to take the horses and
carriage. Julian escorted Regina in, smiling at her surprise.

"This is one of my favorite places, Regina. The chef is
magnificent, for she is the wife of the owner and will not be
bought away with huge salaries," he teased the owner, who
beamed happily. "I have ordered some paté maison,
braised chicken the way you like, and some of our own
wines, which the owner has. He also has a surprise dessert."

They enjoyed the meal very much, neither caring that it

was served on a red-and-white checked tablecloth or that
the table service was rather battered. Around them were
French workingmen from nearby offices 'and shops, eating
heartily and talking amiably of their work. Regina liked the
informal atmosphere.

The surprise dessert was cherries jubilee, made from
fresh home-grown cherries and light-as-air pastry. The wine
was Julian's 1893 vintage Rosé Verlaine. Regina stroked
the label as the bottle was emptied.

"This year you will have many more, Julian, the best
harvest yet," she said solemnly. "To the vintage." And she
raised her glass to him.

"And to my beloved wife," he said softly, smiling his
radiant, charming smile at her. His green eyes glowed yellow in the candle flames.

They drove home in midafternoon, and Julian insisted
that Regina should rest. She was nervous for fear Simone
would come or call, but so far no one had called and there
were no messages. Julian said he would notify the Longstreths they were here, if Regina wished.

"Yes, as you wish, Julian," she said rather wearily, and
lay down in her negligee.

He frowned at her worriedly. "You are so tired, my
dear. Was the cold air too much for you?"

"No, I enjoyed it so much, Julian. I—I should like to see
the Longstreths but not this weekend. Perhaps . . . next
week, early, before we go." Surely Simone de Lamartine
would call on her or leave a message before then. Still, how
could the woman know Regina was already in Paris, unless
she had some sort of spies?

"I have appointments on Monday, Tuesday, and
Wednesday," Julian said. "I think we may return on Thursday to Verlaine. Will that suit you, my dear?"

"Yes, of course, Julian. Fine."

She closed her eyes, and he left the room. To her surprise, she wakened later to find she had slept for four
hours. It was past seven o'clock.

Ninette crept in. "Ah, you are awake. Monsieur said to
let you sleep. You wish dinner up here?"

"No, I will dress and come down." She rose feeling phys-
ically rested, although her spirit was still weary as she
thought of Simone.

They dined quietly at home and retired early that night
to separate rooms. Julian is tired, she thought. She was
lying awake, tossing and turning, when he came in.

"My dear, I could not leave you tonight," he said, standing over the bed. "Do you mind? May I come to you?"

He was so humble it made her feel like weeping. "Yes,
please, Julian. If you are not too weary," she added. "You
should have a rest, not I. It is you who are working too
hard these days."

He lay down with her, having removed his robe. He
drew her into his arms. "Maman was furious with me and
scolded me," he said with a smile in his deep voice. "She
said, 'You are a married man, Julian, and with a beautiful
wife. How can you ignore her needs for your grapes? You
are worse than your father, for at least he came to my bed
at night and paid me compliments, no matter how busy he
was. Have you forgotten you are a man?' And, of course, I
said that when I look at my so-beautiful wife, I feel very
much a man, and very proud. You are lovely, in body and
soul, Regina, and I am the most fortunate of men."

Tears came to her eyes at his compliments. She hid her
face against his chest. "I am a foolish woman," she said,
her voice trembling. "Dragging you here—taking you from
your work. Forgive me, Julian."

"I forgive you everything, except not telling me that you
wished to come to Paris and have some fun," he said gently. "I want honesty between us, my dear. I want you to be
happy at Verlaine. I thought you *were* happy, but Thérèse
says you are working too hard, and you must be taught to
slow down and enjoy life. I also think that American
women are inclined to drive themselves from morning to
night. This is not a frontier, my dearest. I do not want you
to work your fingers to the bone." He raised her hand and
kissed her slim fingers.

"I don't—really, Julian."

He drew her closer and moved his hand tenderly over
her body under the silken nightdress. His palm cupped her
rounded breasts. He bent and kissed her bared throat and
shoulder. "I want you, but not if you are too tired," he
whispered, his voice urgent.

"I am not . . . too weary, Julian. But you—"

He laughed a little. "I could be dying—as the man in the
poem *Maud* said, you remember?

My dust would hear her and beat,
Had I lain for a century dead,
Would start and tremble under her feet,
And blossom in purple and red.

"That is the way I feel when I see you, hear you, think of you, my darling."

His musical voice in her ear made her tremble, and she forgot everything in the world but him. He was so tender, so passionate, he seemed so much in love with her. But how could she be sure of it? She shut out the thoughts, clinging to him desperately.

"Oh, Julian—I do love you—I love you so very much. You are all the world to me. No matter what—I love you so—" Her voice broke, and he felt the tears against his chest.

"My love, my sweetest treasure, please don't weep. Aren't you happy with me?" he asked anxiously, and kissed the tears away, whispering tender reassurance to her.

He kissed her until the tears stopped, until she trembled, but not from weeping; from ecstasy. He caressed her until her body burned with fire, and she drew him down into her arms and held him fiercely to her. It seemed that nothing could come between them.

His whispers were sweet in her ears. His words of passion quieted her anxiety. The love between them was hot and sweet that night, lasting for a long time, until finally the sweet rush of desire had calmed them both. Then he held her in his arms and they slept together, her head on his shoulder, his muscular arms tightly about her, holding her even in slumber.

CHAPTER TWENTY-TWO

They spent a quiet Saturday. Ninette went around measuring rooms in the townhouse for rugs and draperies while Regina wrote down the numbers. Julian went with them for a time, making suggestions for changes in color and design, but then he retreated to his study to work on his notes.

On Sunday afternoon the Longstreths came, at Julian's invitation. He knew how much Regina enjoyed them. Vicky was bubbling over with pleasure at their arrival, and Ken was quietly happy.

"How splendid that you've come!" Vicky cried. "I didn't expect you until Christmas at least! Do let us go out tonight. We have found an exciting new place in Pigalle!"

They did go out and enjoyed it. Vicky studied Regina shrewdly, and when they excused themselves to the powder room found an opportunity to say quietly, "What is wrong, my dear? I am troubled for you. You do not look yourself."

Regina tried to smile, but her mouth trembled. "I cannot tell you, Vicky. I am sorry."

"Well—" The older woman hesitated. "I am usually at home during the day. If you want to come any time, to talk, please do. My dear, there are such shadows under your eyes—"

"You are . . . very kind," Regina managed to say, and they left the powder room, returning to the men.

The new place was very amusing and had several pairs of Apache dancers, who fascinated them all. They drank and were merry, not returning home until past two in the morning.

Regina slept late the next morning, and Julian came to her room at about ten o'clock as she was yawning herself awake.

"My dear, you look brighter, but we did have a late night. Why don't you remain in today and get more rest? I promise you a lovely evening, if you will!" He was smiling, sitting on the side of the bed.

But, Regina thought, Simone might call.

She smiled. "We will see, Julian. Where do you go to-day?"

"To interviews with three more brokers," he said. "I scarcely know how to choose between them. I wish Monsieur Carnot were here to advise me."

She roused herself to say naturally, "Julian, don't hire anybody right now, please. Why don't you take down all they say, and whatever deal they will make, and consult with the others when you return to Verlaine? If they realize they must compete for your business, and it will be large, they might make a better offer. I think that is what Father would do."

"Of course!" he said, pleased, and bent to kiss her cheek. "You are hereby appointed my financial adviser," he teased her gently. "You should have been a man, you would have been a great business success. But I—" and his voice dropped huskily—"am very pleased that you are . . . so lovely a woman." He pressed a kiss into the soft warmth of her neck.

When Julian left, she rose slowly. Ninette came to help her, but as they were trying to choose a dress for the day, a note was brought up by one of the footmen. Ninette took it at the door, and a shadow came over her face.

"A note for you, Madame," she said without expression, gazing anxiously at Regina as she brought it to her.

The handwriting was the same, bold and slanted. Regina's hand shook a little as she opened the letter.

My carriage will come for you at eleven o'clock. Please come outside and meet me at the end of the drive. Simone de Lamartine.

Regina glanced automatically at her little gold watch on the end of the gold chain. "Quarter to eleven! Oh, heavens! Hurry, Ninette, the blue dress will do—and my hair—"

Ninette's mouth was stern with disapproval. She dressed Regina quickly, fastened up her thick brown hair in a coronet, and set a shady hat on her head with hatpins. Regina almost ran down the steps and out the door. Ninette was following her.

"No," said Regina firmly. "I go alone!"

The butler was staring, upset and disapproving. Ninette

said, "The monsieur, he will be most angry and alarmed!"

"I will return before long," said Regina. There was a closed carriage at the end of the drive. She went out, hesitating as a groom got down and opened the door. Then Simone leaned forward in the carriage, her lovely face intense and her eyes very dark.

"Get in, Madame. We do not have far to go," she said.

Regina did as she was told. The door was shut and the groom went up to his high seat. Simone was silent, leaning back in the corner of the dark carriage. She wore black today, and seemed a shadow.

"Your note was very mysterious, Madame," said Regina stiffly.

"It was necessary. I could not risk anyone seeing what I wrote," said Madame de Lamartine. Her face was pale and grave. She drew her black veil down over her face so that Regina could not even see her expression.

"What is there for me to see? You can tell me now, here in the carriage. I have no wish to go to your home, Madame."

"So haughty yet! Wait until you see what I have to show you." Simone's voice was calm, yet Regina could read a sneer in it. She felt shaky and insecure. The cold damp air of Paris was reaching to her bones.

"I wish an explanation now, Madame!"

A delicate shrug was her only answer. Simone de Lamartine was gazing out the other window of the carriage. Regina settled back in the carriage, her lips tight, her teeth clenched to keep back angry words.

The horses *clip-clopped* from the pavement onto a cobblestone street, Regina saw they were entering a mews. Inside the courtyard the carriage came to a halt.

The groom descended heavily and opened the door. He helped Regina out, then Simone de Lamartine.

"This way," said Simone, and led the way, holding up her black filmy skirts. She kept the veil down over her face, which was further shadowed by a wide black straw hat.

They entered a hallway, walked up some narrow stairs, and paused at the door to an apartment. Simone knocked. The door was opened to her by a neat older maid in a black and white uniform.

Regina felt ill with tension. She glanced about the small

hallway, noted the full-length tapestried panels, the magnificent gilded desk for reception notes. They went on into a
large drawing room, stepping onto a Persian rug of glorious
crimson, blue, and gold.

The furniture was gilded, with crimson satin on the sofas
and chairs. Scattered about were small tables of mahogany,
and many delicate bits of sculpture, jade, ivory, and
bronze. In one corner near the French windows was a gold
Chinese screen.

"Please be seated, Madame la Baronne," Simone said as
she went to a golden bell pull. She pulled the rope and a
maid came in, a younger girl. "Coffee for Madame," she
said.

"No, thank you," said Regina curtly. "You said you had
something to show me. Please do so, that I may depart."

Simone de Lamartine took off her hat, handed it to the
maid, and crossed to the gilded mirror to arrange her hair
deftly with her slim long fingers. "Bring in the boy," she
instructed.

Regina started. Simone turned from the mirror, her face
calm, watchful.

The maid bowed and withdrew. There was a brief silence, and then the maid returned with her hand on the
shoulder of a boy of about six years old.

Simone's face softened. She smiled tenderly at the boy,
who came over to stand at her side. He glanced shyly at
Regina, then turned his face to Simone.

"*Mon petit*," she crooned to him. She drew him to her,
then turned him gently so he faced Regina.

Regina felt the blood draining from her head. She was
dizzy, sick, her nerves were snapping.

"Tell the lady your name, *mon cheri*," said Simone.

"My name is Pierre de Lamartine."

"And your age?"

"I am six years of age, Madame." He was grave, with a
little boy huskiness in his voice. Tall and slim, he was already handsome. He had light-brown hair with a slight
wave—like Julian's, thought Regina. His eyes were brown,
not green, but his face was just as Regina would have
imagined Julian's in his youth. The very way he crinkled
up his eyes when he smiled, the shape of his mouth, his
nose—it was Julian in miniature.

"*Bon*," said Simone, satisfied. "You may go, *mon petit*, and tell Hortense to give you your luncheon. She may also serve us coffee in here."

"*Oui, Maman.*" And he skipped away in relief.

Regina was glad she was seated, for she could not have stood. Her legs felt frail and weak. She felt sick to her stomach.

So this was the real reason why Julian clung to Simone. She had had his child! His son! A fine, tall, strong lad—he must be proud of the boy! Oh, my dear God, thought Regina, in agony. No wonder there was such a close bond between them; she was not just his mistress, but the mother of his child as well.

Only the lack of money had separated them—for a time! When the harvest came in, rich and splendid, Julian might have enough money to annul his marriage to the outsider, the foreigner, and marry the woman who was already the mother of the heir to Verlaine!

All the suspicions, all the doubts were confirmed. This was why he had not had her instructed in his faith. This was why the priest had not been requested to perform a binding Roman Catholic marriage. One day, he would divorce her or annul the marriage for lack of a child, and with the money he had received and the rich harvests of the vines he would marry the woman of his choice, the woman for whom he had waited many years.

The older maid wheeled in a silver coffee tray and set it before a chair, bringing Regina out of her thoughts. Simone seated herself gracefully and proceeded to pour. The china was delicate porcelain, white with a gold rim and a design in crimson.

All of the most exquisite taste, thought Regina. She had no doubt that the rest of the apartment was lavishly and beautifully furnished, probably with Regina's money.

Julian's mistress—and his child—lived there.

"Is he not a darling?" Simone asked after a pause. She handed a cup of coffee to Regina, who accepted it automatically, placing it on the small table at her side. Simone smiled, slowly, a catlike stretching of her crimson mouth. She lifted her own cup to her lips, watching Regina alertly over the rim. "You see the resemblance? I saw when he was born, that he was truly a Herriot. My poor Hilaire was overjoyed, he could not see it. But others would have, so

we kept the birth a secret. I told Hilaire that I had received
threatening letters about the child from some of his jealous
relatives. They had thought to inherit! He was persuaded to
allow me to keep the child in Paris, here. When Hilaire
died, no one knew about my darling Pierre except me and
Julian—and a couple very close friends. But he is heir of
the de Lamartine estates—and of Verlaine."

So this was why Julian had been reluctant to allow Simone to sell Lamartine! Simone did have an heir—a
child—and the boy was Julian's.

Simone waited for a reaction from Regina. Not receiving
it, she went on.

"Pierre remains in Paris. He now goes to a private
school here. When I am at Verlaine and Lamartine, he
misses me very much. But I have good help. Hortense is
devoted to him. And of course, Julian comes as often as he
can."

Regina drew in her breath, and it hurt her heart. Her
chest felt clenched, stifled; her vision was blurred. She
pressed her hands together.

"When . . . the child was born . . . did Julian promise—" she began hoarsely.

"All Julian promised was that we should never be in
want. He pays for this apartment, for Pierre, for his schooling, his clothes, the servants. But I wanted more—I wanted
marriage, to acknowledge Pierre as the heir to Verlaine.
But he refused me this." Simone put her hand to her face
briefly, and her mouth trembled a little.

"He—refused marriage," said Regina slowly.

"Oui. I thought when Hilaire died that Julian would
come to me after a proper period of mourning. Instead I
heard that he was hunting an heiress! He searched out half
the heiresses of Europe, but they would not do for him!
No, they didn't have enough money for his beloved Verlaine and his treasured vineyards!"

"He said—he knew—that they did not have—enough
money—" Regina repeated. "The wars had ruined their
fortunes—"

"Unfortunately, yes. A Frenchwoman I could have dealt
with," said Simone bitterly. "They understand the need for
money, the need for pride, for one's responsibilities. He
might have married a Frenchwoman and acknowledged
Pierre. But no, he had to go to America and search out an

American girl who had more money. And he found you. He said to me that he could not tell you about Pierre, that if I tried to tell you, he would hate me forever! You would never understand about his love for Pierre, he told me."

Regina put her hand to her throat. "But he could have married you—he could have—"

Simone shook her head sadly. "I went to him, I went on my knees to him," she said, and her eyes filled with tears. Simone's proud hard eyes, so full of tears. If there was any doubt in Regina's heart about Simone's love for her son, it died then. "My Pierre, I would do anything for him. I went to Julian, I begged him shamelessly to marry me, to give Pierre his rightful name. He refused me. He said no, he had to have money for Verlaine. So he went to America— and married you. And he had the gall to see that I was invited to the wedding! He has his subtle way of torture, Julian. You may not have seen this side of him, the French *gentleman*."

Regina was silent. Simone finally went on with a sigh.

"Yes, he has his ways of torturing a woman. He flatters, he kisses, he caresses, he vows he cannot live without her love. Then he turns about and forgets and ignores her. He goes to his vineyards—his true love, Madame! He has no other. Not even his son."

The words died in the warm beautiful room. Regina felt stifled, as though she were choking.

"Why did you tell me this, Madame?" she finally managed to ask coldly. "What difference should it make in my marriage?"

"You are a proud woman. I am making one last effort to give my son his true name, Madame. If you will leave Julian, divorce him, he might then marry me."

"Why now, when he would not before?"

"Because he has hope now that Verlaine can earn money from the wines. If Verlaine can become self-supporting— and he already has your dowry to assist him—then he will not need you, Madame! You are an American, you must be homesick for your own country and your own people. If you will release him, I think he will turn to me. Then we can be happy, Julian and I, and Pierre."

Regina managed to get to her feet. "I must consider this, Madame," she said. "I . . . will let you know. Or Julian will."

Simone rose also, gracefully, lithe as a leopard, or a black panther, thought Regina. Simone, in her dramatic black, her magnolia-petal skin shining against the fabric, her mouth crimson, her dark eyes huge and haunting with the tears in them.

"I will thank you forever, Madame, if you will but give Julian back to me, and to his son," she said simply.

She accompanied Regina to the carriage. "Take Madame home," she said with a wave of her hand to the coachman.

Regina huddled in the dark carriage. She did not know what to do. As the coach turned into a familiar avenue near the townhouse, she realized she did not want to go home. She rapped on the ceiling to get the coachman's attention. He opened the vent and leaned down.

"*Oui*, Madame?"

She gave the Longstreths' address in a choked voice, and had to repeat it. "*Oui*, Madame," he said stolidly, and turned the carriage around.

The horses trotted along the avenues, up one, down the next, along a narrow street past shops and sidewalks full of smartly dressed women. The Frenchwomen, with their painted lips, their knowing eyes, their narrow ankles and smart clothes, thought Regina bitterly. She was a babe in the woods here in Paris.

Regina could not think clearly. Her worst fears had been realized, and more. After the harvest, she thought bitterly, Julian would surely discard her anyway. With a good harvest, he would no longer need her or her money. He could be free to marry Simone, with money aplenty to keep them both and all Verlaine—for his son Pierre.

The carriage stopped, and the groom got down to help her out. She fairly staggered up the steps of the Longstreths' townhouse. The butler showed her in at once, and sent for Mrs. Longstreth.

"Regina, my dear!" Vicky came into the room, and stretched out her arms as she saw Regina turn to her. "What in the world is the matter? Oh, my dear!"

It was comfort, and Regina sorely needed it. "Julian—" she managed to say, and swayed on her feet. Vicky took her in her arms, hugging her tightly.

"My dear, sit down. Have you had tea? My dearest Regina, we shall talk later. No, no, sit down and rest now."

Vicky sat helplessly beside her, holding Regina's hand, while the tears poured down Regina's white cheeks.

Tea was brought in. Vicky made Regina drink some, and added brandy to it. The strong drink helped her to calm herself enough to speak.

"Shall I send for Julian?" Vicky finally asked anxiously.

Regina shook her head wearily. "No, no. I will go—home—presently. Oh, God, I wish I could go home—to America!" The words burst out. She thought of her dear father, so anxious for her welfare, even her stepmother, bustling and hasty but concerned over her. A welcome would be there, and a haven.

"What is it, darling?" Vicky said quietly. There was understanding in her eyes, even before Regina told her.

"It is—Simone de Lamartine," said Regina. "I went to—her apartment—on her request."

"And found she is—Julian's—" Vicky hesitated delicately.

"Mistress," said Regina baldly. "But—oh, worse, Vicky—"

"Worse?" asked the older woman blankly. "Was he there with her?"

Regina shook her head. Her heart seemed to beat in slow painful strokes. "No. Vicky, she showed me—their son. Six years old, so like him. Oh, God, so like him, except the eyes. The very cut of his face, his nose, his mouth. . . ."

Vicky sat silent, appalled, her eyes wide. She did not seem to know what to say. Distraught, Regina put her hands to her cheeks.

"I can't think what to do," she said. "I think—he will discard me. The harvest will be good—he won't need more money. Oh, Vicky, I want to go home—to America."

"Have you spoken to Julian about this?" Vicky asked gently. "Have you asked him what he means to do?"

Regina said wearily, "No, I just came—from her place. I could not bear to go home. I don't know—" Her voice rose hysterically. "His son! And I had hoped to give him a son! Why should he want a son of me? He has a fine boy, a fine boy!" And she began to laugh uncontrollably.

Vicky got up and went to the door. She spoke to the butler, then returned. Her face, so delicately pretty, was set and hard. "I have sent for Ken," she said. "Be calm, my dear. Drink some more tea and brandy. Have you eaten today?"

"No. I feel sick." She put her hand to her stomach. "I should go home—but where is home?" she said drearily. "Oh, Vicky, I knew he went to Simone often—but this—I never dreamed this—"

She began to cry then, and tears streamed down her cheeks. Vicky soothed her as best she could and was relieved when Ken came in about an hour later. Vicky conferred with her husband in the hallway, then both returned to Regina's side. Ken's jolly red face was unnaturally grave and angry.

"Did you know about this?" Regina demanded, sitting up on the sofa. "Men always know about their friends. Did you know?"

Ken averted his gaze from her tear-swollen face. "Yes, I'm afraid so, a lot of us knew that he pays for her apartment, he goes to see her in Paris, and of course when he is at Verlaine, he looks after her estate," he said wearily. "I'm horribly sorry, Regina. We were worried when we saw what a nice girl he had married. He is quite a splendid fellow, except for that weakness of his—"

She sank back into the cushions. "Everyone knew!" she whispered.

"Not about the son, I didn't know that," Ken said. He sat down awkwardly. "Regina, I'm sorry. Is there anything we can do? Do you want me to talk to him? I mean, it would be awkward, but he should do right by you—"

"How? By murdering his mistress and his son?" she flared, and began to laugh again, in a strange wild way. Vicky patted her hand.

"Regina, my dear, what would *you* like to do?" she asked. "Do you want to go home for a while?"

"Home? To New York?" Her handkerchief fluttered as she wiped her eyes and tried to calm down. "Oh, I wish I could!"

"There is a ship tomorrow from Le Havre," said Ken Longstreth. "We could take you to the port. This time of year there might be a vacant cabin—"

"Oh, yes, yes, yes," muttered Regina feverishly. "I want to go home!"

Vicky said quickly, "She should talk to Julian first, Ken! Talk it out. Maybe he would give up Simone—"

"Maybe pigs will fly," said Regina inelegantly. "No, I don't want to discuss it with Julian. He is so . . . persuasive. If he has kept it from me, he would find some way to— Oh, no, I don't want to talk to him."

Vicky and Ken conferred quickly, then turned to Regina. "All right, my dear," said Ken. "I'll send a carriage for you in the morning, about eleven. I'll come myself! I'll get a ticket for you, and we'll take you to the port ourselves. I wish we could sail with you, but my commitments—"

"No, no, I cannot expect that," said Regina. Leave Julian? It would be tearing out her heart. But she could not face him again, she never wanted to see his charming deceitful smile. "But if you would get me a ticket—and see that I can get to Le Havre—"

It was arranged, and they sent her home in their own carriage. It was only about three in the afternoon when she arrived at the townhouse door. As if in a daze, she looked at the clock in the hallway. Had it been only a few hours? It felt like years.

She crept upstairs to her bedroom. Ninette soon came, to see her tearing off her dress, muttering to herself.

"Oh, Madame, you are not well?" exclaimed the maid. "What may I do for Madame?"

"Pack the trunks," Regina said quietly. "We will be— leaving—tomorrow."

"I think Madame should go to bed," Ninette said, firm for once. She helped Regina put on her nightdress and a robe and creep into bed. She brought up hot bricks wrapped in cloth, and a tray of hot tea. She packed quietly, at Regina's fretful insistence.

Regina could not sleep. She rested there against the pillows, her eyes shut, planning frantically. She had her own passport; her father had arranged that, in case she wanted to travel on her own. Married women usually went on their husband's, but Frederick Pierce had ideas about that.

Ken would get the ticket. Money, she would need money. No, Ken would think of that, he was so practical. If she could just get her trunks and valises packed. Ninette had most of them packed, so it was just a matter of having them ready before Julian realized. If only he went off the next morning for his appointments—

It would help deceive him, if she got up, had dinner, and acted naturally. She called Ninette, who came in at once.

"I feel better, Ninette. Take out the wool dress, I have been chilled all day. Has Monsieur le Baron returned?"

"His carriage came in a few minutes ago, Madame."

"Fine. Lay out the dress, please."

When Julian came upstairs, his face reddened by the September wind, Regina was dressing for dinner. She even managed to smile at him. If she did not look directly into his eyes, it was easier.

"My dear, Ninette says you have been ill!" he exclaimed, looking anxiously at her in the mirror.

"I went to the Longstreths for a chat with Vicky. The carriage was cold and I got a chill, that is all, Julian," she said quite calmly.

"But you look so pale!"

"Vicky said that also. I think I've been doing too much, Julian. I shall be glad to go home," she said, and smiled, thinking bitterly that she would be very happy to go home—to America!

"Thérèse was right," he said, putting his hands on her shoulders. It was all she could do not to fling them off and tell him what she thought of him! "We work you too hard. Please, Regina, do slow down. Verlaine has stood for more than eight hundred years. It can stand a little more wear and tear! When we get home, you will slow down, won't you? To please me?"

"I'll make a bargain with you, Julian," she said, tossing back her head. "I'll slow down when you do!"

He bent and kissed her cheek, and moved his lips to the lobe of her ear. She shivered at his touch. "I promise—as soon as the harvest is over," he added automatically.

"What appointments do you have tomorrow?" she asked as casually as she could, rising from the dressing table stool.

"Oh—a broker in the morning, a banker in the afternoon. Two more brokers on Wednesday." He frowned. "I'll be glad when that is all over."

"I think I'll stay in tomorrow. Monsieur Silver assured me he understood all the measurements."

"Good. You rest all day, and then we might go out tomorrow evening, if you like."

He watched her anxiously all that evening. She ate some dinner, managed to drink coffee with him in the drawing room and listen to his talk of the brokers without taking in a single word.

Finally she said, "I do believe I am sleepy. I'm going to bed, Julian. Don't come up yet, I know you want to go over your notes."

He came over to her as she stood to leave the room. He kissed her cheek, then her lips, so tenderly that she wanted to cry and scream and rage at him. "Good night, my adored. Sleep well. I shall try to be very quiet when I come up. And sleep late tomorrow. Rest all you can. I cannot forgive myself for letting you take this mad trip to Paris. We shall find you more amusements at Verlaine, I promise! The fall and winter seasons shall be gay."

She managed a smile. "Good night, Julian," she said steadily, knowing she was saying "good-bye" to him in her heart.

CHAPTER TWENTY-THREE

Julian went out at about ten the next morning. Regina had risen and put on a warm woolen dress of lavender with white piping. It would do to travel in.

She ordered Ninette to finish packing, though the girl was obviously bewildered and suspicious about the order. Ken and Vicky arrived in their carriage at eleven o'clock.

The trunks were carried down by the amazed footmen. Ninette tried to protest, even tried to force herself into the carriage. "But, Madame, who will look after you? Where are you going? What shall I tell Monsieur?"

"Tell Monsieur I have gone home—to America," said Regina grimly. "I am sorry, Ninette. You have been a good girl. Farewell."

And she turned her face away as the maid began to sob. Ken was overseeing the packing of her trunks into a second carriage. He tried to tip the servants, but they refused it, eyeing him with dark suspicion.

"Did you leave a note for Julian?" Vicky asked as they set out at last for the train station.

"A note? What for? To tell him he has a son? He already knows that," Regina replied wearily. "I'll write from America—perhaps. . . ."

They just made the boat train, and porters hastily loaded the trunks and cases. Vicky and Ken accompanied Regina, though she tried to protest.

"We will see you onto the ship and make sure you have a good cabin," Ken said firmly. "I must say—this has shaken me badly. I thought Julian was the one man I could really admire. Though I knew about Simone. But to deny his son—"

"Oh, do please shut up, Ken," Vicky urged, with an anxious look at Regina. "My dear, what else can we do? Go to talk to Julian?"

She shook her head. "No, he will be angry. He doesn't like his plans upset," she said drearily. "He will get over it sooner or later."

They could be friends with him later, if they chose. Ken liked Julian, Vicky enjoyed his company. Just because his blind American wife had finally opened her eyes was no reason for all his friends of many years to drop him.

The train trip seemed longer than three hours. Regina stared out the windows, remembering the other trip when she, as shy a bride as one could be, was learning to know Julian and to love him. He had pointed out the ports, the fishing villages, a small ship out at sea, the fields, the apple orchards—

The train pulled in at Le Havre, and Ken saw to the loading of the two trunks and many cases. Both Ken and Vicky went with her to her cabin in first class. It had a charming little deck of its own, and Vicky said, "Oh, you can enjoy the air without going out."

"But you should go out on deck and walk," Ken said quickly. "Promise me, Regina, you will walk about. September can be stormy, and you may get seasick if you sit in a chair or lie down much of the time. Do get some exercise."

"I'll try," she said, and smiled. They had brought a basket of fruit and some flowers, and she thanked them, trying to pretend she was a tourist going gaily back to America after a wonderful holiday. But when the final boat whistle blew and the Longstreths went ashore, after hugging and kissing her, Regina felt very much alone.

The stewardess came in to introduce herself, and took in the fact that the Baronne de Verlaine was traveling without a maid.

"Madame, may I offer myself?" she asked politely. "I will be happy to assist you at any time."

Regina thanked her and asked if she would unpack. She felt rather sick and foolish, and wanted to lie down. The girl unpacked efficiently and left her in a darkened cabin to rest.

Ken's dire prediction came true. The September equinox brought storms swirling across the Atlantic. The ship lurched and pitched, day after day, night after night. Regina stayed in her cabin, eating little but cheese and biscuits, and drinking hot tea.

But she did go out on deck when the weather cleared, and walked up and down until she was glad to return to her cabin. Curious looks were cast at her, whispers reached

her ear. "The Baronne de Verlaine, a rich American," she
heard. "Yes, traveling alone. Isn't she smart-looking? . . .
Beautiful . . . She speaks French very well, I hear . . .
Alone . . . Alone."

When she finally ventured to the dining room, she found
she had been seated at the table of the First Officer. He
greeted her kindly, saw her to the chair next to his, and
made her feel comfortable. There were two other couples at
the table, one American, one French.

The Americans had been traveling over Europe and did
not speak much French. Regina heard them attempting to
make themselves understood, and roused herself to inter-
pret for them. It kept her busy and amused.

They asked finally about her husband. "Is the Baron de
Verlaine—ah—coming later?"

"He is very busy with the grape harvest," she explained.
That was the explanation she had worked out, to keep their
curiosity at bay. "He cannot come at this time."

The Americans were very talkative, and full of their little
adventures. They had met an amusing German in Munich,
who had shown them around and urged them to remain for
a beer fest. "Herman wanted to stay." His wife beamed and
laughed. "But imagine, a beer fest, and us in the middle of
it! I said, 'No, Herman, we have to get home to the children.'"

The "children" were in their forties, with children of
their own. Pictures were brought out to be shown and admired. Regina stared at the photo of one child, a solemn-
faced boy of about five, and felt a pang of grief so intense
she wanted to weep.

"How attractive they are," she managed to say, returning
the pictures.

"The Baronne does not have a child yet?" ventured the
Frenchwoman.

"No, Madame. I was just married last March."

"Ah, a bride, indeed, a bride," they murmured.

Regina thought of how much she had grown up since
then. She had become a woman, a married woman, had
learned to love a man with passion and her whole heart—
only to find he had lied to her, deceived her, lived a lie of
such immensity—

* * *

Being on the ship was like being suspended in time. No one could reach her with angry letters. No one could confront her to torment her with questions or accusations. No one could demand that she speak, or be silent, or go to parties, or work, or go to bed early or late.

She did as she pleased from morning to night. It became a set pattern of its own. She lay awake much of the night, then was lulled to sleep by the motion of the ship. The stewardess came in with a cup of hot tea about eight o'clock in the morning. Regina drank it, got up when she wished, dressed herself, arranged her own hair. I will get accustomed to it, she thought. She did not want to be waited on all the time.

If the weather was not rainy, she strolled on the deck, and then went to get some breakfast, which was served until ten. Then she strolled some more or played cards with someone. Luncheon was at one. After that, she sat in a deck chair and talked to fellow passengers or was silent, as she chose.

Tea was served in the afternoon between four and six, and sometimes there was a concert of pleasant music. She often went with the elderly French couple who made no demands on her and were pleased that she enjoyed their company.

Then she dressed for dinner in one of her more formal dresses. As she struggled with buttons and snaps, she wondered how Ninette had done them so quickly and deftly. If she had much trouble, she rang for the stewardess, who came and helped her. She ate dinner some time between eight to ten, and then attended another concert or a little party in the captain's rooms. Regina was asked to go to dances, but she refused. She did not feel like dancing. No one pressed her, but she saw the looks from attractive men of all ages, and half a dozen nationalities. Once I get a divorce from Julian, she thought, I will never marry again.

She tried not to think of Julian but things kept reminding her of him: the turn of a man's head, a look from dark eyes, the quick walk of a young man along the deck. In the midst of a conversation with a woman she had met, Regina caught sight of a tall, brown-haired man and without warning, tears came to her eyes. She pretended it was the keen wind.

Should she have stayed? Once he'd found out that she

had left, he probably had made his plans to marry Simone.
He would want his son to be his legal heir.

Would anyone miss her? She thought about them, missing Thérèse and her sharp wit, Maman and her gentle con-
sideration, Aunt Agnes and her all-seeing eyes, even absentminded old Uncle Oliver. And Eric, did he miss her?
She hoped he would not sink back into his previous isola-
tion. She thought of his worried brown eyes, the look he
had given her when she had rushed off to Paris. Had Eric
sensed her fear, her unease? Did he know about Simone?
He probably does, she thought. They must all have known,
really. One could not keep such a matter a secret.

Regina had to find out some time. But perhaps they had
all thought she would be so foolishly and deeply in love
with Julian that she would close her eyes to the situation.

The truth was that she *was* deeply in love with Julian.
She shivered and drew her shawl more closely about her
slender shoulders. How long did it take to fall out of love?
She had fallen so quickly, but could she fall out just as fast?
She feared not.

Sometimes at night she reached out for him in her sleep.
She would awaken slightly and think he was in the next
room, but then she would feel the motion of the ship and
she would know—Julian was far away. She would probably
never see him again. Not see his handsome face, the mustache that lined his upper lip, the slow smile he gave her,
the way his green eyes changed to yellow when he was
moved. Not see him coming to her in the dusky lamplight
and bending over her bed, whispering, "Regina, I cannot
stay away from you tonight—"

The memory of his hard muscular body next to hers
brought the sting of tears to her eyes. She could almost feel
his arms closing around her, his big hands moving slowly
over her silky body. His hands had always been a little
rough, for he worked with the soil and his hands showed it.
But they were always gentle, always anxious to please her.

Julian always tasted sun-warmed, she thought, closing
her eyes against the sun glinting off the blue waves. When
she had put her lips to his throat, as he held her, he tasted
of the sun and warmth and grapes and the clay soil in
which he worked daily. Sometimes she tasted wine on his
lips.

Julian and his vines. He would do anything for them,

and for Verlaine. She sighed, and thought she could understand him a little. He had a passion for Verlaine. He had not thought an American heiress could be hurt by him; perhaps he had not even considered that matter. Americans were supposed to be hard and tough. They could take anything—

Well, maybe I can, thought Regina. She had gone through a great deal as a child, and maybe she could withstand this also and come through it, smiling one day.

One day.

What if she had remained, savored the long days and the nights with Julian? Remained, to find out from his lips that he no longer wanted her, that he was eager to make his son legally his own, to leave Verlaine to him?

She flinched, and her face tightened to a white mask. People looked curiously at her, as she sat in the deck chair, gazing unseeingly out to the far horizons. *The Baronne de Verlaine,* they whispered. *So alone. . . . An American girl. . . . Wealthy. . . . So alone. . . .*

The days rolled on slowly, and finally the ship approached New York. They would arrive the next morning.

The stewardess packed efficiently for her. Regina silently blessed Ken for giving her both French and American money, and she was able to offer generous tips to the stewardess, the dining-hall waiters, the deck stewards, and the porters.

She was ready the next morning, standing quietly in her navy-blue dress and a fur coat, for the late September morning on the dock was cold. A steward came to help her gather up her possessions and to see her ashore. He assisted her through Customs and into a carriage.

Looking about in dull amazement, Regina was glad to find that New York was no different than when she had left. The same streets, the same carriages, the trolley cars drawn by horses, the busy crowds crossing at every intersection, the bustle and hustle and business that was New York made her feel a little calmer.

The carriage rolled up to her father's house. Footmen came out, and grooms from the stables, to exclaim in surprise. Her mother was out at a luncheon, someone said, and her father was working, of course. They gathered her up and brought her inside.

Her room would be made ready in a few minutes. A

maid was brought from downstairs to assist Madame. Her father was sent for from the office, against Regina's protests. She could see him tonight.

Frederick Pierce came home about three o'clock. By that time, Regina had eaten lunch, mechanically, had had tea, and had lain down. Her room looked the same, except that the furniture had been covered by dust sheets. But the maid put fresh linen smelling of lavender on the bed, and made Regina comfortable. It seemed odd that Giulia was not there. She wondered again how the Italian maid was feeling, away from New York and her family. Perhaps Sally would let her have Giulia back again.

When she was told that her father was home, Regina went down to meet him in his study. He hugged her for a long while, then held her back. "You're pale, my girl," he said tenderly. "Want to talk about it?"

"Yes, I guess I had better," she said wearily. She sat down and told him the whole story.

Frederick Pierce listened with growing amazement and anger. "And then she showed you the boy? His boy, his lad?"

Regina nodded. "Yes, he is the image of Julian," she said, her hands clasped. "So—Papa—I could not remain. I wanted only to come home. I think—with his bettered financial condition and all—he would have cast me aside. He will want . . . his son."

"What did Julian say?" demanded her father furiously. "Did he make excuses for himself, eh? Did he?"

"Julian? Oh, he would have, I suppose—"

"Would have? What do you mean, miss? What did he say?"

"I did not stay to confront him. Ken Longstreth told me there was a ship home the next day, and they offered to help me get on—and I wanted to come home, Papa." Her lips trembled and a tear rolled down her white cheeks.

Her father took her in his arms and reassured her gruffly that she was welcome. But he demanded again about Julian.

"I cannot believe you did not confront him! Where is your courage, my girl?"

"I had none left, Papa. He can be so charming—and I—I do—did—do love him yet. I didn't want to hear him say why he—he rejected his son—why—" She shook her head wearily.

He gazed at her thoughtfully. "So you didn't even stay to fight it out, eh? To hear his reasons?"

"No, Papa." Her voice was barely a whisper.

He shook his head again and again. It did not sound like Regina. But she was so weary and so thin; he did not like it. He said mildly, "Well, I'll write to him, and I'll have an answer, why he treated you like this. Yes, I'll have something to say to him! Why, George and Bernie thought the world of him, came back full of good things to say, all about how well you were getting along with Julian and how nice his family was. They told me how hard Julian worked, and the plans for the cooperative and all—"

"Yes, I really thought he might—forget Simone de Lamartine. Until I found out about the—the boy—" She choked over the words.

"Um, yes, that makes a difference. So, the cheat Claude is out, and Julian's money situation is better, eh? And you think he doesn't need you anymore?"

"That's about it." It hurt, like a clean knife cut, the way her father said it, but it was good to hear, anyway. It confirmed her thoughts, cleansed the wound. Honesty would help her to heal.

"Well, I'll write to Julian and see what the lad has to say for himself," grunted Frederick Pierce. He hated to have his plans go awry, and he hated more to be taught he had made a mistake in his judgment of a person. He had thought Julian a fine man, a good man for his Regina. It hurt him that such a bad mistake had been made. He hated to see his girl crushed and pale like this.

But he could not blame her for coming home. It was all too much of a mess. By God, Frederick Pierce would have a thing to say to that man. He said as much to Regina.

"He cannot help it if he loves her, Papa," Regina replied gently. "He—works hard, he supports all of Verlaine, he tries very hard. He has to have his—love, his affection—and his son. I can . . . understand that—"

"But George got the idea that Julian was crazy about you," her father mused, with a frown.

That hurt. Regina finally got up and said, "I will leave you for now, Father. I want to rest. Mama will be home soon, I suppose."

"Yes, yes, but don't let her nag at you now, my dear! She means well, she really does."

"I know. I'll see you at dinner, Papa. Forgive me for dragging you from your work."

"Why shouldn't I come home from my office when my daughter comes home from France?" he asked and escorted her as far as the stairs, with an arm about her waist. "There, now, you get some rest, and be perked up when your mother comes home."

"Yes, Papa," she said, and picked up her skirts to walk slowly up the stairs.

She rested for a time, but could not sleep. She closed her eyes and saw Julian's face, gentle, concerned, as it had been the last time she had seen him. Browned by the sun, with lines about his mouth.

"Oh, Julian, why could you not let her alone?" she whispered. Simone had been the wife of another man. Had Julian loved her so desperately, he could not resist her? It must have been that way.

Regina felt she could understand undying love—but she only hoped her love for him would not be that kind. She wanted to get over it as soon as possible, and learn to forget so she could sleep at night and laugh some day. That was all she could hope for.

CHAPTER TWENTY-FOUR

Regina found the days long and empty, but the nights were even longer. She had little to do. Emilia Pierce fussed over her until Frederick told her gruffly to let the gal alone. He was fretting that he had written to Julian but had received no answer from him yet.

Giulia returned to her. Emilia Pierce had written to Sally and begged for the maid "for Regina, if you will, dear," and Sally had generously sent Giulia at once.

"With a groom and a footman, ma'am, if you will!" said Giulia, amazed at her good fortune. She did not know how long she would be in New York. But she was with Miss Regina again, and she could visit her family every week.

The warm Italian family roused Regina's envy, and she smiled wistfully over Giulia's accounts of them. It sounded a little like Julian's family, warm and close, quarreling mildly but loving each other.

Giulia found that Miss Regina needed distraction, so she told her many stories of her family. "Now, my brother, Vittorio, he runs about and makes trouble with the girls," she said with gusto. "Mama, she says what Vittorio needs is a wife, and she will see that he marries. He says, 'Mama, I want fun,' and she tells him, 'Fun, is it! You will marry and work hard for your wife and the *bambinos* that come!'"

Emilia saw to it that Regina went out. They took Giulia with them to the opera, and Regina and Giulia also went to concerts, in a carriage by themselves. But Regina refused to go to dances or to big dinner parties. Emilia complained to Frederick.

"I want to show her off! She is, after all, the Baronne de Verlaine! I wanted to take her to Mrs. Astor's party and she said no! No, to Mrs. Astor!" Emilia looked shocked.

"Let the gal alone, she's grieving," said Frederick.

That was not the only thing wrong. Regina was sick promptly every morning. Giulia looked at her wisely but said nothing. It was not her place to tell her mistress what had happened to her.

Eventually Regina roused from her daze and began to understand. Her body no longer functioned the way it had. She was sick every morning—yet by ten o'clock, sustained by tea and toast and egg, she felt better than any time in her life.

Then she knew. She was going to have a child, Julian's child. She counted up—it must have happened in August, when they had been so happy together and Julian had slept with her often. That meant she was two months' pregnant. She would have a child in May—and Julian would not be with her. What if she had a son? Would Julian want him? Or was he quite content with Pierre, his son by Simone?

Somehow it hurt all the more to think of it. She was pale, but her body grew. Giulia encouraged her gently to eat the right foods. The girl from a large family knew about such matters, and she had much common sense.

Emilia's shrewd eyes soon took note of Regina's condition. "You're pregnant," she said to Regina one day. "My dear, why didn't you tell me?"

"I just realized—recently," Regina told her wearily.

"Are you going to write to Julian about it?"

Regina shook her head. She knew that Frederick had told Emilia little beyond the fact that Regina had become disillusioned, and had left her husband. Emilia was full of curiosity, but Frederick had given her stern orders not to fuss over the girl. But this was too much. She had to do some fussing.

"Regina, do you know how to take care of yourself? I think you should see a doctor soon and make sure everything is all right."

She arranged for a doctor to come, who studied Regina's pale face, took her pulse, and gave orders for some tablets. "Some iron," he said briskly. "You seem unnaturally pale. And get out and do some walking, except on the days when it is too cold and windy."

Emilia inspected Regina's wardrobe critically. The girl needed more clothes; most of them had been left in France.

"You should have some new dresses, Regina."

"I don't need anything, Mama," said Regina listlessly.

"Yes, you do, for the baby's sake," said Emilia. She was

in her element. She was needed! I'm really a mama to Regina, she thought proudly, for the girl needed a mother now. "You should stop wearing those tight corsets, and your dresses should be loose in the waist. Tasteful, but loose. That way the baby will not be constricted."

"Mrs. Pierce is right," Giulia murmured respectfully. "I have worried about the tightness of your dresses, Miss Gina."

The dressmaker was sent for, and Regina submitted to having new dresses made. It did make a difference; she felt much better with the softer garments about her. The dressmaker was clever, and fashioned garments that could be made wider about the waist as Regina grew. And no corsets were needed. The thick velvets, the soft satins, and the everyday woolens were made full, falling to the ground from Regina's shoulders; smart and fashionable, but not revealing.

Regina went out less and less, however. She and Giulia took brisk walks in the morning and again in the afternoons, and sometimes they went to art galleries or concerts. But Regina felt self-conscious about her figure. She had always worn tight-fitting dresses and now she felt suddenly shapeless, even though her figure had barely begun to change. She thought everyone was staring at her.

Her father was gruffly nice to her, and very careful. He pampered her, bought her a ruby necklace and earrings, brought small presents home frequently.

However, the days went so slowly and Regina's thoughts went more and more to Julian, and to Verlaine. How were they managing now, with the harvest in full swing? She had longed to help them, and now they were without her. Was all going well? Did any of them miss her? Would Julian neglect the villagers again, without Regina to remind him gently of some need or other?

She could have helped at the harvest. Julian would be in the fields from morning to night, directing the work, deciding which fields should be picked first, which ones left for later. Eric was probably out helping also, directing the wagons of grapes into the vats, watching the thick juices squirt from the grapes, making sure the fermenting began properly, watching carefully for the exact moment when the fermenting should stop, and the must be poured into the oak casks. Had Marcus been able to purchase the oak casks they needed? Did they have enough of the smaller barrels?

Would Thérèse be able to manage alone the feeding of the many farm workers, as well as running Verlaine smoothly? Of course she could. She had done it for many years in the past. But she might resent the fact that she had to do it all alone again, after Regina had promised to help her.

And what of Maman? Would she try to do too much, and become ill again? She was too old and frail to do so much.

So Regina lay awake night after night, worrying, fretting, wishing secretly that she had not been so impulsive about leaving. "I jumped too fast, it was my fault," she mourned. "If only I had been more adult and—and dignified! Maybe Julian would have wanted me to stay, even with Simone—"

Then she would shudder and close her eyes, pushing away the memory of the beautiful face, the stunning black hair, the rounded figure in dramatic black chiffon.

"No, I could not have stayed—not like that! It would have been humiliating. And if I had a child, and Julian preferred Pierre—and made Pierre his heir, instead of my child—" She tormented herself with this night after night.

When Giulia crept into her room late in the morning, she would find Regina fast asleep, the sleep of exhaustion, with purple shadows under her eyes.

Then one late October day, a letter came from France. The butler himself brought it to Regina as she sat in the drawing room, some embroidery in her lap.

"Madame, a letter—from France!" he gulped.

She started violently and sat up straight, reaching eagerly for the envelope. Yet one look told her it was not from Julian. Julian had not written at all, not even to answer Frederick Pierce's angry letter.

The letter was in the elegant wavering handwriting of the Dowager Baroness de Verlaine.

Regina tore it open eagerly, her hands shaking. The butler discreetly left the room, though he longed to remain.

"My dearest daughter," the letter began.

Regina bit her lips, fighting back tears. She could take anger, coldness, but tenderness was another matter. She wiped her eyes, then read on.

We all hope you are enjoying your visit to your
dear family in America. May the weather be pleasant
for you, and may you be gay and enjoy dancing and
parties.

Regina's mouth curled. She sighed, and kept reading.

Julian decided to begin to harvest one crop of the
red Cabernet franc grapes. He is most anxious about
them. They are ripe, yet he does not wish to harvest
but half of them. He decided to risk much, but said it
was your advice, my dear child.

Eric and Marcus concurred with him in this. They
are all most excited. The weather has continued sunny
and even hot, which is good for the grapes, though
wearing for the grape workers. The first crop has been
plucked, and Eric watches like a fond parent over the
must. He let it ferment only a few hours and then directed that it be placed in the new oak casks. One can
only hope the grapes will do well.

Julian then went to the whites, which are now overripe, as they must be. He worked from morning till
night, as always, and the wagons were piled high with
the beautiful creamy-white Chenin Blanc. These also
were fermented only a few hours—I believe Eric said
eight hours—and then allowed to stream into the barrels. Marcus directed the placing of the barrels. He
said they must remain there for six months, or more.
We are all hopeful that the weather will remain splendid and the harvest will continue.

Julian works so hard! I am sure he misses you, for
his face is grave and he never laughs. Thérèse sends
many fond messages, and hopes you are having a
splendid holiday.

When may we expect you home, my dear? We miss
you, all of us, so very much. Aunt Agnes has continued your good work in the village, and not a day goes
by without someone there speaking of you, or sending
blessings on you, and prayers for your safe and speedy
return to us.

Regina paused again to wipe her eyes and blow her nose.
She was reassured that they missed her, yet she felt uneasy.

Surely they knew why she had left! Surely they all knew about Julian and his mistress and his child.

The letter had a few more paragraphs. She managed to compose herself and finish it.

Little Jeannette speaks of you often, and brings me her doll Regina to say her prayers with her. Thérèse has such good news for us: She expects another child, she and Marcus. How overjoyed they are! We could only hope for you, our dear one, that you and Julian will one day be so blessed.

We think of you often. You are in my prayers every night, my child. Julian misses you so much, I know, for he is silent and aloof every evening. He comes home so tired and quiet. If only you were here to encourage him to rest a bit more— But there, I will not nag you, my dearest!

The harvest promises to be glorious. Julian says the fortunes of Verlaine will be one day restored. Monsieur Carnot and his son have chosen a broker, and all approve. And only fifteen percent, my dear! What wonders! Madame Tillemont shed a few tears with me when she heard the joyous news. And we owe all of this to your good ideas and suggestions. How can we ever thank you enough? Your father raised you well.

All of us here at Verlaine send our best greetings and wishes to you and to your dear family. Pray, give your father and mother my best regards, and also your dear brothers and sisters. We bless you and hope to see you one day quite soon.

Fondly, your Maman

Regina was now wiping away tears, but they fell faster than she could check them. She sat with the pages clutched in her hands. Then she read the letter again, and yet again, worrying out the meaning of each word, fretting that it might only be politeness that had made the Dowager write.

Yet politeness might have been served by a shorter note. Warmth came through every sentence and line.

She went over it again, to absorb all the news. They had harvested half of the reds, as she had suggested to Julian. He had taken her advice! And the whites were being harvested, and all goes well there, she thought. She pictured Eric in his wheelchair, anxiously wheeling himself about the winery, directing operations with Marcus coming from the fields to advise. And Julian coming home wearily every night. If only she might be there to encourage him to eat, to have a little wine to relax, to assure him that all was going so well.

She looked at the date on the letter. Early October. They must have started harvesting soon after Julian returned home from Paris.

There was still the second lot of reds to do. He would be working through October, which was almost over. Had the weather continued fair? Had they had sunshine, or had the rains come to spoil the delicate mist on the grapes, the bloom that was so essential to the fermenting process?

When her father came home, she amazed him by demanding, "Papa, do you have newspapers from Europe? How has the weather been in France?"

He sat down, spread his big hands on his knees and stared. "And what does that matter, miss?"

"Oh, Papa," she said impatiently, waving the sheets in her hand. "Maman says they are harvesting. It is important that there should be no rain until the grapes are all in! Have they had rain?"

"Good heavens, how should I know?" But he sent for his invaluable secretary who promised to find out. He came the next day with the news. He had studied the newspapers in a private library of a financier with interests in France. The weather had continued fine; there had been no rain in the Loire Valley.

The letter sustained Regina for a time. She read it over and over, until the pages threatened to tear. She longed to be with them, helping as she might. She could at least have helped Eric in the winery. Or she could have helped Thérèse to load the wagons with food to go out to the vineyards, to feed the workers and Julian and Marcus.

Her cheeks glowed for days, and her eyes were bright once more. Frederick winked at Emilia and nodded. She was missing them. Maybe things would work out all right.

But October faded, and rainy days came sweeping through New York, leaving puddles in the streets and refuse along the gutters. When Regina went out, she was huddled in a thick coat and Giulia was always winding a scarf about Regina's throat. The dreary days were coming, and the long winter—and still there was no message from Julian.

She did not know how to answer her mother-in-law's letter. Should she say that she could not return to Julian, not since she had learned about his son? Should she beg to come back, and ask her to tell Julian she was with child? She dithered about it. She did not know what to do, how to write.

And she had bad dreams at night. She would be sleeping peacefully and then begin to dream she had returned to Verlaine. Then as Regina was dreamily entering the rose drawing room and looking about her with pleasure at its beauty—Simone would appear.

Simone in stark dramatic black chiffon, radiantly beautiful, her magnolia-skinned face glowing with happiness. At her side was her son, dressed in white, Pierre with an angelic face.

Then Julian came in. He walked past Regina as though he did not see her. He went right to Simone, kissed her cheek, and then knelt to hug his son. Regina cried out, "But look at me, I have a son also. Look at me, Julian!"

He did not turn around; he was hugging the boy, Pierre. He gestured imperiously for Regina to leave. "I don't want your child, I don't want your child," he repeated.

She woke up with tears streaming down her cheeks. She was shaking and shivering in the bed, so she drew up more covers to warm her. Yes, that is what he would say, she thought. He doesn't want my son. Why should he? He already has a fine son, just like him!

The nightmare haunted her. She lay awake until morning. And the nightmare came again and again. It varied a little, but always Julian rejected her, saying "I have a son. I do not want your child."

Early in November her father's secretary came to tell her, "The rains have begun in France, Madame. Do you think the harvest is finished yet?" He had taken a keen interest in all the events, from hearing about the grape harvests.

"I don't know," she said numbly. "I don't know if they are finished with the harvest. It's November. If the harvest isn't yet done, the reds will be ruined."

And, she thought, it would be my fault. She had advised Julian to wait and have a second harvest of the later over-ripe grapes. If it all went badly, would he blame her for that also?

CHAPTER TWENTY-FIVE

The second week of November was even colder and more rainy. The winds swept rain across the island of Manhattan, and Regina stayed indoors day after day.

Even Emilia Pierce grumbled about going out. She was due at a morning tea to plan a charity event that morning, but she grumbled at dressing in warm woolens and a fur hat before setting out in a carriage through the flooded streets.

Regina wore a new woolen dress of soft crimson, with bands of dark-brown velvet cleverly embroidered around the loose sleeves and the full skirts. Not expecting visitors on such a wretched day, she had left her hair down, fastened back with a brown velvet ribbon.

She settled in the drawing room with her sewing. She and Giulia had been cutting out and sewing some baby garments, and Regina enjoyed the feel of the soft cottons and linens, sewing the little sleeves, taking pleasure in finishing the hems with crocheted work in lacy patterns.

About noon, she heard the butler going to the door as a carriage drove up. "Oh, no," she muttered. Was there time to escape, to run upstairs, so no grand society matron would see her like this? No, the door was opening. She heard voices in the hallway.

Emilia was not home and Frederick was at the office. Regina resigned herself, stuffed the baby clothes into her sewing basket of rose-patterned cloth and straw, and went to the door of the drawing room. She would just have to apologize for her appearance.

Then she gasped. At the door stood the butler, Horace, directing the moving in of a trunk and several cases. The footmen were scurrying around, and a maid was curtseying.

The tall man in rain-drenched coat and hat turned about. She heard his deep voice saying "Any room will do—is Madame Herriot at home?"

"Julian!"

He looked up and saw her, and she wanted to cry out
again. His face was tanned, but so weary, so drawn and
grave. His green eyes seemed to have acquired lines around
them. He was so thin his cheekbones stood out.

"Oh, Julian, you are soaking wet! You never take proper
care of yourself! Come in quickly and come to the fire!"

She went over to him, and reached out to touch his wet
sleeve. The concern she felt overshadowed her uneasiness.

"I am soaking, yes, Regina. Perhaps I should dry out,
then come to speak to you—" He was hesitant, his gaze
steadily searching her face.

"No, the fires are not lit upstairs," she said impatiently.
She turned to the butler. "Horace, the brown and gold bedroom, take the luggage up, and see that a fire is lit and hot
water brought up presently. Julian, do come to the fire."
She directed him toward the drawing room.

Horace said, "May I have the coat of the baron?" He
removed the dripping overcoat, the top hat that ran with
water. Gravely, he directed the moving of the luggage, and,
satisfied, he watched Regina lead Julian to the drawing
room.

The room was cosy, with the fire burning brightly. Regina turned to call again to a footman, "Do bring in hot
coffee, and a bottle of Papa's best brandy."

He bowed and went off hastily. Regina motioned Julian
to the fire. "Stand here and get warm," she said. "Oh,
Julian, where did you come from?"

"From France, from the boat—" He did not smile, and
his eyes never left her face. She finally sank down on the
sofa, self-consciously making sure the work basket was
closed. "I did not go to a hotel. I wanted to see you at
once."

"Oh, Julian." And she began to realize all the difficulties
between them.

Perhaps he had come to ask her for a divorce, to start
that long process. Her heart seemed to freeze within her.

The footman brought a silver rolling tray with a pot of
hot coffee, cream and sugar, coffee cups and saucers of
white porcelain with gold rims. He set it before Regina. She
poured out coffee and handed it to him, and he carried the
cup to Julian at the mantel.

Julian set it aside for the moment, as it was too hot to
drink. "Brandy, sir?" asked the footman, producing the

bottle. Julian shook his head absently. The footman bowed and left the room, closing the door after him.

Julian held out his reddened hands to the fire. Regina gazed at him hungrily. It seemed years since she had seen him. Yes, he was thinner; his coat hung on him. She wanted to ask why he had not taken care of himself but she bit her lips. She had no right to be anxious, to show her concern.

He drank his coffee, then finally sat down beside the fire across from Regina. "Ah, that is better. I always seem to find New York in nasty weather," he said with a faint smile. "You recall—last winter?"

She nodded. She had been thinking of that snowy day when Julian had walked to their home rather than risk the horses' safety.

"So," Julian began, then, with a sigh: "I found it difficult to realize you had left me, Regina, and so suddenly, without a clue or a letter. I questioned Ninette, and what she told me sent me to Simone de Lamartine. After much questioning, she revealed that she had told you something of the child, Pierre."

Regina flinched. "Yes, your son," she said in a low tone.

"No!" said Julian, not loudly but firmly. "It took more questioning to discover the lies that had been told for years, it seems. What a shock to me, to discover that Kenneth and Victoria Longstreth, and many friends, even my own sister Thérèse, all believed I had been keeping Simone as a mistress! What a blow to discover that one had thought oneself a man of honor, only to find that all believed him to be a rake, a cheat, a womanizer, a liar."

His voice was calm and dispassionate, as though he had thought it all over; yet his tone was sad.

Regina stared at him. Was he going to deny this? She felt chilled, quivering, her hands clasped together. "But, Julian—they all knew—"

"Knew what that liar Claude had told them," he said flatly. "Yes, Regina. It was Claude who had an affair with Simone years ago. He still visits her on occasion. He gave her a child, and they hid him away. She told you that her husband knew of it. That also was a lie. Hilaire de Lamartine was elderly, but no fool. He would have known at once the child was not his. He had not had relations with her, because of his illness."

"He—did not know?" Regina whispered. Julian shook his head. His light-brown hair was ruffled, but he did not notice it.

"No. Claude paid her for a time. He spirited her away during her later pregnancy and obtained an apartment for her in Paris. She simply told her husband she needed a long holiday and left him. When she returned, she carried on as before. However, Claude became weary of her demands and her bills, the bills for the nurse, the apartment, Pierre's illnesses. She threatened him, but he only laughed. Then she came to me."

Regina shivered. Julian saw it this time, rose and put a light woolen afghan about her shoulders. Then he returned to his seat.

"Her husband died. I told Claude I thought he should marry her, for the sake of the child. But, no, he was having too gay a time for that, he said. He would not be burdened. Simone was furious, and upset. I agreed to support the child, pay for the apartment and for the boy's schooling until he is twenty-one. I hope he will turn out well. However, with a mother like Simone and a father like Claude, there is not much hope for the poor lad."

Julian sounded convincing. But Regina kept wondering if she should believe him. Could she trust him? She watched him gravely, watched for every expression. She was doubting, wanting so much to believe this miracle, yet—could she?

"After Hilaire died and Claude refused to marry Simone, she then came to me," said Julian after a pause. "She said that I was unmarried, that I wanted a son and heir. Here was a Herriot, a fine boy who even looked like a Herriot. I must marry her, she said, and adopt Pierre as my own. I refused, disgusted. I am a strong believer in the power of heredity. Claude's father was weak, a gambler who absconded with his company's funds and disappeared. I had hoped to keep Claude too busy to cheat me but still he did. There is little good in him. And so the boy has such a heredity that only strict schooling will keep him from following his father's path."

"But she—wanted you to marry her—"

"Yes. I would look after her lands, and she thought I would carry the burden of that forever. No, indeed. Besides, Claude was causing trouble. I refused her, though she wept and screamed."

That must have been the scene that Thérèse had overheard, and misunderstood. Regina's heart was beginning to lift. Julian spoke in such a simple direct way, she could not help but begin to believe him.

"When all this came out, after you left me, Thérèse and Marcus told me that Claude had dropped hints, sent out little jabs about me and Simone. Evidently he wanted to cover his own mischief. He let them believe I went constantly to Lamartine to see Simone. Eric told me that Claude was constantly saying little things that would make one think there was—intimacy—between me and Simone. However, Eric said that he had come to realize that Claude was a liar. So he discounted all that Claude said. I wish the others had had such a belief, and more faith in me."

The sadness in Julian's deep voice made Regina bite her lips against the tears. She too had believed him guilty, and had not had faith in him.

"What—will happen now?" she asked quietly. "You will not help her now?" She hoped he would not. It might prove what he said.

"No, Regina, I gave my word to help the boy. I will continue to pay for him, for the apartment, for his schooling, until he is twenty-one. However, finding that Claude had arranged all the deceit that they visited on you—"

"Claude did? Not—not her?"

"It was Claude's idea. Simone was reluctant; she is shrewd. She thought if I found out what they had told you, how they lied, I would cut off their funds. But Claude persuaded her out of his desire for revenge, and he has always had a charming tongue. I even think she may have been a bit jealous of our—our happiness together."

"Oh, Julian! I am sorry—"

"I was sorry that you had not trusted me. But more sorry that you did not remain to talk to me, to confront me. Regina—why did you run off like that? It was so unlike you. It lacked courage, I thought. Why didn't you ask me what I had done?"

She gulped. "I was sorry later, Julian. But then—I was so shocked, so hurt—I thought you would divorce me—when you no longer needed me."

"What? Divorce you?" he asked sharply. "What made you think so?" Now he did look distressed.

"Well—Thérèse said when we did not marry in your church—"

He looked furious, and there was a grim set to his mouth. "So? What of that? Later you would have taken instruction from the priest. If you wished to become Catholic, it would have pleased me, but I did not wish to rush you, not when so many matters were new to you, our language, our way of life, our home—"

"But, Julian, I often felt a constraint between us," she felt compelled to say.

"Yes, for the manner in which we married. I felt you were reluctant, that you had been pushed into this. For me, I had begun to love you early," he said simply. "Yet how could I speak of love and ask for a large dowry in the same breath? I felt a beggar at your gates. But if I could work hard, if the fates were kind, then I might restore Verlaine's fortunes, and come to you with an open heart. I tried to show you I loved you, and I thought you responded."

"Oh, Julian, I did! I do love you—so much," she finally said. He left his chair and came over to sit beside her. He put his arms about her gently and she leaned against him.

"I wanted to believe that you loved me," he murmured against her hair. "How I adore you! You look so beautiful with your hair down like this, to your waist. How beautiful and sweet you are." He stroked the length of her curly chestnut hair.

She hated herself for her jealousy, but she had to say, "What about Simone, Julian? You always welcomed her to Verlaine, you sat her at your right, you went over often to help with her vineyards—"

"I admired her for a time. I thought she was gallant, struggling against odds. She was paying for her mistake, I thought, having to keep her own son hidden in Paris. But now— She has a cold selfish heart. For what she did to you, I shall never receive her again at Verlaine."

The simple declaration shocked Regina. "Never? But while she lives at Lamartine—"

"I have had an offer for Lamartine, which I am urging her to accept. There is a Frenchman who wishes another estate for his younger son. He came, and I showed him Lamartine, and talked to them of the vineyards, the harvest, the cooperative. They are both enthusiastic. The boy is about twenty-five. He wishes to marry and settle there. He is a farmer, he works hard. Marcus likes him immensely. I shall urge Simone to accept his offer for Lamartine, and then we need never see her again."

"Oh, Julian—" She sighed in immense relief. Not to have the stunning widow at her doorstep! What a different view of her future that would bring to Regina! "But did you not want her to keep Lamartine for—for Pierre?"

"The boy will have to make his own way. When he is older, I will speak to his instructors and see for which profession he shall be trained. I do not intend to waste my time working so much for Lamartine, while Simone and Claude play their ways through life. I am sick of them both."

When he spoke so, in quiet but firm tones, she realized the extent of Julian's disillusionment with the pair. They had lied, cheated, fooled him for years. Now that he had discovered the depths of their intrigues and what they had tried to do to his marriage, he was finished with them.

She could not help but be glad of it.

"Oh, Julian, I am so happy—so happy you came, and it is all straightened out."

"And you will—return to me?" he asked hesitantly.

"If you—want me to come."

He groaned. *"Mon Dieu.* What else have I been saying these hours?" he asked impatiently, and held her closer. He pressed an urgent kiss to her cheek.

"Julian, I have something I had better tell you," she said hurriedly as he squeezed her. She withdrew a little from him, pushing him gently with her hands on his chest.

His face darkened. "There is not another man, is there?" he asked swiftly, glaring at her, his green eyes gleaming yellow.

"No. That is, not a man. . . ." And she began to giggle a little with sheer happiness.

He stared.

"Julian, I am—that is, you are—I mean, I am going to have a—a baby—your child."

The color slowly returned to his tanned face. "A baby? Our child? Oh, Regina, my darling, my adored! I cannot believe it! But when?"

"I think it is in May," she said shyly, coloring deeply at the happy look in his face.

"Oh, *mon Dieu,* I am the happiest of men! My adored, you have made me so happy! I was sick at heart, coming here, worried about what you would say. And now how happy I am!" He bent and kissed her lips tenderly, as though afraid of hurting her. "You have been well?" he asked anxiously.

"I was a bit sick, but Giulia and Mama say it is normal. In the morning I get sick," she explained. "But by ten I am all right."

He frowned a little thoughtfully. "We had best not travel. If anything happens—"

"I will ask the doctor. He is very sensible and kind," she said. "I am sure he will know if it is safe to travel. And now that all is settled— Oh, Julian, I do want to go home, to Verlaine!"

"That makes me happiest of all," he said quietly. "I had feared so much that you had turned against us, that you hated the quiet life at Verlaine, that you were bored and seized the chance to—to escape."

"Oh, Julian, no! I love Verlaine, I have missed you, and everyone, so much. Tell me all the news!" she cried. "We have talked and talked, and you have not told me how Maman is, and Eric, and dear Thérèse—she also expects a child."

"Yes, in May!" he said, and began to laugh. "What a commotion there will be! Two children in May!"

"Oh, it is splendid! They will grow up together!"

"Thérèse and Marcus want the lodge. They wait for your return to help them plan the furnishings. But I will not let them work you so hard."

"Oh, I should adore helping them refurnish the lodge!"

"Eric is well. He helped so much with the harvest. Regina, can you believe it? He has more use of his arms, and even of his legs! The exercise has been so good for him. The doctor came to examine him, and says he may be able to walk again with the help of crutches! It is a miracle!"

"Julian, is it true?" she gasped, turning pale with excitement. "Eric, walking!"

"Not really walking, my dear," he said more soberly. "But he can get in and out of his wheelchair with less aid.

When he gets crutches, if he can use them, he will hobble always. But he will be able to ride in a carriage, to get out more. He is so excited, you can imagine! All he needs, he told me, is for his dear sister to return and share in his pleasure."

"I shall, I shall. And he shall ride out with me to the vineyards, and along the country roads and to the village," Regina declared.

She asked after the others, wanting all the news. He was telling her about the village when Horace knocked at the door and announced luncheon.

They went into the dining room where they were alone. The others would not return until later. They continued talking, over the delicate omelette the cook had concocted for the return of Monsieur le Baron. Milk for Regina— Giulia had recommended it—then wine later for them both. "Not Verlaine wines," Regina sighed with a twinkle in her eyes. "But almost as good."

"Your father keeps a good cellar."

"Tell me about the harvest! Did you get all the reds in before the rains?"

"How did you know about the rains? No matter; yes, we harvested all the night, and the reds were all in when the rains swept in. We got the last of the must into the crushing vats as the rains began. Regina, I think it will be the best harvest Verlaine has ever known!" he said with deep satisfaction.

"Oh, I am so glad. So very glad! Papa believed in you always, Julian. He knew you would do it."

They talked about the harvest, and he told her about the number of barrels of white, the number of reds in two separate pickings. They discussed what to do about holding the reds. The whites usually sat in barrels for six months and then were bottled.

"But the reds—I don't know," Julian mused. "I think I shall experiment, Regina. We shall test them again and again, and bottle some early and hold some longer in the oak casks, perhaps two years. I have been talking to some men who produce a fine rosé, and it may be that with two years the wine will be at its best."

That talk carried them through the elegant luncheon and back into the drawing room. They had so much to say, sitting side by side on the sofa, gazing into the fire or into each other's eyes.

Emilia Pierce came home, tired and cross from her gloomy tea, as she expressed it. But when she learned that the Baron de Verlaine had arrived, she went into ecstasies and immediately began to plan dinners and balls.

"No, no, I beg you, Mama," said Julian charmingly. "I just wish to remain *en famille*."

"So I will send for George and Bernie at once." Emilia beamed. "I know they will enjoy a good long visit. Dear me—a houseful of guests. How delightful! You will stay for Christmas, will you not?"

"Mama, we want to go home to Verlaine for Christmas," said Regina, as Julian looked at her uncertainly. "We will be here for Thanksgiving, then sail for home in early December, if that is all right, Julian."

"That will be splendid, if the doctor agrees." He smiled. "Then I can consult with your father about the banking, and with George."

Frederick Pierce came home from the office at five, as he always did, and was quietly happy to see his daughter so radiant and Julian so gently attentive. All had gone well at last, he realized.

They had an early dinner, for all of them were exhausted. Julian slept in his separate room, but came to Regina's room early the next day.

She was still in bed, her hair woven in long braids. "Oh, Julian, why did you come?" she asked. "This is the time I am always sick."

"Then I will help you, my dear." He smiled mischievously. "You are not going to keep me away with any excuses." He played with her braids, teasing her about her pink ribbons. "You look about ten years old today. What shall I do if you get younger every day and I get older?"

He bent and kissed her cheeks, then her mouth. "My sweetness," he whispered. "How I have missed you!"

"Oh, Julian, I missed you so much!"

"Not as much as I did," he said firmly. "You will see the doctor soon, and know all is well for traveling?"

"*Oui*, Monsieur," she said demurely.

His voice lowered. "For I am most anxious to carry you off with me, Madame! I will abduct you to my secret castle and keep you forever by my side. That does not displease Madame?"

"Darling," she responded, and wound her arms about his neck to kiss him. She did not even notice when Giulia peeped in, only to disappear quickly and silently.

Regina knew only that she was the happiest woman in the world; Julian's wife, his love, soon to have his child.

Someday she might tease him that he had waited to come to her until the harvest was over! But she knew why he had done so. He was proud, and this time he wanted to come to her with more to offer.

She did not care about it anymore, but Julian did. He wanted to come with the harvest in hand, with hopes for their future and Verlaine's. Now he was free to express his love for her.

She had hurt him badly by running off and not trusting him enough to talk to him about the matter that troubled her. She vowed she would never do such a thing again. If any problems came up, she would go to Julian and they would talk them out. It was the only way to make their marriage work. And she wanted very much for their marriage to work, and to last a lifetime.

A lifetime. It will scarcely be enough for me, she thought happily, as Julian's lips nuzzled tenderly at her throat. A lifetime to live with Julian, to help him all she could, to raise their children, to help Verlaine become what he wished it to be. To live with Julian—all her life. That would be joy and paradise enough for her.

MADELEINE A. POLLAND

SABRINA

Beautiful Sabrina was only 15 when her blue eyes first met the dark, dashing gaze of Gerrard Moynihan and she fell madly in love—unaware that she was already promised to the church.

As the Great War and the struggle for independence convulsed all Ireland, Sabrina also did battle. She rose from crushing defeat to shatter the iron bonds of tradition . . . to leap the convent walls and seize love—triumphant, enduring love—in a world that could never be the same.

A Dell Book $2.50   (17633-6)

At your local bookstore or use this handy coupon for ordering:

 **Dell** Bestsellers

**The first novel
in a new series**

A sweeping saga of the American West

Esther left New England a radiant bride, her future as
bright as the majestic frontiers. But before she could reach
California, she had lost everything but her indomitable
courage and will to survive. Against the rich tapestry of
California history, she lived for love—and vengeance!

A Dell Book $2.50 (11035-1)

Class Reunion

RONA JAFFE

author of
The Best of Everything

"Reading Rona Jaffe is like being presented with a Cartier watch; you know exactly what you're getting and it's just what you want."—*Cosmopolitan*

Annabel, Chris, Emily and Daphne left Radcliffe in '57 wanting the best of everything. They meet again 20 years later and discover what they actually got. Their story is about love, friendship and secrets that span three decades. It will make you laugh and cry and remember all the things that shaped our lives.

"It will bring back those joyous and miserable memories."
—*The Philadelphia Bulletin*

"Keeps you up all night reading."—*Los Angeles Times*

"Rona Jaffe is in a class by herself."—*The Cleveland Press*

A Dell Book $2.75 (11408-X)